"YOU ARE THE MOST EXASPERATING MAN I KNOW!"

"You have not known any other man but me, *wife,*" Eben pointed out.

"I have not known *any* man," Raven corrected him, "and certainly not you! This marriage was your idea and it is not hard to see why you thought it up!"

"The situation is easily remedied. And I will be glad to show you just what you've been missing."

"Thank you, no," Raven said. "What you suggest is something I can live without."

"Spoken like a true virgin," Eben said with an exaggerated sigh. "Will you not at least kiss me then? It will give me something to think about during the interminable hours I am forced to lie upon my invalid's couch."

"One kiss," Raven reluctantly conceded. "A brief meeting of the lips . . . and nothing more."

"Of course." He grinned wickedly, pulling her close against him.

Other Books in
THE AVON ROMANCE Series

Brazen Whispers *by Jane Feather*
Devil's Moon *by Suzannah Davis*
Falcon on the Wind *by Shelly Thacker*
Moonfeather *by Judith E. French*
Moonlight and Magic *by Rebecca Paisley*
Playing with Fire *by Victoria Thompson*
Spitfire *by Sonya Birmingham*

Coming Soon

Captive Rose *by Miriam Minger*
Rugged Splendor *by Robin Leigh*

Rough and Tender

SELINA MACPHERSON

AVON BOOKS NEW YORK

ROUGH AND TENDER is an original publication of Avon Books. This work has never before appeared in book form. This work is a novel. Any similarity to actual persons or events is purely coincidental.

AVON BOOKS
A division of
The Hearst Corporation
105 Madison Avenue
New York, New York 10016

Published by arrangement with the author
Library of Congress Catalog Card Number: 90-93395
ISBN: 0-380-76322-2

First Avon Books Printing: February 1991

Printed in the U.S.A.

RA 10 9 8 7 6 5 4 3 2 1

For Ken and a love that transcends time.

BOOK 1

The Journey

Chapter 1

Indiana Territory
August 17, 1807

The day had been uncomfortably warm, the air still and so oppressive that even the simple act of drawing breath took a supreme effort. Though he lay upon the narrow cot in the comparatively cool shade of the cabin, the heat seemed to drain Henri François Delacour of all his body's fluids. His skin felt hot and dry as paper, and his lips were parched. He just lay there, thinking of the cool water his daughter had brought in from the creek that morning. From his position on the cot he only had to turn his head to see the bucket that rested on the rough trestle table.

How heavenly it would taste right now! He was not greedy. A dipperful would satisfy his awful craving for a little while. If only Raven would come . . .

She was a dutiful daughter and far too young and beautiful to be tending to the needs of a sick old man. She had turned nineteen this very day, and should be wearing beautiful, stylish clothes and dancing with handsome young men. It was her right! and he, Henri, had stolen it from her. This agonizing thirst he felt now was his penance for depriving his little girl of her youth.

Of course, in the beginning it had seemed no more than indulging one of the child's whims. Since her dear mother's death Raven had become the very light and substance of his life. He had petted her and spoiled her. She had only to show interest in something for Henri to go out of his way to tutor her. Because of this she could ride and shoot as well as he. And if she was less than adept at womanly arts, well there was plenty of time for that later. He would see to her education when she was older. In the meantime, he would enjoy her company just a little longer. She made a fine companion, and was not given to complaining like some females.

Very gradually the years had slipped away. Raven grew up and grew wild. She delighted in the unlikely company of the hunters and trappers and Indians who stopped by Henri's post to trade. Some were dangerous men, some merely lonely for the talk of a woman. Still, Henri had kept a wary eye on his beautiful daughter.

Henri had noticed the men's eyes following her trim figure and decided that it was time to arrange for her schooling. It was dangerous for her here. He shuddered to think what might occur if some renegade happened by while he was off hunting. He was all that stood between her beauty and harm's way. And now he was helpless to protect her.

Henri had never had the opportunity to bring up the subject of formal training to his headstrong daughter, and he knew in his heart that Raven would not agree to go in any case. She knew nothing of city life, or of academies for young ladies, nor did she want to know. She was content with the skills she had and wanted nothing to do with being turned into a gentlewoman to slave for some man hand and foot. Besides, she knew enough of cooking and cleaning to take good care of Henri without any assistance from a man, and could read and write in both French and English, thanks to her father's tutelage. That in itself was more than most women could do.

The idea of schooling for his daughter had been put aside by Henri when the illness took hold of him three weeks ago. Day by day it became less and less important. He weakened more each day, and it was a herculean task just to haul himself from the cot when Raven changed the linens. It was obvious to him that he wasn't going to recover. Soon, his only child would be left alone, and there seemed nothing to be done about it.

Raven's predicament preyed upon Henri's mind. So much so that he found himself beseeching the Blessed Virgin to deliver his child from danger. If only he was assured of her safety, then he could die peacefully. But it had been so long since he had actually prayed that he thought She might not hear his desperate pleas.

"Mother of God, deliver us," Henri croaked. Water, he needed water. If only he could bestir himself from the cot and reach the bucket, the cool water would relieve his thirst and make him a little stronger.

Eben had developed a strong respect for the little sorrel mare he had purchased in St. Louis. She had carried him back into the mountains when he'd parted company with Meriwether Lewis and William Clark, and had served him valiantly.

Cadence, he called her, for she had a delicate way of placing her feet when she cantered, the rhythmic clip-clop reminding him of military drums. She was a pleasant animal with a keen intelligence and an easy disposition, and Eben valued her highly. To his way of thinking she was the first step in seeing his plans for the future to fruition. She would produce a fine string of blooded foals for the breeding empire he intended to build. Within ten years the name St. Claire would be synonymous with quality horseflesh, and he himself would be modestly wealthy.

Cadence was worth ten horses similar to the young stud who trailed behind him on a long tether. The stallion was only half broken and as cantankerous an animal as Eben had yet to come upon. He called the stud Willow, and a more apt name Eben could not have found, for the horse remained as green as a willow switch.

The stallion would stand to be mounted and allow a rider to lapse into a false sense of security, then just as soon as the rider's guard was down, he bucked or bolted or stopped so suddenly that the rider went flying headlong into the dust.

This last had happened to Eben twice and he had walked up to the stallion, vowing to see him gelded at the first available moment. But the horse had seemed unimpressed and had rolled his eyes and pinned his ears back, looking very mulish.

No wonder the seller had insisted on a price for both animals and had refused to discuss selling just the mare.

It mattered little if the stallion was worthy or not. The mare was his gem, his beginning.

The land was fairly level and he let his thoughts turn to the future. In his mind he pictured the house he would build, strong as any fortress, but possessing an elegance that would catch the eye. He blithely ignored the intruding thought that he had no one with whom he could share his plans. The longer he was alone, the less importance he placed on family.

Of course, in all the years that had crept by since Jase's capture, Eben had never quite given up the idea of finding him. But he no longer wished to start a family of his own. Ivory had spoiled that for him the night she had taken the merchant into her bed. And while he could now admit that he had not really loved her, the betrayal stung him just the same. He had lost his trust in women, and now that it was gone, he knew that he would never regain it.

He still enjoyed a woman's favors, yet the type of companionship he needed had a monetary price. It was one he was willing—no, eager to pay. At least he knew what to expect from a whore. He could buy her time and her body—the transaction had a kind of honesty to it—and he knew what to expect. But when a man was foolish enough to care for a woman he became a kind of whore himself. He could expect to give his heart, his time, his trust, and in turn would be paid back with deceit and betrayal. Eben concluded that he would rather live alone and take his pleasures when his body drove him to it, than put his trust in another woman.

His mind was so caught up in his musings that for a moment he forgot the tight hold he had on Willow's rawhide tether, and urged Cadence down a slight incline and into a shallow, rock-strewn streambed. At the sight of the water the animal behind balked, then reared, his sharp hooves coming forcefully down against the mare's rump.

Cadence screamed and lunged forward, wedging her foreleg between two jagged rocks. The mare went down heavily with rider cursing, but just before she rolled atop him, he managed to kick free of the stirrups and ended his descent in an impromptu icy bath.

"You bloody mule!" Eben bellowed at the stallion.

It stood on the bank, blinking stupidly at him, as if pondering why he now stood dripping. Eben's temper soared and he snatched his knife from its sheath, advancing with an evil leer that looked strangely at odds with his drowned appearance. "I'll geld you here and now and be done with your jackass bend of mind!"

On the far side of the stream, Cadence had risen. She nickered softly and stood trembling. Eben grabbed Willow's bridle and forcefully twisted the braided leather tight across the animal's nose. "Another foolish move like that will see you bait for the crows, by God!" he warned.

But changeable Willow had already lost his stubborn whim and followed along like an obedient hound, across the streambed and up the far bank where his master then secured him.

Eben walked back to where the mare waited. The very fact that she had gained her feet meant the leg wasn't broken, but upon a closer examination he saw that it was cut and bruised, and already beginning to swell.

Glancing at the lowering sky, Eben wondered at his luck. His gem, the foundation for his fortune, was lame.

This was her nineteenth birthday, but Raven was in no mood for celebration, indeed, her heart was leaden with the weight of her dread. In a short time her world had turned upside down, and it seemed that soon the hand of fate would deal her another wry twist.

Only four weeks ago her father had been robust and active. Now he seemed almost a skeleton. His flesh was being rapidly consumed by the fever that wracked his body. Raven had been trying to vanquish the silent foe that threatened to rob her of Henri, and in the same instance doing battle with the fear she felt at the very idea of being left alone; but she knew that in the end she was bound to lose. She could only keep him comfortable and wait it out; she could only learn to deal with her solitary existence when it came.

Off to the west there was a low growl of thunder.

She quickened her pace along the path leading to the creek. The storm was slowly advancing and if she hurried she would have enough time to bathe before returning to the cabin with the water. It was her daily ritual, and the only time she took for herself. To deny herself her bath would make the evening seem an eternity. It was such a small luxury—one of the very few she now could afford to enjoy.

Even before she reached the deer trail leading down to the water, Raven began shedding her clothing. Her dress was a simple, round-necked affair with a high waist and cap sleeves. A drawstring at the neckline held it in place, so it was only a few seconds later that she flung it to the ground.

Naked, Raven waded into the water. It was deliciously cool after the heat of the afternoon. It lapped at her thighs and hips, feeling soft and luxurious as satin. Raven had seen satin once, fashioned into a sumptuous lady's gown, but she had never owned anything so extravagant and could only imagine that it would feel like the caress of the cool water. Someday she planned to own such a gown. She pictured herself whirling through a crush of dancers on the arm of a handsome gallant. Someday, she promised herself, after this nightmare she was living was over.

Raven had still not returned and Henri's thirst was terrible. He felt he would expire forthwith if he did not receive immediate relief. With a feeble hand he drew back the covers and after some effort struggled to a sitting position.

Mon dieu! What the effort cost him! But he fought the urge to lie back down and die. Determined to reach the cool water, he kept his gaze fixed on the handle of the dipper. It gave him the strength to lurch to his feet and take a few halting steps toward the table before he stumbled and fell heavily to his knees.

Henri lay there dejectedly with his eyes closed. He had failed. The bucket was within spitting distance and yet he could not reach it. Moaning, he sensed rather than heard the swift footfalls of someone entering the cabin. Henri's head had lolled to one side. He opened his eyes and saw close to his shoulder a pair of dust-covered boots that had seen better days. Slowly, Henri's gaze followed the long length of buckskin leg upward. The leggings the man wore were made Indian fashion, complete with breechclout and fringed seams, as was the hunting shirt. Henri noticed the beadwork that embellished the shoulders and the front of the shirt. It looked Shoshone, but how could that be? The Shoshone lived far to the west of the Mississippi, and many days from here. It puzzled Henri so that for an instant he forgot his thirst and continued to stare at his unexpected visitor. His eyes fastened on the stranger's wide leather belt. Hanging from that belt was an evil-looking hunting knife with a long and curving blade. Perhaps if he could not persuade the stranger to fetch him some water, he could ply the knife to end his misery. At last Henri's gaze lit on the man's face. It was a visage deeply tanned with a lean and hungry look and eyes as blue as ice chips. Then there was no more time to look, for strong hands were lifting him with surprising gentleness to the cot.

Eben had no more than placed the old man on the cot than his boney hand rose and pointed at the table standing in the center of the room. "M'sieur, please, water. Over there."

Henri watched as the stranger went quickly to bring him a full dipper. He was then drawn upward and supported by the arm the man placed behind his shoulders. "Slowly," the stranger cautioned. Henri drank and sputtered.

Once the dipper was drained Henri sighed. He

was lowered to the cot, and the man replaced the dipper then came to stand beside him. The stranger's cool eyes were regarding him, but he seemed loath to speak. Henri, however, was not so reticent. Providence had at last smiled upon him and sent him this golden haired, bearded stranger in lieu of an angel.

"Thank you, m'sieur, for your assistance," he said. "It was a kind deity who sent you to me in this most trying moment of my life."

Eben disregarded the remark and asked, "Do you live here alone, old man?" He thought it unlikely, for the one large room was spotlessly clean. The only thing out of place was a small pile of bed linens near the door.

"*Non*, m'sieur, I live here with my daughter, Raven. You will please excuse my lapse in manners. We have few visitors these days, so I tend to forget. I am Henri François Delacour, a Frenchman by birth and a trader by profession. I have been here some years but do not recall your face, m'sieur . . . ?"

"St. Claire, Eben St. Claire," he replied. "I haven't passed through here before today."

"Ah, M'sieur St. Claire! It is a name with character. Some believe that a man's name molds his character in later life. The Indians, for example. They believe that whatever name they bestow on a child will instill in it those traits. St. Claire. . . . Is it French, perhaps?"

The stranger shook his head. "Scotch-Irish."

A tough breed, Henri knew. Many of those trading with him over the years had been of the same background. There was something in the mixture that seemed to breed a violence as ruthless as any the Indians could lay claim to. Henri only hoped that this man was different. He had few options open to him and could not afford to be too discriminating, but neither was he eager to place his daughter's future in the care of an unprincipled ruffian. He would need to tread carefully.

"Will you fetch up a chair and sit a little? As I said before, we don't get many visitors and news is always welcome."

The request was not an unusual one. Contact with the outside world was often infrequent, and travelers were a ready source of information, news, and gossip. "My animals are still out front, and one is lame. I saw your smoke and thought to buy a night's lodging in your barn or shed. I can pay you for the trouble."

The Frenchman waved Eben's offer aside. "I would not think of taking payment from you, m'sieur. You are my honored guest. You say your mount is lame? If it can wait a little while, my daughter will be returning. She has some knowledge of healing with herbs. She will be glad to see to it, I am sure. Would you care for something to drink? There is a demijohn over there on the shelf. Bring it and a chair and settle your bones for a little while."

Eben found the wicker-bottomed jug and extracted the cork with his teeth. The distinctive odor of brandy floated up to tease his senses. It had been long since he had tasted anything except the green liquor that passed for whiskey on the frontier. Drinking more than a swallow meant taking your life in your hands. It was sometimes mixed with gunpowder, colored with leaves, and it tore down a man's throat and singed his vitals like hell's fire. He tried to avoid it when possible, and had lately resorted to dreaming of the fine liquor Zeb stocked in his cellar at the inn. He resisted the strong urge to tip the jug right there and found a metal cup for the old man. He wasn't an uncouth bastard, no matter what the old Frenchman might think.

Henri received the cup with a grateful smile. *''Salut, mon ami!''*

Eben hooked his forefinger through the jug's handle and rested its full weight on his forearm. The liquor went down like warm silk and blossomed in his belly just as flowers open their petals to the warmth of the sun. He lowered the jug and sank into a chair. ''I haven't had anything so fine in ages,'' he said by way of appreciation. ''I guess civilization does have its advantages.''

''You are traveling eastward, m'sieur?'' Henri's hopes were building. The stranger drank like a gentleman, though country style. Henri would gain as much information as the man was willing to give. But the matter must be approached with diplomacy. He would need to apply all of his considerable persuasive powers, and if that did not gain the desired results, then he would resort to bribery.

''Aye, to Pittsburgh, then upstream a ways, along the Allegheny.'' The brandy was having its desired effect, and Eben's tongue was loosening a little. If not for the liquor, he would probably have cut off the man's questions. He was not a man given to talk about himself, especially with someone he barely knew. Yet, here he was, sipping the Frenchman's sweet liquor and giving ready replies. The frontier had that effect on a man, he supposed.

There were times when the loneliness had nearly driven him mad. Those were the times when he had longed to see Castle Ford again, to sit with Meggie in her kitchen and smell the fragrance of spice that was ever prevalent there. It was a vein of thought Eben was vastly uncomfortable with. He had a great deal of pride—his greatest fault Meg had always avowed, and likely to be his downfall—and it pleased him to think that he needed no one. He stood alone and took what life handed to him and turned it to his advantage. So why did he feel the strong urge to return to Castle Ford?

And if he arrived at the inn, what reception might be receive? Zeb McAllister was likely to be put out with him for jilting his only daughter. Eben's honor would not allow him to malign the woman's name, no matter what she had done. If he showed up suddenly after four years what might the older man think? Eben had meant to write during his absence, yet Meg had never learned to read, and what would he say to Zeb that would make up for his casting Ivory aside? It was a sticky situation and one that perplexed him, so he had thought it wise just to postpone writing the letter. The old Frenchman's voice cut into his musings.

"M'sieur does not find the brandy to his liking?"

"I find it very much to my liking. Why do you ask?"

"You do not drink, and you wear a frown, as if the liquor does not sit well with you. I regret that I have nothing else to offer. . . ."

"Liquor does strange things to a man," Eben mused aloud. "For some reason it brings reflections to mind that I would rather forget. It also loosens my tongue, and I'm not a man given to idle talk."

"That I can see, my friend," Henri said, "but alas! I am a man not destined to be long upon this earth, so I hope you will humor me and give your tongue free rein a little while longer."

There was more than a grain of truth in the other man's words. Eben felt the urge to humor him, though he felt no pity. Every man faced death at some point, and this old Frenchman would greet his end in bed with his loved one by his side. He had seen men die far less desirable deaths. Eben raised the jug again. When he lowered it the Frenchman questioned him.

"If it is not prying, might I ask where you have

come from, M'sieur St. Claire? I noticed the beadwork on your hunting shirt. It is some fine handiwork; Shoshone, perhaps?"

"You have an observant eye. It is indeed Shoshone crafted, and I've been to the Pacific Ocean. I went out with Captain Lewis and his men. It was the wife of the interpreter, a young Shoshone girl, who made this shirt for me."

"Ah, how very fascinating! M'sieur is a great *voyageur.* You must know the country very well indeed, and be well skilled in providing for yourself and your companions. Do you travel with companions, M'sieur St. Claire?"

Eben shook his head and tilted the jug for a short swallow. The liquor was sweeter than any nectar he'd ever drunk. It far surpassed the fine Scotch whiskey the judge kept in his cellars at the inn, the whiskey he'd been aching to sip again. This brandy warmed his insides and made him feel extremely mellow—it was good to relax after years of sleeping with one eye open and both ears cocked. "I'm alone," he admitted.

"This is good," Henri murmured without thinking. Then he noticed the young frontiersman give him an odd look, so he hastened to put his fears to rest. It would do no good to make the man suspicious. "It is just that my daughter is shy and would be ill at ease if there were more for supper than just we three." He noticed the younger man relax. "You have been gone long from home, have you not? Your wife must be most anxious for your return."

"I have no wife, thank God," Eben said. "And want none," he added, eager to make his point. "You seem uncommonly interested in a man you do not know, and I have replied patiently. Now it's my turn to question you, Monsieur Delacour. What do you want of me, for surely there is something?" He held up a hand when Henri made to protest. "Pray, don't claim boredom because I won't buy it for a minute."

"Very astute," Henri said quietly. "It is true, what you suggest. I asked because I need to know. My daughter's security depends upon it—upon you, *mon ami.*" Henri sighed, as much from the effort this long talk cost him as from being caught in his game. "I have a proposal to lay before you that will serve my purpose and benefit you as well."

Choosing his words as carefully as he could, Henri related the facts as Eben listened. "As you have seen, I am dying. When I am gone my daughter will be left alone. This world is cruel, m'sieur. I would not leave my only child at the mercy of wolves. It is a parent's worst nightmare—to leave a child unprotected, perhaps unable to fend for herself—"

"I fail to see what any of this has to do with me," Eben interjected.

"You are the only white man to happen by in many weeks, since long before I fell ill. How many weeks will it be, I ask you, before someone else comes by? I cannot wait, m'sieur. You are my only hope to save my daughter from this horrible fate! You must take her with you when you leave here—you must! There is no other way! She needs a strong protector, and you are that protector."

Henri had anticipated many reactions, but not the one he now received. He watched in bemused silence as the younger man tossed back his tawny head and howled his mirth to the beamed ceiling. It was some moments later that Eben finally sobered. "By Christ," he said, giving way to a final chuckle, "I've been many things in my life, but never a nursemaid to a half-grown miss! What the devil would I do with her? I know nothing about the needs of females."

"Why, *mon ami,* they are just like us, only softer, of course," Henri said.

Aye, that they were, Eben thought. And likely to complain at the least little inconvenience. He detested the idea of dragging a pigtailed lass five hundred miles through rough country and hearing her nagging him every step of the way.

"She need only be protected from harm and given a bit of food and water. It is not so difficult, eh? Raven is a good and dutiful girl and will give you little trouble." This was an outright lie, but Henri was forced into telling it. If Raven could be handled by anyone, it would be this man. He had an unswerving gaze that seemed incapable of guile, if it did seem a trifle cold. His features were stern, yet Henri knew he was capable of laughter. And lastly, when he had helped him, a stranger, back to his bed and given him water, he had displayed his generosity of spirit and a gentleness that was at odds with his rough exterior. Yes, Henri thought, satisfied, this Eben St. Claire would do very nicely indeed!

His arms folded across his chest, Eben was shaking his head. "What you ask of me is impossible. I can't do it." Even as the words left his mouth he felt guilt at saying them. The old man was pitiful, begging for his daughter's life. But to take on a tender young female was more than he felt he could handle. There had to be another way. "Surely there is some other recourse," he said. "Close neighbors or relatives—anyone who would take the girl in."

The old man shook his head sadly. "No one, and time is dwindling rapidly."

Eben swore softly. "Even if I agree, what the hell will I do with her once I get her there? Have you thought of that? I'm bound for Pittsburgh, and being a bachelor, I can't take the girl in!"

"And neither would I ask you to," Henri said. "All she needs is decent lodging, someone she can depend upon to help her adjust to her new life. In a few years when she is of an age, she can marry. It is all I wish for her."

"You certainly paint a rosy picture, old man," Eben said. "But how do I know the girl will comply? Women are adept at using unfair tactics on a man to have their way. Tears and tantrums, vapors—" He shuddered at the thought of being burdened with some weeping, swooning creature. "I have a bad feeling about this."

He was showing promise. Henri decided it was time to add incentive. "I will pay you handsomely for your trouble. A thousand—no! Fifteen-hundred dollars in gold. Just to see my little girl settled. I have saved a tidy sum to leave her as a dowry. She will be able to live modestly on what is left."

It was against his better judgment, Eben thought, but the lure of the gold beckoned. "And this girl is obedient, you say?"

"But certainly!" Henri hurried to affirm.

"And docile?" Eben asked. "I won't coddle some sniping harpy."

"As meek of manner and docile as a spotted fawn." Henri thought it seemed to satisfy him. Like a fat trout the younger man swam about the baited hook. Patiently he waited.

Eben paused to consider the old Frenchman's offer. The promise of so much gold was extremely tempting, and all he need do is coddle the old man's brat as far as Pittsburgh. If they traveled hard, how long would it take? Of course he would need to have another horse for the girl to ride because the stallion was unsuitable. The more he thought of it, the better the money looked. Added to what he already had salted away in St. Louis it would make a good beginning. He was startled to hear his own reply, "I'll take the girl to Pittsburgh, but not a foot further. If you wish for her to go elsewhere, then she can be put on a stage from there. It's the most I am willing to do."

"And you will be nearby, to see that she is well?" Henri prodded.

"I suppose it isn't out of the question that I check on her welfare now and again. I even know of a woman there who might consent to keep an eye on her." He was thinking of Sally Sourwine who ran a boarding house of sorts. For a nominal sum Sally might find the girl a decent home and see to her education in the womanly arts, whatever she needed to know to get her a husband.

"I put my trust in you, m'sieur," the Frenchman said.

"My solemn oath." Eben had warmed to the bargain rapidly with the promise of monetary reward. He extended his hand and took the shriveled one that the Frenchman offered.

Henri's dark eyes danced. "Then it is done!" he said. "And I can die in peace. Now, there is but one more thing I would ask of you, *mon ami.*"

"Christ, man! Don't tell me you've another daughter!"

The younger man looked so appalled that Henri chuckled. "*Non,* M'sieur St. Claire, only fill my cup again and we will drink to seal our bargain."

"That's the first thing you've said so far that makes any sense, old man." For the first time since arriving, Eben smiled.

Chapter 2

The wooden buckets were clumsy and hard to carry. Their very awkwardness made Raven walk twice as fast as she normally would have just to reach the cabin. With each step the heavy wood bumped against her calves until they were bruised and sore. The rope bails had at first raised blisters, which had by now hardened into a horny ridge of calluses just below her fingers on the palms of her hands. Raven didn't really mind the calluses, for they protected her tender hide from more chafing. It was only when she thought of someday wearing a satin gown that she looked at her hands and sighed.

By the time she reached the end of the path and came to the clearing, Raven was winded. It was a long walk from the cabin to the creek. She realized that she must have dallied too long at her bath when she noticed the dark clouds overhead. The storm was no longer far off to the west, and she was likely to get caught in it if she did not hurry. Despite that knowledge, the pain that knifed through her side forced her to stop for just a moment and put down her burdens. She would rest just long enough to catch her breath before continuing on to the cabin. Yet the bottoms of the buckets had barely touched the earth when she snatched them up again. Tied to the post ring in the cabin yard she saw two sleek-looking horses. Someone was there, and Henri was totally unable to defend himself.

There were no candles lit and the fire had nearly gone out, so the interior of the cabin was dim and the shadows deep. Rushing headlong into the gloom, Raven found herself temporarily blinded. Luckily she knew the large room and where each piece of furniture was positioned. It was with considerable shock that she collided with an obstacle placed directly in her path, where it had no right to be.

The thing was big and hard and unmistakably male. It could not be Henri, he would have been bowled over by the force of the impact. It must be the stranger, the owner of the horses. The hands that reached out to steady her were so warm and strong that Raven recoiled from the unaccustomed touch. Her sharp backward movement jostled the buckets and caused an audible slosh of water that brought tears of frustration to her eyes. The water she'd worked so hard to obtain washed over the man's boots and puddled on the floor. All her labors had been for naught.

The stranger seemed not to notice the trouble he'd caused. He was far too busy ogling her breasts, revealed by the damp cloth of her thin calico bodice. She stared up angrily at him. Her eyes had adjusted to the light now, and she could see where his pale gaze roamed! Whoever this clumsy beast was, she blamed him for the entire mishap.

Eben was still trying to tear his gaze away from the round fullness of her breasts when she launched herself against him with a strength amazing for one so small. She landed a few well aimed blows before he finally managed to catch hold of her wrists. "Goddammit, hold still!" he commanded.

She struggled violently in his arms and cursed him roundly in French.

Eben's command of French was not extensive, but he knew enough words and phrases to understand that she intended to see him emasculated if she got hold of a knife. Holding her was like holding a slippery fish. Judging from the sharp jabs of her elbows—her only weapon, he surmised—and the murderous tone of voice, she was quite capable of trying to carry out her threat. The little wildcat just might decide to use his own knife to execute her planned surgery, and he'd be damned if he intended to spend the rest of his days as a eunuch!

"You're as slippery as an eel," Eben said, laughing down at her. Her language was atrocious for a young woman. The oaths she hurled at his head were more than colorful, they were damned inventive! By God, where had the little she-demon learned such things? He hadn't heard such foul talk hurled from the rough, bearded mouths of the *voyageurs*.

"Old man, can this spitting, clawing catamount by any chance be your daughter?" Eben asked casually, then howled when the girl sank her sharp little teeth into the underside of his wrist. He was sure she brought blood, the vicious little thing! "Be still, or so help me I'll turn you over my knee and tan your hide!" he growled at her.

"Papa! Has this brute harmed you?" She stilled in his unwelcome embrace as if she were listening intently for the old man's reply, then when she felt the man loosen his hold on her she drew an elbow forward and jammed it as hard as she could into his midsection. She smiled at his gasp as his breath left him suddenly.

Tightening his embrace, he held her so close that she could feel the muscles of his chest flex against her back with his every movement. He laughed humorlessly, his breath fanning the side of her throat. "It seems to me that she needs taming more than protecting."

"Raven, *ma fille,*" Henri cried from his cot. "Desist! You insult and abuse an honored guest! Where are your manners? M'sieur St. Claire," he said to the buckskin-clad frontiersman, "I beg you to forgive my daughter's rudeness. I am afraid that without her *maman*'s guiding hand she has grown a bit wild."

"That's readily apparent," Eben said.

"Apologize to m'sieur, Raven."

"But, Papa—"

"Immediately!"

"*Moi s'excuser,* m'sieur," she said. Somehow she did not sound the least bit contrite.

"*Anglais!*" Henri barked, his voice gravelly with anger.

Raven snatched in a shocked breath. He sounded ashamed of her, her dear papa. She softened her voice and spoke over her shoulder to the man who held her so familiarly. "I ask your pardon, M'sieur St. Claire. My conduct was most unbecoming. Will you please release me now?" His hand had slipped down to rest on her hip, his fingers pressing against her flat little belly. Was the contact intentional or accidental? It didn't really matter, for Raven longed to slap away the warm, hard hand.

"Aye," he said, "I'll let you go. But first let's have a look at you." And with that he turned her to face him. One hand fell to her shoulder so that she could not pull away from him, the other came up to cup her chin and tilt her face upward, forcing her to meet his eyes.

What Eben now looked upon very nearly took his breath away. Here, gazing up at him with a mixture of belligerence and ingrained hauteur was by far the loveliest young woman he had yet to behold.

His scrutiny was kept intentionally curt, his eyes displaying not an ounce of the warmth that was suffusing him from being so near her—touching her.

Her features were delicate, her nose slim and straight, her chin rounded, and all derived from her Gallic ancestors. Yet there was something else not quite as obvious, something in the proud tilt of her head, the flashing dark eyes so full of fiery spirit as she glared at him.

Eben knew he was staring, but he could not help himself. Her lush red lips parted, revealing the small, perfect teeth with which she had bitten him. Desire flared up inside him and he started to lower his head to taste the sweetness of her mouth when he remembered the Frenchman.

She was watching him warily through the thick fringe of her sooty lashes, trying to see behind his pale inscrutable eyes to his intent. Had she truly had the knack to look beyond his cool facade she would have blushed to the roots of her hair.

"Bastard!" the girl hissed, her eyes shifting to the figure on the cot, then back again. She smiled sweetly up at him when she saw she'd not been found out.

Eben laughed outright at the insult. He saw her raise her stubborn little chin and slit her eyes malevolently against his cutting stare. "I'll let you go, but I warn you, take care what you do, little cat. I won't take kindly to being attacked."

He released her and in a calculated show of bravado she stood where she was, rubbing her abused wrists and shoulder and looking daggers at him.

Her boldness seemed to amuse him and he gave her a grin that was decidedly wolfish. His teeth looked very white against the darkness of his beard. His eyes sparkled pale blue in the sun-bronzed face, devoid of even a trace of warmth. She found his eyes chillingly attractive, and as she stared back at him she wondered abstractly if this was how a bird felt when it was hypnotized by a serpent.

But he was not a serpent; he was only a man and

made of flesh and blood just as she was. The thought put her feelings of fear and trepidation in perspective. She relaxed a little, though she did not take her eyes off him, and even shook back her blue-black hair so that it fell down her back in damp disarray. Had she known just how tempting she looked, she might not have been so confident.

Eben got his feelings under control and deliberately dismissed her. "You didn't tell me that the girl had Indian blood," he said to Henri, for all the world as if she weren't there.

Raven bristled.

"I saw no need, m'sieur," Henri said. "Her *maman* was French and Delaware, so Raven is but one-quarter Delaware, and as you can see for yourself, her French blood takes precedence."

"I agree it would take a trained eye to see it," Eben murmured. He was looking at her again. "She could pass for a true daughter of France, were it not for her hellish temper. Seeing her in action, one knows she is part savage. But that's all right, I'll soon take it out of her."

Raven had seized a straw broom and now thrust it into his hands. "Here!" she said hotly, "you made this mess, you clean it!"

Eben gave her back the broom and crossed his arms before his chest, gazing down at her as if she were crazed. "May I remind you, little hellcat, that you ran into me. Sweep if you will, I shall see to my mount as I was about to do when you came flying in here. That way I won't be in your way." He turned to Henri. "If you can tell me where your spring is located I'll fetch some water for my mounts."

It was Raven who answered. "You bumbling oaf! Why do you suppose I was carrying the buckets? The only water to be had is in the creek, that way." She pointed in a southeasterly direction.

He smirked at her, or so she thought. Actually Eben had only smiled, his mouth curling at the corners in a peculiar kind of half smile she would soon become familiar with. He exited as she began plying the broom with a great deal of force, knowing that she would have much preferred to have attacked him with it instead.

Just as soon as the frontiersman had gone, Raven threw down her broom and rushed to her father's side. "Papa, who was that horrid man?"

"Salvation, *ma petite,*" Henri replied. "We must talk. There is so little time left us, and so very much I need to say. Promise me that you will listen without interruption until I have finished."

Raven guessed he was going to speak of his imminent death and her future. She feared her father's plans for her somehow included that arrogant man. "Papa, you need to rest now. We can talk later, once this person has gone his way."

"*Non,* we must talk now," Henri said. "And you will listen."

"Papa, please," she said. Something dark and sinister lurked just beyond his next utterance. Raven found herself wanting to put her palms over her ears as she had done when she was a child. But she wasn't a child; she was a woman, and she made herself listen.

"Soon we must part, Raven," Henri said, smoothing her hair as he always had. "I am going to join your *maman.* No! Do not be sad, *cherie!* I am not sad to go, only that I must leave you alone. But now, now you will not be alone. M'sieur St. Claire will look after you, see you settled in a new place where you can be happy. I have made all the arrangements; the bargain has been sealed."

"Bargain, Papa? What bargain?" Raven asked, suddenly alarmed. She knew of the casket of gold coins that Henri had buried under the floor of the cabin, and she knew which board to pull up to find it. But had her father, in his eagerness to absolve his guilt at leaving her alone, told the tall stranger of the fortune in gold? Raven had looked into the frigid depths of the man's blue eyes; she had recognized his ruthlessness.

"The price is set. Fifteen hundred dollars for M'sieur St. Claire to take you to Pittsburgh. It is so small a price, *ma fille,* to have my worries borne by another capable of the carrying. The remainder of the money will see to your living expenses once you arrive in Pittsburgh. There, you will have a decent home, some frilly dresses to lighten your woman's heart, and other young ladies with whom you can gossip. Who is to say? If fate is kind, you might even meet a young man there, someone who catches your fancy. I should like to think of you married and content, Raven. M'sieur St. Claire has agreed to arrange the details in my stead."

Raven gasped. Her father must have lost his mind. It was the illness, she quickly decided. He wasn't responsible for his actions, and she was not going to be held to any bargain he had made in this condition. Then it occurred to her that perhaps it was not all of Henri's doing. The suggestion may have been the frontiersman's. Yes, it was something he would do, she thought. "What makes you think that you can trust this man, Papa? He seems very treacherous, if you ask me. A man who might take advantage of someone more vulnerable than he." As he had when he had held her imprisoned. She felt sure he had wanted to kiss her, and no doubt would have had Henri not been present to witness his scoundrel-like conduct.

"You are wrong about him, *ma fille.* He has a kindness in him, this man, though for some reason he strives to hide it. Perhaps he believes, like you, that if he is found to be vulnerable someone may attempt to take advantage of his good nature."

Henri saw her mutinous expression. She had formed a strong dislike for the man named St. Claire and would not be swayed by his words. Henri wondered if it was indeed dislike that his daughter felt for the frontiersman. From his vantage point on the cot, Henri had witnessed the entire scene. He had noticed more than what he was sure the frontiersman or Raven were aware of themselves. From the moment their eyes had met and clashed, there had been a special kind of tension in the room. Perhaps this was what Raven fought, instead of dislike.

"You did not see him, Papa," Raven protested. "Nor did you look into his eyes. He is very cruel."

"He was angry. There is a difference. And as you were busy cursing him quite viciously, I believe he was justified," Henri told her. "No man enjoys hearing such rough talk slip off a woman's tongue, Raven. M'sieur was not exactly eager to become your guardian. I had to cajole him into believing that you would cause him no trouble, that you were sweet-natured and uncomplaining. He knows now that I have lied. I wonder if he will refuse our agreement or rise to the challenge of 'taming you,' as he put it."

"One can always hope he will back down," Raven said, though she doubted it in light of the lucrative bargain he'd made. "But if he doesn't . . ."

Henri saw the light of cunning enter her expressive dark eyes. "*Mon dieu,* daughter! Desist with this scheming! You are willful and spoiled and I am ashamed that you've come to this pass! By God, I am glad your gentle *maman* is not here to see this!"

The effort of the speech was too much for Henri. He collapsed in a violent fit of coughing. "Go, go," he said once he regained his breath.

Raven saw the blood-flecked spittle on his lips and

felt immediately contrite. He was her dear father, and he was dying. She loved him enough to give him what he wanted, or at least to keep up the appearance of doing so. "I am sorry, Papa. I did not mean to vex you. I will be the ward of M'sieur St. Claire, if that is truly what you want."

"*Bon,*" Henri said in a weak voice. "Now go and bring the casket."

Raven bit her lip to still the argument that rose within her, and went to do his bidding. The board was easily pried loose and the chest brought to the cot. At Henri's nod, Raven opened the lid. A small velvet bag lay on top of the horde of coins. She raised questioning eyes to his.

"Your *maman*'s locket. I want you to have it, *cherie.* A final birthday gift."

"But I thought—"

"*Non,* I could not bear to part with it. It was all that I had left of her." Henri paused to rest, then continued more softly. "Take the gold and give M'sieur St. Claire his rightful share. It is his due, and I will rest easier knowing my debt is paid. The rest is yours."

Raven took the locket from its velvet nest and put it around her neck. The task kept her from meeting her father's gaze. It would not do to upset him further.

Henri was growing weary by now, and so he failed to notice. "There is one other gift I wish to give you," he said. "It is the most important gift of all, more priceless than trinkets or gold."

Raven tried to laugh gaily, but it sounded hollow. "What can it be, Papa, that is more precious than gold? Perhaps I can give it to m'sieur instead of the coins you promised!"

Henri smiled weakly. Perhaps you can, he thought. But he said, "It is love, *ma fille.* I wish for you to find a love like your *maman*'s and mine. One that is deep and abiding. Cherish it, Raven, for it is the one true key to happiness. Nurture it as you would a delicate flower and it will flourish, and never, never, cast it aside for the sake of pride.''

Raven looked lovingly at her father's face, tears welling up in her eyes. ''I will carry your words in my heart, Papa,'' she assured him, although she doubted that she would ever meet a man to whom she would want to give her heart.

''Kiss me now, for I shall seek my rest,'' Henri said. ''Treat M'sieur St. Claire with civility, *cherie.* Remember that he is a guest in my house.''

Raven could hardly forget, for moments later as the storm was breaking outside and her unwelcome guardian burst through the door.

Chapter 3

The small fire that Raven had built for her father's comfort earlier in the day was now all but dead, with only a few live coals glowing red beneath the soft gray wood ash. A handful of wood shavings placed discriminately amongst the coals and a little care would soon rebuild the blaze, and it was during Raven's completion of this chore that Eben reentered the cabin.

He saw his ward bending very near the hearth, seemingly intent upon what she was doing and not noticing him. Curious, but not wishing to interfere, Eben went to stand just behind her. He watched closely as she bent forward, almost over the kindling, and blew gently on the coals. A single yellow tongue of flame rewarded her efforts. "Bravo, mademoiselle," he said softly, "but do be careful, it would be a shame to singe those pretty locks."

She turned to shoot him a glare meant to silence him and smelled the noxious odor of burning hair. Raven jerked her head back so fast that she hit her head on the stone chimney ledge. Sitting down quickly, she rubbed the injured spot. To her consternation, her guardian stood looking down at her with a mixture of amusement and disbelief on his face. He reached down and took her hand in his, drawing her up to stand before him. His hand touched the knot on her brow and smoothed the tiny tendrils curling round her face. "My, but you're a clumsy wench," he murmured softly. "It's a wonder you've survived out here so long. You may thank me for coming to your rescue, otherwise you'd likely maim yourself for life."

He was damp from the rain and carried a clean, fresh smell on his clothes and skin. He still held her hand in his, rubbing her palm thoughtfully. "Are you all right, mademoiselle?" His fingers brushed the calloused ridge; she saw him frown.

Raven would have snatched her hand away from him then, but he held it securely. She looked down at the floor, refusing to meet his piercing eyes. He was laughing at her, she had no doubt. Instead she heard his words come soothingly. "You've had a very great burden to bear, lass. It is all right to lay it down, you know. There are those who would help you if you but ask."

"And just who, m'sieur, could help me? You?" Raven felt like spitting at him, but she didn't because he was a guest in her home. Instead she asked scornfully, "What price does your 'help' entail? Or dare I inquire? Another bit of fondling against my will? Another show of submission from your ward?"

His eyes slid over her face, down her throat to her soft, round breasts. "I cannot imagine your being submissive to any man, even one so obviously your superior."

For the first time in her life, Raven was reduced to sputtering in French. She searched for something bad enough, vile enough to call him, but she could think of nothing. Her tongue ached so to dress him down, and all she could do was watch him as he turned his back on her, taking a seat at the table, where he proceeded to whet the blade of his skinning knife.

"That's something you should try to master," he said without looking at her. "Where you are headed people speak English. I can understand why with your father being French you have not learned English properly, but if you listen carefully you will be able to master it, I am sure."

"There is nothing wrong with my English!" she shouted at him.

"Then make use of it. I won't have you speaking a tongue I can't comprehend. It's distracting."

"I don't give a damn if it distracts you. I'll speak French all I want—" The look on his face stopped her.

"Raven, you're trying a man with little patience to spare. It has been a bad day gone even worse since my arrival. I'm hot and I'm hungry and my horse is lame. Since I came in here you've beaten me, bitten me, and abused me verbally. Now, a mean-spirited man would backhand you and be done with it, but I'll simply issue a warning: don't push me."

Raven saw the stony set of his handsome features. He left no doubt that he meant every word, though he had yet to say how he would punish her. She remembered the feel of his hard arms around her and how he had stared down at her. He might just take his wrath out on her body. Her gaze fell on his broad shoulders, ran down the length of his arms to his hands. His muscles gathered and bunched with the slight movement it took to whet the blade and were visible even beneath the rough leather hunting shirt he wore. To her utter horror, she found the idea not totally distasteful.

Their evening meal consisted of a roasted hare accompanied by small potatoes Raven had grown, and sliced raw turnip. There was not a great quantity of food, so Raven was glad to note that her guardian possessed some table manners. He ate sparingly but did not waste a single scrap, stripping every morsel of meat from the plump hind leg until the bones were clean. She imagined he was accustomed to dining alone, for he wasn't inclined to the type of genial conversation that was usually enjoyed at the dinner table. Even when there had only been just the two of them, Raven and Henri had always talked at mealtimes. Henri was still asleep, and Raven found she missed the conversation, even if the topic was something as mundane as the weather.

Proceeding with care, Raven tried to open a dialogue with her guardian. After all, he was human—just a man, though he didn't belch as he placed his cutlery across his empty plate, as other men did. "You said before that your horse is lame," she said softly. "If you like, I could take a look at it."

He raised his pale gaze to her face and seemed to be weighing her sincerity. After a moment he was apparently satisfied. "It's true what your father said, then? You do have a knowledge of herbs and such."

"Yes, my mother taught me when I was small—before she died," Raven supplied. "It is really a matter of knowing what to use, but much of it is just common sense." While she talked Raven neatly stacked the plates and stood. "Shall we?"

"After you, mademoiselle."

Raven wondered if the man was actually a gentleman in the guise of woodsman. He certainly could be amenable when he chose. He had even shown her a modicum of respect, allowing her to precede him. What she didn't know was that this position provided him a most enchanting sight: the gentle sway of her hips beneath her skirts.

A hard rain was battering the exterior log walls of the cabin. Raven would have gone into the deluge had her guardian's hand not stayed her. She looked at the hand, so large and brown and capable, resting unself-consciously on her bare arm, and was struck anew by the incredible warmth of his touch. There was something about Eben St. Claire that was vibrantly alive and excruciatingly male. She wondered what she would do if the hand slipped up her arm, down to her breast. Slowly she raised her eyes to confront him. He seemed not to notice the pulse that jumped in her throat or the hesitancy in her gaze.

"It's raining very hard, Raven," he told her. "If you've a cloak then you'd better make use of it. I can ill afford to nurse you if you take an ague."

"What about you?" she found herself asking. She actually sounded concerned, and wondered where it had come from. She told herself steadfastly that this man meant nothing to her.

His mouth curled at the corners in a peculiar kind of half smile. She thought that he must have a strict rein on himself at all times, even on his smile. It was a very cold notion. "I am well accustomed to being out in all weather, lass," he told her. "You get toughened by it after a time."

She took a light cloak made of plain black cloth down from the peg on the wall and laid it over her shoulders. Adjusting the hood, she opened the door. "Well, you had better not take an ague, m'sieur, for I can ill afford to nurse *you!*"

Night had fallen prematurely and though there was no lightning or thunder, the wind was gusting hard. It drove Raven's breath back down her throat and whipped the cloak in a wild dance that sent it flying back against her companion's long, booted legs.

Raven stole a glance at the man behind her. His tawny head thrown back slightly, he seemed to derive some pagan pleasure from being in the midst of nature's vented fury. With his sun-streaked locks and his piercing pale blue eyes set off by the tan of his skin, he looked like a god.

Her thoughts would have amused Eben. His ancestors had indeed been pagans, yet hardly gods.

There had not been an ounce of nobility in the strain. The St. Claires were an old family, and as far back as the thirteenth century the family had served the Scottish kings. Cannon fodder, Eben's grandfather had derisively called them. Old James St. Claire had escaped the poverty of the isles and fled to America and a hangman's noose.

James, veritable rogue that he was, possessing a wry sense of justice, had thought it a fitting end after thirty years of living on the fringes of the law. James' son, Cameron, had been just fourteen when his father was hanged for stealing a horse from a lieutenant of the British dragoons. Cameron had made a better way for himself, though his life ended no less violently with his wife's, under a redman's war club. His eldest son, Jase, was no luckier it seemed, for he'd been taken captive in that same raid, and never again heard from, but Eben was determined that the ill luck of the St. Claires would end there.

When they reached the barn Eben hung the lantern he'd been carrying high on a nail. "She's valuable to me," he said as he lay a hand on Cadence's neck. "It would break my heart to have to put her down."

"I wasn't aware that you possessed one," Raven said wryly.

Eben looked at his ward from under lowered lids. "Yes, I do possess one, though I often feel it is a weakness to admit it. My poor organ, Mademoiselle Delacour, hasn't seen much usage, yet there are times when it acts quite queerly, and thus reminds me of its presence." He didn't offer the information that now was one of those times. In fact, his heart had been acting quite strangely since he first laid eyes on her sultry beauty. Instead he dropped to a crouch beside the mare's injured foreleg and reexamined the injury. "What do you think?" he asked.

She kneeled next to him and inspected the horse's

leg. "I think we can save your heart any injury, M'sieur St. Claire."

"Eben."

"What?" She turned and saw he was looking at her. There was no amusement or mockery in his face, just something else she could not define.

"You might call me Eben," he said softly. "It is my given name and sets better with me than 'monsieur.' "

"You do have an aversion to French," she said.

"No, I don't dislike it at all. In fact, I like it very much when you speak it. Even when you are cursing me the words sound soft, like a lover's lament." Eben was amazed that he said that. It must have something to do with her nearness. He was always in control of his life, of what he said, what he did. He was determined not to end like his grandfather and father before him. He intended to make a life for himself, to carve an empire from nothing. Yet somehow, with this small slip of a girl within easy reach, he lost every ounce of will, and his body—and worst of all his tongue—acted on their own. He was astounded and annoyed to find himself acting like her suitor instead of her guardian.

"A lament? What is that?"

"It is a very sad song."

She frowned a little and her arched black brows came together. "When I curse you it makes you sad? I think you are very strange indeed."

Her honesty made him laugh. "It loses something in the telling. Suffice to say that your pretty voice matches the rest of your—uh—of you. I like to hear it, yet I prefer that you speak English. That way you will be better accepted where we will be going. There are still those who remember the old animosity left behind by the French and Indian War."

Raven was looking at the horse's leg now. The animal snorted at the strange smell of her and she sought to calm her by patting her shoulder. "There, *ma cherie*, it is all right." Then to Eben she added, "The ones who remember that must be very old and decrepit. I am not worried." She stood up and went to a shelf which held various tins and bottles on the nearest wall. Raven stood on her toes and reached for one particular tin, but it was too far back on the shelf. She stretched as far as she could, and still it remained beyond her grasp.

Eben came to stand behind her. His shoulder was centered near the middle of her back, his left hand just bare inches from the soft curves of her bottom. He could smell the scent of her hair, the haunting fragrance of wild woods violets, and for an instant he felt an ungovernable urge to take her into his arms, to kiss her, to love her. . . . Never had he known his desire to mount so swiftly, to be so unbearable and so difficult to contain. Never had a woman been so unreachable as this one—his ward, his youthful, innocent, untried responsibility. He had given his word to protect her, and now it seemed that he was the one she most needed protecting against. What in hell was wrong with him? When had he become so debauched as to want to seduce a mere child?

Of course Eben's horror was unfounded. Raven, at nineteen, was hardly a child. And though she was untried and virginal, she still had all the feelings and desires of a woman. Along with her dreams of owning a satin gown, she had also imagined being with a man. She was well aware of what men and women did together. She had even seen a woman taken once by a man. The man had been a trapper, the woman an Indian who was quite drunk on her father's brandy. Raven had been out in the woods when she spied the two, and full of curiosity, she had hidden and watched for a moment. The sex act between a man and a woman was similar to what took place in the animal world, though since people mated facing each other there was more opportunity for other contact, such as kissing or looking deeply into one another's eyes. Of course, none of that had occurred between the trapper and the Indian girl. In fact the event had been singularly disappointing from an educational point of view.

The woman had sighed a great deal, and rolled under him as if she were trying to escape. The man had heaved and grunted for a moment or two before rolling off her inert form. He had readjusted his trousers and left the drunken woman lying discarded on the ground. To Raven, it had all seemed very fast and rather unglamorous. She could not imagine wearing a satin gown and doing such things. Indeed, if there was not more to it than what she had witnessed, she was not sure why people kept on doing it. It had crossed her mind that those two might not have done it properly.

"I can't reach it. . . ." she said, suddenly dropping onto her heels and turning. Eben was standing so close that she had brushed the fringe on his shirt with her arm as she turned. He was looking down at her with a strange expression on his dark face. He looked almost as though he were pained somehow. "Eben, are you ill?"

He sighed. How incredibly sweet his name sounded on her lips. "No, I'm not ill, lass. Here, I'll get it for you." He reached around her with his left hand and for the barest moment held her in the circle of his arm. His head was bent ever so slightly toward her. It would have been no great feat to try her lips then, but still he held back.

She took the tin he offered her and smiled up at him with her huge dark eyes. Her lips parted, looking soft and red. He could see her small pink tongue behind her white teeth. His heart was thudding so heavily that he could barely hear her.

"This is the wrong tin," she said. "See." She shook it and he heard it rattle.

He reached up again and took down the one just beside it. Then he stepped back quickly and made some excuse to go outside, where the pelting rain quickly cooled his ardor. "Five hundred miles," he said slowly to himself, "and it might just as well be five thousand." This journey was going to be pure hell.

Chapter 4

Raven had cleansed and salved Cadence's wound, then wrapped the injury before returning to the cabin. Now she moved about, setting things to rights. The dishes had been washed and stacked neatly away on a shelf, the table wiped and the wash water discarded. There was little left for her to do, and yet she could not sit still. If this M'sieur St. Claire noticed her unease, he gave no outward sign. He was seated near the fire and occupied with cleaning his rifle.

The gun was nearly as lethal looking as the man, and with its dull brass butt plate resting on the floor, it was almost as tall as she was. Finished with her tasks, Raven made her way closer and stood off to one side, observing him at his work.

He seemed totally engrossed with the maintenance of the weapon, though she didn't understand why. It hadn't a speck of dust on it anywhere, even though the brass was dull. Still, he ran a lightly oiled rag over the barrel and down the long stock. "If you wish I could show you how to polish the brass," she said. "In no time it will gleam as bright as new."

He looked up, the rag suddenly stilled. "Now why would I want the brass to shine?" he questioned, his impatience entering his voice, making the question more curt sounding than he had intended. He saw her blink and draw herself up as though offended and he hastened to explain. "Raven, have you ever noticed how alert the dumbest of beasts is to noise or the sign of movement? What if I were hunting and saw a prize buck standing near your creek?" He lifted the gun and sighted at the door, his pale gaze narrowing. "I draw my bead and the sun winks on the shiny brass that you want to polish. It would ruin my shot, and you, milady, would go hungry."

"You needn't speak to me as though I were a child," she said, feeling a little hurt. "And besides, M'sieur St. Claire, I can forage for my dinner if I need to." She put her slim nose in the air and walked off to sit at the end of the table.

Eben grunted and returned to his task, pretending that he didn't notice her presence. But the irritating truth was that he was thinking of her in ways that might not have pleased her father.

From the safety of the table Raven watched him. To her disgust she found that his hands fascinated her. How very brown they were, the fingers long and blunt, and hard as iron when they had gripped her shoulders and wrists. Yet watching them work the cloth almost lovingly over the curly maple stock of the rifle they looked very graceful.

"Your weapon means alot to you, does it not?" she found herself saying.

"Aye, lass, that it does. It was the only gift I've ever received, and from someone I respect deeply."

"From the way you say it, I would guess it must be your father who gave the gun to you."

He glanced up at her as he removed the flint and fitted another in its place. "You would be wrong in your assumption. My own father was long dead when this gun was presented to me. I suppose though that in a way you were also correct, for the man took my sire's place when he was killed. He saw that I was fed and clothed and educated. In a sense he has been a father to me, though certainly with little of the pride or affection that usually accompanies that relationship."

There was a curious detachment in his pronouncements, almost as if he spoke of someone else's life, instead of his own.

"I would have guessed you to be illiterate, M'sieur St. Claire," she said, though not unkindly.

"You have a very annoying habit of judging on sight, Raven. I suppose it has something to do with your tender age and vast inexperience. You'll learn soon enough that appearances are oft times deceiving."

"Why would a man not fond of his charge gift him with so marvelous a weapon?" she wondered. She was glad that he wasn't brushing her off. She was lonely and frightened and needed the sound of his voice. Every few moments she cast anxious eyes in the direction of her father's cot, just to reassure herself that he still breathed, that as yet her life had not changed.

"Because he wanted me to live." He sighed under the weight of his cares and proceeded with less enthusiasm than before. He really did not feel up to relating his life history to this slip of a girl. But sensing that she needed to hear it, he went on. "I am the last of my line, Raven. The St. Claires die out with me. Zebulon McAllister knew that and took it into account. Zeb knew my father well, and he felt a debt was owed by someone for the murder of my parents by the Senecas. He was most able, or willing, to pay it. He saw me grown safely to manhood so that I could renew the line, for my father's memory, and that of my mother."

"And did you? Perpetuate your line, I mean."

His eyes narrowed and his features hardened. "You've your own sire's curiosity, Mademoiselle

Nosey. But no, as I said before, I am the last St. Claire this side of the water."

Instead of being affronted, she laughed. "I can tell you don't like talking this way, but I think I like it very much if it annoys you. Call it my revenge upon you."

"Revenge is a two-edged sword, lass. Remember it. Anyway, why would you take revenge upon me? I am innocent of any blame. I haven't harmed you, now have I? Indeed, I'm your sworn protector." He allowed a slow grin to spread across his hard mouth, giving a twist of irony to his words. "That should give you a measure of security, instead of inciting your anger."

"I did not ask you to be my protector," Raven said.

"Nor did I ask to be it, and make no mistake about it," he told her firmly. "I will be just as glad to see Pittsburgh as you."

"Pittsburgh . . . it has a lovely sound to it," she said with sarcasm. "I can hardly wait to get there."

He looked at her again, sharply this time. "My home is nearby," he said in a warning tone. "It will allow me to drop in on you from time to time to see how your husband is treating you."

"A man of your own choosing, I suppose," she said, irritated that her life was being planned for her, first by her father, and now by this infuriating man.

"Of course," he said. "I've been thinking about it, and it will be the best thing for both of us. You'll be well provided for and off my hands. But you needn't fear, Raven. I like you, so I'll find some kindly man for you who won't beat you or treat you ill. It's your own best interest I'm thinking of."

Raven opened her mouth to refute his lie, then thought better of it. Argument with this stubborn wretch got her nowhere. He was opinionated and bullheaded and she loathed the way he was arranging her life for her. But on this of all nights he was human companionship, and he took her mind off her father's dying. In the moments of silence that followed his last pronouncement she could hear Henri's hoarse, rattling breath. She knew what it meant, but she didn't want to dwell upon it—not now, tonight. Tomorrow was soon enough to face what must be done.

"Try not to think on it," her guardian said softly, as if he read her thoughts.

It was the last thing she had expected or wanted, this bit of plain and honest sympathy. It started tears in her eyes and brought a choked little sob rising out of the depths of her soul. She dropped her head on her arms to hide her shame and was surprised to feel Eben's hands resting gently on her shoulders. She raised her eyes and saw through a prism of tears Eben kneeling before her.

"I know," he said quietly. It was enough to bring her into his arms. She fitted against him surprisingly well, as if they'd been made to be like this, her slender arms clutching him tightly, her soft round breasts crushed against his chest. Eben sighed and closed his eyes, breathing in her haunting sweet scent. She was made for some man's loving, but not his. Her face was pressed against his collarbone and her tears dampened his skin. Soft black curls brushed against his trim beard, catching, yielding to his masculinity, clinging to him as she clung to his body. The familiar quickening of blood in his loins urged Eben to tip up her small face.

Her bewilderment showed. She had stopped weeping, but her breath came very slowly through her parted lips and a faint pink blush had crept into her cheeks.

Eben hesitated a fraction of a moment. He ought to find the strength of will to resist, but with her beauty offered up to him so sweetly, all thoughts of the pledge he'd made to her father were forgotten, replaced by the wonder of the moment yet unfulfilled.

One simply spoken acknowledgment of her pain had brought Raven trembling into this stranger's arms. Surely he was her guardian, surely . . . but he was also very handsome, with the firelight catching bright in his tawny hair, glittering in his eyes so that they seemed filled with starlight. His arms were iron hard, yet gentle when holding her so close to him. She saw from under lowered lids his head bend down, felt the tentative brush of his lips . . . so warm!

Without really knowing what she did, Raven leaned closer until her slim arms were around his neck and her body pressed tightly to his. A shock went through her when she felt the hard evidence of his desire, but she was not appalled as a proper young lady should have been, and she could not pretend to be. It all seemed very natural to her. She was enjoying the heady rush of power she felt at being able to control his response by her actions.

His mouth was very insistent, sending messages she had no will to deny. Beneath his expert tutelage her lips parted even more, allowing the entrance of his tongue. He tasted of her father's brandy, smelled fresh as the rain outside—indeed, there was something about him that was very similar to the outdoors, a sort of untamed power held tightly in check, just waiting to be released. The disturbing fact was that Eben St. Claire intrigued her; she wanted to know all about him, everything.

His kiss, the slow movement of his lips across hers, the coaxing of his tongue, robbed her of breath. Henri had wished for her a love both deep and abiding, one to last a lifetime. But this was something very different. The rapid fluttering of her heart brought on by Eben's nearness, the way his touch seared her skin had naught to do with love. She felt his hands slide down her back to cup her buttocks and urge her hips against his bold length.

Raven felt alarmed and tried to pull away, but his strong hands prevented her. His lips left hers to chart another course as fully enchanting as the one just completed. To his delight Eben found the skin of her throat to be like warm silk beneath his ardent kiss. He slid his mouth along the arching column, feeling the anxious leap of her pulse against his tongue. He was just as anxious as she, and slowly bore her to the floor.

"Eben please," she whispered, her small hands pushing ineffectively at his chest.

"I vow, I'll do my best, sweetheart." His fingers toyed with the ribbon tie that secured her bodice. And then her breast was bared and his golden head descended. The heat of his mouth just grazed the trembling flesh. . . .

Whispered pleas were not enough to stop this lusting beast from rapine, and so a stronger measure was required. Raven's hand slipped behind his neck, her fingers threading into the heavy silk at his nape. She jerked down hard, pulling back his head, and at last, gaining his attention.

"Raven, lass," he said softly. "A man has needs."

"And you would slake your lust on an unwilling woman to satisfy them?" she demanded.

"If that is what you call unwilling, then I should like to see you eager." He slowly grinned and braced his elbow on the floor, supporting his head with that hand. "It will be interesting to see just how long you can resist me." He dropped a lingering kiss upon the coral peak of one trembling mound and when she cursed him, laughed aloud. "And I was thinking this journey would be a dull one."

"You bumbling ass," Raven snarled, "get off me!" She was looking daggers at him now, the pent-up fires deep within her were rising to dangerous heights.

"You will not change your mind?" he taunted.

She swatted at him and he ducked, turning his head away. It was then that the small iron box neatly concealed beneath the table caught his attention. "Now what is this, I wonder?" he questioned softly, his speculative gaze returning to his ward. "What were you planning, mademoiselle, that you kept this hidden?"

"Being under the table is hardly 'hidden'!" Raven replied testily. It rankled deeply that while the fires he had so neatly kindled in her blood had yet to cool completely, he seemed to have already forgotten their recent encounter.

"But neither is it in plain sight," Eben argued. "You were not thinking of cheating me, were you Raven?"

"No," she said, "but you have done nothing as yet to earn your share. When the terms of the bargain are completed, you will be paid, and not a moment sooner. I'd have to be a fool to put the gold in your hands so soon. You'd likely take it and be gone, and I would be left here alone and helpless."

"Alone perhaps, but hardly helpless," he said, his gaze flicking over her. "You certainly are adept at insulting me. Has it occurred to you yet that if I was truly as bad as you say, I would take *all* the gold and go?"

"I can't imagine what keeps you from it," she said.

"My honor keeps me from it," he said levelly.

"Honor?" she asked scathingly. "A strange word indeed coming from the blackguard who nearly forced himself on me just moments ago."

Eben stared at her in dumb amazement. "There was no force involved. Though I suppose it is quite in character for you to refuse to admit your own guilt in what happened! Women of your caliber seldom do."

Raven's eyes narrowed. "Exactly what are you saying?" she demanded suspiciously.

Eben did not reply immediately, but walked slowly around her, raking her from head to foot with his chilly gaze. He halted by her side, close enough that his breath stirred the tendrils at her ear, and reached out to trace one lean finger along the gentle curve of her hot cheek. His tone was low and vibrant and made Raven shiver. "I am saying, mademoiselle, that you are a tease. But do be careful, for I am not a man to turn aside so tasty a morsel when it is flaunted before me so blatantly . . . especially when I am hungry."

Turning on a booted heel, he stalked from the cabin and closed the door on his seething charge. He leaned against the wall outside and let the heavy rain pour over him. His breath came hard as he fought to control his raging thoughts, which were wont to linger on the seeming willingness of his ward just moments ago. He knew it would be a long time before the feel of her soft and fragrant skin would be erased from his memory. Silently he cursed the old man for putting him in this unenviable position.

Sometime later Eben returned to the cabin to find a quiet, much needed haven. Curled childlike on her side, Raven slept. Eben went to stand beside her, looking down into a face that was angelic in soft repose. It seemed impossible that the full soft lips were the same ones that had heaped curses upon his head earlier. Their pink curves registered a sweet vulnerability that was not present in her waking moments. And those eyes, now hidden behind shuttered lids, the lashes thick black crescents that lay upon her cheeks, could not have snapped with fire.

Surely here was the Frenchman's daughter, the poor waif who was in need of a man's protection. Yet as he stood gazing impassively down at her slumbering form, Eben found his mind recalling how she had been before. He admired the spitfire who'd threatened to unman him, and he'd thoroughly enjoyed the woman who for a few brief moments had allowed herself to melt in his arms.

"Two sides of one golden coin have I seen," he murmured softly. " 'Twill be interesting indeed to see what else the wench comes up with." He left her side and went to check on the old man before he lay down to sleep. What he saw did not surprise him. The waxen features bore a stillness that had naught to do with earthly slumber. Death was a silent stalker, for as the girl dreamed upon her pillow, the old Frenchman had just slipped away. Eben reached down and drew the blanket over the corpse's face.

In death, Henri Delacour had smiled. Perhaps relieved at last of earthly woes he had felt happy to die. Or had he seen the passing of his troubles onto the shoulders of another man as a final jest? If this was so, then it was a grim jest indeed.

Chapter 5

The familiar ring of a spade striking earth woke Raven just before first light. Though she knew the implications of the sound, she was not yet ready to face what lay ahead. Instead she crawled from her soft nest of quilts and without looking at her father's bed went about making breakfast for herself and the man called Eben St. Claire.

Soon the sizzle and pop of frying bacon was accompanied by a delicious aroma that wafted through the open door and into the cabin yard to tease the laboring man's senses. In a few moments he was washing the dirt from his hands and splashing his face with tepid water. Wordless, he came to the table and seated himself in the same place he had occupied the night before.

Raven sat across from him and while he worked diligently at satisfying his appetite, she picked at her food. Until now she had yet to look at the place where her father lay and had purposely kept her gaze averted in hopes of delaying the grief she knew she'd feel. Now she felt compelled to look, as if seeing the still and lifeless form would somehow make it all seem more real, her need to make a decision about her future more imperative. Avoiding her guardian's curious gaze she turned her eyes slowly to the empty cot.

Eben saw her look and knew that the impromptu

burial had come as an unpleasant surprise to her. Her small face told him she was appalled, and he suddenly felt the need to justify his actions. In as calm a tone as he could muster, he said, "It was for the best, Raven."

His cool tone unnerved her. The eyes she raised to him had once been soft and velvety brown, now they appeared nearly black and were more than mildly hostile. "What would you know of it? You know nothing of either Papa or myself. You only came here yesterday and now you think you know 'what is best.' Well, allow me to enlighten you, M'sieur *Arrogant* St. Claire, you know nothing! But then, never having had a family to love you, I suppose accounts for your ignorance."

He was watching her impassively. Not a hint of expression was in his eyes or on his lean, dark face. She decided instantly that this was what she detested most about him. How dare he sit there and feel nothing while she openly insulted him!

"What you say is true enough. I've had no family for many years. Still, I've looked upon the faces of those dear to me and seen the ravages that vermin and open air cause upon the dead. I have not much stomach for such sights myself, but since you are so outraged, come. Come! I'll set to work and open the grave for you. That way you can lay bare what is better left covered."

She felt the force of his ire; his meaning sank in and brought tears to her eyes. "You are crude," she said.

"Crude, Raven? I prefer to think of myself as being truthful." He watched her for a long moment. She remained beautiful even when she was weeping. There was no redness in her face, just the tears wetting her lashes and tumbling over each other in their haste to dampen her cheeks. He felt a strong almost violent urge to take her in his arms and kiss away those tears.

Indeed he would have, had he not had an eye toward the future. Leave her he would, and the break would be better clean. If she found her way into his arms again he might not be able to restrain himself. Last night had been hard enough. And so he crushed down the wild impulse and made his voice purposely cold. "Ready yourself, for we leave in the morning. If you must grieve, then do it today. I want no sniffling when we are on the trail." With that he rose and left the cabin.

Raven stared after him, hating him. How could he be so callous in the face of her loss? Henri, beloved parent, boon companion, sage adviser, was gone. Since her mother's death he had been all of that to her and more, and she would miss him terribly. His absence created an aching void that Raven doubted could ever be filled, and certainly not by the overbearing beast just now exiting the cabin.

Her situation settled in upon her like some heavy cloak, bringing with it a feeling of suffocation. Panic threatened to overwhelm her. She was alone with Eben St. Claire! And if he had his way, she would be totally at his mercy. He would take great pleasure in ordering her about, directing even the smallest aspect of her life, then he would jeer at her attempts at defiance. Had he not begun already? His words came soaring back to beat at her frazzled nerves with frenzied wings. "If you must grieve, then do it today. I want no sniffling when we are on the trail." Her circumstance would only worsen the longer she remained.

Yes, he would want to be on his way quickly. The sooner they reached Pittsburgh, the sooner he could be rid of her. All his prattling on about finding her a worthy husband had found fertile ground, and Raven knew without a doubt that he meant what he said. She began to plan. She had to escape this callous and unfeeling brute, Eben St. Claire.

The problem of how to go about escaping plagued Raven for most of the afternoon. To pass the time she busied herself by gathering some of her belongings and going through her father's things. It was while she was occupied with the latter that she stumbled upon the solution to her problem. Tucked away in Henri's trunk was a bottle of laudanum. Raven recognized it by its cloying odor. She clutched the vial to her bosom, wild thoughts running through her mind. If she administered this potion to her hated guardian he would be unable to pursue her until she was well away, and safe.

But how? She could not put it into his food, for surely he would notice the taste. There seemed nothing strong enough to cover the flavor of it, and then Raven remembered the brandy. Suddenly it all seemed very simple, and she need only wait until evening to put her plan into action.

Supper was long past and M'sieur St. Claire was still seated in the same straight-backed chair at the table that he had occupied at supper. He had nothing much to busy himself with this evening and seemed content to study her movements about the cabin as she put her belongings close to the door. "I'm glad to see you show some sense at last," he said after watching her a while.

His voice nearly caused her to start, so nervous was she, but calming herself Raven managed to ask what it was he meant.

"Your belongings are few," he replied. "It saves me from having to go through them and discard anything unnecessary. You can buy what you need in Pittsburgh." Her look of shock was misinterpreted by Eben who laughed. "Forget what you've heard about the place, Raven. It's not a wilderness anymore. There are places where fine apparel can be purchased, pretty things delicate enough to earn the right to caress skin as soft as yours. I vow, you'll be the envy of the entire female population and the bane of many an eager young swain's heart."

Raven looked at him and shrugged, her dark eyes glinting with anger. "Whatever this place is you drag me to, do not expect me to be eager to go there. I confess an eye for pretty things, m'sieur, but not to please some foolish man!"

"Please them you will," he said firmly. "But only one will you choose."

"You are allowing me to choose now? Ha! Isn't that a curious turn? I thought you might auction me off to the highest bidder since your lust for gold is so great."

He looked at her. "You intentionally misconstrue my efforts on your behalf. Of course in truth, I must admit to a need of money, but it is no greater than that of other men. I but take payment for services rendered. And if I may remind you, it was your father who set the price, not I."

Again she shrugged. "I do not wish to argue with you."

"Now there's a first. A woman without a bent for argument."

"Are you always so loose at the jaws?" she shot back.

He was unperturbed by the pointed question. "As a matter of fact I'm not. You seem to have a strange effect on me, Raven. I am not much accustomed to such verbosity, especially around women."

"You have a very low opinion of the female sex, m'sieur," she observed.

"Not the entire female sex, mademoiselle," he countered smoothly, "just the portion I have had dealings with." Now he met her eyes, and she saw their pale depths gleam. "With few exceptions I have found females to be calculating and cold, and basically undeserving of a man's trust. To be blindly devoted to a woman spells disaster."

For a long moment silence reigned. Neither of them seemed wont to break it, yet after a while Raven thought it prudent to offer him the brandy. The moon was full this night and would be making its appearance within the hour. She felt the need to be on her way, far removed from this man and his handsome face, his unsettling eyes, his manner of bald truth. In her heart she felt a thread of fear, perhaps the fear of self-preservation. The memory of his hard arms encircling her the night before, of the pressure of his demanding kiss and the weakness of her own resolve was still fresh in her mind. There was something about him that attracted her, even while it infuriated her. Raven could not lay a finger on the cause, but she feared that if she stayed too long she might lose her heart to him, and pompous ass that he was, she could only be hurt if she allowed that to happen.

To save herself she hurried toward the jug. "May I offer you brandy, Eben? You look weary, it will help you rest."

"I had a taste of it yesterday and found it uncommonly fine. I would indeed enjoy it, lass, and as you say, it should aid my search for rest. Will you join me, or shall I drink alone?"

"It's a rare occasion that I drink more than a little wine," she said, "but yes, I will join you. It is an occasion, is it not, m'sieur? Our imminent departure?" Our parting of the ways, she thought to herself.

She filled his glass, the one containing the heavy draught of laudanum, to the brim, then splashed a minimal amount into the second one meant for her. She took him the glass and stood smiling down at him.

Eben's eyes gently touched her face. No one could match her elegance, her grace of movement. He saw her curving little smile, hardly noticing that it never reached her dark-lashed eyes. He accepted the glass from her and deliberately closed his fingers over her own before she withdrew them as if she'd been scalded.

Her own glass was raised and she said softly, "To your health, m'sieur."

"To the future, Raven." He drank deeply, still watching her as a cat must watch a mouse hole. His glass was half empty now, and he showed no inclination to drain it further.

Raven thought with a jolt of fear that she might not have given him enough of the drug to produce the desired effect. "Shall I refresh it for you?" she asked, afraid that if she prodded him to drink it he would become suspicious. She had turned away to fetch the demijohn, and when she turned back she found he had passed out in the chair. She went directly to his side and put her hand on his shoulder. "Eben?" she said, gently shaking him.

She received not so much as a groan in reply. "You might have picked a more comfortable chair, m'sieur. You will awake with a crick in your neck from sleeping here."

It was amazing, she thought, how suddenly light of heart she felt. She was free of this tyrant, this arrogant bully! She could leave and he would be less one ward. It never occurred to her that she would need him for any reason. After all, she was the daughter of Henri François Delacour, and capable in any situation! Her mind leapt forward, and she envisioned a scene in which she would cross paths with this man again, one day when she was a fine lady, dressed impeccably in a satin gown of such richness that it would render him agog. Perhaps she would even nod politely, if he showed her the respect due her.

She hurried to gather up her possessions—just a small bundle of clothing and a parcel of food to carry her through the next few days. She would need to take one of his horses. Pierre, the ancient nag that had served them these many years could barely urge his rheumatic bones above a walk. He was far too slow to aid in her escape, and so Raven felt compelled to leave him behind. Her guardian could sell him or turn him loose to forage for himself. She took his saddlebags as well, to carry her father's fortune. Feeling a twinge of conscience, she put a few coins on the table as payment for his trouble before leaving.

When she entered the barn, the horses turned their heads and peered at her as if questioning her right to be there so late in the evening. She spoke to them in French, which she thought was a much more fluid language than English. The horses seemed to prefer it also, and looked at her with friendly eyes.

She paused a moment, trying to decide which one to take. She would have liked the mare, for she was a gentle creature, but Eben's words rang in her ears, "She's valuable to me. It would break my heart to have to put her down." If the mare meant so much to him, he might be likely to give chase and try and reclaim her, while he had said naught of the other mount. She decided it the wiser course to take the wiry little gray.

In less than a moment she had the saddlebags slung across his back and tied securely beneath. She placed her old saddle, not Eben's newer, more comfortable one, on the horse. If she only took what she needed there was a chance that Eben St. Claire would just consider himself well rid of her unwanted company. He had admitted that she'd been thrust upon him. To him she was only a burden, more weight to carry, a millstone around his neck. . . . He probably would not follow her, but would offer thanks to God that she was gone.

The horse pricked its ears as she stepped up onto the second rail of the stall and slipped onto his back. He seemed to be waiting for her command, so she nudged his ribs with her heels and walked him from the barn into the gathering night.

An infernolike heat seemed to surround Eben. He was not fully awake, yet he imagined himself having changed places with old James St. Claire. It was an odd notion, he knew, for he had not stolen any horses. Yet his head felt as if it was split in two, and his tongue was thick. His neck was bent to the side and when he attempted to straighten his head, pain shot through him, demanding that he waken now. He lurched to his feet, stumbling as he flew to the door, and just barely reached the side of the cabin before the horrible retching began.

Once the poison was gone from his system, Eben felt human again. His headache was diminishing to a dull throb that centered with a miserable persistence behind his eyes. Thought became possible as the fog shrouding his brain slowly evaporated. Leaning now against the sturdy cabin wall, he thought that he must have drunk too much brandy the night before, though for the life of him, he could only recall having the one glass Raven had given him. . . .

Frowning, he looked around slowly. Raven. That's what seemed amiss. She was nowhere in sight, and the window of the cabin hadn't been opened. He went back inside and looked around. On the table he found the gold, and directly beside the demijohn of brandy was a small suspicious-looking bottle. He took it down and opened it, sniffing the contents.

"Laudanum, the little bitch!" he said. "And to think I was beginning to trust her! By the saints, the wench is cunning," he breathed. "She thought to murder me while she tripped off lightly with the gold!" He forgot his aching head and trotted to the barn where he saw that Willow was missing.

Cadence turned a jaundiced eye on her master and nickered to him. She pawed the floor with her injured foreleg, impatient with her confinement.

"Let's have a look at your leg, girl," Eben said to the animal. "Well, it seems that the black-hearted little wretch is good for something after all. The injury is healing, and sound, I swear."

He led her from the barn and let her crop the tender shoots of grass in the cabin yard while he carefully examined the yard for signs and laughed. "She left a trail a child could follow, and she will live to regret it, I vow."

For the first time since waking the black scowl he'd worn lifted and a wolfish grin took its place. It was only a matter of time.

Night came swiftly to the forest. There was no small interlude of peaceful serenity come day's end when the sky was awash with color and the world settled down to await the night. There was only a momentary deepening of the ever-present gloom, and finally blackness altogether.

It was not the dark that Raven minded. The silvery disk of the hunter's moon would soon be rising above the trees, and even here where the forest canopy was thickest overhead, some small light would penetrate. No, she didn't mind the dark; it was the profound quiet that settled with the dusk that she found so unnerving.

Seated on the ground with her cloak wrapped around her, she listened. For a time there was nothing. The birds had long ago ceased their twittering calls, the squirrels their gay scolding. Nothing seemed to move. Then gradually her sensitive hearing picked up tiny, furtive movements far off in the night. Something was moving about out there, and she had no inkling what it was.

She thought of the nocturnal creatures who inhabited the woodlands, sleeping the days away in their hidden lairs and hollow logs, the dark caves that remained a mystery to those who walked in the sunlit hours. With the curtain of darkness drawn upon the land, they emerged to roam, and it was these furtive scurryings that kept Raven so long from sleep.

For a very long time she lay awake, wishing she had the comfort of a fire. But where the flames might keep the beasts at bay, they would also prove a vivid banner proclaiming her whereabouts to the one she feared the most—her guardian.

Even now he could be out there, watching from the safety of the darkened forest. He would wait patiently for her to nod off, then steal in and take his revenge upon her for duping him. Had he not warned her not to test him? She recalled the cruel bite of his fingers as they dug into her wrists and shoulders. What might he be capable of if he did find her? Would he listen to her pleas for mercy? Or what if she chose not to humble herself and stood defiant before him, uncowed, as she had been before in the face of his ire. Whatever the possibilities, the point was moot, for she had no intention of letting him find her.

Chapter 6

Eben followed the girl's trail until darkness prevented his going any further. Then he unsaddled Cadence and sat using a sturdy tree as a back rest and watched the animal graze. He remembered Raven saying tartly that she could forage for her food if need be, and he wondered if she'd planned this all along. She must have had great amusement at his expense, playing upon his lust for her charms, then using her wiles to attempt his murder. The thought upset him thoroughly, and such anger welled up within him that he felt he might strangle her when next they met.

Although he wasn't hungry, he forced himself to eat some of the venison jerky he carried with him. Besides providing sustenance, the chewing of the leathery meat gave him something to do.

All night Eben sat, and by the time the first gray light of false dawn lightened the skies he was seething with impatience to be gone.

He traveled all that day, following Raven's wide path of broken twigs and trampled grass. Near noon he stopped at the very spot where she had camped the night before. Dismounting, he hunkered down and examined the small nest she'd made. Given the nature of the beastie she was riding, it was a miracle she had made it this far without breaking that lovely white neck of hers.

The urge to hurry was almost overwhelming. The stallion, though ornery, was fleet of foot, and if given his head, could far outdistance the little mare. Cadence's foreleg was healed nicely, but Eben didn't wish to test it. He deliberately kept her at an even pace, knowing that Raven was traveling faster than he dared, yet sure that he would find her before long.

His second night differed from the first in that he slept, waking just before dawn kissed the skies. By the time full light broke he was a mile and a half from his camp and hot on the trail of his runaway ward. His mind immediately filled with thoughts of exacting his pound of flesh for her treachery. What he didn't know was that at that very moment his prey was alone, afoot, and just twenty miles to the northeast.

The scurryings Raven had listened to that very first night had turned out to be a family of masked brigands in raccoon-skin guise. The furry little thieves had stolen into her camp and devoured every last morsel of food in Raven's saddlebags while she slept.

She had awoken a few hours after dawn, soaked by the dew and utterly famished, only to discover that she must hunt for her breakfast. An hour's diligent search yielded nothing more than a handful of acorns the hordes of squirrels had somehow overlooked. The meat was hard and bitter as gall but she ate it anyway and washed it down with cold water from a nearby stream.

All that day as she rode she watched the woods and fields around her, hoping to spy a berry thicket where she could satisfy her gnawing hunger. It was nearing dark when at last her hope was fulfilled.

High along a spiny ridge of earth the thick brambles sprawled, clinging to places that less tenacious vegetation would have scorned. Raven saw the berries and her stomach immediately rumbled noisily, demanding that she dismount and eat, lest she find nothing else palatable that day.

The fruit, she found, was much battered by the hard rain two nights before, and most had mouldered in the heat. Raven picked them anyway, reaching into the thick tangle and plucking the fat, overripe blackberries, popping them into her mouth. Eager to satisfy the gnawing ache in her stomach, she pushed even farther into the thicket, though the thorny tentacles embraced her soft flesh quite painfully.

Soft exclamations escaped her as the thorns dug deep furrows on her exposed arms and tore at her cream-hued muslin gown. Just beyond her outstretched hand the bushes rattled hard and a curious bleating noise sounded as two small bear cubs scrambled away to swiftly ascend a nearby tree.

The cubs kept up their frightened cries, as Raven quickly tried to extract herself from the clutching vines. If the cubs were here, then the mother bear was also close, and that could prove dangerous. The noise they made raised the fine hairs on Raven's arms and caused her skin to prickle with fear. Losing all sense of caution, she gave one maddened plunge and was free of the vines.

The stallion shied nervously as she grabbed for the reins, snorting and giving a high-pitched whinny. She had no time for foolishness. They had to get away, and now! Her fingers caught the very end of the leathers, only to have them dragged through her hand as the stallion reared and made his headlong dash back down the steep grade with all of her belongings looped around his neck, and her last hope flying away with him.

The rest happened very quickly. The sow bear, hearing the cubs' distress, gave a rumbling growl and ran rolling down the hill, six hundred pounds of maternal outrage barreling down on Raven's hapless, frightened form.

The girl tried to back slowly away, but the vines again caught at her clothes and her hair.

With all the clarity of a nightmare the huge bear rose on its hind legs and towered over her to roar its fury. The animal's huge head swayed from side to side in a rage-induced dance, its mouth open wide, revealing long, yellowed ursine teeth.

Bellow after angry bellow issued from the depths of the bear's cavernous mouth and mingled with Raven's terrified cries. The beast was so close that she could smell its rancid breath. And in that instant she knew that she had to break free of the thicket or perish.

Instinctively, one step at a time she began to back away, the animal following. Ironically, before she had gone more than three paces her heel was caught by a protruding root and she sprawled backward in the leaves.

She fell hard, knocking the wind from her lungs. At her side was the precipice, a steep-sided descent down a rocky cliff some eight feet high. With no other escape possible, and preferring whatever fate it held to the one in store for her here and now, she used the momentum of her fall and continued to roll over the edge and into the empty air.

Even with a deep bed of leaves to cushion the fall Raven was stunned by the impact. She could summon no will to move, to even breathe, so she just lay waiting to die.

The bear's bellowing had ceased, or was it just dulled by the ringing in her ears? She didn't know. Nearly buried in the leaves, Raven lay very still as the animal made several feinting charges down the incline at her feet. Then finally, it climbed back up the embankment, paused to sniff the air, then with a grunting whine, shuffled off to find its cubs.

Slowly Raven turned her head slightly and opened one eye. The bear was gone. She turned her face into the leaves again and cried.

"Something isn't right," Eben said softly to himself. He squatted on his heels by a frequently traveled game trail used by animal and man alike and, he was sure, by one very lovely and very treacherous female. There was no mistaking Willow's hoof prints, for the left shoe bore a mark of Eben's own devising—three deep grooves cut horizontally across both ends of the shoe. Horse thieves ran a lucrative business even in these modern times, and the identifying mark was one means of protection.

Eben touched a finger to the print and his brow furrowed in a deep frown. It was the depth of the imprint that had him puzzled. It was almost as if the horse was riderless. . . . Yet from this conclusion arose yet another question.

He turned on one booted heel to squint back down the path. Was this some ruse the girl had used to throw him off the mark? Or was she truly out there somewhere, lost and alone, hurt and unable even to cry out for help? "It will eat away at me until I know for sure."

A single fluid motion brought him to his feet. There was only one way to know, and that involved doubling back the way he'd already come. He went carefully, his pale gaze raking every inch of ground for the tiniest clue.

An hour later his efforts were rewarded. He had found the spot where the horse and girl had parted company. The entire tale was told in a bizarre tapestry of dislodged dirt and leaves and a scrap of cream-colored muslin still affixed to a blackberry thorn.

Eben plucked the prize and smoothed it between his fingers. It was spotted with blood—Raven's blood. She must have been picking the overripe fruit when the bear startled her.

He knelt and measured the width of the paw print against his outspread hand. It was a very large bear, and must have frightened the girl half to death. He saw her slipper prints just a few feet away. The heels had been dug in deep, the toes lifted, and he could well imagine her rocking back on her heels in sheer horror as the beast loomed over her. From there he followed her tumbling descent into the dirt and down the steep incline.

The bottom of the ravine was layered deep with dead leaves. Just to be sure that she was not hiding there, Eben kicked through them. He found nothing, and since there was no blood he had to believe that she had escaped any serious harm from her clawed assailant. She was wandering then, somewhere out there, alone and most likely frightened—at least if she had wit enough to be! Yet her arrogance was such that she probably thought the situation could be turned to her advantage.

Never had Eben met a more headstrong female than Raven, or one that wrung his heart with this violent urge to protect her.

By late afternoon the next day the full weight of her loss was just being pressed upon her. Without the horse she was at the mercy of the land, and the land, she knew, could be ruthless. The previous night she had curled upon the ground and tried to sleep. But the day's ordeal would not permit it. She had shivered from the cold, starting at each noise, and imagined her guardian sleeping safe and warm at the cabin.

Morning arrived and Raven began to walk. If she headed east there was a good chance that she would come across a cabin or farm, and she could pass the time by looking for something to eat along the way. But time passed and her search yielded nothing.

The stream she was wading across was the first of any size that she had come upon, but it was only one of the many she would encounter on her eastward trek.

It had ceased to matter to her that the frontiersman might find her, for at least he would feed her. All day she had searched, and it seemed the hordes of hungry squirrels had eaten every single nut in the forest, and as for berries—though she had yet to run across any more—she was rather leery of berries. And so she went to sleep hungry each night and dreamed of home.

Cold water lapping just beneath her breasts reminded her that autumn was coming swiftly. Already the mornings were chill and foggy, redolent of September. Soon the mountain stream fed rivers would grow icy cold, and without the stallion Raven would be forced to ford them or swim.

As she waded, her skirts were tucked into her belt to free her legs, and keep her from being dragged under where the current was strong. Her soft kid slippers, so unsuited to all of this walking, were held high in one hand. Nearly worn out now, they were the only possessions she had left, besides her mother's locket which hung securely around her neck. All the rest, including the gold, she had lost when the stallion ran away.

With the water tugging at her ragged clothes and her toes feeling out the slippery, slime-covered rocks for the safest footing, Raven thought back over the past few days.

She thought often of the man she'd left behind, wondering if he was behind her somewhere, searching. If she stopped here and now, would he catch up with her? Being his ward could certainly be no worse than the prospect of freezing to death, or the unpleasantness of slow starvation.

He had claimed that he knew enough to keep her belly filled, and as a picture of him sighting down the long barrel of his rifle flashed in her brain she knew it had not been empty bragging.

The irony of the situation was not lost on Raven. She had accused him of being a fortune hunter who wanted her worldly goods. She had longed for freedom, to be rid of his unwanted company, his bald remarks and criticisms. Now, she had all of that, and with each passing minute in the cold river it was becoming clear that what she had now was worth less than nothing.

Where was the great surge of joy at being free? She was indeed free and unhampered, but she was also very hungry—and more than a little lonely. What a great blow her pride suffered as she was forced to admit that the one man she professed to hate was the one she longed most to see again. Had he come striding through the water toward her right at that moment, she would have gladly flung herself into his arms.

But he was nowhere nearby, and Raven was alone, cold, and ravenous to the point of swooning. As she neared the far shore a disturbing thought came to mind. Perhaps M'sieur Eben St. Claire was not even searching for her at all. Perhaps he considered himself well rid of her. Had he not said that the bargain had been all of Henri's doing? That he was eager to see Pittsburgh and be rid of her?

It was his wretched eagerness that had caused all of this, Raven thought darkly as she emerged from the water and sat down on a large smooth rock. She wrung out her sodden skirts and spoke aloud just to hear the sound of a human voice. "If you had not been so hot to marry me off to the first man you found worthy, then none of this would have happened.'' She snorted in disgust. ''What manner of man would you have chosen for me? Someone with a long nose and warts, no doubt!''

From across the river the one she addressed stood quietly watching. He had barely believed his eyes when he saw her wading the stream, a ragged, solitary figure. He had had to suppress the urge to call out to her, fearing that if he did so she would again take to her heels.

Curious, he watched as she rose from the rock and began rooting around in the shallows. He felt the urge to laugh as he looked at her muddied hands. She appeared to be grubbing for roots. Several she pulled out easily, but there was one she was obviously bent upon having that proved stronger than the rest. With determination he found admirable, she pulled and yanked, making grunting noises that carried clearly across the water. Finally the root broke free and a startled Raven stumbled backward and sat down abruptly in the water.

She came up sputtering in angry French to hear laughter, clear, rich, and masculine, ringing through the shallow river valley. It was totally unexpected, and to her infuriatingly familiar.

He had the damnedest habit of catching her at her very worst, making her feel foolish and vulnerable. What pride she had left was considerably deflated. She pushed the wet strands of her tangled hair out of her eyes and cast him a dull glare.

''Well, you unchivalrous buffoon! Will you stand there braying while I starve to death? Go and shoot me a deer. A big deer, for I am very hungry!''

''Do I have your word that you will stay where you are? If I have to hunt you again I'll wring your neck when I find you,'' he called to her.

''I surrender, m'sieur. Feed me and I am yours.'' She saw him sketch a graceful bow and disappear into the forest, calling back over his shoulder. ''A big deer with antlers to hang above the lintel of mademoiselle's new residence."

"You can't eat antlers, and I don't have a lintel," she chided softly. She sat back down on the rock to wait.

Near dark the frontiersman returned. He had a knack of blending in with the forest that she admired. If he stood very still it would be difficult for the untrained eye to spot him. And even when he moved he did so gracefully, almost as if every movement he made was carefully thought out and planned before his muscles executed it. He made no noise when he approached, even through the water. It was Cadence who alerted Raven to their arrival and set her mouth to watering, for slung across the saddle was a small white-tailed deer.

He eyed her critically as he came close, noting her haggard appearance. She was wet and looked thoroughly bedraggled, yet her eyes shone bright as jet in her small face. He couldn't help but wonder whether it was he she was glad to see or the promise of food. Most likely it was the latter, he thought with an odd pang.

"If you gather some kindling, I'll take care of this." He nodded at the carcass that he was even then lifting off the horse. He carried it over his shoulder a little distance up the bank to a likely place to build the fire, then lowered it to the ground.

"You gather the wood; I will dress the deer," Raven offered. It was a chore she was quite adept at performing. And she knew just what cuts to prepare first. She held out her hand, waiting for his knife.

Eben looked at her for a long moment, then unsheathed it and laid it hilt first in her palm. His pale eyes narrowed as she hefted it in her hand, judging its weight and balance. "Don't think that you can finish the task you began at the cabin. You botched one attempt at murder, and it would take a greater strength than yours to kill me."

His statement surprised her. "Kill you?" she said. "Is that what you think I tried to do?"

"Aye," he answered steadily, "if not by poison, then surely by suffocation. When I awoke it was hotter than blazes in that airless coffin you call home."

"Think whatever you like, m'sieur," she said lightly. "But I had no intention of killing you. I only wanted to escape."

"And where did it get you, this grand escape? Half starved, bedraggled, nearly killed by a bear, and right back where you started from."

She did not like his tone, and she put her nose in the air, feeling some of her pride return now that the promise of food was certain. "I nearly succeeded," she insisted.

"Aye, in killing yourself," Eben told her. "What the hell were you thinking? You might well have died out here alone, with no one the wiser. Or worse, perhaps! For Christ's sake, Raven! Didn't your father ever warn you about men?"

"I am learning, m'sieur." Her voice was laden with insinuation. She saw him frown and knew her barb had not gone unmarked.

"You succeeded all right, in stealing my horse and losing him. I found your paltry coins left in payment. What makes you think it is enough to satisfy the debt you owe me?" Then more softly, "Don't worry, I'll exact my due, you may be sure. Where is your precious horde, by the way? Hid or buried, I'd wager." He saw her still expression and guessed the truth. "You lost the gold, didn't you?"

"I might have guessed that it would be my gold that would most concern you."

"Our gold," he reminded her.

"Now that you know it is gone, I suppose I can expect no help from you. It was the only reason you agreed to the bargain in the first place. Now that Papa is gone, you will not hold to your agreement. I knew you were unscrupulous the moment I laid eyes on you!"

"Lower your voice, woman. It isn't wise to advertise our presence."

"What do you care? Perhaps some filthy specimen of manhood will come along and agree to take me off your hands! It was all you wanted, to be rid of me! I cannot think why you came after me, except for the lure of easy fortune!"

"Speak softly or so help me I will gag you," Eben warned in a low voice. "I made the bargain in good faith to a man who was obviously dying. He seemed to care for his daughter, though I now wonder at his sanity. He told me you were a dutiful daughter, who would give me no trouble. A well-meaning lie, but a lie just the same. Had he told me the truth I never would have agreed to so much as look at you. But never fear, Raven. I'm ever a man of my word, despite your low opinion of me. A bargain well met is a bargain I intend to keep, gold or no gold. As for my payment," and here his eyes fairly stripped her of the rags she wore, laying bare her womanly form and turning her cheeks a dull rose, "I will think of something, never doubt it."

Having said his piece, Eben went into the woods, leaving Raven alone with her raging emotions.

Chapter 7

Moments later Eben emerged from the woods. His arms were full of broken, dry branches he had gathered from the forest floor. He arranged them in a small pile, then glanced at the girl to see how she was progressing with their meal. She was bending over the carcass, but instead of plying the blade, she was whispering in the animal's unhearing ear.

"What the hell are you doing?" Eben asked sharply.

She ignored him, speaking softly. "Poor little doe, you have given your life so that we might eat."

"Jesus Christ, girl, don't pity the kill, you'll spoil the meat! Here, give me that damned knife and I'll make short work of it!"

"You snap and snarl about gagging me, yet bluster about when it suits your mood. Perhaps you need the gag, m'sieur." Her eyes brightened. "Indeed, I like that idea very much. I have suffered greatly because of your ready tongue!"

"You have suffered?" he asked in disbelief. "My character lies in shreds, victim to your own forked tongue and you say that you have suffered?" Able to think of nothing more suitable to say, he offered a disgusted snort.

"Forked tongue indeed," Raven said, getting down to work. She talked as she split the hide down the inner hind legs to the hooves. "I have never lied to you."

"A deception remains a deception, whether it was spoken or acted out." Eben remained unconvinced. "You drugged an unwilling victim, thereby resorting to the most vile trickery. And you, looking so innocent and sweet that night, for all the world the perfect ward . . . while plotting mayhem."

"Must you always exaggerate?"

He turned his frosty stare upon her and fairly spat the reply, "Mademoiselle, the headache with which I awoke defies description, let alone embellishment!"

"Well, I am sorry about making you ill, if it makes you feel any better," she offered generously. "I didn't mean to harm you, only give you a sound night's rest so that I could slip away quietly."

"Why?" he asked bluntly.

She raised her chin, her battered pride showing its rips and tears like some battle-worn gonfalon. "I had no other options. You were intent upon seeing me married off to the first man you came across."

"I never said that."

"Now who hands out untruths?" she asked.

"All right then, I never meant it. I mean to see you safely wed, but I would never force upon you any suitor you found distasteful." Eben frowned as he struck flint and steel to produce a tiny shower of sparks. Why must he always defend himself to her? Was it not enough that he was protecting her, feeding her, saving her from her own foolishness? Why did she always misconstrue every word he uttered? If he lived a thousand years he would never understand this perplexing little baggage.

"And what if I do not choose any suitor?" she asked. Even in light of her hunger, she could not help but bait him.

"Take my advice, wench, and do not be so

choosy. With your temperament, you can ill afford to be."

"I am not a 'wench,' as you so indelicately put it. And I don't like being told what to do." She stared sullenly into the first of the flames he was coaxing, and looked back upon her short-lived freedom, which in the light of Eben's noxious company, she was seeing in a more golden light. She was not likely to taste independence again. He would not relax his guard, and in any event, there was nowhere for her to go. She was facing facts, as distasteful as they were. He was back to ordering her around again, deciding her future, and she was dependent upon his so-called "good nature" for her very existence.

"Very well, then don't act like one lowborn, and I will address you properly, as befitting a young lady of quality. Though I must admit, to call you a lady with those manners of yours, would tax anyone's imagination," he told her.

He stirred the fire with a stick, the pale blue of his eyes picking up the orange glow. "Your father seemed a good man, but he did you a disservice by allowing you to run so wild. It would have done you good to have been thrashed now and again."

The last few days had been very hard on Raven and his words wounded her. Must he always criticize her? He never gave her a single kind word. For a moment she struggled with her injured feelings and the threat of tears, then she won out, and to cover her own discomfort asked him, "Did your parents beat you, M'sieur St. Claire? You certainly hold great store by the practice."

"Aye," he answered softly. "My own father laid his hand on my scrawny backside more than once before he died. But the pain was somehow tempered by the knowledge that he loved me." For a long moment he was quiet, and when he continued it was in tones so low that Raven had to strain to hear him. "After that no one cared enough to beat me for what I did. I grew wild, like you, but from a dearth of the affection that you knew."

"Then I am sorry for you," Raven said.

Eben cleared his throat. "Save your pity for someone who wants it. I have all a man needs in this world. I have no time for feeling sorry for myself or listening while someone else does it for me." He had not meant to mention his past. Doing so only opened all the old wounds he thought had healed.

He picked up two chunks of meat and began to roast them. "The future is what's important," he said, warming to what was by now his favorite subject, Raven noticed. "Yours, especially. I feel sure that you can make a fine match, if you will but tame down a bit. A little wildness is sometimes advantageous, but not until the husband indicates he wishes such."

Raven sighed. "I don't think I can ever get used to being dictated to. It's no wonder you haven't a wife, m'sieur. You would treat her abominably."

"It doesn't matter, since I have no intention of taking one," he told her. "Women are troublesome, and you, milady, are a fine example."

"But if you do not marry, you will never have sons to beat. Won't that make you unhappy?"

Eben chuckled. "You do have a way of putting things. Yes, I suppose I will. I once wanted children very much. I had thought to rebuild my family. Unfortunately, the woman I chose was something less than virtuous. She had no honor. After that, I no longer cared. Now I must admit it all seems foolish."

"There is nothing foolish about wanting loved ones around you." She eyed him critically across the fire. "You might make a passable father, provided you abandon the idea of beating the children.

But you *are* rather advanced in age, so you'd better start soon."

"I thank you for the advice, mademoiselle," he said sarcastically, "and for the compliment, left-handed, though it might have been."

"Are you insulted?" she asked, and Eben could see that she hoped he was.

"No. And there is nothing so very ancient about the age of twenty-nine. At nineteen, you yourself are nearly past marriageable age," he reminded her.

She made a face at him. "Marriage! Is that all you think about?"

No, he thought, it was not all. But voicing the eventuality of her marriage to another man kept his desire at bay. It was going to be extremely difficult to do battle with her and with the fires she kindled in his blood. Just looking at her was enough to stir him, to make him wish that she wasn't his ward. Her dowry was gone. All that she had left now was her virtue; he could not rob her of that as well. Even with her hair all tangled round her face and her cheeks dirt smudged, as they now were, she was nothing short of breathtaking. In an effort to redirect his dangerous thoughts he turned his attention to the meat.

As ravenous as she was, she did not wolf down her food, but bit off small pieces and chewed them carefully, swallowing the juices first to accustom her stomach to having food in it once again. It grumbled loudly for more, but she ate slowly, feeling her guardian's pale gaze upon her all the while.

"You should not stare so," she said after she finished the first piece and reached to take the second he was offering her. "It isn't polite."

"I was just debating whether to tie you up tonight or to leave you loose," he said.

"You wouldn't tie me!" she said, truly alarmed. This was one possibility she had never considered.

"I cannot trust you, and I must sleep sometime. I'd prefer not to have to do it with one eye open, lest you decide to further test my patience."

When she replied, she did so in a small voice. She was tired and feeling quite defeated after her ordeal. For the time being most of the fight had been taken out of her. She wanted nothing more right now than to lie down and sleep in security, and he was threatening to bind her. "Where have I to go, m'sieur? I have no one left to me."

"You had nowhere to go before, and no one to help you, but it didn't stop you from trying to flee," he told her.

"Please, Eben." She had not meant to plead, but there it was, out in the open and lying heavily between them. She saw his frown deepen and thought to further her cause. "I will lie close beside you so that you can hear me if I move. If you wish you can put an arm over my waist, only do not bind me."

Sweet Christ, how she tempted him! He had gone very still at her suggestion and had nearly leapt upon it as a grand idea before he stayed himself. "Give me your word that you'll not stray, and I'll trust you. Though God help me, it's against my better judgment!" He motioned to the ground where she was sitting. "Go to sleep."

He watched from slitted eyes as she immediately lay down and curled into a ball, much like a child would have. He shook his head and grumbled to himself, thinking that she would try the patience of a saint. He had barely spent three full days with her and already all he wanted to do was lay her down and rid her of her innocence. How he could abide the prolonged period it would take for them to reach Pittsburgh was beyond his imagining.

He lay down not far away from her and pillowed his head on his arm. But it was a long time before sleep would come to him, and when at last it did, it was riddled with impassioned dreams of a certain raven-haired hellion.

Raven awoke before the first streaks of the new dawn lit the sky. She sat up and stretched, feeling rested, but very dirty. The fine grit that coated her skin and the tangles in her hair had not bothered her the night before, because she had been intent upon slaking her hunger and resting. But now the grime made her shudder. She cast a quick look at her companion and found him asleep. If she hurried, she could be bathed and dressed before he stirred. Silently she made her way to the river's edge.

When Eben woke a few moments later he was alone. A swift glance around showed him that the girl was gone. Thinking that she had broken her word he reached out to feel the place where she'd lain. There was still the barest trace of warmth; she couldn't have gotten very far. He trotted down the path to the river, but came up short at the sight that greeted him.

Raven was standing in the river, the water licking gently at her hips. Her lithe form was presented in profile to his hungry gaze, her round buttocks just slightly facing him, while he had a tantalizing view of one coral-tipped breast. The fitful sun broke through the morning haze, touching her skin with golden light, and Eben found himself burning with envy for those sunbeams. Oh, to be the one touching that satiny skin of hers!

For the life of him, he should leave, but his body seemed to have gained a will of its own and stood rooted on the bank as he devoured the vision she made. He heard her humming softly beneath her breath, some lilting tune that caused his heartbeat to quicken. She wrung out her long hair and shook back its gleaming mass before turning slowly to face him.

If she was shocked to see him standing there, she did not show it. She only stood, meeting his gaze evenly, without shame. He had the odd feeling that she was waiting for something, perhaps to see what he would do. Then when he made no move to leave, she slowly emerged from the water.

"I had not meant to invade your bath, mademoiselle," he said in a husky voice, "but for the life of me, when I awakened—"

She stopped just before him and stood looking up into his face. "You thought I had broken my word and gone," she finished for him. "Your trust in me is nonexistent, m'sieur, while mine in you is seemingly . . . boundless."

"I apologize," he said, unable to take his eyes off her beautiful body.

"It doesn't matter. I am ready to begin, if you are."

"What?" he asked hoarsely.

"The journey . . . to find this wonderful husband you insist is awaiting me."

"Oh, aye, a husband."

She looked at him, savoring his obvious discomfort. "Are you all right, Eben? You look a little flushed. Let me see if your skin is hot." She reached out to lay her hand along his cheek and heard him groan. His longing was plain upon his face. If she lingered much longer he would take her, and she would then have no reason to find a husband.

Very slowly, as if swaying in a sensuous dance, she moved forward until she was standing at his side. "Perhaps this will cool you down!" Swift as lightning she placed her hands on his chest, pushing with all her might and at the same time hooking one bare foot behind his knee and kicking it forward. With deep satisfaction she watched the great plume of water that was made as he fell into the river. "That will teach you not to spy on me, m'sieur!"

He came up with hair streaming water and shook like a dog. "Damn it, woman, this time you've gone too far!" He started from the water, and Raven grabbed up her threadbare gown and took to her heels.

A bright burst of delighted giggles drifted back behind. At last she had outwitted him! Her bare feet flew along the path that led to the clearing, and only after she gained the open ground did she stop. Here, she could safely pause just long enough to dress, though the threadbare gown would be little protection enough from that rutting stag! She quickly found a small stand of trees, three or four clustered close together, that would provide a wall of sorts to place at her back. From there she could watch the path for her pursuer, then flee again if need be. The dunking, though sorely deserved, had inflicted a wound to his hugely inflated pride, and it was quite within the keeping of his character to try a counter coup of his own. If, indeed, he could catch her!

The material of the gown was worn quite thin, and it wadded up at her waist, refusing to slide easily over her still-damp skin. She struggled with it, but could not right the thing without giving it her full attention. An impatient sigh escaped her—she never had excelled in waiting—and she cast one last glance down the path in the direction of the river. There was no sign of Eben. Perhaps the water had served to cool more than his ardor, she thought, and he had decided to bathe himself, or better yet perhaps the clumsy fool had drowned. Her lips curved in a gleeful smile, and without further worry, she gave her full attention to the reluctant gown.

Somehow, the garment had twisted in back and after a moment's work Raven managed to right it.

She settled the skirt in place and dragged one arm carefully through a sleeve, the other poised to do the same, when she was suddenly and without warning seized from behind.

Raven gave a startled scream and struggled in his grasp. Her skin was damp and slippery, as were her captor's hands, and she managed to break loose and run several feet before a hard-hewn arm shot around her waist to drag her back. She was pulled roughly against his hard length and held imprisoned there. "Loosen your hold, damn you, I cannot breathe!"

"That makes twice you've flown from me." Eben's voice came low and angry beside her ear. "But again I have you in my keeping, and I'd say 'twas more than time your wings were clipped."

"You cannot blame your clumsiness on me!" Raven flung back. "Besides, it was fair payment for your lascivious bent. I only thought to cool you down a little."

"You might have drowned me, you little harridan!"

"All right, you've seen me repentant, now let me go." The look she gave him then was one of pure, unadulterated innocence . . . but there was devilment dancing in her dark eyes. Eben found himself warring again with his rising passions, but this time, he fought them down. He could release her now, and suffer yet again at her small hands, or teach her just who it was she was playing with. He quickly chose the latter course, and bore her struggling form over to a fallen log.

"You've not a repentant bone in your body," he told her, "but soon you'll repent your lack of wisdom loud and long, every time you sit!" He had reached the log and bracing one booted foot upon it, proceeded to drag his unwilling charge over his leg while she kicked and scratched to no avail.

Turned on her belly over one hard muscled thigh,

Raven felt his palm connect with her rump. His hands were hardened with calluses, and though moderately applied in comparison to his strength, the blows stung her tender flesh, even through her skirts. She tried to fend him off, twisting on his leg, but the wily beggar always managed to subdue her best attempt. Her already abused backside received yet another enthusiastic swat. "Do you know how much I hate you!" she cried.

"Do you think I bloody care?" Swat!

An outraged yowl escaped the punished one, just before she raised her head. This backwoods buffoon thought that he could chastise her, did he? Well, he deserved some punishment of his own! His left arm secured her while the right doled out the beating, but his shirtless torso was a reachable target. Raven twisted until she could grasp the blade that hung from his belt, slipping it from its sheath, and at the same time sinking her teeth into the tender flesh just below his rib cage. Her effort brought blood, and was rewarded with an enraged bellow and instant freedom, as he dumped her off his leg.

She bounced and rolled and scrambled away in a crouch to put a little distance between them. Through wary eyes she saw him twist and examine the bite, then his own pale orbs swung to her with a chilling intensity. God alone knew what he might do to her now. No matter how he threatened, she had to keep the knife! It gave her something to bargain with . . . something to hold him at bay.

"By the love of Christ, you test a man!" He took a hasty step forward. It was then he saw the knife. "What do you think to do with that, my fine sweet savage? Carve away my heart perhaps, and since you've a taste for flesh, ingest it to add to your brave nature? Or mayhap you need some hair to adorn your Pittsburgh lodge, eh?" His hand flicked the dark blond tendrils that hung damply at his nape.

"Prattle on all you like, fool!" she sneered. "Only keep your distance. My poor backside cannot abide much more of your fondling touch, and if you think I'll go with you now, then you'd better think again."

He seemed to calm a little and relaxed where he stood, resting a hand on one hip; but Raven wasn't fooled, for the cold never left his eyes. "A pretty maneuver, for one so helpless and in need of protecting," Eben drawled. "You've much of the savage in you, Raven. 'Tis high time, I think, for you to leave the squaw behind; it won't suit well where you are bound." He held out his hand then, deliberately advancing a step. "Give me the knife."

"I will not!" she flung back at him, stung that he should name her a squaw. "I need it more than you. The woods abound with wolves, m'sieur." And from the way her glance raked him she left little doubt she was speaking of him.

He laughed low and without mirth, his pale eyes gleaming like colorless shafts of sunlight reflecting off the surface of the water. "Had I truly wanted you, nothing short of hell itself would have prevented me from the taking. Your virgin's stain would be adorning the ground this instant."

"A warning well taken, m'sieur," she replied evenly. "And so I'll consent to keep the knife in my possession."

"The hell you will! Now hand it here, and have a care how you do it. I whetted the blade myself and 'twill slice to the bone with little effort!" He advanced again, intending to have his weapon back. Having carried it these many years, he felt a trifle naked with only the feather weight of an empty sheath dangling from his belt. Further adding to his disgruntlement, the girl had obviously determined to turn this little battle into a full-blown siege.

"I think you brag, but still," she said, "there's no need to test its edge upon your stubborn hide. Move back and give me ground, or I shan't be responsible if you harm yourself."

"You must be daft," Eben ground out, "to think that I could close my eyes at night, knowing I might well wake up dead at your small hands. I'll have it back, and now!"

Eben's temper had been tested sorely in the space of the few days he'd known her, and now tore loose of its normal restraints and plunged him beyond all caution. He stalked her steadily, alert for any opening in which to wrest the blade away.

Raven stepped back, her heart fluttering in her throat like a frightened bird. "Are you crazed?" she screamed at him. "Stay your distance!"

"Willful bitch!" He lunged at her and with a cry of alarm Raven brought the blade arcing up. Had it not been for her own backward impetus at the same moment, her attacker might have been mortally impaled. As it was, and true to Eben's word, the blade bit deep, plowing a deep furrow in his right forearm from elbow halfway to wrist. He cursed and shook the smarting limb, sending spatters of bright blood flying; the glare he sent her way cutting just as surely to the quick. "Give me that knife, goddammit, or you'll live to rue this day!"

Raven swallowed hard. She could stand and hold him off until he bled his strength away, or quickly strive to strike a deal. "You will forget about trying to seek revenge?"

"I'll have that knife, Mademoiselle Hoyden," he persisted, holding out a bloody hand.

"Your stubborn nature will be your undoing," Raven warned.

"Not half so quick as your own! The knife, Raven."

She would not hand it to him, but grudgingly compromised by tossing it into the tall grass at her side. She wasted no time in putting the small clearing between them. If he chose to attack her again, she would at least have the chance to flee. But he seemed to forget her presence momentarily, and after a cursory search, replaced the blade in its sheath and sat to bind his wound.

"You should cleanse it first you know," she said, watching his clumsy efforts at staunching the crimson flow, and feeling as though she should offer her help. There was just something about an animal in pain—no matter how obnoxious. "I could do it for you," she said slowly.

"I think I can well do without your tender ministrations," came his caustic reply. "I should like to keep my arm."

"Suit yourself, M'sieur St. Claire, but the blade was unclean—"

The gaze he raised to her sent chills along her spine. "Save your concern, wench. You see, despite your wild hopes, I've no intentions of leaving you before we reach Pittsburgh. It will give me pleasure untold to dance at your wedding."

"As you like," she said softly. "Just don't blame me if you sicken—" The rest of the thought went unspoken. No matter how he infuriated her, to think of his demise brought on a strange unfathomable emptiness, and Raven was at the moment unwilling to ask herself why such should be the case. She pushed the thought away. He was strong. What could possibly befall him?

Chapter 8

Breakfast that morning was a hurried affair and consumed in silence. Raven ate her portion and was satisfied to keep the space of the small clearing between them. She tried to ignore her guardian's presence, but it was difficult with him watching her so closely. She wondered what he was thinking as he continued to watch her, but she knew she dared not ask. And so she finished eating and rose to tend her immediate needs, but to her surprise, Eben followed. "What do you think you are doing?" she asked.

"Keeping an eye on you," was his swift reply. "You've proven that you aren't to be trusted. And I can ill afford to let you out of my sight. Even for a moment."

"But I need some privacy," Raven argued, her cheeks warming with embarrassment. He seemed to derive some warped pleasure from causing her discomfort. "Must you take away everything I value? You have my freedom, will you take my pride as well?"

"Go on, then," he said, "but hurry up. We've delayed long enough. I'll saddle Cadence. If you're not back here by the time I'm through—"

"Do you think it wise to ride like that?" Raven asked, indicating the bloodstained wrap. "Perhaps you should rest."

"Rest . . ." He stepped close before she realized his intention and traced a finger down the long column of her throat. "But I'm not tired, Raven. So unless you've some suggestion as to how to occupy this proposed leisure time that will otherwise satisfy me . . . I suggest we be on our way."

Raven turned and fled into the trees, the low sound of his laughter ringing in her ears.

The sun was going down when Eben finally drew rein and made camp for the night. There was enough venison left over to last for several meals, and with the tension between them leveling off, Raven began to build the evening's fire.

Eben sat apart, and as he was intent upon rooting through his small store of possessions, ignored her. Covertly, Raven observed his actions.

His lean face looked tense, but once he had found the article for which he searched, he seemed to relax. It was a silver flask, and he held it mockingly aloft as if to toast her. "Mademoiselle of the sore backside," he growled, "a tribute to the softness of your derriere!" He tipped the flask and drank deeply in the hopes that it would lessen the throb of his injured arm.

Beyond the fire Raven sniffed her disdain. "The liquor would serve you better to cleanse that cut, I think, than to warm your gullet." It was good advice, but she knew that he would ignore it.

"Your concern fairly warms my heart," came Eben's cold reply. "Put your fears for my safety to rest, Raven. I've survived far worse than this small scratch."

A fool's utterings! she mused. From where she sat Raven could see that the crude binding was oozing red, but she prudently held her tongue. There was simply no arguing with him when he'd set his mind on something.

She turned away, and he nursed his flask, and soon a stilted quiet settled between them, broken only by the sizzle of the meat juices dripping into the flames. When the dripping slowed, Raven took her share. The meat inside was pink and tender. She ate with relish, but noticed however, that her companion abstained. "You are not eating," she said.

"No, I am not eating," he replied tersely, waving the flask at her. "This evening I prefer to drink."

"Drink yourself into a stupor for all I care," she said. He was hurting no one but himself.

"Are you never quiet?" he snapped impatiently. He was not feeling the least bit well, and it made him irritable. "Sweet Christ, woman! Your constant sniping wounds a man more deeply than any blade could! 'Docile as a spotted fawn,' your father described you." He gave a derisive snort, letting her know what he thought of that description. "A blazing, harping shrew, is more like it! I hope that old man's conscience hurts him greatly for pawning his problems off on an innocent man!"

More than any of his ravings about her numerous flaws could, the reference to her father wounded Raven. Henri had meant well, placing her into this ruffian's ungentle care, but oh, how the man's treatment stung! Since coming into his keeping, she had been maligned and misused, beaten and nearly raped—or so her mind now justified—and now he dared to wish unrest upon her gentle, caring parent! It was too much! Tears stung her eyes and she turned away, not wanting him to know how surely his barb had struck its mark.

Eben leaned back against a tree and watched her, his eyes reflecting the firelight, but revealing none of the conflicting emotions she caused within him. Never before had a woman possessed this power to anger him beyond all reason, nearly to the brink of desperation—not even Ivory. With women he was cool and aloof, sometimes unnoticing, but always uncaring. He went his way, and their words and deeds left him unaffected. But somehow Raven was different. She taunted and she teased him, she insulted him and even dared to defy his orders. Her every word and every action seemed designed specifically to penetrate the shell he'd formed around himself, to draw him out . . . and did.

Whether Eben liked it or not, the fact was that Raven was one woman he simply could not ignore.

Sleeping or waking, she was with him. Tantalizing visions of her looking like some water sprite, rising naked from the river as she had that very morning, seemed destined to linger around the edges of his thoughts. The gay, tinkling sound of her laughter as she ran from him was wont to echo in his mind. Her softness, her beauty, even the swiftness of her anger tempted him almost beyond redemption. He wasn't sure that she was even aware of the effect she had upon him, but after giving the matter some thought he decided that she was either totally innocent or excellent at torture, for torture him she did. And Eben also knew that had his anger not ridden him so hard that very morning, had he not felt the urge to teach her a lesson, the episode with the knife would have ended quite differently.

Among other things, Eben found his volatile ward a problem. But until they reached Pittsburgh and he could safely give her care into another's hands, the problem was his.

The second day of travel was much like the first. With a hard hand Eben shook Raven awake at first light, and after a hurried breakfast they set off again.

For an hour or two Raven held herself erect before him on the saddle, trying to keep from touching him. But as the morning advanced and the day turned steamy the effort proved too much. She was forced to wage a constant battle with the buzzing horde of deer flies that swarmed around the horse. Wherever one chanced to bite, a red welt was raised, and after an hour of swatting at the elusive pests, Raven began to envy her guardian the sturdy protection of his leather garb. For what seemed the thousandth time that day, she slapped and cursed at the persistent pests, and finally it yielded results and her guardian stopped the mare.

"Get down," Eben ordered. His head was aching and his voice sounded slightly slurred.

Raven gaped at him in horror. "You wouldn't leave me here? I'll be eaten alive!"

"That's what I'm trying to prevent," he said. "Take the leather satchel from behind the saddle. You'll find a pair of leggings and a shirt in there that you can wear. They've never been worn and the leather might chafe, but it will be a damn sight better than this flimsy thing you're wearing now."

Raven felt a surge of relief that threatened to overwhelm her. Impulsively, she threw her arms around his neck and hugged him before sliding to the ground. She completed a hurried search for the garments, then tossing her delighted thanks back over her shoulder, ran into the woods.

"And throw that pitiful rag of yours in the bushes!" Eben called out after her.

For once Raven heeded his orders, and was soon divested of her tattered dress. Smiling, she tossed the worn gown into the brush and donned the leggings. Their previous owner, Eben, was long and lean and so the lower garment fit her closely. She was glad that he was tall, because they left her buttocks bare, as well as her pelvic area. No loincloth had been provided, but Raven had no need for one. Eben's hunting shirt was long and hung nearly to her knees, providing her with more than modest coverage. Indeed, she had to fold the sleeves back twice, and the leggings as well. She looked down at herself and laughed. This rough frontier garb was a far cry from a satin gown, but she was glad to have it.

Emerging from the woods, Raven went directly to where Eben waited. In giving her his clothing he had done her a service, and so for now she would try not to vex him. She found him oddly hunched in the saddle, and when he looked at her his eyes were glassy. "You're taking ill," she admonished lightly. "You should have let me tend your arm yesterday, you know."

"I know," he said. "But yesterday I didn't trust you."

"And what about today?"

He sighed. "Today I may not have a choice," he said.

"We could camp here," Raven suggested. But she saw him shake his head. When he spoke it was with effort, and she noticed how his breathing seemed slow and labored.

"As long as I can sit a horse we'll go a little further." He offered her his left arm to help her mount, but she declined, taking Cadence's bridle instead and guiding her to a nearby stump which she used as a mounting block. She settled herself before him and he clucked to the mare, who ambled slowly off.

Eben leaned heavily against her. Raven felt his breath stir the soft tendrils at her cheek. His chest was pressed against her back and his thighs molded tightly to hers, their fevered length searing her skin through her leather clothes. His uninjured arm rode at her hip and draped over her leg to rest on the pommel. The familiarity made her cheeks grow red, but in the light of his illness, she could not find it within her to rebuke him.

It was nearing twilight when they finally made camp for the night. Raven was the first to dismount, deftly bringing her right leg over the pommel, then sliding to the ground. Eben's descent was slower and far less graceful. He seemed to have lost all coordination and had a great difficulty extracting his left boot from the stirrup. He cursed softly in his effort to free it and bumped against Cadence, who nervously shied away. He might have been dragged to the ground or trampled then and there had Raven not intervened.

With a hand on the bridle she held the mare steady and helped to free his boot, for which she received an evasive shrug. "I'm a little tired," he insisted.

"Indeed," Raven said, tying Cadence's reins to a low-hanging branch. "You are also more than a little sick."

Eben shrugged again. "A passing bout of the ague," he said, knowing full well it was something far worse than that. He sat down, his back braced against the sturdy bole of a tree.

He had to admit that he was feeling quite ill. His skin felt hot and dry as parchment, and his vision was blurred. A nap would help refresh him, he thought, and replenish the strength he seemed to have lost. But first he had to reassure himself that the girl would not run off the moment he closed his eyes.

With burning gaze, he watched her move about the camp, preparing a fire for their usual nightly fare of venison steak. The fringed leather clothing fit her sweet curves like a second skin, and gazing at her he felt his body react. The firelight gilded her skin and coaxed the blue highlights from her shimmering tresses. It seemed to accentuate her soft feminine charms, while concealing her bent to violence, much like a velvet cat's paw, which sheathed the feline's razor-sharp claws. He saw her look his way, a troubled glance that was far removed from the usual hate-filled looks she reserved for him. As if on cue, he spoke.

''Raven, lass, will you leave that alone for a moment and come over here?''

Raven positioned the improvised spits fashioned from supple birch rods over the fire before fulfilling his request. ''What is it you want of me?'' she asked, looking down at him from where she stood.

''First of all I want you to sit here by me. There is something we must discuss, and much I need to say, and I want you to listen carefully.'' He patted the ground beside him with his left hand. The right, Raven saw, was positioned across his midriff, the bandage stained with dried blood.

''You make it sound very serious,'' she said, taking not the seat he offered, but one at a few feet away. It was bad enough to be pressed so intimately against his work-hardened length throughout the day's ride, and she had no intention of sidling up to him now.

He glanced ruefully at the bandaged arm. ''I'm afraid it may well be,'' he admitted.

''Had you heeded my warning and left me alone, your arm would not be injured.'' She frowned ever so slightly, knowing how callous her statement must sound. The truth was that she had never meant to harm him. She had taken the knife for her own protection, and nothing more than that.

''I am your guardian, Raven. And as such, I could not let you have the upper hand. A guardian bears the same responsibility to protect and chastise a ward as a parent does a child. You were begging for a comeuppance from the first moment we met. I would have been remiss in my duties as your guardian had I allowed matters to continue as they were.''

''Justify your actions all you will, Eben St. Claire!'' Raven said hotly. ''But the fact remains that you are not my father, and I am no child! I wish you would remember that!"

"Would that I could forget," he muttered beneath his breath. It was pressed upon him constantly as she swayed against him on the horse that this was no half-grown girl who was his ward, but a lovely young woman, well-formed and aching to be tamed. As the days passed he found it more and more difficult to recall the promise he had made to her father to protect her. Especially since it seemed that he was the one she most needed protection against.

This kind of thought made him angry. "Are you as good at shooting a gun as shooting off your mouth?" he demanded.

"My father taught me well. Why do you ask me that?" she wanted to know. "Can it be that you wish me to shoot you, m'sieur, and put an end to your misery?"

Eben caught the impish gleam in her dark eyes and knew that she was teasing. Still, he was feeling just ill enough to consider it. He gave her as frosty a look as his fever would allow and told her to fetch his rifle and shot. In a moment she had lain the things before him. "The piece is loaded, so take care how you handle it," he said.

"The knife was sharp as well, but I was not the one who got cut."

"Your tongue, mademoiselle, cuts and slashes more deeply than the keenest rapier! Now shoot the damn thing so that I can oversee your reloading procedure." He watched as she picked up the rifle and sighted it at a tree where a fat gray squirrel scampered. The weight of the piece made her bead unsteady. "You need a rest unless you've a mind to waste a shot. Use this tree, and make the first shot count. Remember, you may not get another."

Without replying Raven rose and leaned against he same tree her companion used as a backrest.

The squirrel scurried back across the limb toward his hole, anxious to be away from the intruders. Raven took a deep breath and held it to steady her aim, then slowly squeezed the trigger. The gun went off with a roar and a small sulfur-smelling cloud rose from the frizzen pan. At the same instant, bark flew from the limb and the squirrel tumbled to the ground and lay still. She looked at Eben with all the hauteur she could muster. "Are you satisfied?" she asked.

He pinned her with his feverish gaze. "You've shown me that you can hit a squirrel, but do you think that you can kill a man?"

Raven turned pale. "You are jesting. Your injury is not that bad."

"I'm not talking about myself," he said. "But if someone threatened you, could you bring yourself to kill him?"

"Yes," she said, "if it is necessary, but it surely won't come to that. You are strong—"

"I'm none so strong today, I'm afraid," Eben said slowly. "Perhaps tomorrow I'll feel better, but if I don't—"

If he didn't . . . The uncompleted statement sent a shock of fear running through her. No matter how repugnant his company was, she was loathe to lose him—to be left utterly alone in a wilderness. Like it or not, she had become dependent on him. "Let me see your arm," she said. "I can gather some plants and make a poultice."

He held up his good hand to stay her. "Another minute or two will not make a difference, Raven. The arm bothers me, it's true, but not half so much as my worries concerning you."

"You have seen that I can protect myself," Raven said. "You needn't worry about me. Now seek your rest while I get the herbs. The wound in your arm has waited long enough, and there is the squirrel to clean."

"Bother the damned squirrel!" he growled. "And tell me how you expect me to sleep when the moment I close my eyes you'll cut and run?" he asked.

"I would not leave you while you are incapacitated," she said, giving him a look of disgust that he should think so ill of her.

"Somehow I doubt that," Eben's tone was dubious. "But if you are willing to swear, then I will chance it."

"Will you allow me to see to your arm?" she questioned.

"After we finish our talk."

"All right then," she relented. To argue against his stubbornness would not do either of them any good. "You have my word upon it. Are you satisfied?"

"It's a beginning," he said. "I've noticed some fresh sign of unshod ponies crossing the trail we've been following, and I'm afraid we may be getting uninvited guests. I want you to be prepared. Keep the rifle near you at all times. In fact, you'd be wise if you slept with it in hand."

"Don't you think that's a little extreme?" Raven asked.

"If I did, I wouldn't suggest it. You'll need the rifle, Raven. It will remain your best defense against any threat. The only other protection I can provide you with is a nominal one. What you said the other day about the woods abounding with wolves is very true. There are many who would take advantage of a young woman alone, especially if they think of her as being unspoiled. One as fair as yourself would bring a king's ransom to some enterprising fellow. Slaves are valuable commodities, Raven. Especially pretty white women, so you must be on your guard. Try to rouse me if anyone comes, red man or white, but if you can't then tell them that you're my wife."

"What!" The suggestion was outrageous.

"Don't argue with me, lass," he warned. "I know what's best. I am not guaranteeing that your claim of being my wife will protect you from every harm, but there are some who would hesitate to rape another man's wife. Especially if she can bark a squirrel as well as you can."

The offer of his name, even in pretense, made Raven uncomfortable. How could she claim to be his wife when she detested him as she did? She suddenly wished that they could go back in time to yesterday morning, before he had spanked her, before she had retaliated by taking his knife. Until then he had been just another trial to be borne, a hardship to tolerate. But now he had quite suddenly become someone to worry about, and as she noticed the ashen cast of his normally tanned skin, that worry deepened. It was just his talk of unscrupulous men roaming about in these woods that caused her to experience unease, she told herself steadfastly. And it had nothing whatsoever to do with her feelings for him—whatever they happened to be.

He was watching her expectantly. "Well?" he asked. "Will you promise me that much?"

Raven shrugged to hide the discomfort brought on by this conversation. "I have already promised to stay; I suppose I can promise this as well." She paused and heard his sigh of relief. "But do not get ideas that this gives you rights where I am concerned."

"You have the rifle, my lady wife," he said with mockery, pleased that she did not turn immediately shrewish. "Your warning is well taken."

Raven reloaded the rifle and propped it against the tree, within easy reach. It seemed to satisfy him, and he raised no further objection to her tending his wound. She unwrapped the makeshift bandage and found the arm was swollen, the gash an angry red. "Keep the flies away until I get back," she said, then took the soiled rag to the small brook beside which they had camped. She rinsed the cloth and wrung it almost dry, then with the fading light of day to aid her, searched the banks of the rill for the herbs she needed.

The long spear-shaped leaves of wild comfrey grew here in abundance, and Raven gathered several. They were as long as her forearm, and several times as wide. One leaf would make a poultice, and the portion she did not use tonight could be dried and carried with them for later.

When she returned to the camp she found that Eben's lids were drooping. He had moved closer to the fire, and his rifle rested across his knees.

"What manner of weed have you found?" he asked. His pale gaze followed her movements about the camp as she searched his belongings for the alcohol she knew he had. When she found the flask she went to sit beside him.

"It is called comfrey," she answered, tearing a small square from the still damp bandage. "It aids in healing. My mother used to say that it would grow a new tail on a cat."

His heated gaze roved over her and a somewhat pained smile creased his lips. "My little cat, I rather like the tail you have."

Raven said nothing, but set about her work. She soaked the small square of cloth with whiskey from the flask, then proceeded to cleanse the wound and the arm around it. The gash itself was drawn together in a pucker and would leave an ugly scar, a token of their time together. The flesh surrounding the wound was swollen and inflamed, and the redness seemed to extend up his arm in long streaks. Raven frowned. "How are you feeling?"

"A trifle warm," he replied, though privately he thought that watching her seemed to have lent him as much heat as the fever.

"Does your head ache also?" she asked. She had finished cleaning away the dried blood and mashed a leaf and stem of the plant on a flat rock to extract the juices. The whole of it was then applied to the injury, and that bound again with the recently laundered cloth.

Eben's appreciative gaze roamed leisurely over her. "Aye," he rasped. "And other places ache as well."

Catching his meaning, Raven smiled. Did his lusting never stop? She moved away and a companionable silence stretched out between them. For once he was no threat, and Raven could relax in his company. She cooked the meat and took his portion to him, but he refused. "Remember what I said," he reminded her. "And keep the rifle handy."

"Try to sleep," Raven replied in a soothing voice. "I will keep watch." She saw him nod and his lids came slowly down. In sleep his features lost some of their hardness and he seemed almost boyish, a world away from the callous man she knew. She peered at him—with his eyes closed against her, she felt safe in doing so—and wondered just where the mocking, arrogant brute of a man she so detested had gone? Surely there was not a trace of him in the smooth lineaments of his handsome face. Her mind wandered back over all their confrontations, and she wondered if they had arisen because of something she evoked within him. Or did he act so boorishly with every woman he met? If so, then it was no wonder he remained unmarried. For what female in her right mind would put up with a man like him?

Close to the warmth of the fire, the young frontiersman stirred. He rolled onto his side and shivered, in his dreams complaining, "Ivory, lass, the bed is cold."

Raven's eyes widened at the utterance. Obviously she was wrong, and there was at least one woman who found him appealing, despite his pompous ways. She wondered who this Ivory was and what she meant to Eben. Could she have been the woman he had spoken of as being unfaithful? It roused Raven's curiosity.

As she lay down to sleep she tried to picture the woman Eben would have chosen. In her mind's eye she saw her as some pale and winsome creature, a woman too weak of spirit to defy his headstrong ways. When she slept her dreams were hauntingly filled with images of Eben, but disturbingly, the woman in his arms had hair like jet and eyes that were filled with fire.

Chapter 9

Streaks of rose and goldenrod adorned the morning sky when Raven awakened. Everything was peaceful and still, hushed into silence by the breathtaking dawn sky. Despite the gentle quiet, she sensed immediately that something was terribly wrong. Spinning around, she reached for the rifle, but it was no longer where she'd put it before she'd lain down to sleep. Soberly, she looked up into the face of the brave now holding up his prize.

He was obviously greatly pleased with the weapon for he brandished it proudly before his companions and said something in a dialect that Raven didn't understand. She wished that Eben were awake and well, so that he could tell her what to do. But then, had her guardian been well, this never would have happened.

She rose quickly, not knowing what other course of action to take, and held out her hands, speaking in rapid Delaware, then repeating the same thing in French, hoping that one of the languages would be understood.

"The rifle is mine and I would like to have it back now. Without it my husband and I will go hungry."

"What do you do with this white eyes buck, little doe?" It was not the man with the rifle who addressed her, but a muscular man on a speckled pony. He spoke to her in French and seemed not unfriendly.

"The man may be a white eyes, but he is a great hunter, and he is my lawful husband," Raven lied. Of course, she only lied about him being her husband, for he was unsurpassed as a hunter.

"Which law, little doe," Chaubenee asked humorously, "the white man's law or the law of the people?"

"God's law," Raven said. "We were joined together by a Jesuit priest."

"Ah, then you are indeed his wife," Chaubenee said.

"Or perhaps his widow," another chimed in, and all the braves laughed.

The others, who had remained on their horses, now dismounted. They milled around the camp, some gathering around Cadence to speculate over her worth. Alarmed, Raven cried out for them to leave the mare alone, but they paid her no attention, so she turned instinctively to Chaubenee, who seemed to be the leader of the band. "Please, leave the mare with us. She's all the chance I have to get my husband out of here. Without her he will surely die."

An ugly little man with a greasy headscarf pulled low to cover one eye snorted with malice, then said to Raven, "If the man is to die anyway, then we should hasten his departure. This yellow hair will look good fastened to my lodgepole."

While he continued to leer at her from his one good eye, Raven warned him, "If you so much as touch him, I swear I will kill you."

"Your little doe has fangs, Chaubenee," he said to the big man. "But Tenskwatawa is not afraid of a mere woman," he told her, but nonetheless he moved aside.

Recognizing the name Tenskwatawa from news

gathered around the trading post, Raven knew immediately who she was dealing with. "So this is the great prophet of the Shawnees. Have you sunk so low as to murder those unable to defend themselves? If so, then the People must indeed be desperate for leadership."

"Unable or unwilling?" The prophet sneered. He walked over to Eben's prostrate form and stood looking down at the young frontiersman with one malevolent eye. "I think your man is a coward, who pretends to sleep, much like the opossum who fears being hurt by those superior to it."

He raised his moccasined foot and brought it near Eben's injured arm; but seeing his intent, Raven swiftly swept the long-handled knife from the sheath at Eben's belt and leapt toward the little man, knocking him to the ground and bringing back the blade for a killing blow.

"I said that I would kill you, little man," she hissed, her eyes glaring angrily. "Unlike some, my words are not empty ones."

There was a stir among the men, and for the barest instant, Raven looked away. It was during that space that Tenskwatawa hit her, knocking the knife away. "Witch!" he yelled. "This woman is a witch! Stay back, lest her evil infect you!"

The man who held the rifle brought it to bear on her breastbone, pulling back the hammer. She thought that at any moment she would feel the cruel sting of a bullet, and nothing more. She held her breath, looking daggers at them all, and waited to die. They would never see her show cowardice before this threat, even though she was more frightened than she had ever been in her life.

"Hold!" The cry rang like thunder through the small clearing, startling Raven and bringing looks of unease to some of those caught up in the shameful badgering of an innocent girl. The man responsible for staying Raven's execution was a tall and extremely handsome Indian. He was dressed in the same simple garb that Eben chose, a fringed hunting shirt and leggings, with only a breechclout to cover his loins and moccasins to protect his feet. His arresting countenance was devoid of paint of any kind, but was fearsome indeed in his wrath.

"Have you nothing better to do?" he demanded. He went to snatch the rifle from the one who held it still. "We are not on the path of war, and this woman's possessions are not plunder!" He held it out to Raven.

"She speaks the tongue of the French," Chaubenee said to Tecumseh.

"Little sister, I apologize for their rudeness," Tecumseh said. "Here is your rifle." His clear hazel eyes watched her with more than passing interest as she came and took the gun from his hands. "You are to be commended for your brave defense of your husband. Perhaps I could recruit you to our ranks. I think this one small woman would serve me better than the lot of you."

"I would never follow that man," Raven said, casting her baleful glare toward Tenskwatawa, who had seemed to shrink even further in stature with the appearance of his brother.

"He is not in command here—though I don't doubt he would like to be." This remark was uttered less harshly, and it drew laughter from the men. "What is wrong with your husband, little sister?"

"He cut his arm and it has made him ill. Whatever poisons were in the wound seem to have entered his blood. Do you know what I can do for him?" she asked hopefully.

Tecumseh shook his head. "The one among us who is a shaman is the one you do not trust."

Raven glanced at the prophet, who was looking

smug. His eye glittered evilly. "I would not put Eben's life in his hands," Raven said firmly.

Tecumseh looked down upon this petite woman and wondered at the urge he felt to help her save this white man, her husband. He hated whites with very few exceptions, and the Galloway family of Urbana was numbered among the few he felt deserving of his trust. "There is one, not far from here in which your faith would be well placed. I was going there . . . if you wish you may ride with our cavalcade."

Raven immediately seized upon Tecumseh's suggestion. Tecumseh had saved them both from certain disaster. Eben had warned her of the dangers she might have to face alone. Perhaps the next encounter with strangers lurking in the woods would not end so fortunately for either of them.

The day was a fair one, and the cabin door stood wide open to admit the fresh air and the late summer sunshine. Sixteen-year-old Rebecca Galloway stood in the doorway, blue eyes bright with expectancy, for surely her suitor would come today. He was ardently courting her, this proud chieftain of the Shawnee, and if she could tame him it would be a grand feather of accomplishment in her cap.

Not that she didn't like Tecumseh the way he was, for she was very much an admirer of beauty, and he was beautiful of face and body. About him there was an air of nobility that took some people aback, but not Rebecca. She saw him as an exotic prince, come to pay his suit.

In the kitchen of the spacious cabin, James Galloway was just finishing his breakfast. He saw his daughter rise slightly on her toes and knew that she had seen something out of the ordinary. "Becky, what is it? Is someone coming?" he asked, rising out of his chair.

"It's Tecumseh, Pa," Rebecca said, "and someone is with him."

"Indeed, I can see that," James said with amusement in his tone. The long column of more than a score of Indians certainly constituted "someone."

"I don't mean them, Pa," she said impatiently. His eyesight was failing him, but he was too vain to wear his spectacles. "Look there, alongside Tecumseh. There's a man on that sorrel mare that looks like your friend. I remember him from years ago, when I was just a girl, he stopped by the cabin to visit. Why, he looks ill—Mother! Mother!"

Elizabeth Galloway came from the bedroom, a slight frown marring her face. She was a tall woman, a little bent now from the work of keeping her brood alive and healthy. Her beauty was fading with the advent of the years, from too many babies and too little care. Her hair, once bright and golden like her daughter's, had dulled to the color and consistency of straw, and her blue eyes had lost a little of their sparkle and were lined about the outer corners, as was her mouth. She bustled to the doorway, where her husband and eldest daughter were craning their necks to view their visitors. "Have you two nothing better to do with your day than to lounge about in the doorway?" she chided good-naturedly. "Honestly, James! Go and make them welcome! Rebecca, put the coffee on to boil and get down the sugar tin, enough for all, you hear?"

Rebecca went reluctantly to do as her mother had told her, though she did so slowly, and with many an anxious glance at the doorway for the tall figure of her beau.

Outside, James and Elizabeth greeted their guests. The usual were there among Tecumseh's traveling retinue. Chaubenee, Tecumseh's good-natured friend, Shabbona, the chief's right-hand man and also the grand-nephew of Pontiac, the celebrated

Ottawan chief, and one that James knew only as Four-Legs were all there. Some of the others James recognized by face but not by name. James gave his hand in greeting and spoke his welcome, waiting.

"We bring you a present, James Galloway," Tecumseh joked. "We found him in the woods by the quarry."

James looked at Eben, who was slumped over his mount's neck. His right arm was swollen and an unhealthy color. "I know this man," James said. "Will you help me get him into the house?"

Tecumseh nodded to Chaubenee, who went to drag Eben bodily from the horse. The rough treatment brought a startled curse from the injured man that made Elizabeth's ears burn.

"This is his woman, *squa-thi neeshematha,*" Tecumseh said, indicating Raven. "They are yours now."

By this time Rebecca had finished the coffee and added to the black brew a sickening amount of sugar. She doled it out to each man, serving Tecumseh first as courtesy demanded. She smiled coyly up at him from under her pale lashes. She had heard him address the pretty young woman as his "little sister" and was none too pleased with his attention to her. "Will you stay awhile?" she asked him.

"No, Rebecca," he said softly. "I cannot stay. I stopped only to bring the white eyes to your father. James Galloway's honor is such that he will not allow the needs of this man or his woman to be neglected." He saw the disappointment on her face. "I will be coming back when the moon is bright."

It would not be seemly to argue, though Rebecca longed to do so. Business always came first with Tecumseh, but once she accepted his suit, all of that would change. "I will wait for you then," she told him demurely.

Raven came from the cabin where she had seen to

Eben's immediate comfort and went to stand beside the tall Shawnee. She could see Rebecca Galloway watching her with a tense look on her face. The girl's jealousy was apparent, even from a distance. Raven ignored the glares that were being cast her way. She wanted only a word with Tecumseh before she went back into the cabin, but she knew that she must wait for this man to speak first.

"Take care that your man keeps his arm, *match-squa-thi neeshematha,*" he told her. "He will need it if he is to fight for his people."

"I will, and thank you," she said.

He mounted swiftly and called a farewell to the Galloways, then headed off toward the west.

Raven watched him go before she returned to the cabin and Eben.

"When did this happen?" Elizabeth Galloway questioned gently. She was about to bathe the wound, but paused long enough to glance up at the buckskin-clad girl who hovered at her shoulder before she returned to her task.

"Three days ago," Raven said softly.

Elizabeth took off the makeshift poultice and sat back to view Eben's wound. "Dear God," she murmured, taking in the long gash and inflamed flesh. "How on earth did this happen, child?"

Raven averted her eyes. "I tried to tell him to take more care with his knife, but he wouldn't listen to me."

"Well, now that I think on it, I can't say that I'm surprised," Elizabeth commented dryly. "Men are such bumbling fools when it comes to their own health. I'm frankly amazed that this young man is still breathing. He always struck me as having far too much stubbornness for his own good." She paused to wring the rag out over the basin before continuing. "The chief says that you're his wife, but

I would guess that bride is a more accurate word, judging from your shyness."

Raven blushed and looked down at her hands. Her fingers were conspicuously devoid of a ring. "We are just newly joined," she fairly whispered, hating to lie to this kind woman.

"Well then, you have your work cut out for you," Elizabeth observed. "Your husband is going to need a lot of love and tenderness to see him through this ordeal." She smiled slightly. "And, for that matter, a little prayer to the Almighty might not hurt either."

She rose from her chair and took up the basin and rag. "I'll go and make some beef tea," she said. "We can't have him falling away to nothing, now can we? Not when he's got some fighting to do." With a kindly look, Elizabeth laid her hand on Raven's arm. "Now don't you fret too hard," she said softly. "Your man's going to be just fine. Fighting is what these frontiersmen do best. We women just bank the home fires and bide our time. Now, sit and watch in case he should waken and not know where he is. I'll be back shortly."

Elizabeth left the room and Raven sighed beneath the weight of her concern. She *was* terribly worried about Eben. He lay quietly enough, but his arm was so swollen, the flesh an angry red. What would happen if it grew black and putrid? She couldn't stand the thought of him having but one arm and knowing it had been her own impetuosity that had caused it, however unintentionally.

She knelt by the bedside and took his good hand in both of hers, squeezing it tightly. "You must get well," she whispered, "you must!"

"Ivory . . . where is Meg?" he mumbled. His fevered eyes opened slowly and he glanced around the room, then looked at Raven. "Oh, 'tis you, Raven. I thought I was home, in Castle Ford."

"Not Castle Ford, but you've been here before, have you not? You know the Galloways, Elizabeth and James?"

He sighed. "So tired." His pale gaze swept over her. He was indeed tired, tired of fighting his feelings for her when all he wanted to do was pull her close to him. Slowly, as dripping water insinuates itself into impenetrable stone, this capricious female was making her way into his life. And all of the armor he'd used these many years to prevent such a thing from happening was becoming useless against her.

The reasons why this should be so eluded him. She was young and pretty, it was true, but there had been others just as young and pretty in his life, and if his memory served him correctly, of a far sweeter nature than Raven. Yet none had stirred his passions to the unbearable heights that Raven did, nor kept him teetering on the brink of violence as she seemed to do. He wanted her badly . . . he wanted her gone. Yet the thought of spending his days without her to share them caused a hollow feeling that could only be attributed to the fever. It was all so very confusing. Just trying to untangle his thoughts and feelings made his headache intolerable.

If he survived this crisis, he would try to sort it all out. And once Raven was safely in Pittsburgh, with a steady man to stay her wild ways, his own life would return to normal.

"I hope that you're not too tired to eat," Elizabeth Galloway said from the doorway. "It's good that you're awake, Mr. St. Claire. It will make it easier on your bride, here."

Raven felt his questioning gaze turned on her and blushed. Thankfully, Elizabeth Galloway seemed not to notice and Raven accepted the bowl containing the strong broth.

"No one has died in that bed before, and I would not take kindly to have you be the first," she continued.

"I'll try not to . . . disappoint you," Eben said with a weak smile.

Chapter 10

With the advent of night Eben's fever rose and nothing Elizabeth Galloway or Raven tried seemed to ease his fever. He tossed upon the Galloways' featherbed as if upon a torture rack. It pained Raven to see him this way, and she began to worry in earnest that he might die. Her only comfort was the stalwart Elizabeth Galloway, who never seemed to waver in her belief that her patient would rally.

"I'm going to send James for some cool water from the well," Elizabeth said, pressing the rag she'd been plying into the younger woman's hand. "There's but one way I know of to lower a fever, and that's to bathe the hot with cool."

Raven hastened to place the rag against Eben's brow and Elizabeth laughed softly. "Dear girl, not just the head, the whole . . . he's naked beneath that coverlet. Strip it off and bathe him. I'll be back in a little while."

Elizabeth left Raven gaping at her. "This is a fine revenge, m'sieur," she said to him as she inched the sheet down. "I'm glad to see you're still asleep. Were you awake I am sure you would enjoy venting your mirth at my expense!"

While she talked she rinsed out the rag in fresh water, wrung it out, and ran it down his neck and over his shoulders, not halting her work until she met again with the barrier of the sheet. When this was done she lowered the sheet again, this time leaving it draped modestly over his loins.

She washed his chest with its light furring of dark hair . . . then moved lower, over the flat surface of his belly. Again the sheet barred her continuing, and again it was moved further down, this time to the top of his thighs.

Now nothing was left to Raven's imagination. Her warm gaze soon followed in the rag's wake, touching him where she'd never dream of touching him when he was awake and watching her. He was so magnificent, with his broad shoulders and lean hips.

The surge of pride she felt when she looked at him only served to confuse her. Surely there was no reason for it! He was her guardian and the bane of her existence! So why should performing this wifely chore make her feel like a spouse in truth? As she worked the cloth over his smooth tanned skin she allowed her mind to wander. What would it be like to be his woman? To share his bed and have his babes? She imagined a tow-haired lad or lass with eyes of palest blue and felt her heart thaw in her breast.

"What are you thinking?" came a raspy whisper from the bed. "You have such an odd look on your face . . . a look of radiance I have never seen before. Can it be that you see my demise and the end of your hated bargain?"

"My thoughts and feelings have been of no importance to you until now," Raven replied, irritated that he should catch her daydreaming when her thoughts had been of him. "Instead, concern yourself with getting well."

"That's not true, Raven," Eben said. "I have thought only of your safety since entering into the bargain with your father." He shivered. Never in his life had he been so miserable. He felt hot and cold and ached all over, and all she wanted to do was argue. "It will not matter soon, in any case—your problems will be over. I doubt I can survive this."

His talk of dying made Raven uneasy. The pain of Henri's death was still fresh, and though Eben meant nothing to her, she could not let him go. She picked up the wet cloth again and after wringing it out, sponged his brow. "You surprise me, m'sieur," she said chidingly. "After all we have been through together I would not have thought you would surrender this easily."

"This is one fight I cannot win."

"I see," Raven said. "I suppose then that you are wise to quit. It is easier than a good fight." She dropped the cloth back in the basin, and it sloshed water on the sheets. "I suppose you will want someone to sit by your side and hold your hand while you get on with this business of dying."

Her pointed remarks penetrated Eben's fever-induced haze and brought a frown to his dark face. "You make it sound as if I have a choice."

"Do I?" Raven raised her brows in surprise. "Well, that was hardly my intention. I only meant to give my understanding to a man whose hours are limited. If you prefer I will just sit quietly and wait."

Eben scowled. "You have never been so acquiescent. I do not think I like this side of you."

"And how should I be then?" Raven asked. "Should I weep and gnash my teeth? Should I praise your cowardice on high and vow that you did all you could to save your life when just the opposite is the case?"

"You are raving," Eben stated hoarsely. "I took the blade from you when a coward would have fled."

"You were a fool," she told him, pushing deliberately to make him angry. "It had nothing to do with bravery."

"Must you always nag at me, woman?" Eben demanded. "Even in my sickbed I can find no peace from your harping! I rue the day we met!"

His anger would give him something to concentrate on besides dying. Raven turned away to hide her smile and was surprised to feel Elizabeth's work-worn hand on her shoulder. "It's just the fever talking, dear," she said. "He'll be his old sweet self in no time." She brushed past Raven, who wondered just how well this woman knew Eben, and stood beside the bed. "Mr. St. Claire, do you think you can drink this for me, or shall I spoon it into your mouth?"

"I can manage," Eben said, taking the cup she held out for him. His hand trembled slightly, but he brought the cup to his lips without spilling a drop. He drank the tepid liquid and shuddered, pulling a face. "Sweet Christ, what is that?"

Elizabeth stiffened. "Willow bark tea," she replied, "and because of your condition I will overlook your lapse . . . this time."

"I beg your pardon, ma'am, but this concoction of yours is rank," the patient mumbled.

"Medicines rarely taste good, young man," Elizabeth said. "But I expect you to drain that cup all the same. It will help rid you of that fever and lessen your aches from within, while this poultice works on drawing out the poisons."

Eben drank the bitter brew and handed back the cup.

Straightening, Elizabeth looked stern. "You should not be so hard on your wife, Mr. St. Claire," she said softly so that Raven could not hear. "She is only a girl and to name her a nag when she is concerned for your health is unkind. Every man needs a gentle push in the right direction now and then. And though it may not always seem so, there is love behind it."

"Wife?" Eben asked, unsure what she meant until Raven spun around and glared at him. "Oh, aye, Raven," he said.

Elizabeth glanced at the girl, who shrugged lightly. "He's been out of his head almost from the moment we met. I am unsurprised that he should forget our nuptials so soon."

The older woman clucked her tongue. She went to Raven and put an arm about her slim shoulders. "Come, dear, I've a freshly brewed pot of peppermint tea waiting in the kitchen." She ushered Raven from the room and left Eben alone. His mouth watered at the mention of the tea, but he dared not request any for fear Elizabeth would bring him more of her willow bark tea. As he settled back into the pillows and closed his eyes he felt his aches lessen, the muted sound of the women's voices drifting in from the kitchen soon lulling him into a restless, dream-filled sleep.

Meggie was frowning, her freckled brow was furrowed deep and her kelly-green eyes fairly snapped with her barely repressed ire.

It had been that way since he had come to the inn to live. Meggie, just a half score of years older than Eben himself, had taken up the role of counselor, confidante, and elder sister. Eben always knew from her expression whether she disapproved of his actions or not, and just now the scowl she wore on her thin face would have rivaled that of his late sire.

Her anger showed in every fiber of her being, in the way she handled the dough she was kneading for the day's bread, the short jabs her bony fists were executing, the tiny geysers of flour that spurted from the bread board now and again. "I've never told you what to do," she said sourly, "and I'm not about to begin now."

Eben laughed. "You always tell me what to do, Meg," he said, pleasantly. "I suppose I've come to expect it."

"Not that you ever listen to me!" Meggie paused to wipe her sweat-dotted brow on her forearm. A smudge of flour whitened her temple and was left there, unnoticed. "Eben, please, stay away from that girl."

"I can't, Meg," Eben said quietly. "She's in my blood. I can't say that I love her—I don't know what love is—but I know that other women pale beside her. For me, no one else compares."

He walked to the table and stood looking down at Meggie, the only person in the world that truly cared about him, besides Ivory. More than anything, he didn't want any harm to come to Meg. But he was eighteen now, and just returned from the army. He was a man, with a man's desires, and more than anything, he desired the judge's daughter.

"Flaming hair and grass green eyes!" Meggie muttered. "A hundred years ago she'd have been burned as a witch! I wish to God the practice could be revived!" Meggie paused to lay the finished dough in the larded wooden raising trough, covered it with a clean linen towel, and turned again to Eben. "She's poison, Eben, and she'll taint your life if you get mixed up with her. Already she's been with men—God only knows how many!"

He frowned heavily. "You can't know that," Eben said.

"I do know it! Everyone in the county knows it, even Zeb, though he strives to ignore it!" Meggie replied. "For pity's sake, Eben. Have a good long look around you. There are dozens of girls who would jump at the chance to be with you, decent girls who could bear you fine little ones."

"But Ivory—" he began, only to have her cut him off.

"Huh! Don't think that little rip will bear your babes! She'll not ruin her figure for any man! That vixen knows every trick in the book, and she'll ply them all, against you!"

"No . . . Meg, listen," Eben said. He was so hot. Meg had turned away, he could see her stiffen her spine as she always did when she was angry. "Ivory isn't a whore . . . she isn't. She's in my blood, Meg. I . . . want to marry her. . . ."

Something cool passed over Eben's face. He sighed. Why was he so weary? His chest felt weighted down, every breath felt as if it were his last. His heart seemed to jar his whole being with every beat. He thought he heard murmurings, soft and slightly distorted. Meg was somewhere nearby. If he could only convince her . . . "Meg?"

"Ssshhh," the voice said. "Rest and get well."

Somewhere deep inside him burned the light of recognition, though it didn't quite illuminate the dark corners of his weary brain. He knew only that the softly accented words were soothing, and that he willingly obeyed them, sinking into a deeper, dreamless sleep.

Seated on the very edge of the bed, Raven heard his willing sigh and saw him slip out of the grip of his delirium. She had listened to his mindless confessions, yet she was curiously devoid of emotion. Indeed, she felt empty now that the struggle was over. She felt a hand on her shoulder, gently sympathetic, and raised her eyes to meet those of James Galloway.

"Mrs. St. Claire, why don't you get some rest?"

he asked. "See? The crisis is past, his fever has cooled somewhat."

Raven saw tiny beads of sweat dotting Eben's pale brow. She sighed, not even fighting with the kindly gentleman who was urging her to her feet and guiding her to the foot of the bed.

"Elizabeth prepared this pallet for you," he said. "It's close to the bed so that you can hear Eben if he wakens."

"Thank you, Mr. Galloway," Raven said softly. "You and your wife have been very kind."

"Eben is a good friend, Mrs. St. Claire," James told her. His brow creased as he wondered just how much he should reveal. It must have been difficult for her, hearing Eben speak another woman's name. And there was always the possibility that she didn't know. "I've known him a long while, since my army days," he said carefully. "He has been rather unlucky in the past. It's good to see that has changed at last."

"Yes," Raven agreed, sinking down on the pallet. Changed, she thought, but had anything really changed? Or was the man sleeping nearby still in love with this woman Ivory?

Raven closed her eyes, but sleep wouldn't come. His words moments ago reminded her of what he had said when she had questioned him about having a wife waiting for him. *"I have no wife, nor do I want one. . . ."* Since he had not wed the woman, what had kept him from it?

He must have loved her to have wanted to marry her, Raven thought. If he had felt love for this unknown woman, then how could he bring himself to force her into wedlock with a man she didn't love just for the sake of respectability?

James Galloway had intimated that things had happened in Eben's past, hurtful things, that made him deserve happiness now. Eben himself had said that he didn't trust women. What had Ivory done? Raven fell asleep pondering the question and when she dreamed, she dreamed of flaming red tresses curling out like cruel tentacles to choke her, and laughing green eyes that bore not a trace of pity for their unfortunate victim.

Chapter 11

The sound of voices raised in conversation drifting in from the kitchen woke Raven that morning. Hearing the sounds so indicative of family life drew her off the thick bed of quilts and to the kitchen door, where she paused.

There, seated with his back to the wall and looking a little gray faced, was Eben. Seated on either side of him in a tight semicircle were the smaller Galloway children, some round eyed at the presence of this ragged looking stranger, others plying him with curious questions. He replied slowly, a little haltingly, and noticing this Elizabeth shooed the children from the room, directing them to do their chores.

"Go on and leave Mr. St. Claire alone!" she said. "Mind, he's just out of his sick bed, and against my advice!"

"Do as your ma says," said James, and the children filed reluctantly away.

Raven stood for a moment longer unnoticed in the kitchen doorway and watched him. Weariness born of illness etched lines round the outer corners of his pale blue eyes. His arm, swathed in bandages, was supported by a sling tied around his neck that could just be glimpsed beneath the open shirt he wore. One sleeve of his shirt hung empty. He must have felt her eyes on him, for his gaze slowly rose until it met with hers.

He had been in the act of lifting his coffee cup to his lips, but he paused now, his cool stare warming as he took in her soft dishevelment. Raven thought she knew the direction his thoughts were taking and felt a shock run through her. Just one look from him had the power to make her tremble. The chair next to him was vacant now, and she saw him hold out his hand, palm upward, fingers reaching.

She drew a shaky breath and started forward, feeling uncertain how to act. The Galloways thought she and Eben were married but it was all a lie. In the throes of delirium he dreamed of another woman, not her, and he would just as soon see her wed to another man. So how could he look at her that way? she wondered. Was it his heart that told the lie, or his eyes?

Slowly her hand crept into his—stealthily, he was thinking—the very same way she had crept into his life, without him ever knowing it was happening. "Good morning, wife," he said quietly.

"You should not be out of bed," she admonished softly.

He gave her a weak grin, a bare facsimile of his old wolfish smile. "A wife's place is not to nag her mate. Just ask Elizabeth and she'll tell you."

"I thought we spoke of that last night," Elizabeth said coolly. There was something about this couple that didn't seem right. She noticed a certain reluctance in Raven that most brides did not possess and wondered at the cause. And even though Eben St. Claire clearly displayed all the signs of an eager young bridegroom, there was something undefined in his attitude—almost as if he did not take his vows seriously. Elizabeth had tried to take the matter up with James, but he had laughed and said it was Eben's way to be gruff—a fact the girl was obviously aware of, or she wouldn't have married him in the first place! Elizabeth wasn't so sure. "Raven is only concerned for your health. And she has every right to be. After all she is your wife." She turned to Raven, smiling now, "Nag him all you want, my dear."

Elizabeth set a plate before her heaped with eggs and summer sausage and fresh baked cornmeal biscuits. It was far too great a portion and Raven said so.

"Go on and eat, child. You'll need your strength, even if it's just to hold your own with that bull-headed young man of yours."

Eben sipped his coffee and watched his "wife" from under lowered lids. He thought he'd never seen her looking lovelier, unless perhaps that morning at the river. Her hair was slightly disheveled from sleep and fell in gentle black disarray to her waist. It begged to be stroked, and Eben could not resist the urge to tuck a stray tendril behind her shell-like ear.

She met his gaze then, her soft brown eyes appealing. Without a word she begged him not to carry his game too far, but Eben was enjoying it and was loath to give it up so soon. He leaned back in his chair and after watching her for a time in silence, said, "Since I'm bound to sit in this chair awhile longer perhaps you could fill me in on how we got to Old Chillicothe. It's a considerable distance for you to have dragged an unconscious man."

"Just as you suspected they would, our visitors arrived," Raven told him. "But there were no problems. I deal quite well with Indians."

"Aye, and I seem to recall hearing someone remarking upon my hair color and what lovely decoration it would make," Eben said dryly. "One of your bosom friends, no doubt."

Raven's impish gaze ran over his long flaxen locks.

It waved like thick silk at his nape. "I see you still have it, m'sieur."

James had been watching the exchange and now commented. "Raven's made quite an impression on the chieftain, that's for sure. He introduced her as *match-squa-thi neeshematha.*"

"Chieftain?" Eben repeated. "Anyone I know?"

"By remark, if not by sight," James said. "Tecumseh brought you in, Eben. Quite a sight you made too, what with Raven there holding you on your horse and a score of braves as an escort."

Eben digested this in silence. He wondered just what it was that Raven wasn't telling him. Watching her watching her food as if she expected any moment it would leap off her plate, he knew that she was holding back something. He decided to let it go for now, as he lacked the strength it would require to contend with her stubbornness. However, the sudden picture that came to mind of Raven holding off Tecumseh's contingent with that untamed tongue of hers made him shudder.

She evidently saw the reflex and mistook it for pain. She covered his hand with hers and looked worriedly into his eyes. "Eben, you really should be in bed."

The soft note of concern in her words tempted him. "At the moment I can think of no place I would rather be," he replied.

Raven's color heightened. She would rebuke him for his insolence, but Elizabeth Galloway was watching them with what Raven thought was suspicion. To bring the truth to light now would raise too many questions, and her life was complicated enough with just Eben to deal with. She did not need a stranger, no matter how well-meaning the woman might be, prying into matters better left alone. And so she stood up and went to help him out of his chair. He leaned heavily on her, his good arm draped over her shoulder in such a manner that as they left the room he could fondle her breast without the Galloways seeing. "Will you stop!" she hissed at him.

"Do you really want me to?" He smiled down at her, his pale eyes glinting.

"I think your fever has returned," she said. "For otherwise you would never be so foolhardy."

"Aye," he agreed, "I do feel hot." They reached the bed and she felt his breath caress her ear. "And you, Raven, are you warm as well?"

"You're incorrigible," she told him, trying to wriggle from his grasp, but his good hand slipped lower, down her stiffened spine to the small of her back, to the gentle curve of her buttocks. "Eben, please, the Galloways," she said in quiet protest, but Eben wasn't listening. Very slowly he urged her against him, at the same time nuzzling her hair and breathing deeply of her sweet fragrance. His head dipped down and his lips brushed against her ear, the roughness of his beard tickling her skin.

"It's very good of them to give up their bed to us, don't you agree?" he breathed against her. He took her lobe into his mouth, causing her to gasp. The flood of warmth that shot through her turned her blood into a surging tide and made her knees feel weak. For a moment she swayed against him, her small breasts crushed to his hard muscled chest.

Summoning her flagging will, she drew a shaky breath and forcefully removing his hand from her hips, stepped away. "You've played your little game long enough, m'sieur. Now get into that bed!"

He reached out and took her hand. "Come with me."

"Eben!"

"All right, but first a kiss!" he pleaded. "Try as I might, I can't recall the kiss that sealed our vows. I would have another now, given by my wife to her beloved spouse."

"Where have I heard the warning, 'do not push me too far!' "

"Have I married a frigid woman? Woe is me! 'Tis the bane of many a man's marriage, a husband's nightmare! A woman who will not so much as willingly kiss her husband!" He leaned forward to rise from the bed, cradling his arm in its sling. "I'll just return to the kitchen and more genial company."

"You, m'sieur, are the most exasperating man I know!"

"You have not *known* any other man but me, wife," alluding that she was solely his. "Besides, I am unique, the last of a dying breed."

She cast a glance at the doorway and seeing it still empty, presented him with her haughtiest look. "I have not known *any* man, and certainly not you! This 'marriage' was your idea, and it is not hard to see just why you thought it up!"

A man caught up in his longing for a beautiful woman will hear what he most wants to hear, while adroitly ignoring the rest. So it was with Eben, and with his blood running high, he patted the mattress beside him. "The situation is one easily remedied. And I will be glad to show you just what you've been missing."

Raven's gaze swept over him. "Thank you, no. What you suggest is something I can live without."

"Spoken like a true virgin," Eben said with an exaggerated sigh. "Will you not at least kiss me then? It will give me something to mull over during the long, interminable hours I'm forced to lie prone upon my invalid's couch."

He was sitting on the edge of the bed, his knees apart. It was between them she at last came to stand. "One kiss, and you will stay in bed?"

"Aye, lass, a bargain. Do you find it at all to your liking?"

She refused to reply, but slowly knelt before him. "One kiss," she said. "A brief meeting of the lips . . . and nothing more."

A brief meeting of the lips indeed. Eben let her have her way and subdued a threatening smile as she naively fitted herself against him. Her arms were looped around his neck, but there was a good six inches between their bodies. It would be interesting to see what manner of kiss she thought was fitting for a wife to give her husband. With lowered lids he watched her, and saw her close her eyes. Her mouth met his with a gentle pressure, and remained, unmoving. A kiss to satisfy a cleric, perhaps, but Eben wanted more. He brought his good hand up to slide along her jaw and around to her nape, where it wound into her hair. His broad palm cradled her head and allowed him to take control, deepening the kiss.

His mouth was hot and when it slanted across her own trembling lips Raven could have sworn she felt it sear her very soul. Insistently he urged her lips apart, and to her surprise his tongue entered to boldly spar with hers. His conduct was shocking and caused Raven to utter an involuntary gasp that provided him with unrestricted freedom of her mouth. He was swift to turn it to his advantage, his tongue boldly exploring the silken recesses which no man had dared to try before. There was no denying that the provocative stroking of his tongue was having its effect upon her. It coaxed and cajoled, it teased and caressed, robbing Raven of her will. She melted against him and her lashes fluttered down. For a moment she was unsure what to do, then a feeling of languor slowly stole over her and for once she grew pliant beneath his bold caress.

Knowing that he had at last breached Raven's defenses gave Eben a sense of satisfaction. Having successfully rid her of her ingrained reluctance was just the first step. And in a moment or two he would have her where he wanted her . . . warm and willing on the big bed. With this in mind, he left her swollen lips behind for the gentle curve of her throat. Her skin was soft and tender, too tempting for a man like him! With a painstaking slowness he covered it with kisses, then gently bit her where her neck joined her shoulder.

Raven felt his teeth test her flesh and a pleasurable jolt ran through her. He was too wicked! And she wondered just where this interlude would end.

His hand moved lower, along the gentle curve of her back to her waist and past the hem of his hunting shirt. It was the touch of his hand placed possessively on her bare hip that brought Raven out of her dreamlike state. "You go too far!" she gasped, at once tearing herself from his one-armed embrace.

Undaunted, his pale gaze burned into hers. A few more moments and she would have been his in truth. "You're a hard unfeeling woman, Raven St. Claire," he said. The name was spoken in jest, but he found he liked the sound of it very much. She moved a little away from the bed and with a sigh he watched her. He could still feel the smooth globe of her derriere as it nestled in his palm—surely a perfect fit—and the vital heat that radiated from her skin. Instead of satisfying the longing that burned within him, the kiss he had requested, then purposely prolonged, had only served to fuel his body's fires. He wanted her in the worst way possible, and had they not been in the midst of a bustling crowd of a family, he might have tried to force the issue. As it was, he would settle for whatever morsel she would give him, first of all her nearness.

"Into bed," she prodded, "and give me no further argument." She watched as he complied, stripping off his clothes and settling back in the big bed. Then Raven turned to leave, feeling a desperate need to get away from him. He had the power to do what no other man had ever done, to dominate her, to make her lose control . . . and it frightened her more than she cared to admit.

"Raven, lass?"

"What is it now?" she asked impatiently.

"I'm stiff from lying in this bed, maybe you could rub my back, wife."

It was the last thing she wanted to do just now, to touch him again. The casual way he called her his wife, combined with his heated kiss had pushed her to her limits. She was trembling inside and wanted badly to escape the room. Those pale blue eyes were as sharp as any hawk's, and he would surely see the discomfiture his kiss had caused her and guess the truth. "Later, perhaps," she said, seeking to put him off. "But now I must help our hostess with the dishes."

"Another moment then," he coaxed, patting the bed beside him. "Sit with me a little while, can you? The truth is that I'm fairly bored out of my skull. I'm unaccustomed to lying abed all day, and yet as you have so sweetly shown me, I haven't the strength to be up and about." He smiled up at her, his mouth curling slightly at the corners.

"You are using this as an excuse!" she said in an irate whisper. "And you have even less strength for what I'm sure you have in mind!"

"Raven, please, I've something urgent to tell you."

"Then tell me quickly, for I must go."

"Come closer, it is for your ears alone." He could see that this latest ploy was not working, so he bent forward as if he would rise, then doubled over with a soft groan, cradling the bandaged arm. He heard the small gasp she uttered and then she was beside him, trying to look worriedly into his face. He laughed at her intent expression, he could not help it.

But Raven was not amused. She snarled at him and pushed on his shoulders with all her might, shoving him backwards as he sought to protect his arm from further injury—this time in reality.

There was a solid thunk as his head connected with the thick cherry headboard, but Raven's anger was so great that she never looked back as she made her stormy exit.

Elizabeth raised her brows in mute question at Raven, who took up a clean linen square and began to dry and stack the plates that the older woman was washing. Feeling pressed by that look, Raven felt the need for some sort of explanation. "He deserved it," was all she could manage, but it sounded lame, even to her own ears.

Nothing could keep Eben in bed beyond the morning of the third day. His strength was slowly returning, and with it, his boredom at being confined increased. He was short-tempered with everyone, even the mild Elizabeth, who argued to no avail that he was far from recovered from his ordeal.

After their last confrontation Raven tried hard to maintain a safe distance between them. When he was about she found chores to occupy her in other parts of the house. She even took to helping Rebecca, though neither of them had any special liking for the other.

She spread clean linens over the children's trundles and swept floors with a straw broom while Rebecca prattled on about inconsequential matters. More often than not, Raven listened with half an ear, barely taking account of what the girl said, as her mind was already occupied with thoughts of her obstinate protector. It bothered her that her dislike of him was slowly evolving into something different. No longer could she look at him without noticing how handsome he was or the way his eyes seemed to kindle when he looked at her. She was attracted to him—a hard thing for her to admit, even to herself—and not at all sure that she wanted to be.

From the very first she had known that allowing herself to be taken in by Eben St. Claire would lead her to certain disaster. He was still the same arrogant, unfeeling beast who had bargained her safekeeping against a cache of gold. Only now it was not money he was lusting for, but her! To allow him into her life would only bring her heartache, and that she could do without.

On the morning of the fourth day Eben accompanied James to look at his holdings. His stamina was returning, and very soon he would be bidding farewell to his friend and his family. It would be a relief to go, for Eben's conscience was smarting from his dishonesty.

He never lied without a damned good reason, and indeed would not have lied to the Galloways had he been in his right mind at the time of his arrival. But now there seemed no easy way out of the situation. He would lose face by admitting the truth, and thus it was easier to just let them believe that he and Raven were husband and wife and hope that they never discovered his perfidy.

The fields on the Galloway farm were lush with produce, the trees hanging full of nearly ripe fruit. Everything had a bountiful air, from the new calves in the fields to the Galloway children spilling from the neat log dwelling. To his surprise, when viewing it with James, Eben found he was envious.

"It's a good life, Eben," James was saying. "But then you'll see, you'll see."

"Aye, I suppose."

"Have you got your eye on some land?" James asked. "A man must have land to live and prosper, land to pass on to his sons and daughters . . . to his grandchildren."

"That's a long way ahead for me, I'm afraid," Eben said. He would never see sons or daughters, let alone grandchildren. It made him oddly sad, then irritated with himself. He had reconciled himself to all of this years ago. James was right though. He had to start thinking about getting some land—for himself, for his empire. His capital was not as extensive as he wished, and the gold the Frenchman had promised him had been lost, but he still had enough to make a start. It made him feel somewhat better, though he couldn't banish altogether the hollow feeling that there would be no one in his life to share it with him. No one to witness his triumphs or to soften his failures. James had that in Elizabeth.

Eben's pale gaze swept the land spread out before him. Aye, he told himself, James Galloway had all of that. But Eben St. Claire could have at least part of it. The rest he would have to live without.

Later that evening he was feeling restless and he asked Raven if she would walk out with him to take the air. He had hardly glimpsed her in the past few days, and he knew that she was avoiding him and perhaps was still angry at him for wanting more than she was willing to give. More than anything he wanted to be alone with her, to walk with her beneath the stars, to talk with her in privacy where they need not pretend.

The dishes were done and James was reading while his wife plied her shining needle through a rent in one of his shirts. When she heard Eben's suggestion she smiled. She knew the cause of his restlessness to be a lack of privacy. Newlyweds suddenly thrust into a crowded household were bound to have certain frustrations, especially a healthy young man like Eben.

Elizabeth glanced up in time to see Raven hesitate. What the girl needed was a gentle shove in the right direction, she thought. "Go on, my dear," Elizabeth said. "You certainly deserve a respite. You've near worked your pretty little hands to the bone, and this house has never looked so clean. Besides, the night is beautiful. Why, were James's rheumatism not so affected by the night air we would be out stargazing, isn't that right, Papa?"

"Rheumatism? Why, Liz, you know I don't have—" A stern look from his wife made him halt in mid-sentence. "Oh yes, my rheumatism," he said with some amount of chagrin. To emphasize the point, he rubbed at his elbow. "It's been so good lately I nearly forgot I had it."

Raven could feel Eben's gaze upon her, but she refused to look at him. "It's likely to be cold out there this time of evening," she muttered.

Then he was beside her, running his hand up her arm. "I will take special care that you do not catch a chill," he assured her. "Now come."

The hand that had caressed her now closed over her wrist. He was giving her no choice. She could steadfastly refuse to go and make a fool of herself before these kind and gentle people, or she could walk out with him in the beautiful night.

Once the buckskin-clad pair had gone through the door James began to chuckle. "That's real sweet, ain't it, Liz?"

"I don't know, James," Elizabeth said, frowning down at the tiny stitches she had made in the torn garment. "There is something about those two that just isn't quite right. Do you know that when I spoke to him the other day and assured him that Raven loves him, he seemed astonished to hear it! Now why would he marry the girl if he knew she didn't love him?''

''People marry for many reasons, Mother. Not all are as fortunate as you and I. Eben always was oblivious of such things. I don't know that I have ever seen a more determined, single-minded man when he sets his mind to something. It makes me wonder if he has stopped looking for his brother. Used to be all he talked about—though in truth, he talked little.''

''Well, it's not him I'm worried about. It's that sweet little thing he's wed. If indeed he has wed her at all!''

''Oh, now Mother!''

''Well, I won't say more, James! But mark my words, if he hurts that dear child, he'll someday regret it!''

Chapter 12

The Galloway home was very close to the banks of the Little Miami River. It was here that Eben finally halted his strides and turned to face his angry charge. The moon was high and full and a delightful shade of yellow orange, a harvest moon. It was beautiful, reflected as it was on the rippling surface of the river. He wanted to tell her now that the loveliness of the night paled in comparison to her own sweet beauty, but by the look on her upturned face he could tell that there would be no soft words between them.

She wrenched her wrist from his grasp and stood rubbing it while she glared up at him. "Well, you succeeded in dragging me here. Now what do you want?"

"Just to talk with you, away from the others," he said. He wasn't sure just how to put what he was feeling into words, so he seized upon the first thing that came to mind. "There is something that has been preying on my mind since that first night when I awoke, and we need to have it out between us."

He sounded very grave, and Raven wondered what he meant. "Is this what keeps you awake at night?" she asked.

He frowned. So she was aware that he hadn't been sleeping. He had thought her oblivious of his restless turnings upon his lonely bed, his thoughts full of her. One night he had even sighed her name aloud. She must have heard it. Why then had she ignored him? And what now, since she knew? He couldn't very well admit that it was she who kept him from his rest.

"In part," he said evasively, "but truth to tell, it is something Elizabeth said to me that has cost me much peace of mind. Her remarks set me to thinking, and you are the only one who can clear away my turmoil."

His frown deepened and a muscle in his cheek began to jump. Why was it so difficult for him to communicate with the little wench as he wished to do? He had never been less than direct, and here he was, sounding as if he were approaching some dire inquisition, instead of asking her how she felt about him!

Raven looked into that dark frowning visage and imagined all sorts of things. Foremost in her thoughts was the idea that he might be thinking of leaving her here instead of taking her to Pittsburgh, as he had promised. She had not wanted to go with him in the beginning, but neither did she want to stay here. Elizabeth and James were kind, but she didn't belong with them. Eben, had he guessed her thoughts, would have swiftly informed her that neither did she belong with him. Raven was unsure at this point if she belonged anywhere.

Cursing low he forced out the words. "She said that you cared for me, Raven."

Relief showed in her small visage. At least he was not thinking of leaving without taking her along. She struggled to form an answer that would satisfy him. Not an easy task. How could she tell him anything, when she was not sure herself what her feelings for him were? She liked him well enough, of course, in spite of all their fighting. And his kisses set her heart to racing and made her knees feel weak. But that was hardly enough to constitute affection, and nothing that she could admit to feeling without having him hold it over her head the entire way to Pittsburgh. Prudently, she said nothing.

Eben saw her uncertainty and gave an inward sigh. "Of course I knew she must be mistaken. She must have come to that conclusion because you played your part so well. That is all that it was, isn't that so?"

He hoped he didn't sound as anxious as he felt. To his shock he had found the game they played extremely satisfying, except for creating so many falsehoods. He had all but one of the benefits of naming her his own, without the restricting bonds of wedlock—and that one he wanted most of all. It had surprised him just how warm his heart grew whenever he thought of her welcoming him into her, of how loath he was to consider handing her into another man's safekeeping. Yet he could hardly beg her to share his life of struggle. He wasn't even sure that he wanted to.

In the back of his mind Ivory lurked, and all the pain of her betrayal waited just to be recalled. He somehow doubted that it would ever go away, this suspicion he felt for all womenkind. The faithless woman had ruined him for marriage and a family, normal pleasures other men enjoyed.

Raven let her breath out slowly. "Elizabeth was mistaken," she replied. "Why, I barely know you. How could I possibly care for you?" She broke away from him and walked a little way along the riverbank, stopping beneath the overhanging limbs of a gnarled oak. Here the moonlight could not penetrate, and it was dark and safe. There was a chance that he would not see the confusion that she felt.

Eben followed her as she knew he would and stood very close. He was looking over the water and wondering why he felt this deep disappointment when he should feel relieved.

"I was concerned for your life," Raven continued. "If something happens to you, how shall I get to Pittsburgh to find this wonderful husband you constantly rail about?"

"It's good to hear, and eases my mind no small bit," he admitted. "I would hate to see your feelings get all tangled up with me. I'm not a man who is well suited to being bound to anyone, Raven. And I fear I would make a terrible husband."

"Well, lay your fears to rest, m'sieur, for in all truth I would not want you." She saw him raise a dark arched brow, just the way he had done to her back at the cabin when he labeled her a tease. "If I must have a husband, then it certainly would not be you." She touched his shoulder and peered mischievously up into his face. "You are far too demanding for my taste . . . too bossy and not at all tall enough!"

His hand snaked out to catch her arm and he leaned toward her, his face just inches from hers. "Not tall enough, madam? Are you accusing me of not being man enough for you?"

Raven giggled and tried to break away, but she could only go as far as he would allow. "I did not say that . . . exactly."

"Ah, but I believe that is what you implied and now you must pay for insulting me." His head came swiftly down and before Raven had time to form a protest he covered her mouth with his. This time she was not shocked by the invasion of his exploring tongue, and curiously welcomed it. The injured arm was out of its sling and so there was nothing to separate them. Raven felt him press her close, felt the hard wall of his chest that forced her softer form to yield until her breasts were crushed against him. The kiss went on and on until all of her conscious thought was wiped away, leaving just the two of them and the ravenous hunger of passions for the moment unrestrained.

"Is this not recompense enough?" Raven questioned against his lips.

"It is only partial payment because your debt to me, my dear, is quite large." He parted the shirt she wore at her throat and urged it down until her breasts were bared to his heated gaze.

"What do you think you're doing?" she protested, trying to cover herself. What little moonlight penetrating the limbs overhead cast shifting patterns of light and shadow on her skin and made her eyes look huge and luminous. He thought he saw something flicker behind the thick fringe of her lashes . . . something akin to fear. Gently he brushed her hands away. "Let me," he whispered, unable to remove his gaze from her magnificent breasts.

He dropped to one knee before her, intending to sample the waiting delicacy, but she stayed him just inches from her breast by entwining her fingers through his flaxen locks and gripping them rather forcefully. He looked up at her with a bemused expression, then Raven saw that wolfish grin of his spread across his hungry mouth. Before she knew what was happening his arm came around behind her knees and he swept her legs out from under her. Raven's cry of alarm sounded as she tried to break her fall—however needlessly, for Eben deftly caught her and laid her down upon the mossy bank.

"Your fire only serves to inflame me, sweetheart," Eben murmured, bearing slowly down upon her. He knew that she would have scrambled from under him, had his hand not rested quite securely on her heavy tresses. He lay half atop her now, and for a long, drawn out moment his gaze traveled over her quivering form. Her shirt was gaping open and the shifting moonbeams just breaking through the trees played across her skin in a silvery dance that stirred his blood considerably. His head dipped down to sample the cool delight.

Merciful Mother of God, Raven's mind screamed, if she permitted him to take such liberties with her body she would surely be lost! She opened her mouth to plead with him, but at that very second his ravenous lips found her breast and Raven's intended outcry was transformed into a breathless gasp.

Calculation and ruthlessness seemed to be his way in everything, and it was translated quite clearly into this seduction of her as well. He somehow seemed to know exactly what to do and where to touch to set her body aflame. But she also knew very well that if she surrendered to the passionate yearning his ministrations summoned up within her, she would be lost. He would use her to assuage his lust, then toss her away as if her feelings were of no consequence. She wrestled with her inner turmoil in silence until she felt the gentle but insistent probing of his fingers in the valley between her legs. "Can you bring yourself to rape an unwilling woman, Eben?" The quietly spoken query burst forth, and Eben immediately stilled.

Deliberately he ran his tongue around the stiff little coral bud of her nipple, his eyes searing hers like pale blue fire. "Tell me then that you do not want me."

Stifling a moan of pleasure, Raven looked into his face and shook her head. "The price you demand is one I am unwilling to pay."

Eben groaned loudly. "My little cat, you will surely drive me insane," he said. But he got to his feet all the same, pulling her up with him. "You do indeed remind me of a cat," he said against the sweet smelling fall of her hair. "The way you curl around me, your warmth and softness . . . your teeth and claws." He held her in the circle of his arms and dropped a kiss atop her head.

She pulled away just enough to look up into his face and loved how the moonlight silvered his eyes. "You like cats?" she asked.

"You sound surprised."

"I didn't think there were men alive who would even tolerate them. My father detested them. He would never allow any at the cabin, and I always wanted one," she said.

"Aye," he said, "I tolerate them, but you are right about most men not liking cats, so don't betray me to anyone, lest they think my manhood in question. If you swear you won't, I'll tell you why it is."

Raven couldn't help but smile. "Anyone who knew you would never doubt your manhood."

He laughed low again and was about to kiss her again, the question of the cats forgotten in the light of passion, when she put a hand across his mouth.

"The cats, m'sieur," she teased. "You have roused my curiosity."

"Swear to me that you won't betray me."

He was smiling and still at play, but suddenly Raven was very serious. "Death before betrayal," she said softly, "my father's family motto. I will honor it, I vow."

Eben drew her head against his breast and sighed.

She saw his brooding expression and questioned softly. "You don't believe me, do you, Eben?"

"Promises are easily made and more easily broken, lass," he said. "But it doesn't matter, for I was but teasing."

She was a little hurt that he should reject her vow, but she kept it hidden. "Will you tell me then? Why don't men like cats?"

"It is simple, really. Most men like to feel strong and all protecting of everything they own, their dogs, their livestock, their children, their women.

Then along comes the cat. And a more independent creature never lived. She hunts her own food, and only comes to be petted when it gratifies her to do so. She is never at anyone's beck and call. And a man feels suddenly resentful, mistrustful of her haughty air. *That* is why men don't like cats."

"But you admit that *you* like them."

"I am not most men," he told her. "I can admire a cat's independence, because she doesn't depend upon me for any of her needs, unless she wants to be stroked," he added with a wry grin. "She doesn't howl mournfully when I leave her or beg for scraps from my table. It leaves me free, you see, to do as I will."

"Yes," Raven said thoughtfully. "I do see." She saw very clearly. He wanted no strings to tie him down. No faithful hounds and no woman waiting for his return. Hearing it put this way only served to bring more questions and doubts to Raven's already troubled mind.

His voice broke into her musings. "I see that James has taken his rheumatism to bed. The light is in the loft." He stood back from her and adjusted his trousers to more comfortably accommodate his erection. He wanted her so badly that it was almost painful for him. His pale eyes sparkled as he held out his hand to her. "Well, little cat," he said, "shall I make you purr?"

She looked down at his outstretched hand. "Thank you, no. I'm going to bed now—alone. Good night to you, m'sieur."

Eben leaned back against the tree and watched her walk away. It was a long time later that he made his own way into the house.

The following morning Tecumseh came.

It was early and the family had yet to finish breakfast. All were gathered around the large table in the kitchen, and the conversation hummed. Childish voices jangled pleasantly as the children teased each other, provoking Elizabeth to intervene gently. James spoke with Eben about some subject of common interest, and only Raven was quiet. She was the first to notice the tall Shawnee who had stepped into the doorway of the house and stood quietly waiting.

It was hardly her place to welcome the guest; nevertheless, Raven went to him. This man had spared Eben's life and her own and she was grateful.

"Little Sister, I see that your husband is well now," he said, looking down at her. In many ways she reminded him very much of his own sister, Tecumapese.

"Yes, he is well, and for that I owe you many thanks," Raven said. "If you hadn't come that day—" she began, and saw him break into a brilliant smile.

"My brother, Tenskwatawa, would likely be dead now," he supplied. "Tenskwatawa is more ready with words than competent in battle—or defense. Talk is his only strength, I fear, and it does little to outweigh his weaknesses."

"I was only protecting my husband," Raven said. She was very aware of Eben's keen interest. He was watching them closely, and no doubt taking in every word. Slowly he came out of his chair and joined them.

He took his place at Raven's side and she saw him incline his head ever so slightly in polite deference to the Shawnee chieftain—definitely not a gesture of submission, for there was nothing submissive in Eben. "It seems I owe you a debt," Eben said quietly. He cast Raven a sidelong glance. "Though until now I didn't know to what extent."

Tecumseh saw the tiny smile playing around the corners of the woman's mouth. She was headstrong, and it would take a man of great will to tame her. Meeting the cold eyes of this man who claimed her, Tecumseh judged him equal to the task. "I did nothing but defend my men from your woman. She is a great warrior who will bring pride to your name and strong sons and beautiful daughters to your house. In the face of danger she fought like a panther."

Eben's gaze slid to her face as he replied. "Aye, 'tis a comparison I myself have made from time to time."

Raven looked down at her hands and was aware of her face warming with a blush. There seemed no safe reply for her to make to any of this.

James came over then and unknowingly rescued her by asking the chieftain if he would honor them with his presence at their table. Tecumseh accepted. It would be an affront to refuse to eat with his host, and though he was pressed for time, he hoped to have words alone with James's daughter, Rebecca.

The remainder of the meal passed without incident, but often Raven felt the questioning stare of her guardian run slowly over her. It was almost as if he were seeing her for the first time, and it made her feel nervous inside. When the meal was finally concluded and the men gone into the other room to smoke, she gave an inward sigh of relief.

All through the evening hours Raven brooded about the moonlight tryst she'd shared with Eben. From the revealing conversation about cats she knew he wanted nothing at all to do with having a home or family, so why then did he continue to pursue her? Did he think that she would be content to share his bed then be passed to some other man like unwanted goods? Not so long ago he had prattled on about his honor, but it was becoming obvious that he thought she had none. And the more she thought about it, the angrier she became.

She was sitting as far away from Eben as she could get without leaving the room and pretended to watch Elizabeth who was busy at her needlework. That the woman was a master with the needle was evident, but as Raven's gaze saw the sharp instrument glide in and out through the fabric of the quilt squares, she could only think of snatching it away and sinking it deep into Eben's stubborn hide.

Elizabeth must have noted her thoughtful frown, for she raised her gaze to Raven's face often, and each time she lowered her eyes again her own frown got a little deeper. Elizabeth was an observant person and there was little that escaped her notice. That there was some trouble between this pair was readily apparent, and though she refused to pry, it occurred to her that there was a way to take the girl's mind off her troubles for a little while.

She tucked her hoop into her sewing basket and rose from her chair. "Raven, would you come with me?" Elizabeth asked, jarring Raven out of her musings.

Raven got up and with a single glance at Eben, left the room.

Candle held high to light their way, Elizabeth went quickly up the stairs. At the top of the stairs was a wide hallway. Set high in the wall was a window, and just beneath the window was a cedar chest. The older woman handed Raven the candle and knelt before the chest.

"Every woman should be able to bring something into her marriage. Now, I don't know your circumstances, and I'm not suggesting you confide in me, but I can see that you have little and I hope that you will let me give you this." She lifted a quilt from the chest and spread it out so that the girl could see it. The cream-colored background was resplendent with embroidered stags and pheasants and oak leaves in scarlet and gold thread.

"It's lovely," Raven said softly. "But I can't accept it."

"But of course you can. It's for your marriage bed, dear."

Raven felt a lump form in her throat. How could she tell Elizabeth that there would be no marriage bed for her like that shared by Elizabeth and James these many years? She would be wed to some man without a single thought to her dreams or desires, and any marriage bed she possessed would be devoid of love or warmth. She opened her mouth to speak, knowing she must give some explanation, but the words just wouldn't come. Instead, she turned and fled down the stairs, out of the house.

Elizabeth made her way downstairs a little more sedately and stood with the folded quilt over her arm, calmly watching Eben. "Well, what are you waiting for?" she said. "Go on, man, go after her."

By the time Eben found Raven her tears had dried. She was standing on the riverbank, staring at the water and shivering. She wouldn't look at him. He wanted to say he was sorry for last night, but he wasn't. He could no longer deny the strength of his longing, nor would he—but neither would he lie to her or provide her with false hopes as to the future. It would not be fair to either of them to make promises he could not keep. "It's a cool night to be contemplating a swim, don't you think?" he asked finally, keeping his tone light.

"I'm not thinking of swimming. I just needed a moment alone, is all. Is there anything wrong with that?"

"I suppose not," he allowed. "Unless one is shivering of cold."

She shrugged. She had no cape to warm her, but

she wasn't going to remind him of it. He might think she was making demands upon him.

"What did Elizabeth say to upset you?" he asked.

"What does it matter?" she asked softly.

"Does it have something to do with this?" he asked, unfolding the quilt Elizabeth had thrust into his hands and draping it around her shoulders. "It was a beautiful gift, a thoughtful gift. I can't imagine why it would cause you any upset."

"It is intended for a marriage bed, Eben. Our marriage bed. We never should have lied to them."

"Then there is only one thing to do," he said.

"What is that?" Raven asked.

"We must thank her, together," he said. "Then once we reach Pittsburgh you can fold it away for your real marriage bed." He stepped closer and put his arms around her. Her back was pressed to his chest. It was selfish of him to want her, yet he couldn't help himself.

"Yes," she whispered miserably, "for my *real* marriage bed. Elizabeth and James are happy sharing their lives together! Knowing I will never have that kind of love, I can't help feeling envy."

Eben sighed. "There is no reason why you should not find love, Raven. Once you are married love will come—"

"Oh shut up! I don't want to hear what you have to say about it! You think that you can arrange my life so that it suits you, and I am sick of your interference!" With that she turned and fled, leaving Eben to wonder just what he had said to anger her.

Chapter 13

A week later they arrived at the point where the Allegheny and Monongahela rivers met to form the mighty Ohio. Almost immediately Cadence sensed the change in the air and picked up her hooves in a sprightly prance that caused Raven to smile and clutch Eben's waist a little tighter. It was almost as if the animal were on parade as she cantered down the dusty Pittsburgh thoroughfare through the maze of pedestrian traffic, around a huge brightly colored wagon with a circular canvas roof the likes of which Raven had never seen, and which Eben informed her was a Conestoga. The enormous contraption had been negligently parked in the street, all six horses—massive animals made for pulling heavy weights up and down the mountains to the east—standing in various stages of dozing, their tails switching and shoulders twitching to keep away the deer flies which buzzed menacingly around them. Their harnesses were decorated with hame bells that flashed in the sunlight and jingled pleasantly with every movement of their heavy muscles.

In passing the wagon Raven turned for a last look at this strange sight and saw that a woman and two children were peeking out the back. The woman stared as they rode by, but one of the children, a small girl of about five, grinned and waved. Raven returned the greeting with a smile and wave of her own, but as she turned back she found Eben's sidelong glance turned on her.

"What ails you, wench, that makes you twist and turn and fidget?" Despite the sternness of his glance there was a note of joviality in his voice that made Raven want to hug him. He seemed in a rare fine humor and she tried hard not to think it stemmed from thoughts of leaving her. Because of this place and the bustling excitement all around, it was easy to push such thoughts behind her.

"I want to see everything!" she said, flashing him a bright smile.

He returned the smile and spoke to Cadence, who picked up her pace and gaily tossed her head. He liked her mood much better than the one she'd been in since their departure from the Galloways. She seemed much given to tears lately, and he knew not how to cope with tears. When he saw her cry as he had that night at the Galloways and she refused to tell him what was wrong he felt helpless, and to a man who was independent of God and man for his own survival it was a loathsome feeling.

Women were such strange creatures, he thought. They laughed or wept at the oddest moments and never reacted to anything rationally. If he gave her a gift she would weep, as she had at receiving the quilt from Elizabeth, and when he was in a towering rage about something, she snickered in his face. Her behavior baffled him, and it preyed upon his mind that he was far more occupied with her than he should have been.

He was almost home now and needed to redirect his thoughts to laying the foundations for his future. He needed to visit his attorney while in the city to see if there was some news of Jase, and to visit the land office to determine what land was available, if any. Thinking about it, he should have felt some amount of excitement that his dream was close to being realized, yet strangely all that concerned him was Raven's presence, Raven's excitement, Raven's well-being and happiness. All of his thoughts focused around this confusing bit of feminine charm, and he wasn't at all comfortable with it.

Blissfully unaware of her companion's thoughts, Raven continued to enjoy the vivid spectacle of the town. Not every aspect of the scene was pleasing to the senses, as she was swiftly discovering. Like any other city where the human masses crowded in upon one another, there were the usual problems of refuse disposal—Pittsburgh's solution seemed to be tossing the garbage into the open thoroughfares where the half-starved mongrels that were everywhere fought over the scraps. The stench of rotting refuse combined with the odorous melody of outhouses, pigsties and slaughterhouses and ever-present coal smoke to assault the unsuspecting nose of the visitor.

"Doesn't the smell bother you?" Raven found herself asking.

"Mightily," he replied over his shoulder, "but I suppose when one has lived here long enough one would get used to it."

Raven's spirits fell a little. Was that what she was expected to do? Get used to it? Her immediate excitement at seeing this strange new place began to pall. Soon she would be abandoned in this rough-cut metropolis with all of its bustle and stink, and he would ride away, taking his fresh outdoors smell with him. Would the man he chose for her smell of coal smoke? she wondered. After Eben, she didn't think it would be easy to get used to that. If ever she could.

They were heading away from the river now, down a narrower avenue toward another broad way called Liberty Street. If possible, it was even more congested than the one before. Draymen and their heavy wagons carried goods toward the wharves where they would await loading on one of the many flatboats that plied the rivers upstream, as the connecting link to the smaller and more isolated towns and villages, and down, into the broader flow of the Mississippi to the gulf.

Eben seemed oblivious of his surroundings, Raven noted, and seemed not to see the shining faces of the young ladies who strolled on the arms of the more affluent gentlemen of the town along the paved pathways that flanked each side of the street. Bright as the flowers of summer they looked in their pretty pastel gowns and straw bonnets with streamers of pale ribband.

With the subtle chafe of her leather garb to remind her of her circumstance, Raven suffered a twinge of sharp envy. Dressed as she was, she looked more savage than lady, and would not have drawn a second glance from any of the beaver hatted swains she saw. More than ever she longed for the return of her gold. If she but had the means to dress like a lady of fashion, and could turn the heads of other men, might it not make her more attractive in the eyes of her rough companion? Perhaps even worthy of his heart?

Of course there was no gold to procure these lady's things and not even gold for a fitting dowry. She recalled his avarice when they'd first met—or at least it had seemed to be that—and wondered if he'd marry her if he stood to gain her lost fortune. She decided not, for above all things, what this man cherished most was his freedom.

They had passed numerous buildings with gaily painted signs advertising food and lodging for weary travelers, but the place where Eben finally stopped was more a house in appearance. It was a two-story frame house painted white. The small, discreet plaque on the gate proclaimed, SALLY SOURWINE, PROPRIETRESS.

Raven was looking upward at the windows of the second floor when Eben's hands closed around her waist. One of the windows was occupied by a curious young lady who appeared to be watching them. Though it was easily ten o'clock in the morning she wore only her wrapper, and Raven could see that her hair was unbound. "What is this place?" Raven wondered aloud once she was set on her feet.

He gave her a wry smile and with his hand riding on the small of her back, they went up the walkway.

They had not even reached the door when the portal was flung open and that same young woman rushed out to meet them, squealing with unabashed delight and throwing herself into Eben's arms to kiss him passionately.

Raven watched with mounting anger as the brazen creature glued her scandalously scantily clad form to his, her plump white arms winding around his neck so that he wouldn't break the contact, even while her lips continued to ravage his. Suddenly Raven realized what kind of place Eben had brought her to. She saw his lashes lying momentarily against his tanned cheeks before his hands came up to unclench hers from behind his neck. At last he set her from him. "Hello, Cassie," he said.

By now Cassie had noticed Raven's murderous expression. She didn't know what claim the girl had on the handsome frontiersman, but she was looking daggers at her now. "I didn't know you had a little sister, Eben. Bring her inside and we'll give her some milk while you and I go upstairs."

"She's not my sister, Cassandra, and I don't think the lady likes milk. Do you, sweet?"

"I like milk well enough," Raven said with a smile, gazing up into Eben's face. "Now, if you are done trifling with this harlot, perhaps we could go inside."

"You'll forgive the slight, won't you, Cassie? I am afraid Raven has quite a temper." He saw the fury in her dark eyes. If he didn't know better, he would have sworn the wench was jealous. With his arm around her stiff shoulders he urged her up the walk and into the house. He didn't know why her possessiveness should please him, but it did.

The young woman who had kissed Eben was the very one to show Raven to her room on the second floor. It was the most sumptuous room Raven had ever seen, but she was careful not to show her awe as she walked to the window and looked out over the town that was to be her home from this day forward. It was not the view that drew Raven but the need to be alone, to distance herself from the woman, Cassandra, who seemed wont to linger—waiting for Eben, Raven thought irritably.

But Cassandra wasn't waiting for Eben. It was the young dark-haired woman who held her interest. For a long time now Cassie had wanted to make some man fall in love with her so that she could quit being a whore and settle down. But whoring was all that she knew. She didn't know the first thing about attracting a husband, and wasn't likely to learn when the decent women of the town ostracized her and her kind. There was no one to talk to . . . and then came Eben St. Claire, with this pretty young girl in tow.

She recognized immediately that Raven was no whore. Despite her men's clothing she was genteel in her mannerisms and soft-spoken. When she had named Cassie a harlot the word had been so prettily accented that Cassie had forgotten to be angry. She wondered if it was her soft speech that made Eben care for her. He had never shown the least amount of genuine warmth toward any of Sally's girls, despite his generosity with coin once his baser needs were satisfied. But here he was, displaying all the signs of caring for a girl who seemed not even to notice.

It mattered not that Raven wished her gone. Cassie had a mind to know the young woman a little better before she left her. And the easiest, most direct route seemed to be through conversation. "It's not a very impressive view, is it?" she asked from across the room.

"I've been here all my life, but this place just never gets any better," Cassie continued. "I'd like to go someplace where they din't use coal to heat with. Someplace where the snow would be white in winter, instead of gray with soot. Where do you come from, if you don't mind my askin'?"

"Far from here," Raven said. "But it looks like I'll be staying on."

"I doubt that. Eben isn't from the town. He lives upriver somewhere. I never been there, but I heard about it. It's still wild up there, you know. The wolves come and steal the children right out of their beds and carry them off. I don't think I could live there, leastwise not alone."

"Wolves don't steal children," Raven said.

Cassie laughed lightly. "Sure they do! But you don't need to worry. Your babies will be safe. Eben would never let anything happen to his children. He'll make you a fine husband."

Raven's lashes swept down to hide the disappointment she knew would be in her eyes. There was no hope that he would ever marry her.

"Has he been your protector long?" Cassie questioned.

"No, not long."

"You're lucky to have him, you know."

"Yes, lucky." But not for very long, Raven thought.

The door opened then and Eben came into the room. He looked at Raven and inclined his head toward the door, indicating that Cassie should leave them alone. The young whore left them, after one last wishful glance. Then the door closed behind her and the two of them were alone.

He crossed the room to where she stood, and for a long moment he just stood looking at her. She was standing at the window, gazing wistfully down at the busy street below, her small hand clutching the scarlet velvet window hangings. The words he longed to say stuck in his throat. She was so taken with the sights and sounds of the busy town, what would make him think for a moment that she would agree to accompany him to the quiet countryside upriver, away from the hurry and fuss?

"I had never imagined that anything could be so soft," she said, bringing him back from his unsettling thoughts. Like it or not he would have to leave her here.

He saw her stroke the curtain. The plush fabric in no way compared with the peach bloom of her skin or the beautiful fathomless depths of her eyes, but he didn't say it aloud. He was afraid it might sound foolish, coming out of nowhere like it did. "You're angry with me for bringing you here," he said instead.

"To this whorehouse," she said flatly. "Yes, I am angry."

Her words sounded so fierce to his ears. They had so little time left them, he wanted these last days with her to be special somehow. "I meant no insult, Raven. 'Tis only that I have an aversion to bedbugs. Here at Sally's the rooms are clean and you can bathe when you wish."

Raven snorted indelicately. "Bathe indeed. It isn't

my comfort you're thinking of, but your own! I saw the way that trollop threw herself at you! You are only waiting till my back is turned so that you can sneak into her bed!"

Eben didn't hear the hurt in her words. He never got past her accusation. He wanted her with something akin to desperation, yet knew not how to have her, and here she was accusing him of lusting after Cassie, a common whore. Having Cassie in his bed was easy; he could have bought and paid for her a hundred times had that been his wish. But he could not buy Raven's affection or her loyalty, for that matter. His pride was smarting, and he struck out the only way he knew how.

"Sneak, mademoiselle? I have no need to sneak. There are no strings binding me to you, no vows to say if I sleep alone or with ten women!"

"It would be very like you," she said, turning again toward the window. She had not meant for them to fight, but she couldn't seem to stop herself. The words came pouring out, sounding vindictive and mean.

"I did not come here to be badgered," he growled, raking his hand through his hair. "Sally wished to know if you wanted a bath brought up, but since you're in this hellish mood I'll leave you be. Perhaps when I return you'll be more reasonable."

He turned to leave, but stopped when he heard her words pounding at him. "Reasonable! I'm supposed to be reasonable? Who, I ask you, ensconced me in a whorehouse? And you imagine yourself my guardian?"

"No harm will come to you, here or anywhere, so long as you heed my advice."

"And just when have you ever advised me on any point, M'sieur St. Claire?" she demanded, but gave him no time to reply. "Oh no! You don't *advise,* you command, and expect me to obey! Well, let me remind you of this, in case you've forgotten. You are not my father! You can tell me what to do all you want, but I don't have to listen."

His eyes were narrowed as he watched her, clear evidence that her barb had struck its mark. "Perhaps that has been the crux of the problem all along. I am *not* your father. And I have not had one fatherly thought about you since I first laid eyes on you. But then, being a parent sometimes is to be blind to a child's faults, and I am not blinded to yours. You are willful and spoiled and self-centered, and thanks be to a merciful God that you are *not* my daughter! Had I given life to a child with your traits I would drown it!"

"Get out!" Raven cried. "Go to your whores, and stay clear of me! I hope that tongue of yours blackens and falls from your head! What would you know of fathers and children anyway? You, Eben St. Claire, the last of his line! It's probably all a lie! You never had a father, did you? Did you? Well, I had one! And if willful and spoiled is part of being loved and wanted, then I can claim it all! But what about you, Eben? Have you ever in your life been loved or wanted?"

He was still looking at her and even after her tirade had passed away, he just stood, wearing that same stony expression. She thought she saw him draw a ragged breath, and he blinked once, but it was done so slowly that she wasn't sure. Then his voice came low and grating to her ears. "No, never have I known anything like that, and never will I. But mayhap it's best that way, Raven. I don't have need of anybody, you see. Not even you." And then he turned and left the room.

The door closed softly behind him and he headed down the stairs without making a sound. It was as if a spirit was passing, he thought, leaving no echoing footfalls, no trace of his being here, as if he never had been at all. When his life was spent, there would be no more left behind than that. A sharp wave of melancholy came over him as he went out the front door and down the street.

She had brought this on, he thought angrily, this keen awareness of her and the emptiness of his life until she came into it, and he hated her for it. He had been content before to fill his days with backbreaking labor that earned him no more than a hard bed on the ground. His own sparse comfort and safety had been paramount in his mind then, and all seemed simple and right.

But from that very first day when he had looked down with wonder into that incredible face of hers, he had begun to hunger for more than he had, much more. From that very moment she had been uppermost in his thoughts. Now he was wishing all of that to change, and for one instant he saw clearly that he was the selfish one.

Damn him for a softheaded fool! She was no better, no worse than any other female, and if he allowed it she would run him to ruin! Already she was making him doubt his own wishes, placing thoughts in his head that had no business being there! Before his dream had been just to build his empire, now he had thoughts of sharing it. And that willful black-haired beauty was at the root of it all.

She had possessed him, with her bewitching loveliness and her fiery spirit. And like a man possessed he was in need of a sound cleansing. There was no River Jordan here to cleanse away these sinful thoughts, but there was the Whale and Monkey, and the whiskey was cheap and plentiful. His long and angry strides took him there before he even realized his thirst, and he was soon washing away all vestiges of their quarrel.

The whiskey was raw and potent, and by the time the sun was resting on the western hills Eben was ready to face his wildcat again. He leapt from his chair with an agility amazing for one who'd just drunk three-fourths of a bottle himself—or so he thought, when in truth he stood slowly, only to topple sideways into the nearby wall. He was righted by one of his newfound companions and sent on his unsteady way with a few calls of encouragement floating out behind him.

Selma Abrams and her sister, Calla, had just locked the door of their small shop when a thunderous pounding threatened to crash it in. Calla was in back, putting the kettle on the fire for tea, but at the noise she emerged and looked at Selma, who just looked hesitant.

"Well, don't you think we should let him in?" Calla asked calmly. "The door can't withstand this heavy broadside all night, and he does seem determined."

"What on earth would a man like that want in a women's clothier?" Selma whispered anxiously, peering out the side glass at the young ruffian who was causing the noise. "He might be bent on rapine, sister!"

"Nonsense!" Calla said, but Selma was quick to notice the queer little smile that played over her sister's lined mouth. "Just a moment!" she said loudly, unlocking the door.

"Evening ladies," Eben said, glad that his tongue was working well. "I am in dire need of some female trappings."

"Truly?" Calla questioned, while Selma looked worried.

"Aye. Trappers—um—apparel! A gown, something pretty for a pretty wench, and whatever goes under."

"Well, we do have some gowns that are ready to wear, but first we shall need to know the proportions of the young lady you speak of," Calla told him. She saw that her words caused some consternation within his muddled brain, for he frowned in deep thought.

Eben looked at the woman and decided she was far too plump to be anywhere near to Raven's fine proportions, but the other one, the one who looked like a scrawny little hen about to flap her wings and squawk, was another story. He stepped forward and grasped her upper arm, dragging her close to him.

Selma didn't dare breathe, she was so frightened. This tall ruffian was so obviously a Westerner, maybe even one of those horrid Kaintucks they had heard so much about! But to her surprise, he only laid his chin atop her head, then held her at arm's length and nodded to her sister.

"She's the right height. The lass' head just clears my chin when I hold her close."

He released Selma, who nearly swooned, then raked her with his frigid gaze. "Aye, and thin like her too, only not as scrawny, and with softness in all the proper places."

"How much softness?" the brave Calla questioned to Selma's dismay.

"Just enough to entice a man, and none to spare."

"Then the lady is petite and gently curving," Calla pronounced.

"Aye. Well put and to the point," Eben said.

"I have a few items over here, if you would care to look at them and choose," Calla said. There were several hooks on the adjacent wall where gowns of various color and style were hanging. "A day dress, perhaps?" She held out a gown of fine white muslin with a pink sash for him to inspect.

"It's pale," Eben said.

"It's all the fashion these days," Calla said, but saw him shaking his blond head. He knew just what he wanted. With an inward sigh, she wished all of her female customers were so decisive.

"Something that's fit for dancing," he said, hardly believing his own ears. "Aye," he repeated, liking the idea of Raven in swirls of satin and lace, "a gown fit for a full dress ball."

"Well, those kinds of dresses are usually commissioned, but I do have one here in the size you need. I'll be only a moment."

Eben waited patiently while the woman disappeared into the rear of the shop. In a moment she returned with the gown he needed for Raven draped over her arms. It was a rich shade she explained was called bittersweet, being neither rust nor red, and Eben knew that it would suit Raven's vivid looks perfectly. His lass was no pale milk-and-water miss, but a woman worthy of the name, sparkling with life and needing something to accent her best attributes. This gown would set her pale golden ivory complexion to shimmering like the finest of opals without overshadowing her black locks and her luminous dark eyes.

"What price do you ask for it?" Eben asked. Not that it truly mattered, for he would have it for her no matter that it took his last copper penny.

Calla murmured a price and he counted out the coin with a little extra to make up for disturbing them after hours. He was feeling much lighter of spirit, and as he left the shop and made his way unhurriedly to the corner of Virgin Alley and Wood Street where Sally had her house, he even began to sing. It had been long since he had felt good enough for a serenade and his voice was a wee bit rusty, as Meg would have said. But still he sang. Every ribald song he had learned during his days in the army came pouring out in his off-key baritone until windows all along the street were flung open and calls and curses mingled in the evening air.

The drunken balladeer seemed not to notice as he weaved along. He was going to so overwhelm his lady that she would forgive his earlier behavior without his even having to ask.

Chapter 14

The bath was doing wonders to elevate her spirits. The scented water was luxury beyond anything Raven had imagined. After she had indulged herself sufficiently and soaked away every last grain of dust that had attached itself to her skin and hair she would seek out this Sally and thank her. But for now, she just wanted to savor her newfound cleanliness.

She was leaning back against the high rim of the tub when the first volley of drunken singing drifted in through the open window and assaulted her ears. She listened, thinking the voice was somehow familiar. The closer it came, the stronger that impression became, although she knew only one man in this entire town, and she was sure that he would never bellow the ribald stanzas of this serenade.

Feeling very odd and a little frightened, Raven rose from the tub and still wet, wrapped the linen towel around her and made her way to the window. Her heart plummeted to her small bare feet. It was Eben, and he seemed profoundly drunk. His normal light-footed gait was wavering now as he came slowly up the walk. He stopped, sensing her presence, and looked up at the window with his bleary gaze, grinning as he saw her duck back inside.

''Hail, wench!'' he bellowed loudly. ''Come down from the window yonder and fetch your Romeo!''

"Mother of God," Raven muttered, "I can't believe he is doing this." She flew for her clothing, but he had found his swift tread again, and she heard a great commotion and much laughter in the foyer downstairs. It seemed that all of the occupants of the house not otherwise occupied at the moment had turned out to watch him mount the stairs, if indeed he could. Raven could hear the calls of encouragement from some of the girls before Sally came out to put an end to the merriment.

"Eben James St. Claire, are you disrupting my house?"

"Hell no, Sally. I mean to surprise the little wench, but I have to find her first. I saw her from the window outside, but I don't know where the hell she's gotten to. Mayhap she flew again, I don't know. She was horrible mad at me."

Sally shook her head. She had never seen him quite this drunk. It was amazing that a young thing like Raven could so affect a powerful man like Eben. "Cassie, come along and take his other arm. We'll get him up to bed."

He still had the box the gown was in, though it was rather mangled by his rough embrace. He handed it to Cassie. "Hold it for me, will you, lass? It's grown heavy since I got it."

Cassie giggled as she took the box and laid his arm over her shoulders. Sally took the other in the same manner and the threesome mounted the stairs. After a tortuous climb they stood before the door to Raven's room.

"Raven, lass, open the door," his booming voice came from the other side of the panel.

Slowly, the door edged open to reveal Raven bound in a sheet. Her hair was still dripping from the washing she'd given it moments ago, and her skin was glowing. She looked somehow shy and vulnerable, and even in his befuddled state, Eben thought that he loved her. He felt his heart turn over. It lodged in his throat and made speech impossible.

"He's all yours now," Sally said, giving the cue for Raven to take over. Cassie followed in her employer's wake, but her eyes misted curiously as she gave a last glance to the ill-matched pair.

"Raven . . ." Eben said. "I'm yours, if you want me."

"Eben, where have you been?" she asked, guiding him into the room and shutting the door.

"Fetching you a present, love." He glanced down at his empty arms, but the box was mysteriously gone. "That's funny, 'cause it was here just a moment ago. . . ."

Raven saw the long box by the door. "Is that it?" she asked.

He looked around and nodded once. "Aye. Will you open it now?"

Raven took the box to the bed while Eben sank into a chair to watch her. He hoped that it would mend this rift between them. He had never been good with words—the softer ones—that females seemed to need to hear. Action was more his way.

The box was crushed beyond saving, but thankfully the string that bound it had held fast, saving the contents from ruin. Raven's fingers were suddenly unsteady, so she had difficulty in undoing the tight knots. She turned around, about to ask to borrow his knife, when she saw that he was sleeping, his head resting on the high back of the armchair.

She smiled, looking down at him. Relaxed in sleep his face was devoid of its usual hard lines and bore an innocence that belonged to the loveless boy he had once been, not the hard, driven man he was. Her heart melted in her breast, and she knelt and kissed his bearded cheek. "You are not really so tough, M'sieur Romeo. There is a softer side that shows through your thorny armor every now and again."

She took his knife from its sheath and fairly skipped back to the bed, her feet barely skimming the carpeted floor. She hummed contentedly, severing all four strings that kept her from her waiting treasure and finally laid aside the blade. She lifted the lid of the box and drew in a startled breath. There, lying on a bed of filmy tissue was a gown of deep hued satin—the stuff of all her girlhood dreams.

With gladdened cries she lifted it and spun toward the nearest glass. Holding its shimmering folds before her, she gazed at her reflection. Had Eben been watching her then he would have noted that her eyes outshone the brilliance of the gown by far. Now she had her heart's desire, and she began to scheme.

Without so much as a single hint from her he had known her innermost desire and fulfilled it. He must care for her. Why then wouldn't he tell her so or make a commitment to their future? Time was her enemy now if he still had his mind set on leaving her, but was her friend if he did not.

She placed the gown back in the box, which she put on the other chair so that she could still admire it. She went to the chair and shook Eben awake. Bleary-eyed, he looked at her. "Raven, have you changed your mind and decided to keep me?"

"Come, I'm going to help you to bed." She slipped an arm beneath one of his and tugged upward until he stood. He swayed on his feet and laughed drunkenly as he at last sprawled on the bed.

"Ravish me then, if you must. I have no will to fight you off!"

"Imbecile, shut up and go to sleep," she said at his buffoonery. But she was smiling as she listened to his snores.

* * *

The dawning of the next day brought untold misery for Eben. The morning seemed reminiscent of one not too long past and made him open his eyes and look to see if Raven was still about or vanished. She was there beside him, curled in the bed like a small cat, her dark head burrowed into the soft feather pillow. It was a shame to disturb her sleep, but he knew he was going to be sick and it was difficult to be violently ill and quiet at the same time. His head expanded and contracted painfully as he shot from the bed and found the chamber pot—empty thankfully—and emptied the vile aftereffects of the whiskey he'd consumed the night before.

The sound of his retching woke Raven, and she sat up in the midst of the big bed, smothering her yawns with her hand as she waited for him to recover. When at last he left off hugging the chamber pot she was there with a cool damp cloth to press to his whitened brow. He groaned low and lay down on the floor.

"Good morning, M'sieur Romeo," he heard her bright voice saying.

He opened one bloodshot eye and looked at her, then closed it again. "If there is one single ounce of mercy in you, you will lower your voice to a whisper. I think I am about to die and would like to lie here and do it undisturbed."

Romeo, she had called him Romeo, Eben was thinking. Where on earth had that come from? He searched his mind and could produce only the fuzziest of recollections of the night before and most of that long before he left the Whale and Monkey. Then slowly it began to surface in his whiskey-dulled brain like tiny bubbles in a deep, dank pond. He saw himself holding an old woman—shriveled she was like a prune!—close against him and feeling her quaking on her spindly limbs. But what the devil had he wanted of her?

"Raven, did I get here under my own steam last night?" he asked in a raspy whisper. He had to know what transpired and if they should now be fleeing the town before the constabulary was notified.

"Yes. Alone and very, very drunk," she said.

He opened his eyes to slits and contemplated her with his pulsing orbs. She was seated cross-legged on the soft feather mattress, the covers all around her and her hair hanging softly over one bare shoulder so that she could toy with a silken strand as she watched him. "You overstate the obvious. From the expanding and contracting of my normally solid skull I can determine that I drank the tavern dry."

He closed his eyes again and uttered a soft groan. He could feel her gaze fixed upon him and knew that she was but waiting to spring something on him like some evil-tasting physician's draught. He knew it was better to take his punishment quickly and be done with it. "What is it?" he asked. "I can tell you want something of me. Pray God it's nothing physical." He chuckled low in remembrance, and when he saw her lift a curious brow, explained. "What an irony. The first and only time you take me to your bed and I am useless." He laughed again.

"You surprise me, Eben. Where did you learn all those songs? And the Shakespeare that you so horribly mangled, I should like someday to read it. Papa had only a volume or two in French—"

"Raven, lass, put me to your sword swiftly. Don't twist it slowly to watch me writhe."

"It was nothing so bad," she answered sweetly. "You came down the street singing at the very top of your lungs. When I heard you I came to the window, and there you were in all your drunken glory, bellowing up at me to come and fetch my Romeo."

For a long moment he lay very quiet, and Raven thought perhaps he had gone to sleep. Then she heard him give a low snort of laughter that must have cost him much in comfort, for he immediately put his hands to his head and winced. "Romeo," he said slowly. "I had all but forgotten. They said he died of poison, but I'd bet that he was down at the Whale and Monkey."

Raven giggled and found his eyes upon her. "Sorry," she said. "Is there something I can get for your headache?" He had brought this on himself, but in the light of his wonderful gift, she felt her heart softened toward his plight.

"Only quiet," he said. "Be a good lass and find something to do that will occupy your morning. If I live, we'll sup on the town and you may wear your fine new feathers. Would you like that?"

She flew from the bed and hugged his prostrate, groaning form. "Oh, yes! I would indeed!"

"Gently, sweetheart," he reminded with a pained grimace. "And, lady, should I succumb, plant my bones somewhere in the floodplain. 'Tis home to me and I would be happier to be washed by the waters each season."

She knelt beside him and peeled back one eyelid to look directly into the bloody orb. "M'sieur St. Claire, if you succumb I will be very, very angry, and I might be inclined to stick you headfirst down a posthole."

"Jesus, wench!" he said, flinching away. "Have some consideration!"

She left him alone then and dressed in her leather garb as swiftly and as silently as she could. The day stretched long before her, an endless empty chasm to be filled with . . . something.

Raven found Ernestine, the black cook owned by Sally, to be a surly woman. Grudgingly, she plopped down a loaf of fresh baked bread and a knife when Raven entered and bade the girl to "git her own, fer the house din't raise till noon."

Raven raised a fine black brow at her ill manners, but said nothing. As the cook turned her attention to scolding her young son Henley, Raven cut a thick slice and slathered it with butter and hurried out of the kitchen. There seemed to be no place she belonged, no place she could go to pass the time. She wandered aimlessly out onto the porch and sat down on the steps to break her fast and watch the morning.

Even at this early hour the streets were filled with people. For a long time while she nibbled her bread, Raven just watched them passing by. But once she had finished, this activity grew tiresome and she again was faced with the problem of how to fill her morning. The possibilities were limited. She *could* creep back to the chamber she shared with Eben and sit quietly watching him sleep, or she could sit here on the steps all day watching the townspeople go by . . . or she could take a stroll and see the place for herself. The idea swiftly caught her fancy and soon she was on her way.

She looked back once to get her bearings and saw the sun glaring off the window of their bedchamber. Behind that glass her guardian lay sleeping. If he knew that she was going off alone he would be angry, but it had been his wish that she find something to do. Besides, what could possibly happen to her in the broad light of day?

For several hours Raven just wandered about the town, not thinking where she was going. Before she knew it, she was walking along the rough boards of the wharf that bounded the Monongahela, threading her way through the piles of goods and great hogshead barrels awaiting shipment south.

It was the most colorful scene Raven had ever

seen, and it was exhilarating to be able to walk freely among the men, to look at the many boats tied up at the wharf, and even to hear the rough talk of the men and an occasional strain of music from a fiddle kept on board the flat-topped vessels to aid the men in their work. It never occurred to her that she was in any danger being here alone, until she felt her spine prickle and saw the small man's evil leer.

When Eben finally picked himself up off the floor he saw that Raven had gone. He didn't think for a moment that she had again escaped his keeping—not after her ebullient mood of that morning. He had offered to take her out on the town, and she had warned him not to disappoint her. The gown, sitting in its box by the bed, had done much to mend their tiff of the day before. Now, if only he could rid himself of this headache!

He sought Ernestine out in the kitchen and bade the woman good morning. She only scoffed. "Aftanoon is mo' to the point, suh," she said.

"I was out very late, Ernestine, so 'tis my morning." He could see for himself that Raven wasn't there. Perhaps the woman knew where she had gone. She seemed to know everything else that went on in Sally's house. "Have you seen my ward, Raven, anywhere? She's a tiny little thing with coal black hair and big brown eyes and a sassy tongue. I thought I might have found her here."

"You might have, was you here 'bout four hours ago," Ernestine told him. "She took some bread and off she went, out the front door."

As Eben heard the words he felt a distinct chill. Knowing the girl's propensity for trouble he had to find her—fast. He strode from the house and nearly fell over Ernestine's young son, Henley, who was lolling on the front steps. The boy looked up with round eyes as Eben drew a coin from his pocket and held it up so he could see. "Henley, lad, have you seen Miss Raven this morning?"

Henley nodded. "She come out the house and set awhile, then she went up that way." He pointed to Wood Street, which led straightaway to the Monongahela. He was about to open his mouth to remind the man about the promised reward, when he heard it hit the steps beside him. He scrambled to pick it up and secret it away in his breeches pocket, then turned to say his thanks, but the man was gone.

Willard Semples left Delbert in charge of the flatboat and along with Ox made a direct path for the nearest tavern. He hadn't gone far when he saw the girl. She was tender aged, hardly out of her teens, and dressed in frontier style deerskins. The leather dress combined with her soot-hued locks and soft brown eyes to give her an exotic air that immediately drew him, and in that instant he forgot all about his earlier craving for a bottle. "Well, lookee here, Ox," Willard said, closing in on the unsuspecting girl. "Din't figure they'd let half-bred wenches roam the streets. Let's us just siddle up and say hello."

Of the two Semples, Ox had inherited only a fraction of Willard's brainpower and the greatest portion of his common sense. He lagged back, uncertain, and tried to turn Willard's attention away from the pretty woman. For some undetermined reason Ox knew the girl would bring them nothing but trouble, and he tried to steer his brother away from her. "Hell, Willard," he said in his slow manner, "I thought you was dried up. Why don't we git some whiskey first. She'll be here when we git back."

"What's wrong with you, Ox? You lost your taste fer females since that damned St. Claire kicked your ass downriver? Hell, I'd not have thought it of you, but if you're skeered then you go on. I'll enjoy the bitch all myself."

"Willard, that fella would have done fer you if I hadn't stepped in. You had no business doin' what you did."

"I was only frolickin' like always. A man has a right to frolic when he's been away so long from fun. Besides, how was I to know that he was winning square. Seemed to me that the frosty-eyed bastard was cheatin'. Anyways, he beat you. How the hell could you let him beat you, Ox? You must weigh twicet as much as him!"

"He knowed all them Injun tricks, and din't fight honest like no white man I ever met up with," Ox complained. "You know I don't like Injuns, and I don't like the looks of that girl there neither! Let's go get some whiskey, Willard, and forget about her! The girls at Sally's place'll be glad to see us, don't you think?"

"Yeah, but this here one looks real fresh." Willard's gaze raked the slim back, the rounded hips, and lean legs of the girl, who was just turning to meet his gaze. He could almost feel her writhe beneath him as he peeled away those hide trousers she wore. He never had a woman dressed like a man, and it excited him so that he barely heard his brother's reasoning. "I got me a taste for a fresh mountain lily, and this one here's mine."

Willard didn't look to see if Ox was coming along. It didn't matter now. The lust was on him, and his eyes were darting from her to the alleyway across the busy street where he could drag her. He walked right up to her and as she turned away, grasped her arm. "Hullo, miss," he said, smiling up into her face. "Seein' how you're all alone, I thought you might want some comp'ny. Me and my brother, here, we're real good with the ladies."

Raven looked down into the thin face of the little

man. He was very dirty, his straw-colored hair stringing greasily from under a battered hat, his clothes stained with sweat and grime and emitting a horrible odor that made her turn her head to escape it. After Eben's clean inviting smell this man made her stomach churn. She looked down at the hand clutching her upper arm and spoke as calmly as she could. "Let go of me, m'sieur, I'm not in need of company."

"But we ain't even got friendly yet, so how can you know that? Let's take a little walk across this street. I see a place where we can be real private like."

"If you don't let go of my arm I'll scream," Raven said. She was beginning to wish that she had never left the front stoop at Sally's house.

"They ain't gonna give you a second look, less it's to cheer me on. Look around you, honey. Do you see any ladies down here? By coming down here you're asking fer trouble, and you just found it in Willard Semples."

They had nearly reached the alley when suddenly Willard stopped. "Who's in there?" he cried, then pulled Raven in front of him. The shadows were deep, almost black in places, and coming from the bright sunlight into the stygian depths of the passageway, he couldn't see. In his arms, Raven struggled violently. Her cursing rang through the alley and reverberated off the brick walls of the buildings, masking the slight sound of someone or something moving forward. "Must have been a rat," Willard said and gave Raven a shove. "Get on in there!"

For a small man, Willard Semples was strong, and the shove he gave Raven sent her flying backwards to stumble and fall over something. The object was close to the wall and as she brushed against it it moved ever so slightly, unnerving Raven so that she screamed.

Willard was close, but bent upon having the girl. He was in the process of unbuttoning his trousers, but when she screamed he paused in the act to hit her in the mouth. "I told you nobody would hear," he said, freeing his rigid member and pouncing on her.

His hands tore at her clothing and his fetid breath fanned her face. Raven gagged and prayed that Eben would come to rescue her. Then all at once she heard a choking sound and the weight that was Willard Semples was lifted off her. She scrambled back against the far wall and huddled there, sobbing raggedly.

Willard was helpless as he was hauled off his feet and slammed against the unyielding brick wall of one of the buildings. He lost his breath, but more from fear of this grinning demon who held him fast than from the force of the impact. There was something vaguely familiar about the snarling face, the glittering pale blue eyes. But as he felt the push of metal against his most beloved parts, it came to him. The eyes of this stranger were the eyes of that New Orleans bastard, St. Claire. Without even thinking, the words came tumbling out. "M-mister St. Claire, please, have some mercy on me. I didn't know you wanted the bitch, or I'd never have bothered her."

The man said nothing but the razor-sharp blade was slicing skin and Willard whimpered aloud. "Kill me then, but fer God's sake leave me with my manhood! This just ain't Christian, mister!"

"Aye, but rape is," Eben snarled, moving the blade with precision. A bit more pressure, a swift movement of his hand and this man would never threaten another woman. Eben was furious enough to do it; indeed, he knew that he drew blood and caused a considerable amount of pain from the howls issuing from the man's mouth. Yet it was Raven's soft and muted sobbing that stayed his hand. He had to see to her needs and he couldn't afford to dally with this trash all day.

He removed the knife without releasing Willard and marched him swiftly across the street to the wharf. "How did you know my name?" Eben demanded. He was sure he had never seen the man before; he would have remembered if he had.

Willard attempted to smile and put the other man at ease. He had never seen eyes so chilling, and he tried to avoid looking in them. It had been the same that night in New Orleans. "I just guessed. I knowed a fella that looks a lot like you—the face, the eyes. Only he had black hair, not blond. His name was St. Claire."

"Where?" Eben demanded, and when the answer came too slow to satisfy him, he shook the smaller man hard.

"New Orleans!" Willard squealed. "Married into landed gentry, or so they say."

"How the hell do I know you're not lying?" Eben growled at him, his grip tightening cruelly.

"What would I lie for?" Willard fairly whimpered. "Look, mister, all you got to do is go down and ask around. The feller had friends and was well known. I know 'cause I axed about him after he cleaned me out at cards." He didn't elaborate on having called Jase a cheat, or how Willard and Ox had waylaid the other man in an alley after dark. If they were kin, this one might decide to take up the grudge on the other's account. The riverman sagged in relief when he was abruptly released, but his relief was short-lived. Before he could run, the sole of Eben's boot was planted roughly against his scrawny backside and Willard was propelled into the air, clear of the wharf. He hit the water with flailing arms and set to screaming that he couldn't swim.

"It's as Christian as I get," Eben called out to him.

Eben turned his back on Willard and headed back to the alley, brushing past Ox, who was hurrying to fish his brother out of the river. He found Raven, her face streaked with tears, just emerging into the sunlight. She flew to him and he hugged her close, pressing his cheek to the top of her disheveled head. "Are you all right? Did he hurt you?"

She shook her head, finding it hard to speak. She felt him heave a ragged sigh and heard his voice come low. "What am I going to do with you?" he asked.

She sniffed and snuggled even closer. "You could take me with you," she said.

It was a little while before he answered. "Aye, I suppose I could."

Chapter 15

Later that same evening Raven dressed in the bittersweet gown for her first evening on the town. Eben had promised to take her to dinner once he'd concluded his business with his lawyer, but it was nearing seven and he still hadn't come for her. She sat down on the bed, then just as quickly jumped up again, afraid that she would wrinkle her gown. Pacing only increased her anxiety, and so she went once more to the cheval glass to check her appearance. The woman who gazed back at her might have been a stranger, so different did she look. Cassie had helped her dress and arrange her hair, and the wild, untamed locks were now subdued into a sleek and fashionable chignon low upon her nape. The barest touch of Spanish paper had been artfully applied to her cheeks and lips, and this subtle hint of rose brought a sparkle to her velvety brown eyes that Raven liked very much. In her girlhood fancies she had always dreamed of being garbed as sumptuously as she was now, with a handsome man as escort. But never had she dreamed that man would be Eben St. Claire.

The very thought of him made her stomach flutter with nervousness. He was always so critical of her. What if he did not approve of her appearance? A firm knock sounded on the door and the knob rattled threateningly. "Raven, aren't you ready yet?" Eben's impatient query sounded through the door.

She gave her reflection a final glance and went to unlock the door.

Eben had been in the act of checking his timepiece when the door was slowly opened. Raven was standing hesitantly in the doorway, looking more beautiful than he could have imagined. His gaze swept slowly over her, from the sleek crown of her head to her small slippered feet. The color of the gown was perfectly suited to her, as he had known it would be, and provided a generous display of creamy bosom. Somewhat reluctantly his gaze returned to lock with hers, and he saw her lips part as she drew a deep and steadying breath. "Mademoiselle," he said in a voice both rich and deep, "you are breathtaking indeed."

At the compliment, Raven smiled, her lashes only partly masking the admiring glance she bestowed upon him. He was dressed in soft leather trousers that clung to his long muscular thighs, the trouser legs tucked into gleaming Hessian boots that fairly capped his knees and were cut away in back for ease of movement. A soft shirt of unbleached linen had been recently added to his meager wardrobe as well as a jerkin that matched his trousers. With his tawny hair brushed back and just caressing his shoulders, Raven thought him extremely handsome. It came to her then that had she not known how irascible his temperament tended to be, she might have enjoyed a mild flirtation with him. But she had learned from experience that to tempt Eben St. Claire was to tempt fate, and she didn't think she was prepared for the consequences this action might cause. Demurely she offered her hand. "You are in a rare fine humor," she said.

"And why not? That wharf rat gave me the first solid lead I've had about Jase in years. Fifteen years ago, my brother was captured by the Senecas and I've been looking for him ever since." Eben took her hand lightly in his large one and bowed over it, a graceful gesture that he saw surprised her. His eyes glinted with humor. "You were expecting someone else?"

"Yes," she said, smiling sweetly up into his dark countenance. "An illiterate backwoods oaf I was forced to spend some time with a while back. I wonder what has become of him."

"Backwoodsman, perhaps," Eben said. He returned her smile and the outer corners of his eyes crinkled. "But illiterate oaf, hardly! That was your assumption, and a wrong one at that—"

Raven leaned in toward him, boldly placing a small hand on his chest. "Eben, I do not wish to argue with you, tonight of all nights."

"Now here's a change," he said, tucking her hand into the crook of his arm. "Let's go, shall we? I'm starving." But what he neglected to tell her was that the unquenchable hunger burning so brightly in his belly had little to do with food.

The sun was barely visible above the low western hills as Eben emerged from Sally's, the lovely Raven holding tightly to his arm. The evening was quieter than daytime in the city, dusk having only moments before darkness descended. Even the air was soft and smelled freshly of the rivers. The Black Bear tavern was adjacent to the courthouse square, a single block from Sally's, and when Eben questioned softly if she minded the stroll, Raven shook her head. Anything to prolong the evening, she thought. Her dream had been achieved, and strolling down the dusty avenue with Eben tall and strong beside her made it feel strangely complete.

She couldn't help but notice the heads that turned their way. Not only did several gentlemen in elegant cutaway coats sweep off their beaver hats as she passed, but their female companions dimpled coquettishly at her escort, who pretended not to notice.

The tapers were just being lit when they arrived at the tavern. Eben spoke aside to one of the serving girls and Raven saw her pretend to sway unsteadily so that for the briefest instant she fell against him. Eben inclined his head, seeming not in the least upset—while Raven quietly seethed. "If you will," he said to remind her of his request. She winked at him and hurried off, her broad hips swaying dangerously, leaving them to follow in her wake.

"It would seem that you have been here before," Raven said coolly. The sight of the blowsy maid rubbing against his lean muscular body had upset her, though she could not imagine why it should.

"I'm not unknown in town, if that's what you mean," he answered.

"Nor disliked."

"Why, Raven, does it surprise you that every wench I meet fails to share your aversion to my company?" He stared down at her averted face and admired how her cheeks grew pink under his close scrutiny.

"I enjoy your company well enough," she defended, "but you can bet that she wants more than that."

They went down a short passageway that led to a private dining room. Here awaited them a spacious table spread with snowy linen. In the very center was a branched candlestick and a small bowl of late summer roses. A setting of china and silver had been placed at either end. Eben seated Raven and went around the table to take his own chair. "Bring us some wine, will you? Something light and sweet to tease my lady's palate." Only when the servant had gone and the door was closed once more did he reply to Raven's last remark.

His pale gaze looked strangely warm in the candlelight as it roamed over her. When his leisurely perusal was completed, he allowed a smile to spread slowly across his lips. "And why does the thought of me enjoying that young lady's favors rankle you?"

"I did not say it did!" she said a little too quickly. "And besides, a tavern wench is hardly deserving of the term 'lady.' You might choose your doxies a little more carefully, m'sieur, or you'll end up with the pox."

Eben's smile deepened into a grin. "It seems I have chosen, but the one I want is far from being a doxy and unfortunately has yet to admit her attraction to me."

"How can you be so sure that she *is* attracted to you?" Raven asked in feigned lightness. "It could be that your boundless conceit is coloring your view of things—as so often it does. Perhaps this woman is only being kind in not rebuffing you more harshly."

He shook his head, and the candlelight caught in his tawny waves, gleaming like purest gold. "It's far more than that," he said. "I've felt the wild flutterings of her heart when I hold her, like a frightened bird attempting to escape its cage. Her lips are soft and yielding beneath my kiss, and she melts against me perfectly. And yet she resists her more natural urges."

"It sounds to me as if you frighten her, m'sieur," she suggested. She would not meet his gaze, but instead watched the door behind him as it opened and the servant came in to pour the wine. Hearing him talk this way about the intimate moments they had shared set her to trembling.

"Frighten you, why ever would I frighten you?" Eben asked, not waiting for the girl to leave. This was something he had not considered.

The serving girl giggled, and Eben frowned at her. "See to bringing the meal, damn it. Had I wanted this dinner to be open to the public I'd have invited the town. Now go!"

The girl scurried away under his cold-eyed glance. "Monsieur, must you be so rude and abrupt?" Raven asked, annoyed at him.

"Would you rather she stayed to listen?" he asked hotly. He raked an impatient hand through his hair. His best laid plans always seemed to go awry where Raven was concerned. His impatience with this unresolvable situation made him swear. "I thought you did not wish to argue," he said.

Raven sighed. "It was not my intention, I assure you. But all the blame cannot belong to me. You are at fault as well."

The muscle in his jaw worked violently as he tasted the wine. "Since it seems we cannot seem to converse civilly, I propose that we do not talk at all."

Disappointment filled Raven. Her evening was ruined. Her long-cherished fancies had been dreams only; reality paled in comparison. The satin gown was just a gown after all, her handsome escort a man she could never begin to understand, let alone agree with on any subject. So what was the point in continuing with this pretense? Her eyes bright with tears, she shot from her chair and ran from the room, Eben's angry growl sounding behind her.

She had just fled the warm glow of the tavern for the deep blue of the out-of-doors when Eben caught up with her.

His fingers closed around her upper arm, his fingers biting into her soft flesh. "Where do you think you are going?" he demanded. "We haven't even eaten!"

"I don't want your food, damn you!" she cried, not caring that several passersby stopped to stare.

"I don't want anything from you! If you're so bent on eating, then go and have your fill! Perhaps your little tavern maid will dine with you in my stead!" She stormed ahead, but Eben's long-legged strides easily kept pace as he refused to let her go. They were nearly to Sally's gate when Cassandra spied them from the porch.

"Back so soon?" she called. Her smiling glance touched upon Eben's lean form before continuing on to Raven. "We didn't expect you till later. Raven, is something wrong?" She saw Raven's tear-ravaged countenance as the girl climbed the steps, and Cassie plucked at Eben's sleeve. Reluctantly, he let go of Raven's arm. "What have you done to make her cry, Eben?" she demanded.

"I haven't done anything . . . yet," he said, pulling away from her to follow Raven into the house. She flew through the parlor and up the stairs, and he came after at a more circumspect pace.

Sally's eyes were filled with laughter as she watched him give chase. "Now, you be nice to her, Eben!"

"That's my intention, Sally." What he really intended to do was get to the root of their problem. The evening had started on a sweet note, and ended in a sour screech. If he could not mend what ailed Raven, then he would at the very least be able to name the cause. But when he reached her chamber he found the door firmly bolted.

Inside the room, Raven flounced down upon the bed. The doorknob rattled and Eben called out to her for admittance. "Go away!" she cried.

"Open the door, Raven. We need to discuss this!"

"I don't want to discuss anything with you!" Indeed, she did not want to face him. Her emotions were impossibly snarled around him, and she needed to sort them out. . . . It couldn't be done with him so near. "Go down to the Whale and Monkey!

I am sure they will be happy to see you there! Perhaps you can find some corner to sprawl in after you drink yourself sick, or better yet some blowsy breast to provide you with a pillow!"

The caustic remarks must have stung him into silence, for all was now quiet in the hallway. Raven listened for a moment, then buried her face in the pillow to smother the sound of her sobs. But the action also kept her from being alerted by the soft bumping sound at the window of her chamber. There was laughter coming from the yard below that finally penetrated Raven's self-absorption. She raised her head and turned toward the open sash just in time to see Eben climb over the sill, his face a furious mask.

Instinctively Raven backed away. But when her back connected solidly with the headboard of the bed, she knew there was nowhere left to go. Clutching the pillow for protection, she faced him. "Eben St. Claire, get out of here this instant!"

Slowly Eben advanced upon the bed. He had scaled the small portico beneath the window of her chamber and jumped to grasp the sill, pulling himself up and into the room. He was not about to leave without knowing the reason for her erratic behavior. "Did you really think that a mere lock could keep me out?"

"No, of course not!" she flung at him. "The grand and glorious Eben St. Claire is never to be denied his wishes! No matter that you ruin someone else's life in the bargain!"

"This entire evening was planned with your pleasure in mind, and might I remind you that I went to considerable expense to arrange it."

"Have you ever given a thought to anything but gold, Eben?" she demanded. It was true that he had tried to please her, but the evening had ended badly all the same.

Eben's frown deepened. He had thought of her far more than was proper, yet he could not tell her, would not reward her shrewish bent. "Do you know how very angry I am right now?" he thundered.

Sniffling, Raven glared at him through a shimmering veil of tears. "Do you think I bloody care?"

The irony of her remark was lost on him. He saw her small tearstained face and the way she clutched at the pillow, and some of his anger drained away. She looked very small and vulnerable sitting on the bed like that. And vulnerable was one term he would never have consciously applied to the Raven he knew. But it occurred to him quite suddenly that perhaps he didn't know her all that well. He walked to the bed. "Why did you run from me at the Black Bear?" he asked. "I only wanted to please you. . . ."

How could she answer him when she didn't know herself the reasons? She shook her head, fresh tears starting to course down her cheeks. In an attempt to hide her confusion, she tried to turn away, but Eben's hands placed at her shoulders kept her facing him. "Go away. Please . . ." she said in a voice quite suddenly small.

"Indeed, please," he said softly. "I should like to know. What is it? What is wrong? What have I said to provoke these tears? Have you changed your mind about going to Castle Ford with me?" His hand stroked her hair, loosened the pins holding the gleaming tresses in check so that they fell in a glorious midnight cloud down her back. "Your hair is so lovely, Raven. Soft as down, and it smells like the wood flowers on a dewy morning. You should not restrain its wild beauty, but let it hang free."

"That would please you, to be rid of me." His touch, his tender tone, was having its effect upon her. When he gathered her close to his chest she had no will to resist. She curled close and a secret part of her savored the vital animal warmth of him. She had felt alone for so long, first during her father's ordeal, and then later as she fought to hold herself aloof from him. But slowly he was becoming less an obstacle to be gotten around for Raven and more a flesh and blood man with wants and dreams and longings. As such he was hard to ignore.

"You're wrong," he said. "I want you near me." As he buried his face in the hollow of her throat she felt a warmth suffuse her, welling from the depths of her abdomen and shooting swiftly upwards to fill the empty ache of her breast. "Raven . . ." Her name tumbled from his lips in an anguished groan.

"Eben, you can't—" But his fingers placed over her lips stilled her protest.

"Raven, for this one night give me your willing warmth," he said. "Be the woman I know you to be. Don't hold back, sweet, don't fight me, just this once. . . . " He removed his hand, but gave her no time to reply as his mouth descended to claim hers in a kiss that sealed Raven's fate.

Very slowly she was being lowered to the mattress and Eben's long length was covering her. He kissed her until her lips became soft and pliant, her tongue a foil that timidly fenced with his own.

Inside her rib cage, Raven's heart was beating with queer little jerks, seeming to recognize his mastery over it, even if she did not. She should fight him now, she knew, demand that he release her . . . but instead her small hands stole around his neck to pull him even closer. Her fingers played through the heavy silk of his hair, then wandered down to explore the breadth of his shoulders. Beneath her hands the muscles flexed, rippling sinuously in reaction to her touch.

"This isn't right," she whispered as his mouth moved ravenously down her throat.

"It is natural," he countered, freeing her breasts

from restraint and sweeping the gown away from beneath her. "And it is very, very right."

This time he was determined that she would not deny him. Before she could say another word he claimed her breast, and against the blazing heat of his mouth her argument was stilled.

Never before had Raven felt such warmth. His tongue flicked the sensitive tip like a tongue of flame, and when she felt him roll the erect little bud of her nipple between his teeth she thought she would go mad with the strength of her wanting. It was at that instant that the sensation began to blossom deep inside her woman's core, a tense and anguished yearning that seemingly would never be fulfilled. It made her ache and made her angry that he would so torture her when she was at last granting his demands, however against her will. But as his hand swept downward, over her flat belly and down over the gentle rise of her Venus mound she felt the nagging ache sweeten and become delicious.

In a felinelike gesture, she stretched full length beneath him and moved her knees apart just slightly, unwittingly giving him a greater access.

Gently Eben stroked her to awakening, feeling her virgin's flesh come alive under his careful tutelage. His own blood was surging in his temples, a raging, battering tide that demanded he find a quick release, but knowing how unschooled she was he fought it fiercely down to concentrate solely on Raven's reactions. He wanted nothing less for her than total ecstasy.

Conscious thought had long ago ceased to exist for Raven. For now the world had receded, and left to her was only Eben and the wondrous new experiences they were sharing. He touched her further down, with that same fire that had seared her breast, and with something akin to mild shock she felt his kiss against her belly. He paused just long enough to run the velvety tip of his probing tongue into her navel, and Raven writhed and called out his name. But Eben wasn't listening. He seemed intent upon tasting every inch of skin that lay exposed . . . and one spot in particular that like a rare and valuable treasure until now had remained a secret. He parted the folds of protective flesh and closed his mouth over the hidden jewel.

Immediately, wordlessly, Raven cried out, her fingers tightly gripping his hair. She rolled her head upon the pillow and squeezed her eyes shut. It wasn't fair, it wasn't fair! her mind cried out. The things he was doing to her body would mark her as his . . . and she wasn't his, could never be! Yet she prayed he would not stop. His mouth was incredibly hot and wet where it joined her flesh, a molten torture that went on and on. She could feel him slip a finger into her opening, then two, the silken flesh molding tightly around him, silently urging him to stay.

With exquisite care Eben moved them, gently pressing forward then back, easing the tightness of her passage to accommodate his entry. It would help to ease her discomfort when the time came. The actions of his tongue grew bolder, lengthening deliberately until he felt her gain a shuddering release.

He raised his head. A moment passed, during which his possessive gaze traveled over her lithe frame. "I've waited for this moment, Raven," he said softly. He rose from the bed and as he spoke he unbuttoned his shirt and dropped it to the floor. "I have dreamed about it. And now it is real."

Raven was well aware of his attributes, having washed his naked frame at the Galloways, but it still struck her anew with wonder that a man could look this beautiful. He kicked off his boots and peeled away his stockings, then his hands reached for his waistband. She held her breath. She had glimpsed him while he was still asleep, but nothing quite prepared her for the sight of his maleness standing proud and erect against the dark line of hair that ran from his naval downward when the trousers slid down his thighs and were left a forgotten pile on the floor.

He was very well endowed, and for a moment she was frightened. Then she thought of the many secrets this man knew and felt her fear recede. How was it possible that he knew her body better than she?

There was no time for conjecture. Eben had shed his clothing and he quickly joined her on the bed. He nudged her knees wide apart and settled between her thighs. Then there was only the feeling of skin on skin, his intense and hypnotic stare that caught and held her limpid gaze, the feel of his lips when they claimed hers again.

Never had Raven been so close, so intimate with a man. The languorous feelings he caused had yet to depart her, and so when his tongue passed her lips and plunged into her mouth she welcomed its sweet domination over her own. Further down, at the apex of her thighs he was avidly seeking yet another entry. His manhood had unerringly found its way home and now pressed insistently to be welcomed inside as well. The folds of her woman's flesh, still moist and slippery from his loving, slowly opened, then inch by patient inch he proceeded to fill her.

Raven felt his hands lift her bodily, his arms slipping under her to cradle her as close as if she were nothing more than an extension of himself. He paused, withdrawing slightly, then with a swift downward plunge broke through the barrier of her maidenhood.

The pain was sharp and Raven cried out, struggling suddenly against him and pushing at his chest, but Eben only caught her hands with one of his and with the other smoothed her hair. "It's all right now, little cat. The pain won't come again."

The tenderness of his kiss, the gentle note of caring in his voice soothed Raven as nothing else could, and slowly she relaxed in his embrace. Her body was now accustomed to his presence and molded itself around him like a silken sheath. When he began to move, subtly at first, she felt the tension mount again, and instinctively she met each thrust with a surging upward motion of her hips. The strange exotic thrills she had experienced before from his kiss unfolded now like ghostly tendrils, uncurling in her belly and reaching outward with an elusive grasp to strum along her tightly drawn nerves.

With each inward surge Raven's feeling of rapture intensified, until all thought, all of her being centered on that one sensation and the bliss she was experiencing in Eben's passionate embrace. Steadily, her own desire mounted, rippling waves of ecstasy washing over her until it finally burst forth in an all-consuming flood of unbearable physical delight.

Eben felt her melt beneath him and knew that she had reached her highest peak. Now, and only now, would he allow his own pleasure to be satisfied. He thrust deep into her soft sheath, once, twice, and his raging desire exploded in a hot surge of seed.

Raven's breathing slowed to normal and the sanity and reason that had cowardly deserted her under the overpowering force of his seduction now tugged at the edges of her consciousness. She fell into a kind of half sleep in which tow-haired toddlers played on the dirt floor of a sparsely furnished cabin. In her dream the door was open and sunlight streamed in to dance upon the children's flaxen curls. The rectangle of the doorway darkened and she glanced up to see a familiar buckskin-clad figure. He took her in his arms and covered her waiting mouth with kisses. It was only natural that she respond.

When she came fully awake her lover lay sprawled beside her, his deep chest rising and falling with the natural rhythm of sleep. She stared at him, remembering the dream images that filled her suddenly with remorse. Dear God, what had they done?

BOOK 2

Return the Wanderer

Chapter 16

Castle Ford, Pennsylvania

McAllister's Inn was unusually subdued this evening, due mostly to the inclement weather that had kept all but the very hardiest of the county's citizen's indoors. For the better part of four days it had rained steadily, sometimes falling in a heavy deluge as it was at this moment, and at other times nothing more than a miserable, cold mist that not only soaked through the heaviest woolens, but dampened the spirits as well.

One of those most affected was the Irishwoman just now overseeing the moving of the better pieces of furniture to the second floor. She stood at the bottom of a wide staircase that occupied the center of the huge common room and jabbed with an agitated hand at the newel post that was barely missed by the heavy leg of a chair. "Watch there what you're doin'! If you put a scratch on that handrail I'll skin you alive!"

She turned and glared at the man rising from his chair, daring him to criticize her. "That stairwell is the county's pride, and I won't have them gouging it from their bloody carelessness!"

Zebulon McAllister, proprietor of the establishment and county circuit judge, lowered himself back into his chair with a sigh. "You're nervous as a cat,

Meggie," he observed. "What ails you besides the threat of high water? I'd thought you'd've gotten used to it by now. It's a ritual here, spring and fall, the encroachment of the rivers and creeks. They own the land, you know. A little water now and then is just their way of reminding us. And for myself, I do not mind. It's a small price to pay to live in this verdant, fertile valley. Besides, it gives us a little excitement."

"If I want excitement I'll ask for it!" Meggie snapped. Long ago they had gone beyond the customary bounds of employer and employee, so she felt free to speak her mind.

"Easy with that painting, Jedediah! Honestly! You're the ham-handedest lad I've ever laid eyes upon! Ow!"

"So that's it," Zeb said, his eyes twinkling. "It's the tooth acting up again, is it?"

Meggie wouldn't reply. She was far too preoccupied as she clutched at her cheek with her palm. The pain was needle sharp and thumped with her every heartbeat. She knew what was coming, and she steeled herself not to listen.

"I don't know why you suffer with it, when Sam Ruston can yank it out for you," Zeb said. "A moment or two and it would all be over."

"Oh, shut up, Zeb! I have work to do. I don't have time to stand here jabberin' with you." She watched anxiously as the painting, a hunting scene done in dark colors with a gilt frame, disappeared into the safety of the upstairs hallway.

Everything was to be stacked neatly along the walls. What few guests they had would just have to put up with the inconvenience. Better that than to have the beautiful objects she took such pride in ruined by the muddy waters of the Allegheny.

She looked around with her swift, sharp-eyed glance and saw that only a few plain wooden chairs and small tables remained. It would be a great shame to have this shining puncheon floor awash with murky water, but at least it could be mopped out and rubbed again with beeswax, while it was impossible to salvage ruined paintings or water-stained velvet upholstery.

Meggie started toward the kitchen which joined the common room where Zeb now sat. When she had almost gained the doorway another pain struck her. Zeb watched as her thin figure bent double and another moan issued forth into the quiet room. "Fool, stubborn Irish!" he growled.

"I heard that, ye kilt-wearin' bandy-legged old rooster!"

"Woman, be careful lest you tread too heavily and I lose my patience!" Zeb retaliated, but he smiled slightly as she disappeared through the door and into her lair.

He had grown fond of this banter between them over the years. To look at Meggie now, with all her bossiness and feigned tartness, one would never guess that she'd first come to the inn as his bond servant. Zeb sighed.

That was many, many years ago. Why did time pass so quickly? Why, it seemed just yesterday that his daughter, Ivory, and the lad, Eben St. Claire, were lass and lad and tearing up the countryside, wild as Indians. Now, both were gone from here.

Of course, Ivory wrote an obligatory letter now and again—when she was short of funds—and sometimes came for a visit.

But Eben was another matter. They had not received word of any kind from him since he left the inn four years before—this rankled that scrawny Irish hen and worried Zeb more than a little. So much could happen to a man out there, and Eben had stepped over the boundary of the civilized world into the unknown. Though he would have died before mentioning it to Meggie, the judge thought it quite possible that Eben would not be coming home . . . ever.

The rain was falling heavily outside now. Zeb stared at the deep-silled windows where the water sluiced over the panes in sheets. He could hear the drum of the raindrops on the slate roof of the building. God save any travelers out there in this torrent, he thought.

In the kitchen Meggie made a great show of rattling pots and pans, if only to annoy the judge, who liked his evenings quiet. His talk of pulling the tooth filled her with dread. She would almost rather put up with this misery than succumb to the rough hands of Samuel Ruston, the town doctor.

"Stubborn Irish indeed!" she muttered to herself as she went to find the whiskey she kept hidden.

There was little to be done about saving the kitchen, for all of the shining copper and blackened ironware was hung neatly from the smoke-darkened beams. It was doubtful if the floodwater would creep far up on the walls, if it came in at all, for the inn sat on a little rise of ground above the town's level. Still, it was better to be safe than sorry, Meg reasoned. And so everything valuable had already been put up. There was nothing to do now but wait.

Meggie pulled the cork from the whiskey bottle and took in a small mouthful. She hated the taste of the liquor, but it wasn't taste she was after. Held over the bad tooth, the alcohol soon deadened the pain. When the pain had abated she spat the whiskey out the back door and heaved a grateful sigh.

Her chair sat by the huge stone hearth where several great logs burned. On the flagstone floor, as close as he could get without putting his coat in imminent peril, a great hound lay sleeping. Meggie thought he looked unconcerned about the heavy, swollen rivers and creeks surrounding them. "Not a worry in the world," she said softly as she sat down. "And so why do people moan about having a dog's life, I wonder?"

His large hammer head never moved from where it rested on his paws, but Tracer's eyes did open slowly so that he might consider Meggie, and his thick tail thumped the stone lightly.

"Where might your master be this night, eh, boy? Do you ever think of him? These days he's never far from my thoughts. I wish I knew that the lad was safe somewhere . . . inside, warm and dry. I fear he doesn't watch his health like he ought to. . . ." Meggie's quiet voice trailed away and again Tracer slept. It was true that Eben was much in her thoughts, and in her dreams of late. She had the odd feeling that she might hear from him—a letter perhaps, that someone could read to her, or a message sent by some passing stranger.

It had gotten so bad the past few days that when the door opened to let in some patron, Meggie found she was holding her breath. It must be nerves, she thought now. Aye, nerves, that was the answer.

Emulating her canine companion's ease, Meggie put her head against the chair back and closed her eyes to nap.

The horse turned from the mud-clogged road and headed for the welcoming lights in the distance. Weary beyond belief, the smaller of the two people riding double on the mare rested her cheek against the broad back before her and closed her eyes. She felt the clamminess of the leather as it touched her skin and shivered.

Wet. Everything in the world was wet, and had been for what seemed like years. But only a few days ago they had ended their three-week stay at Sally's, where they had enjoyed bright Indian summer days and cozy warm nights together in bed. The man before her took the brunt of the driving rain, and had not uttered a word for miles. Raven thought he must have been dozing, though how anyone could sleep with the cold little runnels coursing down her collar and trickling over her already chilled skin was beyond her comprehension. As for her own rest, the ferry ride over the turgid floodwater would invade her dreams for the rest of her life.

"You all right back there?" Eben asked over his shoulder. He couldn't see her, because she was hunched so close to him, but he felt her flinch at the small waterfall that fell from his hat brim and spattered her with cold.

"Yes, I'm all right," she replied, but he heard her teeth chatter.

Every head in the common room turned when the heavy oaken door swung open to admit the bedraggled pair. Not recognizing them as locals, most turned back to their games of chance or conversations. Only Judge McAllister surveyed the pair with interest, a look of momentary surprise coming over his features as the oiled cloth was swept off the long rifle the taller of the two was placing in a corner, safely away from the dampness.

Zeb's eyes had yet to be weakened by his advancing years, and now those keen ocean gray eyes went slowly over the tall stranger.

The man was lean as a whipcord, his movements all surety and grace, full of the confidence that had only been hinted at in his youth. His face was shadowed by the low-brimmed hat he wore, and as he turned half aside, talking with his small companion, Zeb could not be sure . . .

Zeb's hand, blue-veined and a little knotty, clutched at the table before him. He came half out of his chair. The man was turning, sweeping off the hat. "Well, I'll be damned," Zeb swore softly. "Eben, lad, is it really you?"

Eben came forward to grasp the man's hand in his. "Aye, Judge, it's me."

"By God! By God, it is!" Zeb exclaimed, shaking Eben's cold hand vigorously.

"I can see you're well," Eben said, looking around, "and preparing for the flood. But where is Meg?"

The judge inclined his head toward the door that led to the kitchen. "I'd keep you here and make you talk, but she has waited so long for this day. And we'll have time for talk later. Go on and surprise her."

Raven had made her way to the bench by the wide hearth and was soaking up as much heat as she could get. Steam rose off the leather clothes she wore, and a puddle formed on the floor at her feet.

From under the brim of her hat she watched Eben talk to the distinguished-looking man with the silver hair and keen gray eyes. He was a handsome man for his age, not bent of stature, but straight and unbowed yet.

She really should remove her hat and greet the man, but she was so cold and her fingers so stiff that she thought to wait a bit here by the fire. Besides, her lack of manners had gone unnoticed by the two men, who seemed to have forgotten her.

Eben was just pushing open the door at the opposite end of the room. He passed through and the panel blocked him from her view. There was a long moment of silence and then suddenly a woman screamed.

The sound was so unexpected that Raven jumped nervously and wondered if she should go and offer her assistance.

She was about to act upon the thought when Eben entered the room again, only this time more hastily, and bearing a limp figure in his arms. He took her to a bench and lay her inert body on it, taking her hand in his. "Meg, can you hear me? Meg?"

It was a moment before the woman roused and struggled to sit up. She looked from Eben to Zeb and back again. "Dear God! I must be dreamin' again. . . ."

Eben crouched before her so that he could look in her face. "It's no dream, Meg. Won't you welcome me?"

Meggie's hand trembled as it touched his cheek. "You're so very thin—too thin. Haven't you been eating?"

He shrugged. "I had a little mishap, nothing serious. It's a long story, and the telling can wait. Just now there's someone you should meet. Can you stand?"

"Of course I can stand! I'm not dead yet, only a little shocked is all." Her initial shock was fading now, and her temper returning. "This could have been avoided, you know, had you not been too neglectful to write!"

"I thought about it, Meg," Eben said. "I just never got around to it."

"What have we here?" Meggie asked when they'd almost reached the bench where Raven sat warming herself, almost dozing. "Why didn't you tell me you had someone with you? Why, the poor lad is soaked to the skin! He'll catch his death sitting here in those wet skins!" She turned and cried, "Nan! Come here, quickly!"

Eben was looking at Meg with surprise. How could she mistake Raven for anything but the woman she was? His pale gaze took a swift inventory of the weary girl. The baggy leather did rather hide the soft, feminine charms he knew for a fact lay beneath, and with that hat pulled low on her brow, her lovely tresses tucked up under it—he saw Meggie's point.

Meggie bawled the servant's name again and this time there was a response. The one who came running was still straightening her skirts and Eben saw several pieces of straw sticking in her hair. He could only wonder that she had been to the stables and gotten back into the inn without getting soaked. He didn't know that there was a straw pallet in the attic next to the eaves, where the industrious Nan earned a bit of added coin.

Nan Smith Kelly noticed the stranger's interested gaze upon her and sidled a little closer. Her amber eyes were warmly appraising as they took in the incredible breadth of shoulder and chest, then traveled lower to his lean hips, where her golden gaze lingered a little longer than was prudent. She was wondering if he was truly as well endowed as he seemed to be, and so failed to notice the hostile gaze being directed at her from beneath the brim of Raven's hat.

Meggie's calling for the servant had roused Raven from her lassitude and now she saw Eben watching this brazen bitch who was busy ogling his crotch! Her miserable state combined with this current twinge of jealousy to make her fume. In silent fury she waited to see if either of the overheated pair would attempt to conceal their lustful thoughts. She was about to open her mouth to speak when Meggie saved her the trouble.

"You lazy witch, get up and ready a room for the lad, and be quick about it! No dallying, do you hear me!"

The Irishwoman's tone was nothing short of venomous and to Raven's amazement she saw the carrot-haired serving wench flinch beneath its lash. She looked from Nan's wide-hipped figure to the diminutive Meggie. A moment ago the young woman had been bold as brass, but here she was, clearly intimidated by this small bit of Celtic temper.

"Yeah, I heard, Miss Cleary," Nan said, now avoiding the amused blue eyes of the stranger. "Which room will I put him in?"

"The one overlooking the west yard at the end of the hall will suit the lad just fine. And heat some bricks while I put the water on for his bath."

The lad . . . him . . . Raven thought, looking around. Of whom was the woman speaking? She saw no lad anywhere near. Then she remembered the clothes she wore, and the hat that concealed her hair and shaded her features.

She met Eben's smiling glance. He was obviously enjoying all of this. While she continued to watch him he stepped to her side and said, "Meg Cleary, may I present Mademoiselle Raven Delacour, my ward. Raven, this is Meg."

"Your what?" Meggie said.

As a form of reply he reached out and lifted the battered hat from Raven's head, allowing her thick black curls to tumble around her shoulders and down her back.

"Well, I'll be," Meggie breathed. She gave Eben a long and searching look.

Raven put out her hand. "Miss Cleary, I am pleased to make your acquaintance. Eben has told me so much about you."

"Mademoiselle Delacour," Meggie said, smiling brightly all the while at Eben. "I really must apologize. It is just that with that hat and those clothes. . . ." But she was thinking, he's done it, he's finally gone and done it! And this time he's chosen well.

"I understand," Raven said. "Unfortunately, the weather did not permit my wearing a gown. I have one now, but it means a lot to me, and I didn't want to ruin it."

"One?" Meggie directed her inquiry toward Eben.

"I will explain everything, once we get her into a

hot tub and myself some other clothing," he told her.

"I'll go and put the water on, but I'll hold you to that promise," Meggie said, and scurried from the room. Raven watched her go. Never had she seen such energy in one being. All of the woman's movements were quick—almost impatient—in their execution. That, combined with her reddish brown hair and bright green eyes set in a face rife with freckles gave her such an air of liveliness that her very entrance seemed to bring some unexplained electrical force into the room.

Raven thought that she was going to like Meggie's vivacious nature, but whether she could be truthful with the woman or not depended upon Eben alone. Lies tended to keep a distance between people—not unlike the distance between her and Elizabeth Galloway.

Eben saw the small frown that flitted over Raven's face. "What is it?" he asked.

"How much will you tell her?" Raven asked.

"As little as possible," he answered softly. He saw her look of relief and knew that she was anxious to bury their recent past. He should share in that wish, but he couldn't get past how lovely she looked with the fire's glow burnishing her hair. He forced his gaze elsewhere—on the judge, who was watching them with his speculative gaze. He would have to get used to the idea that Raven was his ward and nothing else.

Tonight she would sleep in her own bed, in her own chamber, and he would sleep alone. Somehow the idea was unappealing, and his mind kept conjuring up pictures of the soft nest they'd shared in Sally's boarding house that last night in Pittsburgh. He had never imagined that just sharing a bed with a woman could be so—satisfying.

"Did I hear you rightly?" It was Zeb who roused

Eben out of his reverie of unsatisfied longing. "Is the lass truly your responsibility?"

Zeb always did have a way of putting things in their proper perspective—sometimes against Eben's wishes. "Aye," Eben said.

"And will you be staying with us for a while, or tearing off to God knows where?"

The younger man stiffened. "For now we are paying guests here. As for tomorrow, I haven't decided."

"The young lady will need security, Eben. Someplace to call home."

"I'm aware of that."

"Yes, but are you willing to provide for her best interests?" the judge prodded.

Raven was watching this exchange closely. She could see that Eben was growing quite annoyed, though his tone of voice retained an undeniable tone of respect as he answered the older man. She thought she knew what Judge McAllister was after, and given Eben's history as a wanderer, it was questionable if he was capable of giving it.

"I will do my utmost to see her well taken care of."

"An evasion," the judge pronounced in the ringing voice he usually saved for court proceedings. "And what about Jase?"

"What about him?" Eben said, his eyes hardening.

"Will you abandon your quest where he is concerned and see to taking care of this young lady as is fitting?"

For a long moment the query just hung in the air between them, and Raven held her breath. Never had she seen Eben's expression so unyielding.

"No. I won't stop looking for Jase," Eben answered, thinking about the information he'd received from Willard Semples in Pittsburgh. "But there is no reason that I cannot do both. I have hired a man out of Pittsburgh by the name of Hargraves, perhaps you know him. He has contacts downriver, and will handle the matter in my stead. It will free me for a time to see that Raven is settled."

Now the formidable old man turned his eyes on Raven, and she saw him smile. "My dear, welcome to McAllister's Inn."

Chapter 17

Swathed in the voluminous folds of an old robe belonging to Eben, Raven lay curled up in her new bed. There were hot bricks wrapped in flannel at her feet to warm her on the outside and the toddy Meggie had pressed upon her to warm her on the inside, and to make her very drowsy. The people here, Meggie and the judge, were kind, and Eben was near and would remain so for an undetermined amount of time. But best of all, he had stopped promising to marry her off. All in her world seemed rosy this night, and like the pink dawn of a new day, there was not a single dark cloud in sight. She felt wonderful; but she worried that it was all just a dream, that tomorrow she would wake alone at the trading post, knowing that her father was dying and feeling that same half-forgotten desperation she had known before Eben came along. Suddenly she felt chilled by the thought that Eben St. Claire was only a dream.

She sighed and turned in the bed, fingering the soft brown velvet of the robe. When she opened her eyes again, he was there.

She smiled up at him, her eyelids heavy. "I didn't mean to wake you, sweet," he said quietly. "I only came to see that you were comfortable, that there was nothing you were lacking."

She reached out and took his hand, bringing it to

her cheek. "There is but one thing I lack, m'sieur, and now that you have come everything is perfect." She pulled him down until he sat beside her, but she saw he was careful to avoid more intimate contact with her.

"This bed is big enough for two," she said in invitation. "Your skin is chill. Climb in and I will make you warm again."

"Your offer is a tempting one, Raven, but I fear we must talk—straighten out some things."

"You look grave. It must be serious indeed. Have I done or said something to displease you? If so, then I am sorry."

"My little love," he murmured softly, "it's nothing you have done. All the blame is mine alone. I have allowed it to go too far, this attraction between us, knowing in the end that it could lead nowhere. It was selfish of me to take you as I did, but Christ help me, I'd do it again. I would not change a single moment of the time we spent together, but now regrettably all of that must end."

She sat up very quickly. His manner alarmed her. Why was he saying these things to her? Had he lied to her before? Was there a woman waiting for him here who would now make him set her aside? Her heart was shrinking in her breast, and for a second or two she felt as if she'd swoon. "End? But why?"

"Because it isn't fair to you," he said. "I think you deserve far more than the meager life I can give you. Raven, you're a fine woman, a beautiful woman. It would make any man glow with pride to have you as his own. But there is no room in my life for a woman, let alone a wife. I'm not the kind of man who wants to settle down, or needs a home and hearth. I've always had the itch to roam. A man with responsibilities can't come and go as he pleases. If I promised to stay, then some morning you woke to find me gone . . . do you understand what I'm trying to say?"

"You have made yourself very clear." Indeed, she understood him perfectly. In a single night he had taken her virtue and now he wanted nothing more to do with her. He would continue on as he had before, coming and going as the whim struck him without giving her shattered life a second's thought. She was beginning to wish that the husband he had promised her would suddenly materialize and take her far from here. Perhaps then she could get on with her life and forget she ever knew Eben St. Claire!

"Good, because I want no misunderstanding between us." He sighed and rubbed the back of his neck as if it pained him. Zeb had brought it all into focus tonight, and though Eben's feelings toward Raven hadn't lessened in intensity, he felt a new pressure to set her life to rights. It was still not too late for her. She could mend her life, find some decent man to settle down with. The best that he could give her was the title of kept woman. He would not have her hanging her head because of his raging desires. "I just can't give you what you need, lass. I don't have it in me."

He was without a doubt the most stubborn man she had ever met, and she knew that no amount of arguing would sway him. He had made up his mind. She could see it. She tried desperately not to let her disappointment show. There was nothing left to her now except her pride, and she must salvage it at all costs. He could not know of her affection for him, not now . . . not ever. "Perhaps you are right," she said finally. "You would make a terrible husband. I confess I am much relieved. For a moment I thought you might ask me to marry you, and it would have been embarrassing for me to have turned you down after all you have done for me." Her tone was flat, but Eben didn't notice. "Does anyone else know about us?"

"No," he said. "There is no need for anyone to know."

"No. No need at all," she said, looking down at her hands that were folded in her lap.

The tall case clock that stood solidly at the end of the hallway was chiming the hour of eight when the scratching sounded on her door. She had slept deeply after Eben had left her, though not without dreams. Now she sat up in the bed squinting into the buttery autumn sunshine that came shifting through the lace-curtained windowpanes, and called for her visitor to enter.

It was Meggie, and she was bearing a tray laden with breakfast. The smell of the food came wafting to the bed and for one horrible second Raven thought she was going to be ill. She quickly bolted from the bed and went to the window, throwing it open so that the cool air washed over her face. She stayed there a few moments, until the first waves of nausea passed, replaced by a stirring hunger that rumbled and growled.

"Are you all right, dear?" the Irishwoman asked, her tone gentle.

Raven nodded. "I'm sorry, Mademoiselle Cleary. I don't understand why my stomach feels so upset. I suppose it is because I'm not used to eating the moment I get out of bed. Indeed, I'm not accustomed to receiving visitors this early in the morning. I must look an awful sight."

She looked lovely, Meggie thought, with that rose blush staining her cheeks. She could well see why the lad had been unable to resist her. And if her suspicions proved right, it would only hasten Meggie's plans. Eben's want of family would soon be satisfied. More than anything she longed to see him happy. He deserved happiness after what Ivory had put him through. "I've brought some tea and an extra cup. I had an idea that if you weren't averse to company we would sit and chat while you eat."

"That would be wonderful! I have never had a woman friend, not since my *maman* died. Unless of course you count Cassandra, and she was a harlot. I confess I didn't like her very well. She told me all about this place, and how the wolves entered the homes and stole the babies from the safety of their cradles!"

"Don't trouble yourself about the wolves, my dear. They're not so bad as they once were. The menfolk take care of that, as you will see. Tell me more about this Cassandra. How did you meet her, her being a whore and all?" Meggie asked, leaning forward.

"She was one of Sally's girls, the place where we stayed in Pittsburgh." Raven could see the look of disapproval flitting over Meggie's freckled brow and knew she shouldn't have mentioned that. "It was all right, Mademoiselle Cleary, Eben was there with me."

"Do call me Meg. Eben took you to a house of ill repute? That man has a lot of explaining to do."

"There's no need to be angry. His reasons were valid. He said the sheets were clean and free of bed-bugs."

"Aye, well, it's over now," Meg said wryly, promising herself she would speak to Eben about his *reasoning,* and very soon. "Come, you'd better get down to eating or the food will be cold."

There were two dainty chairs placed at either side of the cold hearth and Raven took one of them, while Meg positioned the tray on a low table between them, and sat in the other. She poured tea from a china pot into the two cups and handed one to

Raven. "I took the liberty of adding a sprig of mint to the brew. I hope you like it," Meg said.

Raven added a spoon of sugar and stirred thoughtfully. "It must have been a great shock to find that Eben had come home with me in tow."

"A shock that he had come home at last, dear. You were more of a pleasant surprise." Meggie raised her cup to hide her smile.

"I'm afraid that I was a surprise to him as well. He didn't take well to the idea of being my guardian. Indeed, he hated it, and all he talked about was marriage."

"Marriage?" Meg questioned. Could her mind and Eben's be running on the same track?

"He went on and on about finding me a husband," Raven said. "It made me very angry with him for a time, but I think he must have forgotten about it, for he hasn't mentioned it in a long while."

"Eben can be very obstinate at times," Meggie said. "When he sets his mind to something, he's impossible to sway. He and the judge had many altercations because of it when Eben was younger. It used to infuriate Zeb that he couldn't win his arguments with Eben."

"And what about Ivory?" Raven couldn't resist asking.

Meggie choked on her tea. "Now, how on earth would you know about her?" Meg asked. "Surely Eben didn't—"

"No. He doesn't even know that I know about her," Raven said. "He was very ill, and it was her name he called—and yours."

"Her name is rarely mentioned in this house, and never in front of Eben." Meggie paused. She could relate the facts—what she knew of them—if it would aid the girl. But there was much she didn't know about what had occurred the night Eben left Castle Ford. He had been coldly furious, but tight lipped, and from the look he had worn, no one, not even Zeb, had dared to question him.

Meggie opened her mouth to speak, but someone rapping on the door kept her from it. Before she could call admittance the door opened and Eben strode in, taking in the cozy scene. "Well, I see you've found a friend," he said to Raven.

"I rather like having someone to talk to," Raven replied.

"Well, your talking is ended now. I want you dressed. You're coming with me."

"And what are your intentions?" Meggie asked acidly. "If it happens to be another bordello, then Raven is going nowhere with you! Honestly, Eben! What on earth would possess you to so corrupt this innocent child?"

Raven swallowed and waited for the explosion, but it never came. He only frowned at the Irishwoman. "There was no harm done, Meg. I was with her the whole time." He turned his gaze on Raven. "Don those buckskins and be quick about it. Meet me downstairs in five minutes or the canoe will leave without you and you'll have to swim to town."

"Canoe?" Raven repeated, but he was already gone and she could hear the clatter of his boots on the stairs. For once she hurried to obey, and in a moment she was dressed and hastily combing her tangled locks. She washed her face and went to the window. The scene that greeted her made her gasp.

Where land had been the night before, now was only water. Nothing save the highest ground, about three feet of grass surrounding the stone building, was out of water. McAllister's Inn had become an island fortress overnight. He meant to take her out in that turgid muddy flow! She felt a thrill of excitement shoot through her as she ran and kissed Meggie's cheek, then bolted from the room and down the hallway.

Left behind, Meggie smiled.

* * *

"Hold her fast, Jedediah!" Eben said. He was standing in a foot of water, but he came forward quickly, a smile on his lean face as he took in Raven's animated expression. Her excitement was contagious, and not for the first time he was seeing the world through her eyes. She made him feel young and adventurous, something he hadn't felt in a long, long time.

He had thought his youth had fled him years before, at the small holding a few miles up the winding course of Plum Creek. The eight-year-old boy he had been had bled his childhood into the dust beside his mother's pitiful remains with every tear he'd shed.

The way she had looked, one arm reaching, stretched toward the body of her fallen husband a few yards away, had been forever seared into Eben's brain. The carnage of that day had given him grim purpose; it had set him upon a course he had never broken from for a single moment—until the day this precocious minx had come to fill his head with her presence.

Now, instead of his first waking thought being of that horrid, bloody evening, it was of her. But keeping with his nature, Eben didn't give much thought to the implications of this particular truth. He only continued to bask in her radiance and push away any thought of her exiting his life for good.

She was waiting for him on the steps, her eyes round with awe. He stood a moment looking up at her. "Frightened?" he asked.

"I am going with you?" she asked. He gave her a nod. "Then I am not frightened."

He swept her up and carried her to the waiting canoe. She settled herself in the bow and he climbed in after her and took up the paddle. Soon they were shooting along, quick as an arrow in flight, Eben's powerful arms lending the impetus to the graceful little craft.

They traveled north, away from the inn, and for several miles, from shore to shore there was nothing but water. It was difficult to determine where the still backwaters ended and the swift flow of the river began. It gave her an inward chill, looking out across the swirling brown mass. One tip of the canoe, a single missed stroke could send them spilling into the dangerous flood. Unconsciously her hands clutched the gunwales till her knuckles whitened.

Eben noticed her unease and kept close to the eastern shore until they reached the town.

Castle Ford was little more than a village built upon a small crescent of land that hugged close a curve of the river. One main street lined with houses and shops and built around a town square was all that it comprised. It was unimpressive compared to Pittsburgh, yet had a certain rustic charm to it, Raven thought, an undeniable friendliness.

They glided up the main street between the houses, and children wading and splashing on the fringes of the water called and waved to them. Another canoe was coming toward them from the opposite direction and the black-haired gentleman at the paddle hailed Eben in his nasal tones.

"Hello! Is that you, St. Claire? For God's sake, man, I had no idea you were home again! Who is that pretty young thing there with you?"

"If you give me a minute's breather, I'll introduce you, Sam. The young lady is Raven Delacour, my ward, and this lanky fellow is what passes for the town doctor. Though by God, I think he's more fit to practice on the livestock. His name is Samuel Ruston."

"Miss Delacour," the young doctor said, "lovely

day for boating, isn't it?" He gave her a flirtatious smile that kindled in his black eyes and transformed his gaunt face until he could almost be termed handsome, then turned back to Eben. "You'll be acting as captain at the Grand Circular Hunt, of course."

"I hadn't heard," Eben said, "but, aye. I wouldn't miss it."

"Well," Sam said, "I'd best be on my way. Haddie Cary has picked today to go into childbed and I must be in attendance." He tipped his hat to Raven and called a farewell. "Miss Delacour, I look forward to claiming you in a dance at the Hunter's Ball."

Raven watched him dip his paddle and head downstream and out of sight. Then she turned her eyes on Eben. "I like him. He's very friendly, but what ball was he talking about?"

Eben again plied the paddle, answering back over his shoulder. "The hunt he mentioned is a great gathering of local men. They come from all over to hunt the wolves and other predators that threaten the livestock. It's held one night, then the Hunter's Ball is held the next."

"There must be a lot of shooting."

"Actually very little. Only the officers are permitted to carry weapons—firearms, that is. The lesser ranks can bring their dogs and a staff or club if they feel the need. Otherwise 'tis mostly bells and horns and a few pots and pans that are brought so we can make noise."

Raven had never imagined the like. The thought of grown men traipsing through the woods at night with only a horn to toot, or a pan and spoon to rattle was ludicrous. "But why can they not arm themselves? A wolf is hardly intimidated by a bell or a horn!"

"There is one very good reason for most of the

men not being armed. Most are quite drunk by the time we set out in the circles, and they would likely end up shooting each other instead of the catch."

"Oh, I see." She didn't really, but she was determined to witness this event for herself. "But Sam mentioned that you were to be a captain, and that means that you can take your rifle. Therefore, we will be safe."

"We?" Eben asked, looking over his shoulder at her.

"But of course I shall go with you."

"Women are not allowed to attend, Raven. It's far too dangerous."

"*This* is dangerous also, Eben," she reasoned. "But I am safe because I'm with you."

"It's unheard of and I will not allow it." It was the same tone of voice he had used when they first met, before they had made love, before she had begun to fall in love with him. She opened her mouth to speak, but closed it again when he said, "Mademoiselle Delacour, young ladies do not attend wolf hunts, they attend the Hunter's Ball. Now, not another word!"

Raven bit her lip and held an angry breath, glaring at his back. But her anger was soon diluted by her curiosity as he beached the canoe.

They had pulled up before a small cottage set directly against the hillside. The huge virgin growth all but surrounded the building, lending it a cozy air, a feeling of shelter despite the floodwaters lapping greedily at the building's stone foundation. Eben grounded the canoe and leapt out to pull it onto the high ground. He started up the path toward the house, but stopped when he realized Raven wasn't following. He turned and stared at her. "Well, are you coming?"

Until now she had been unsure of what he had

expected of her, but now she stood and stepped onto the grass, practically treading on his heels. When they arrived at the door, Eben lifted his hand to knock, but the panel opened before his knuckles ever touched wood. A tall, rawboned woman stood in the doorway, looking stunned. Raven saw her search the pocket of the apron she wore with unsteady fingers, producing a pair of fragile looking wire-rimmed spectacles, which she perched on her long nose.

''Well, dear me! Eben St. Claire, I thought you'd gone on!'' the woman said. ''Have you been to the inn? Does Meg know you're home?''

''Hello, Elise,'' Eben said, ''and the answer is yes, to both of your questions. Are you open for a bit of trade today, or have the waters bested you?''

''Ha! If the day arrives that I can't stand a little wash, then I'll pack up and move back to Philadelphia!'' Elise pronounced. ''Of course, I'll open up. Come in, come in.''

She disappeared inside and Eben indicated to Raven that she should precede him into the cottage. She was still unsure just why they were here, but she began to get some idea once they were inside.

The room had formerly been the parlor, but the enterprising Elise had turned it into a storeroom with shelves lining all four walls from floor to ceiling. On the shelves were bolts of cloth and lace, ribbons, and even small nosegays fashioned cleverly of brightly colored silk—everything a lady of fashion would require to outfit her from head to toe.

Raven walked around the room, fingering a length of satin here, a bit of silk there. She paid no mind to Eben, who was speaking to Elise in rather quiet tones. She had no idea that while she examined the seamstress' wares, the cool gaze of her guardian never left her.

''Jewel tones suit her best, don't you think,'' Eben

was saying. "Ruby, sapphire, emerald . . . the richness of the deeper hues accentuate her coloring. But she'll need some day dresses as well. And dainty underthings . . . chemises and the like. Something soft, Elise, with a bit of lace and ribbon. Nothing that would chafe a lady's delicate skin. Do you take my meaning?"

Elise Goodman's brown eyes sparkled. She did indeed. She had known Eben St. Claire for many years, as long as she had been friends with Meggie, and she had never known him to show more than a passing interest in any woman; unless one could count the judge's wayward daughter. Even then, he had purchased but one gown for the woman, and had left its selection up to Elise.

But here he stood, watching the girl with his keen-eyed gaze, instinctively imparting bits of wisdom foreign to his male nature about color and fabric and bits of pretty things—all of which he had obviously put a great deal of thought into. He cared about the girl more than he knew. And Elise, being fond of Eben and a good friend to Meg, intended to see that he got just what he wanted. If it helped him win his heart's desire, then it would be worth the extra effort.

Eben and the woman, Elise, had finished their discourse and Raven turned—her hand still lying on the fine, soft pile of vermillion velvet which she had been admiring—thinking it was time to go. To her surprise Eben appeared at her side and reached to take down the bolt. He unwound a goodly length and draped it over Raven's shoulder, then his hands turned her toward the mirror she had not noticed. "Does it strike your fancy, sweet?" he asked by her ear.

"It's very beautiful," Raven said. "It reminds me of Sally's curtains." She caressed it before handing it back to him. "What are we doing here?"

"You can't go through the rest of your days dressed in my buckskins. A young lady must have *and* wear young lady's clothing. It's what's expected, it's what you deserve, and I'm seeing that you get it."

She bit her lip and leaned toward him, shooting the older woman a surreptitious glance. "But I have no gold, m'sieur. I cannot afford the lowliest linsey-woolsey, let alone this! And I will not incur more debts to you. As I recall, the last time you demanded a payment it was more than I wished to pay. I will not be at your mercy again," she whispered fervently.

"Let's not bring past discrepancies to light now. We are here to get you out of this damned leather garb, not rehash the past."

"That, m'sieur, is why it concerns me!" she informed him, wondering what he might demand in payment for this display of generosity.

"Raven," Eben warned, "you need new clothing, and I am going to provide it for you whether you like it or not. That, sweetheart, is what a guardian is for." He handed the bolt of velvet to Elise and took down several more in different shades. A fine, soft wool was chosen and added to the pile for cold weather, then several silks and muslins and finally Raven's beloved satins. There seemed to be no end to his selections, and Raven began to worry in earnest.

He was spending an exorbitant amount on this new wardrobe. But why? A niggling suspicion surfaced and began to take root in her brain. There seemed no other explanation. He was providing her with a sort of dowry, thinking no doubt that she would attract a husband much more readily if she were beautifully clothed.

She began to take the bolts of cloth he had chosen and put them back on the shelves. The deep vermillion was most difficult of all to part with, but she hardened her resolve and grasped the bolt, only to find it would not budge. One brown hand held it firmly.

"What are you doing?" he asked.

"Putting these back where they belong," she said.

"The woman is daft," he complained to Elise. "Can you think of another living, breathing female who would refuse such gowns when generously offered?"

Elise shook her head and smiled. "You had better keep her, Eben. She is rare indeed among women."

"Will you excuse us a moment, Elise?" Eben said, taking Raven's arm and urging her off to one side. "You have my attention. Now what is the reason behind this? Why would you refuse what I willingly give?"

Raven avoided his gaze because she felt sure that he would be able to read her thoughts. "I see it as a bribe," she said softly.

"Bribe? What the bloody hell do you mean?"

"You are only trying to assuage your conscience," she asserted.

He placed his hand under her chin and tipped her face up so that she met his eyes. "I have no conscience. Thus I feel no guilt. I do this only because I wish to. Did it never occur to you, Raven, that I might take pleasure in seeing you garbed in gowns befitting a lady of quality? It's true that you are mine no more, but I want you nonetheless. And I want you . . . in this." He held up the cut end of the vermillion. "Tell me now that you will wear it . . . for me."

She looked stubborn and averted her eyes. "I will wear it," she said, "but not for you."

"I suppose I deserved that," he said, then turning

to Elise, who waited patiently in the other room he called, "I'll be here at three o'clock to fetch her." Then he was gone.

Elise came to Raven and offered her her friendliest smile. "Now then," she said, "what say we have a nice cup of tea before we begin?"

Chapter 18

As soon as the river crested, it immediately began to recede, and was soon flowing swiftly in the boundaries of its shallow banks once again. By nightfall life in the village began to return to normal. The raging water had completed its encroachment upon the lives of the people of Castle Ford, reminding all just how tenuous a toehold they had on the land, and that it was the forces of nature that truly owned the valley, not humankind. Grants and patents, deeds and bills of sale meant less than nothing, and life could be snuffed out as swiftly and easily as moistened fingertips snuffed a candle's flame. This point was driven home that very evening not long after Eben and his ward had returned to the inn.

McAllister's Inn had escaped the worst of the flood and only the cellars had been touched by the murky tide and needed to be tidied. Zeb's best stock of good Scottish whiskey and fine claret which usually lined the earthen and stone walls of the cavernous cellar now crowded Meggie's pantry off the kitchen. In any other similar circumstance, the Irishwoman would have been snappish at the upheaval of her orderly world, but when Eben escorted Raven to the kitchen, they found her seated in her chair by the fireside.

Eben knew immediately from her look that something was wrong. Her face was drawn and pale, and her freckles stood out like flecks of mud in vivid contrast. "Sarah Fletcher's boy is missing and feared drowned," she said. "She came to Zeb and asked that he organize a search for the lad. They gather at first light."

Sensing her deep disquiet, Eben gently gripped her shoulder. She covered his hand with hers and stared into the fire. "It's a great comfort, just your being here," she told him.

"I'll go speak to him," Eben said. "There might be something I can do."

Meggie sniffed and nodded.

"I'll just go to my chamber," Raven said. She felt as if she were intruding, witnessing the woman's sorrow. But when she started to leave the room, Meggie delayed her.

"Stay, Raven, I would be glad for the company. I'm sorry for my tears. I suppose that I'm soft-hearted underneath, though if you let it slip to Judge McAllister, I'll deny every word of it." She tried to smile. "I feel so very sorry for Sarah. There seems no end to her loss. I don't know how she bears up under it all. She lost her husband, Ned, in the spring two years past, a victim of a fever. Then her oldest boy succumbed to a fever in the lungs. Now her Timothy, the youngest, is missing. This leaves her all alone out there to work the place. There has been so much sorrow in that family, and all to hang on to those pitiful acres of land! Sometimes it just seems as if the price is too high."

Raven drew up a chair and sat down beside Meggie, thinking about what she said. Was it this place that demanded such high payment from people or was it merely the amount of determination of the people? she wondered. In effect, Eben was paying too, for his want of land. And in the end was the price he paid not as great? He would thrust her away in order to grasp at a dream. Fool that he was he didn't seem to realize that love was the strongest foundation any man could build his dreams on. She sighed, involved in her thoughts, and drew Meggie's notice.

"Forgive me, Raven, dear. I was so involved in all of this . . . I should have been thinking about you. You must be tired after your long day. Supper is delayed because of all this. Why don't you run along to your room and lie down a little while."

"I am a little tired," Raven said. Tired, but strangely exhilarated. Eben's admission that he still desired her had caused it, she knew. That, and the amount of money he was spending on her. It must have been a small fortune he'd spent at Elise's store and she worried that he could ill afford it. Yet it pleased her, for she reasoned that he must care something for her if he was willing to lay out so much coin. A simple guardian would not strive so hard to please—no, there was more to it than that, much more! Had he not been so hardheaded he might have saved himself money, for though she adored the clothing he had chosen for her, she would have settled for a simple cabin in a quiet glen and the rough leather she now wore, if only he would make her his own. She wanted his love, she wanted his name, neither of which could be bought!

Meggie saw the frown that flitted over Raven's face, the look of pained concentration, and knew a thrill of fright. "Are you all right, dear?" she hurried to ask. Only when Raven nodded did Meggie relax.

Everything, Eben's entire future, was riding on the continued good health of this girl and the child Meggie suspected she was carrying. As soon as she was sure, she would go to Eben. Meg knew that he would make the girl his wife. It was his bairn and only right! But if he proved reluctant, there was always Zeb. The judge had a knack of getting to the point with Eben, and though it galled the younger man to have matters clarified for him by the older, Zeb's pointed remarks usually produced results.

Little did the girl know it, but she had two powerful allies in the judge and herself, Meggie thought. When Raven was gone, Meg sat down again and began to plan.

The evening meal was eaten in the kitchen. To the casual onlooker the gathering of patriarch, bond servant, and former foundling may have appeared odd, but to Raven it all seemed very right. The judge occupied a seat at the head of the table, and Eben sat at his right hand and across from his charge. Meggie chose her own seat, on Eben's right and diagonally across from Raven, where they could converse easily without interrupting the men's talk. It was all very informal—democratic, Zeb called it—but Raven thought it smacked of family.

A fragrant steam was curling into the air from the cut Meg was making in the roast haunch of venison. Leaner than beef and tastier to one who'd been raised on it, the smell caused Raven's mouth to water. She was hungrier than she had been since Eben had found her in the forest, and there seemed no explanation for it, since she had eaten at noon. She waited until the platter came to her, then forked several slices onto her plate. Whole, boiled potatoes fried in butter to a crispy golden brown accompanied the meat, along with several other kinds of vegetables and tender muffins made of cornmeal.

With a growing curiosity, Eben watched Raven fill her plate. When she had eaten before, it had been with a sparing hand. But now she seemed intent upon stuffing herself. He could see by the attention she gave to her food that her hunger was real, but what had caused this sudden change? He had no inkling what type of ailment could bring about this swift change in her appetite but he was determined to find out. If she was ill, then he would have Sam take a look at her. Whatever it was, he hoped it could be fixed.

His gaze narrowed thoughtfully as he surveyed her. She certainly looked as if she were in good health. Dressed in the gown he had bought in Pittsburgh, she sparkled like some rare autumn jewel. Her cheeks still bore a faint trace of pink from their outing that day, and when she chanced to meet his gaze her eyes looked black and huge beneath the heavy fringe of her lashes. She fascinated him, mesmerized him, and he had no idea just how long he had been studying her until Zeb nudged him back to reality.

"What's wrong, lad? You don't seem very taken with what's on your plate," the judge observed. "Why, look there at Raven. She does justice to Meggie's fine fare." He saw Raven lift her gaze, smiling at him, and he winked. "I like to see a girl with a hearty appetite." He looked sharply at Eben. "But then you always did prefer them reed thin, as I recall."

The allusion to Ivory soured Eben's mood instantly. His mouth turned down in a slight frown, and his eyes grew frosty. "You speak as if you know what's in my mind," he said.

"Better than that, I know what should be," the old man quipped.

"I'm not that great a fool, Zeb, to let others direct my thoughts. I plot my own course, and that is what I follow. I'm no longer a lad, old man, and I neither want nor need your directives. Save it for your court." Before any of the three left at the table could speak he rose and stalked from the room. In less than a moment the front door banged behind him.

Raven sighed and put her napkin aside. "If you'll excuse me, I find that I'm suddenly very tired."

Zeb stood as the girl left the room, then sank into his chair and awaited Meggie's wrath.

The cave was high up on the hillside, well hidden among the rocks. Eben was not sure what drew him there, he just headed out of the inn and began to walk and soon found that his feet had carried him deep into the forested hills that curved along the length of Plum Creek to the east of the hostelry. Years ago it had been his favorite playground, a place to secret himself away and play the games all youngsters play, to dream a young lad's dreams. . . . Once, it had even saved his life, for here was where he'd been the day his parents were murdered, the day that Jase disappeared from his life. . . .

Each time he returned to Castle Ford he went to visit the cave. It was in a way a sort of penance—a tempering that steeled his spirit, his will . . . a forced reliving of that black day and all the good and bad that it entailed.

He would never let himself forget, to lapse into the small, everyday comforts and pleasures that could lull a man into a sort of forgetful complacency, a willingness to just go on, to allow the dead to rest undisturbed, unavenged. There were times when he grew tired of carrying the past, times when the weight on his soul became just too heavy to bear a moment longer. Those were the times when he longed to be like other men, to find himself some jolly, red-cheeked lass and settle down—though the thought disappeared as swiftly as it came into his mind. He knew he was not, would never be, like other men.

God alone knew just how much he needed Raven, but there was far more to consider than just his own basic desires. And part of that had to do with this place. It was a large part of what drew him to the cave, he now knew; here he would try to put things in their proper order.

Even in the dark, he had no difficulty finding the entrance. The overhanging slab of rock that jutted out was cold beneath his hand, like marble, he thought, like the grave. Only the starlight glimmering through the leaves showed the gravity of his expression. A look of deep pain came over his lean countenance before he bent and disappeared beneath the hillside.

Inside the small cavern it was unearthly cold and black as pitch. The room was large enough to accommodate his height, and he stood unmoving as his eyes adjusted to the darkness, allowing his other senses to jog his memories. Back along the farthest wall the small trickle of water remained. It dripped into a modest puddle and had done so for years, just enough to satisfy the thirst of a small animal or a half-grown lad who was frightened out of his wits.

He had heard the water that day when he'd run here . . . afterwards. For a long while it had been the only sound inside the cave. He had ceased sobbing by then, and the hatred and mistrust that would be his companions for many years afterward had yet to set in. He had felt nothing then, except for the cold and unreasoning fear he had suffered as he crouched there, alone. The water had sustained him for several days, but in the end it had been hunger that had driven him out into the open—not hunger for food alone; hunger for human companionship, for his own kind.

Eben moved slightly and something crunched beneath his feet. His mouth quirked a little. He knew that his precious horde of snail shells were now powder beneath his booted feet. Not that it made any difference. Everything valuable to him at that time in his life was gone now, just powder, just dust. Only the memories remained, and one small niggling flicker of hope that his agent in Pittsburgh would find some tangible part of his past still living.

He stood for a long time just listening to the quiet when he noticed a small, furtive movement in the very rear of the cave. It was not an animal sound, accompanied as it was by the weary little sigh, so faint he could barely hear it, for all the world like a child's sighing in his sleep. He searched his pockets and found his tinderbox, then bent with the bit of cotton and struck the flint to steel.

A spark or two shot orange in the blackness, catching and blossoming into light. Eben swore as the bit of cotton flared, then went out. But it had been enough for him to see the lad curled and shivering in his sleep. He knew then that the cave had worked its magic again, sparing the life of another besides himself. The slumbering boy was none other than Timothy Fletcher.

Sarah Fletcher was standing in the inn yard when Eben brought Timothy home. The crowds had to part to let the pair through—every man within a five-mile radius had turned out to search—and all watched joyfully as the woman hugged the boy and cried.

Off to one side Raven waited. She saw Eben come up the steps and followed him inside. "Your shirt is soaked with dew," she said quietly. "You really should change. You don't want to catch an ague, do you?"

"I know. I suppose you have no wish to nurse me," he answered, and saw her shrug. "Raven," he said, taking her hand in his, "what I really need after last night is a dram of whiskey. Meg keeps a bottle in the kitchen. Bring it to me, will you?"

In a moment she was back with a small glass and

the bottle. She pulled the cork and splashed some of the liquor into the glass, handing it to him. He thanked her and drank it down.

She had questioned him about the boy and she now knew about the cave, though nothing of the significance it had had in his life. What she didn't know was why he had gone there. She asked him, as quietly as she could, seeing the pensive mood his fatigue caused, fearing that she might anger him, yet at the same time needing to know. "Why did you leave here last night, Eben? Why did the judge's words upset you?"

He only shook his head and held the hand she'd laid on his damp shoulder. He brought her fingers to his lips and placed a warm kiss there, glad that she was with him and in this quiet mood. "We are ever at odds, the judge and I. Don't think about it, everything will be fine."

But will it? Raven wondered.

Sarah Fletcher came into the common room of the inn—a place she would not have ordinarily entered for she hated taverns and liquor. She approached Eben, who was just rising out of his chair to face her. The words came slowly as she strained to hold back her tears. "God bless you, Eben St. Claire!" she said. "You have given me back my son, and I owe you a great deal for that. Pray, sir, if ever there is any way that I can repay you, you have only to name it."

Eben was embarrassed by the woman's gratitude. "Mrs. Fletcher, there is no reason to thank me. I but found the lad by chance—"

"No, no! I am sure that if it weren't for you my Timmy would have died! I cannot explain what a son means to his mother except to say that you will understand when you have children of your own. Again, sir, God bless you!"

Silently Eben watched the woman go through the

common room and out the door. Outside, Zeb was tapping a keg of his best whiskey for the men who had gathered to search for the boy and who now milled in the yard, talking and laughing, and ready to celebrate. Eben had no desire to join them, to hear the congratulations again and again for taking part in an accidental rescue. He was weary and solemn as he turned to Raven. He was thinking how good it would be to be alone with her, that he could rest better in her arms. But he had set her aside by his own volition, and no matter how much he wanted to, he just couldn't retract the words of that noble and detested speech.

St. Claire Manor
Orleans Parish, Louisiana

Jase St. Claire heard the barnyard cock's high-pitched cry, a most fitting herald to a dawn that had yet to break across the eastern sky. Here in the garden off the west wing the dew lay heavy on the grass, wetting the fine moroccan leather of his boots. His night had been sleepless, his mind laden with disturbing, half-forgotten images—shadowy spectres that he thought had been exorcised long ago. Yet they had come again, out of the past to disturb and to unsettle his otherwise orderly world.

Years had passed since memories of his past had surfaced. When he had taken Catherine Blaise Breaux to wife all of that had been pushed aside while he concentrated on rebuilding Rivercrest, Catherine's ancestral home, now known to all as St. Claire Manor.

Catherine was his world now—Catherine and the boys, he mentally corrected himself; and he was more than just disturbed at this intrusion from the past, he was angry. What right had those bloody images to surface now, just when all was so right, so perfect? He pushed his fists deeper into the recesses of his coat pockets and turned to enter the house, the cock again singing out behind him. As he had known she would be, Catherine was waiting for him in the darkened study.

Even in the dim light of dawn he could see the silver lights in her beautiful turquoise eyes; he could also see the worry there, and it only added to his discomfort. She didn't speak to break the spell that lay between them, but only sat in his chair behind the desk, her white lawn night rail puddling in soft folds around her slim bare feet. She watched him cross to another chair and sink down, raising a hand to his furrowed brow. Without his saying a single word she knew what was in his mind. At last she spoke, "You will go, Jason."

He slowly nodded. "Yes, dammit, I will go. I have to." For a long moment there was stilted silence between them, then he added, "Christ help the bastard if he proves to be an impostor." He took out the crumpled letter then and began to read it again.

It had come roundabout and bore, among other things, watermarks that in places blurred the fine scrawl of the solicitor. Pittsburgh, by God! It was far too close to be ignored. The basic content informed its recipient in New Orleans, a colleague of this Hargraves that his client, one Eben James St. Claire, was searching for his brother, Jason, thought until now to have been deceased. David Grooms, the New Orleans–based solicitor, was of course aware of the prominent Jason St. Claire and something of his background, and had come calling yesterday to pass on the missive. The rest was left to Jase. He could go north and look into the man's claims, or he could burn the letter and get on with his life. How many times had he balled the damned thing, intending to do the latter, only to have Eben's youthful face float up before him. It was enough to drive a sane man mad!

"It *is* possible, Jason. He could be alive." Catherine's words came at him, reinforcing his doubt.

"I know it," he said quietly. "And that's what plagues me."

Chapter 19

The first days of October ticked off one by one while the leaves bloomed brilliant and began to fall. November came and the air was crisp and sweet with a sharp tang of autumn that quickened Raven's blood. Every day that passed she saw her belly grow a little rounder. Her hearty appetite in the evening and the sickness that plagued her in the morning were no longer mysteries to her. Though her pregnancy went unnoticed by most, there was one person at the inn who worried her. Each morning Meggie's almost hesitant knock at her bedroom door caught Raven still in bed. And each day, as soon as her feet touched the carpeted floor she experienced the familiar illness.

This morning in particular Raven noticed the woman's eyes upon her, weighing—judging perhaps. But instead of feeling shame, Raven felt only a mild annoyance that Meggie would pry into her privacy.

After a time the sickness passed, and Raven sank down gratefully in the chair by the window and took the tisane Meggie offered her. She sipped it slowly, tasting peppermint and lemon verbena, feeling it calm her stomach. Later she would think of the food-laden tray the woman had brought. Now she only wanted to sit and enjoy the silence. Unfortunately that was not to be, for Meggie had other ideas.

"Have you told him?" she asked directly, looking hard at Raven.

Raven steeled herself not to flinch and replied with a question, "Told him what?"

"There is no need to play coy with me, lass. Whether you know it or not, I'm on your side. I've seen the signs and recognize them for what they are. Eben is bound to see sooner or later as well. He isn't blind, you know, just a trifle distracted."

"No, I haven't told him," Raven said. "And neither will you." Her dark eyes bore into Meggie's, suddenly frosty. It mattered little what the woman thought of her, there was the child to think about, and how she would shelter it . . . from the world, or its father, if necessary.

"Don't be a fool, Raven," Meg said. "He will make it right once he knows. Eben may be stubborn, but he's a good lad, nevertheless. He'll marry you and give your son a name. Isn't that what you want?"

"More than anything," Raven said, "but I won't have him that way. I will not trap him into marriage. It isn't fair."

"Eben is no fool," Meg said. "He knew the risks when he made you his own. Now he must face up to his responsibilities. The bairn needs a father, Raven, and I fully intend for it to have one!"

"But out of love," Raven said, "not just obligation."

Meggie stood suddenly. "You can't keep this hidden forever, you know. Sooner or later he's bound to notice, and once he does there will be no denying him, Raven. Like it or not, he'll take you as his wife. I know the man well and he'd never let his son be born a bastard."

Knowing Meggie was right didn't ease her mind. She knew she could continue to hide her pregnancy for a month—two at the outside. And that was all the time Eben would have to declare himself of his own free will.

The next morning Meggie's knock didn't come, and Raven wondered if now that her curiosity had been satisfied, she would leave the matter to be resolved in all good time. It was the ring of a hammer striking steel that roused her from her warm bed and coaxed her to the window, clad in nothing more than the fragile, lace-adorned chemise that Eben had purchased for her in Pittsburgh.

Resting her palms on the sill she leaned forward to watch Eben at his work, her gaze warming as it caressed the broad sun-bronzed planes of his back. As the hammer was lifted for another blow a voice sounded, lazy and impudent in its tones, but oddly pleasing to Raven's ears.

She craned forward a little more and saw a tall, dark-haired man come into view. He was handsome in his clean-shaven way, with a clefted chin and wide, sensuous mouth which curved easily into a devilish grin. He was grinning now at Eben and saying something Raven had to strain to hear.

The same ringing blows that had disturbed Raven's slumber had drawn Tyler Lee Jackson to the stable beside the gray fieldstone building. Upon arriving he had seen no one he could ask about the whereabouts of his friend, Eben St. Claire. It had been a half-dozen years since they'd seen one another, and since Tyler was on the outs with his family again, with nothing but time on his hands, he had thought to look him up. Twelve years ago, when they had been wild young bucks, they had forged a strong friendship while serving in the army at Fallen Timbers.

Rounding the corner of the building, Tyler had stopped to survey the scene. Steam rose from the stable's white-hot forge, bathing Eben's lean, brown torso in a fine sheen of sweat.

Tyler shook his dark head in disgust. Why his friend seemed to take some grim sort of enjoyment in physical labor was beyond his comprehension. It had always been his experience that the more gentlemanly pursuits provided the ultimate satisfaction, like gambling, horse racing, and skirt chasing. Enlightened fellow that he was, Tyler knew that what Eben needed was someone like himself to show him the error of his ways.

He saw the young frontiersman ply the long-handled pincers to take a second glowing orange shoe from the forge and place it on the anvil. The hammer was poised in midair, but when Tyler moved forward, his friend turned and shot him a questioning glance.

Tyler grinned. "Difficult to determine which one's the horse's ass," he drawled.

Eben swore softly as he dropped the shoe. "Jackson, is that you, man? By God, I never thought I'd see you turn up here!" He came forward and grasped the Southerner's hand. "It's been a long time."

"Too long, Eben." Tyler laughed aloud, thinking of the last night he'd spent in the company of Eben St. Claire. They had spent the evening in a famed Natchez brothel and it had ended in a brawl. Eben had paid the damages from his own pocket, since Tyler had given his last coin to a pretty little dark-haired whore.

"If you can wait until I finish this we'll go and find us a bottle to wash down breakfast," Eben said. "It's the last one."

"The bottle or the shoe?"

"The shoe," Eben said, then bent to his task.

Tyler stood surveying the large stone structure Eben called home. It lacked the symmetry and grace that Windrow possessed, but the ancient seat of the

Jackson family hadn't a shred of the hospitality or warmth this place exuded. His dark face was impassive as his emerald gaze traveled upward to the open second floor window and stopped. "By all that's sacred," he breathed to himself, "I do believe I'm going to like this place."

Raven saw the stranger's eyes lifting and darted back from the window. But not before he'd had an inspiring glimpse of sheer lawn and white lace, of silken arms and taut coral nipples just visible beneath the chemise. Her face flamed as she hid herself behind the curtain and peeked down at the grinning stranger.

Eben finished his task and dropped the glowing shoe in the trough to cool. He wiped his hands on the leather apron that girded his lean middle and undid the ties behind his back. When he happened to glance at the Virginian, he found him staring upward at an empty window—Raven's window—and that damned lazy grin of his was plastered all over his handsome face. Eben's cold eyes followed the soft billowing of the lace curtains at the window, but he could see nothing. He threw down the apron and cuffed Tyler on the shoulder, a sudden frown clouding his brow. "Stand all day if you like grinning like an idiot," he called impatiently to Tyler, "but I'm starving."

He started off through the yard to the back door, but it was a full minute before the Virginian followed, and hours would pass before Eben was able to rid himself of this sudden wave of inexplicable anger he felt at his friend's impromptu arrival.

"So, what tears you away from your beloved Virginia?" Eben asked, once he and Tyler were comfortably seated at the kitchen table. Eben was buttoning his hastily donned shirt, the whiskey

Meggie had grudgingly doled out sat untouched before him. "Tossed you out again, have they?"

"Sir, you wound me!" Tyler objected, placing a hand dramatically over his heart. "Why, the tears shed by my esteemed family at my parting fairly swelled the James to overflowing!" He raised his glass in silent salute and sipped, waiting for the snort that was sure to follow.

"I can well imagine, given your past history," Eben said dryly.

"Well, if you must know, the sovereign state of Virginia does not always look kindly on her native sons. As it so happens, the Tidewater is still seething for my handsome head. To my disgruntlement, contests on the field of honor are not as highly regarded as they once were. I suppose all that business about Aaron Burr a few years back had something to do with it. Damned if I don't sympathize with the man, even if he is a scoundrel."

Eben ignored Tyler's comment. "And I'm to take it a lady was involved," he said quietly, seeing the other man wince.

"Ummm, yes. My sister-in-law, Julanne. You recall my mentioning Julanne?"

Eben had raised his glass to drink, but he lowered it again. "Did you kill him?"

"Murder my own flesh and blood!" Tyler exploded. "My God, man! What color of rascal do you take me for? Of course I didn't kill him. I just put a tiny little remembrance—right here." He indicated his right ear, very near to the top.

"Sweet Jesus," Eben breathed. "You notched your brother's ear." He shook his head in silent wonder.

Tyler leaned back in his chair. His study of negligence was a farce and Eben knew it. He thoroughly enjoyed this part he played, the careless younger son of a wealthy member of Virginia's landed gentry. The proverbial black sheep. And Eben had to admit that at times it was quite effective in throwing others off guard. Only Eben knew better.

"Well," Eben said at last. Nothing Tyler Lee did really surprised him, but this particular episode was worthy of note.

"Well?" Tyler waited.

Eben's eyes met Tyler's, and the small lines radiating from their corners deepened. "Well, I'm damned glad that you haven't lost your aim. You're bound to need it if you plan on staying here. As for Forrest, I never liked him anyway."

"You never met him," Tyler reminded him.

"What the hell does that have to do with it?" Eben poured more whiskey into Tyler's glass and then refilled his own.

Even before the amber liquid touched Eben's glass, his ward was with great stealth coming down the front stairs and heading for the door to the kitchen. She had two hours to herself before Elise came for the final fitting on the last few garments in her extensive new wardrobe. Raven was determined to roam at will until then. An afternoon spent being pricked with pins, measured and yet again remeasured, was not her idea of fun.

Thus far, she had not gone from the inn unescorted; but because Eben was otherwise occupied, she could escape without his turning that critical gaze of his upon her, or having him deny her permission to wander outdoors.

She halted when she reached the kitchen door, able to hear both men's voices clearly. She edged the door open the littlest bit, just enough to see the long booted legs of the stranger stretched out before him beneath the table.

His clothing suggested wealth, she could see that at a glance. The leather of his knee-length boots seemed soft as calfskin, and as she watched, one lean brown hand came to rest on his slightly bent knee, and for the barest instant the ruby ring he wore flashed an evil red wink.

Just then she heard Meggie's whisper behind her and she started guiltily. "Raven, what in the devil are you doing?"

Raven put a finger to her lips and made a swift retreat. "Going elsewhere to spend my morning," she said. Caught and feeling slightly childish, she tore from the room. Only when the brisk morning wind washed over her heated face did she breathe easily again. As she walked through the meadow that bordered the creek, she wondered just who the handsome stranger was and what connection he had to Eben.

"Are you home for good?"

Tyler's question caught Eben off guard and he had no ready answer. He hesitated before giving a noncommittal shrug. "I can only say that I've no immediate plans to go West again or anywhere else. As to the future . . . who can say what might happen." He was thinking of those great brown eyes of Raven's being turned on him expectantly that day in Elise's shop, and of Zeb's jolting reminders the night of his return. It seemed that everyone had to know in advance what plans a man had for the future, even Tyler. It made him uneasy, having people expect things of him. For the first time in his adult life he felt bound, and to a man accustomed to great freedom, it was not a pleasant feeling.

Tyler saw Eben frown. "Just asking," he said, raising his hands in an attempt to ward off the tension beginning to mount between them. "Hell, I wasn't asking you to marry me. I was curious is all."

"I've had a lot on my mind lately," Eben said. It was the only form of explanation he would offer.

Tyler laughed. "Would you care to tell me about her?"

"Aye, but I've no intentions of allowing her within ten feet of you," he replied, ignoring Tyler's feigned look of hurt. He knew the Virginian's reputation with women, and allowing him access to Raven would bring nothing but trouble for the three of them. For some odd reason the very thought of Tyler setting eyes on Raven raised Eben's hackles. "Her name is Raven," he began.

"The name intrigues me."

"And she is my ward." It was said with cold finality and carried with it the same impact as a dash of ice water. Tyler sat a little straighter and shot him a dubious glance.

"It poses a problem, to be certain, but I think I have the perfect solution. If she's of an age, then marry her off."

There it was again—that damnable idea! It had plagued him so much of late that he had almost reconciled himself to it. He couldn't bear the thought of another man touching her silken skin, and there seemed only one solution. For a month now his mind had been playing around the fringes of the possibility, yet every time it touched upon it he recoiled as if he had brushed against a burning brand. "It's hardly as simple as that," Eben said quietly.

Tyler heard the softly uttered statement and glanced hard at Eben, who was staring into the amber liquid still filling his glass. He had barely tasted the liquor and Tyler felt a sudden wave of compassion sweep over him. It wasn't hard to see what malady had stricken his friend, though he doubted Eben recognized the signs for what they were. Sadly, there was but one cure, and that one far from painless.

After a moment or two of silence had passed Eben seemed to rouse himself from his brooding. "What about you?'' he said. ''Will you be staying to attend the hunt, or going off again?''

''I had no idea that your countrymen hunted fox,'' the Virginian said. ''I would have thought the hills and vales to be unsuitable for riding to hounds.''

Eben shook his head. ''It's bigger game we're after,'' he said, bending to scratch the scarred ears of the old hound that lay at his feet, ''and a more durable hound we employ.''

The bulletins were everywhere, tacked in the common room at the inn, nailed to storefronts in town, even posted on the trees along the road. They were impossible to miss and they only served to rub salt into Raven's wounds.

Her life at McAllister's Inn could hardly be called exciting. Eben had chosen to absent himself from her company, sometimes for days at a time, and no one seemed to know where he went or why. Meggie was more often than not busy in the kitchen and could offer no help in solving the mystery of his absence or in easing Raven's loneliness and boredom. That left Nan, the carrot-haired serving wench whose manner reminded Raven of Cassandra, and the judge, of whom Raven was not overly fond.

Her days were empty, without excitement and devoid of all but the smallest of joys. Now came the opportunity she had been waiting for, an event that signified the supreme diversion in her otherwise mundane existence, and Eben had forbidden her to attend. The only excuse he had offered was that he and his pigheaded friends considered it a man's private rite and jealously guarded what they thought a sacred province.

Oh, how it rankled that she could not attend!

As she walked along through the bright morning hours she seethed, forming arguments to use against Eben's hardened resolve, words that might soften his position in her favor. The speeches she thought of were nothing less than eloquent, yet how could she use them to her advantage if he would not let her speak? The hunt was tomorrow. She was running out of time.

A mixture of boredom and excitement drove Raven to the kitchen and Meggie's company later that afternoon. Elise Goodman had come and gone, taking the vermillion velvet with her—the last of her gowns to be completed—but leaving a promise that it would be delivered before the ball. Eben had taken himself and the Virginian off on another of his mysterious errands and Raven was at loose ends.

She wandered listlessly down the rear stairs and carefully opened the kitchen door, peeking in before she entered, to assure herself that only Meg was there. The last thing she wanted now was to run into that dark-haired rake who had stood in the yard that very morning, grinning up at her. The easy way his green gaze had unclothed her had sent a shiver of apprehension chasing up her spine. Whoever he was, he was trouble, and she would do well to keep her distance from him.

Meggie looked up as she entered the kitchen. "I thought you were napping," she said, turning her knife blade against the shining red and green skin of an apple. A pie shell sat near her left hand, half filled with sliced apples and sprinkled generously with flour, cinnamon and sugar.

"I couldn't sleep," Raven said.

"Well, that I can understand," Meggie said. "It's all the excitement over the ball."

"I suppose I am a little excited," Raven allowed. "Meggie, will Eben attend the ball, do you think?"

She sat down in a chair opposite Meggie and reached for an apple and a knife, thinking to help, but Meg gently slapped her hands away. "Do you want your hands to look like mine, all black and stained? Goodness, girl, I'll not see you turned into a housemaid. You're a guest here! Now just relax and think of the babe."

"I think of little else these days," Raven sighed and folded her hands in her lap.

"That's only as it should be," Meggie said. "But, yes, Eben will most certainly be at the ball. Why, everyone for miles around will be there."

Raven felt a little better. She couldn't imagine wearing her wondrous vermillion gown without him being there to see it. She sat quietly for a time and the only sound in the huge kitchen was the scrape of Meggie's knife. Then quite abruptly she asked, "Meggie, what do you think of men?"

Meggie raised her gaze and contemplated the younger woman. "That's an odd question to be asking of a spinster lady like myself, don't you think? What makes you ask it? What has Eben done now?"

"Everything, and nothing," Raven said, lowering her gaze. In the short time that she had known him, he had turned her world upside down, he had fought with her and made her furious, comforted her and made her cry, loved her for a time and then set her aside, yet she loved him more than she could ever say.

"Well, to begin with, Eben is not most men," Meggie said. "But I suppose in truth, what drives him, drives most men. Need. Men are just little boys in men's skins, and they are the neediest creatures on earth. They crave love and understanding, even when they least give it to others. They require a great deal of patience in their women, and, oh, guidance . . . plenty of guidance. Men exasperate me, Raven. I suppose that is why I never felt the urge to marry."

"What makes them want to run the world?"

"My dear girl, 'tis a most unfortunate thing, but they *do* run it." As always Meg's wisdom was expressed matter-of-factly. "However, if one is to be fair at all, then you must admit they have their good points too. They are bigger than us, and stronger, and they can offer the protection we females seem to crave, even if it *is* other men that we need protecting from."

Raven smiled as the stranger's roguish grin appeared behind her eyes. "And what would you do if Judge McAllister ordered you not to do something?" she asked innocently.

Meggie's eyes sparkled with mischief. "Well, then, I'd find a way to do it just to spite him."

Chapter 20

The morning of the Grand Circular Hunt had arrived and as she climbed from her bed and began her morning ablutions, Raven could hear Eben's voice in the yard, followed by the laughter of the stranger. In a moment the back door banged as the pair entered the kitchen. Raven splashed her face a final time, enjoying the bracing cold of the water on her skin, then dried and padded quickly to the large cherry wardrobe containing her newly made clothing. She opened the doors and quickly thumbed through the gowns, catching her bottom lip in her teeth as she tried to decide what to wear.

The knock that sounded on her chamber door startled her, and she called out, asking who it was.

"It's only me, Raven," Eben called. "I missed you at supper last night and came to see how you were faring. Can I come in, or will you keep this door between us?"

"Just a moment!" Raven said. She shot a glance downward to her small, rounded belly. If he saw her disrobed, the truth would be out, and she wasn't ready to brave his wrath. His brown velvet robe lay waiting on the bed like an old and comfortable companion, and she flew to it, belting it loosely around her.

"Raven!" Eben's voice came again. "What the hell

is going on in there? Have you found some handsome rogue in my absence to keep you company?''

The door opened then and a slightly disheveled Raven looked up at him through the small crack, her eyes large and luminous. ''And would it matter to you if I had?'' she taunted.

His hand grasped the door and pushed it open so that he might enter. It had been days since he had seen her, and forever since they'd shared a moment of uninterrupted privacy. He hadn't realized until this moment how very much he had missed her company and in light of his thoughts these past few days, a moment or two alone certainly would do no harm to either of them.

He entered the room and kicked the door shut with a booted heel. ''What, no kiss hello? No warm embrace?'' he asked, keeping his voice intentionally light. ''We've barely seen each other these past few weeks and now you shun me like the plague. Is it true what Meg said?''

Her eyes widened and she stared at him, the color draining from her small oval face. ''What has she said to you?''

Eben frowned at her. She looked stricken. He decided to ride after Sam Ruston directly. If she was seriously ill then she needed gentle care. He could not lose her now! ''She told me you were indisposed when I asked after you. What is it Raven?'' he asked, taking her hand and drawing her closer. ''Is this some female malady that defies a man's understanding, or are you truly ill?''

His concern was genuine and Raven felt a tremor begin where their bodies met—a tingling that began in her fingertips and coursed slowly up her arm. Soon her entire body shook and she tried to pull away, to put a little distance between them, but Eben would not have it. He pulled her into his arms until her cheek was pressed to his shirt front. He smelled of the clean autumn air, and beneath her cheek his throbbing pulse was steady and strong. She began to believe that everything would be all right. He did love her after all, even if he could not say it. She closed her eyes and sighed.

"You have not answered me, Raven," he said. "What keeps you in this room so much?"

"It's only a small matter and will cure itself in time," she said. Her hand had crept around his lean ribs and rested on his back. She hadn't realized how tense he was until she felt him relax. She raised her head to look up into his dark, solemn face and knew that he would kiss her. His lids lowered, shading the light of need in those beloved pale blue eyes, and his head lowered until she felt his beard tease her face. She opened her mouth to receive him, her heart gladdened–

Tyler's fist rattled the door on its hinges. Eben swore. "What the devil do you mean by deserting me?" came that lazy, drawling voice. "I thought we were going down to breakfast! Eben! What are you about in there? Devilment, I've no doubt! Mademoiselle of the lacy chemise, do you perchance need rescuing?"

A blush tinged her cheeks as she heard his knowing laugh in the hall. The man's footfalls slowly faded and she turned back to Eben, who just looked nettled. The moment had vanished.

He released her and stepped back. "Jesus," he swore softly, suddenly looking tired. "I'll not have a moment of peace with him here."

"Who is that man, and what does he want with you?" Raven asked.

"He's a friend most of the time," Eben said, "and at times a welcome diversion to an otherwise tedious existence, but just now he's a royal pain in the ass!"

"When will he leave?" Raven asked.

"Like a bad cold, he's bound to linger," Eben said grittily, his earlier good humor now annihilated by the Virginian's ill-timed interruption. "He's to attend the hunt with me tonight, and with the scent of perfumed female flesh in the air tomorrow I think I can safely say he'll be with us for some time." He stepped to the door and gave her a wry look. "Though I should perhaps post a warning to all the fathers having daughters to beware. It would be a public service." He paused, sunk deep in his own newly made gloom. At last he looked at her. "Will you join us?"

She shook her head. She hardly wished to face that knowing leer across the breakfast table and sensed that things might be easier for Eben without her there. She hoped the man would soon be gone. She could hardly hide in her room forever.

Young Jedediah stole a sheepish glance at his newly acquired "cousin" and grinned nervously. Raiford was perched awkwardly on the swayback of an ancient mule borrowed from the judge's stable named Fireball. Fireball in the past had more than earned his name, yet the steady relentless advance of years had taken the edge off his ornery nature as well as the spring from his now rheumatic stride. All that remained was this plodding old bag of bones who shook with every step and jarred poor Raiford mercilessly.

Jedediah was concerned that Raiford's soft seat would not abide such punishment—but it could not be helped, and Raiford seemed not to mind, for his expressive brown eyes sparkled with excitement. The taut nervous strain had left the fine-boned features, and now Jedediah saw that same bright animation that he had first noticed that wet day weeks before when he had held fast the canoe by the steps of McAllister's Inn.

"You sure that you're all right, Rafe?" Jedediah whispered hoarsely. "If anything happens to you Mr. St. Claire will hide me good!" Their animals were hemmed in on all sides by the sizeable crowd that had gathered outside the White Wolf Tavern in Castle Ford. If Rafe decided to abandon the plan, now was not the time to do it. They would have a difficult time escaping the confines of the crowd without drawing the notice of the one man Rafe hoped to avoid.

"I will be once we're out of here!" Rafe said, careful to keep the hat pulled low. It had been simple enough to seek out young Jedediah and beg for his cooperation, to procure some old clothing and this hat, mount the mule, and ride from the inn to Castle Ford. The hardest aspect of this stolen adventure was sitting here in the bright, revealing sunlight, feeling the slow trickle of sweat between her shoulder blades inch its way downward, and to bear without fidgeting the prickle of the heavy woolen shirt against skin that was more accustomed now to the feather-light touch of fine soft lawn.

All of this brought discomfort to the small-statured figure garbed in a ridiculous mixture of ill-fitting boy's clothing and crowning the scarred back of the mule, yet Raven found that it could hardly compare to the thrill of fright she felt as Eben stepped off the shaded porch of the tavern and headed in their direction. The sea of men parted to let him pass, and Raven fidgeted and tried to swallow the lump in her throat. If he found her out now, he would be sure to send her home.

"Jedediah, where's your pa?" Eben asked once he'd reached them. He patted Jedediah's horse's neck without looking up.

"He wasn't feeling up to snuff, so I brung my cousin Raiford Kenton, from up on the Kiskiminetas."

Raven held her breath and looked at the ground. She could feel that penetrating pale gaze upon her, though seemingly it touched her without interest, for she heard him say, "The lad's a little scrawny for so hard a ride, don't you think?"

"He's little, but he's tough," Jedediah said, his voice cracking.

"Well, he's your kin and therefore your responsibility." He paused a second and then finished. "But look, Jedediah, when they form up into groups, you'd do well to bring young Raiford here and fall in with me. I'll try to keep an eye on you."

He walked away and Raven sighed. Only when he was safely out of earshot did she begin to grumble. "Scrawny indeed!"

She had lost any fear she might have felt at first and now sat glaring at Eben, who was lounging once more against a porch post waiting for the judge to speak, completely oblivious of the dark looks being thrown his way.

Judge McAllister's booming voice cut into Raven's thoughts. "Gentlemen! We've a fair distance to ride, so my opening address will be brief." The loud baying of the hounds nearly drowned him out and he cried, "Hunters! Silence those hounds!" Men scrambled to obey and in a moment order was restored. "You will form companies of thirty men each, excluding your officers. Those of you unfamiliar with the rules of the hunt take heed. Liquor and firearms are prohibited."

There was a full-blown chorus of groans, but Zeb overrode them easily. "With good reason! You all recall that incident five years back when John Bently shot his brother Bob. Now I'll allow that Bob is somewhat lacking in looks, but even on all fours as he was, he could hardly be mistaken for a wolf!" There was rippling laughter as Bob Bently turned red. "Lastly, any celebration can take place tomorrow night at the Hunter's Ball." A murmur of approval rippled along the crowd of men. The quality of the judge's whiskey was exceeded only by the generosity of his hand when doling it out.

"Keep the hounds leashed once we reach Henry Michael's farm. Mrs. Henry values her hens. Now then, are we ready to move out?"

"Aye!" was heard in a roar.

Raven hadn't heard Zeb's speech. She had been too busy watching Eben. Now she saw him make his way to Cadence and swing gracefully into the saddle. In a moment he had maneuvered the mare off to one side and whistled to the hound, Tracer, who trotted over then sat on his haunches, his tongue lolling from his parted jaws.

"Hang back and we'll fall in at the rear." Jedediah fingered his reins. His voice was still hoarse with fear, and Raven saw the nervous darting of his eyes.

"I'll follow you," she replied. But before she had the chance to kick the mule forward something nudged her leg. She turned and looked with shock into the knowing green eyes of the Virginian.

"I liked you better the other day," he drawled. Not giving her time to form a reply, he nudged his horse forward and joined Eben. Yet not before she saw his wink.

Suddenly, despite the ragged, baggy clothes and the light smearing of soot that smudged her skin, she felt naked. Somehow that man with his lazy, impudent grin and wicked dancing eyes could see through her disguise when Eben could not. She stared hard at the two men a hundred yards distant and waited for him to betray her to Eben, but oddly enough it never happened.

The column moved forward to the site where the hunt would begin and Jedediah followed, looking back to make sure that she was behind him. When the crowd reached their destination, they dismounted and tied their horses to various trees so that the animals would not run off during the hunt.

"Spread wide along the ranks! We have a lot of ground to cover on foot!" Eben called to the assemblage. Immediately the small knot of men began to move in both directions just outside the first perimeter of straw. "Most of you have been to a Grand Circular Hunt before, but for the benefit of anyone new to this, I'll explain briefly. This line of straw is the first ring and it is two and a half miles directly through the center. In the middle of this ring is another circle of straw, and dead center inside it is a steep-sided pit. We're going to drive the beasts before us toward the pit. You won't be able to see the man next to you, but stay within shouting distance if you can. If you should lose your way, then cry out. Someone will hear you. But for Christ's sake, don't reverse your way and head toward the cliffs. We don't want to ruin tomorrow night's festivities by having to attend to a funeral."

His speech concluded, he walked slowly along the ranks, speaking with those he knew, nodding to the others, until he came to Jedediah and Raiford.

"Jedediah, keep a close eye on Rafe. T'would be a shame to have to inform his mother that he was bait for some hungry wolf."

"He ain't got no ma," Jedediah said as Eben began to turn away. It had slipped out and he could have bitten his tongue for offering the information, since he could see it piqued the man's interest where before there had been none. Eben turned back and laid his hand on Raven's shoulder, as if in silent camaraderie.

Eben felt the boy flinch away and frowned. "I can see the hurt is fresh," he said and looked at Jedediah. "He seems uncommonly shy. How old is the lad?"

"Thirteen," Jedediah said quickly.

"A hard age for a youth," Eben said. He clapped the boy on the shoulder and nearly sent him staggering. As the lad righted himself, Eben saw the stubborn, almost angry set of his thin shoulders and smiled to himself. Scrawny he might be, almost to the point of effeminacy, yet there was an underlying thread of steel that showed the man he would someday be. "Rest easy, Raiford Kenton," he said as he started to move on. "We'll make a man of you yet."

Raven watched him fade into the twilight, marveling at the man's blindness.

God must have been in a violent mood when he set his hand to molding this land, Raven thought, making her way carefully along. Her pace was slow, her path lit solely by the weak light of her flickering torch.

She held high the flaming knot of pine Jedediah had given her and peered into the unyielding black ahead. The ground rose up sharply now and great boulders squatted like slumbering beasts from a dark and distant past, caught frozen in time and awaiting only the signal for their awakening and the revelation of their age-old secrets.

In her left hand the brass bell Jedediah had insisted she accept was cold reassurance. A pregnant silence surrounded her. Her heart pounding in her ears, she rang the bell and waited.

Nothing happened. Jedediah was somewhere off to her right, out of sight and hearing. Or was he? She stopped and shot a swift glance at the dark walls of the forest surrounding her. The absence of light caused everything to look the same. She had tried to continue on an unwavering course, but with all of the deadfalls and towering rocks, gullies, and malformations in the earth to crawl over or walk around it was nigh impossible.

Eben's words were echoing in her ears, "For

Christ's sake, don't reverse your way and head toward the cliffs!'' Was that what she had done? She experienced a sudden foreboding and her frantic pulse began to race. One thing was certain, she must continue moving.

The other hunters were walking, driving the game before them as they went. She might already be far behind them, too far to catch up. She thought of Eben. Knowing he was somewhere out there in the dark woods made her feel a little more at ease, until she reminded herself that he hadn't the slightest inkling she was here.

She raised the torch high above her head and shook the bell again hard, listening to the loud discordant clanging as it was reflected off the trees and swallowed by the stygian black. She strained to hear some answer—anything!—some human noise that would help her battle this swiftly mounting fear which threatened to suffocate her, to conquer the uncontrollable quaking of her limbs.

But just as before, nothing came. The night closed maliciously in around her. Her heart crept into her throat. Before her the ground sloped steadily upward. Not knowing what else to do, Raven began to climb.

The ascent at the top was almost vertical and Raven was out of breath by the time she reached the deadfall that sat atop the summit. She took hold of a gnarled root to steady herself and looked back down the way she'd come. Her breathing was easier now, the stitch in her side lessening. She didn't know what made her raise her gaze upward, but what she saw made the blood freeze in her veins.

There, crouched and waiting on the trunk of the huge fallen tree was the largest panther she'd ever seen. Beneath her breath Raven muttered a prayer, a hastily mouthed plea to a deity who had long been deaf to her humblest of pleadings. Better that she hope for Eben to save her, than for God to intervene on her behalf. Where was he, that mighty frontiersman, when she needed him?

"Don't move, Rafe, don't even breathe." It was not Eben's voice but the Virginian's, coming in hushed tones from behind the nearest tree. From the corner of her eye she saw him edge around the trunk until he was at her back. The catamount saw him too and before she could open her mouth to scream a warning the cat's muscles bunched and it sprang, launching itself from the deadfall into the air above Raven's head.

She screamed as a crushing weight came down on her, knocking and pinning her to the ground. In her wild struggle to be free she managed to knock her assailant aside, but he grabbed a handful of her coat and pulled her with him. Together they tumbled down the steep ascent.

When finally the two came to a skidding halt Raven lay very still, waiting for the shooting pains that would signal the loss of Eben's child. Only when she realized that she was unhurt and the danger was over did she scream and push at the man who straddled her slim form.

"Get off of me, you blasted oaf!" she shrilled at Tyler.

"Will you hold still? My sleeve is caught." Tyler Lee bent over her, his attention focused on the cuff of his shirt. The button was fastened quite firmly to a strand of her hair, and there seemed no simple way to free himself, especially since she was struggling hard to push him away. "Hold still for just a moment and it will all be over with!" Tyler said, not noticing the lean shadow that just then separated from that of a nearby tree and came to loom like a thunderhead over them both.

"What the hell is going on here?" Eben demanded. He could see the small struggling figure pinned beneath Tyler's much larger one and immediately thought the worst. After all, what other explanation was there? "Of all the depravity—leave the lad be, Jackson!"

"Get off me, you fool!" Eben heard the youth cry, but much to his surprise it wasn't the voice of any boy. The normally dulcet tones now raised in a near-screech were faintly accented with the same beloved lilt that Raven's speech carried. Recognition went through him with a jolt and left him cold.

Not about to stand by and watch his friend maul his ward, Eben snatched his hunting knife from its sheath at his hip and stepped between them. With unnecessary force he grasped Tyler's arm and made a swift arc around the sleeve.

"Ouch, now dammit, Eben!" Tyler protested when the blade pricked his skin. "Just wait a minute!"

Raven was now free and she scrambled up to face Eben's wrath. "What are you doing? Are you mad? Why would you attack him like that?"

Eben stared at her. Not only had she dared to defy him by coming here tonight, but when he sought to protect her from a man who was an acknowledged seducer of women she had the gall to berate him for it! "Perhaps I made the wrong choice," he said coldly.

In the background Tyler was examining the violent parting of his cuff from his shirt sleeve. The cuff, he could see, still hung from Raven's hair.

"Perhaps I should have spared his cuff and lifted your hair," Eben continued, his eyes glittering dangerously. "Given your beloved heritage, you would understand that act more easily."

Raven sucked in her breath. The hateful utterance had stung her just as he intended that it should. "Perhaps you should have. It would have been very like you to save his shirt rather than think of me."

"I think of nothing else these days!" he said grittily, "and when I *do* manage to get away from the responsibilities that have been foisted upon me, you show up!"

"Is that all I am to you? An unwanted responsibility? Then pray, let me relieve you of your burden!" She turned away to hide from him the hurt his words had caused her. She wouldn't give him the satisfaction of seeing her tears, but he wouldn't have noticed anyway, for he was now venting his wrath upon Tyler Lee.

"You were in on this, weren't you?' Eben demanded hotly. "You just couldn't resist the urge to make me a bloody fool in front of her! Where were your wits, man! Had you no thought for her safety?"

The picture of Tyler's muscular frame covering Raven's lithe one still smouldered in his brain. The thought kept coming—if he'd arrived but a moment later . . . He tried to banish it from his mind to quell his ever-mounting anger, but the scene continued to taunt him. What really rankled him was that the scene was an all-too-familiar one that he had lived before. "You must have had a damn good laugh, thinking to betray me with my ward right beneath my very nose."

Tyler knew the warning signs well enough from past experience and sought to calm the other man by putting things in their true perspective. "Perhaps you'd rather that catamount had gotten her instead of me? Look, Eben, I heard the cat's cry a while ago and came to see if Rafe was all right. When the cat leapt from the deadfall I knocked her to the ground and my button got entangled in her hair. I was trying to free us both when you came along. I had no intention of betraying you. Hell, I had no idea she was yours, or maybe I would have." He raked an impatient hand through his dark hair and turning on his booted heel strode swiftly off, back to the others before matters got fully out of hand.

"Is that true?" Eben asked, turning to see that Raven was gone. During the argument she had quietly slipped away. Eben stood and listened to the silence. Then he heard the rustling of dead leaves to his right and knew that she was headed for the cliffs.

Chapter 21

Just ahead Eben could see her slim figure, darting through the wooded copse. The forest was thinning now and the cliffs lay just a few hundred yards ahead, a sheer drop of more than a thousand feet to the river below. He had to stop her before she reached the open grass that crowned the promontory.

"Raven, stop! For the love of Christ, woman!"

She heard his words being flung at her like a handful of sharp stones and sped onward. She was sobbing wildly now, her eyes streaming, her vision blurred. Her folly in loving this cold, unfeeling man was scaldingly apparent. Once her pride had been so great, and now she was reduced to begging for scraps of affection from someone who cared little for her. He saw her quite simply as a burden! her sore heart cried out in wrenching agony, a millstone around his neck! What then would he feel when he at last discovered the truth of her condition? Would he not view the babe with the same impatience? The same bitterness that they should dare to hold him back, tie him down, when his freedom was what he valued most?

These rampant thoughts spurred her onward. She flew from the trees into the open, but the going now was harder than before. Tall, wild grass wrapped about her legs and caught at her coat to detain her.

Eben was close behind her now. She could hear his ragged breathing, the groan that sounded torn from the depths of a tortured soul as his fingers snatched at and caught the hem of her coat. Panting raggedly, he dragged her backwards and into his rough embrace.

He was trembling violently, like a steed that had run a close and desperate race and emerged the victor by an inch.

"Please!" she cried. "Just let me go!"

"You little fool," he rasped. "Why did you run from me? Why?" He was shouting now, but he couldn't help it. The fear that had gripped him relentlessly had been all too real. He had very nearly lost her—and this time for good. The realization robbed him of the smallest shred of gentleness. "Why, damn you?" he growled as he shook her.

She only shook her head and cried aloud, going limp against him.

She found herself pulled closer and Eben sank to his knees in the damp tall grasses, taking her with him, cradling her in his arms. "My God, Raven," he groaned, shuddering. "You might have killed yourself."

"What would it have mattered if I had?" she cried in an agonized whisper. "Surely death could be no more miserable than this constant fighting."

He pulled back and stared at her, clearly horrified. "Have I caused this?"

"I have done it to myself," she said, sniffing.

"Death is final, Raven. And like marriage, it is not to be entered into lightly, nor spoken of in a casual vein."

"How ironic that you should mention the two in the same breath."

"Then I have caused this bleak attitude of yours," he said slowly. "It's because of my damnable speech that first night we arrived, isn't it? Isn't it?"

He held her tightly on his lap—nay, *imprisoned* was a better word—and he now forced her face up so that she could not avert it, nor fend off his query. "Yes, if you must know! I am only a burden to you! You would be rid of me if you could!"

"I spoke in anger," he said. "Seeing you with Tyler shredded my patience. Yea, it's true that I set you aside, and a thousand times have I regretted it! I've missed waking with you sleep-warm in my arms. . . . But thankfully it is a mistake simply rectified," he said quietly. "I retract those hated words. I want you for my own. I have ever since that first day in your father's house. I thought my desire for you would pass, but it hasn't. My need grows stronger by the day. I cannot sleep at night without you invading my dreams. My bed is empty and cold without you in it . . . as hollow as my heart."

Raven heard his words as if in a daze. He was telling her that he needed her in his life, a grand admission for the man that he was. Surely it was tantamount to an open declaration. Her heart was beating wildly when she dashed a hand across her wet cheeks. "Eben, what are you saying?"

His palm cupped her chin as his eyes stared into hers. The icy blue was melting and the emotion flooding forth threatened to drown her. "That I love you, sweetheart, if it means anything to you. My heart is yours for the taking, and all that goes with it."

He loved her. She didn't reply with words. Her arms crept to his shoulders and gently she pushed him backward into the grass. His shirt was hard to remove and came slowly up over his lean ribs, but soon he was free to aid her with her own. "The air is chill," he said doubtfully, even while his hands made short work of her clothing. "You'll catch your death."

"Not I," she said, smiling mischievously. "But

never fear, m'sieur, if you do I shall nurse you . . . gladly."

Her hands were at the waist of his buckskin trousers, her fingers slipping beneath the band, brushing his belly until he drew in a sharp breath. It had been so long since they'd lain together. He could barely wait to feel her gentle warmth closing in around him.

Some of Eben's impatience showed as he pulled her down atop him for a swift, savage kiss. His hands slid down her naked back to her buttocks so that he might end this play, but Raven shook her head. "I think I see your game, mademoiselle," he said low. "You're bent upon torture."

"No torture this," Raven sighed, lowering her weight until her ripe breasts just barely brushed his chest. Her soft, willing lips came down to tease a groan from him, her tongue meeting his only briefly before it was on to other, more erotic pursuits. She kissed his throat and gained satisfaction from the way his pulse leapt, then continued downward to his chest.

Just lightly furred, she found his paps with ease, and rounded one, then the other with her tongue, feeling them come erect with pleasure. But she did not pause for long, instead trailing the pointed tip of her tongue with aching slowness down the center of his taut belly until she reached at last her long-awaited goal.

Eben gasped. Heat seared his manhood, wet and oh so delicious. He tried to speak to her, to tell her of the wild pleasure shooting through him, but found that words deserted him. In this one small act she had robbed him of the will to dominate, to lead, and he knew that he would never be the same. Surprisingly, he found he didn't care.

For Raven it was the ultimate kiss, the supreme act of love. This man was everything to her, and without words she was communicating the emotion which filled her heart. Reverently she accepted him into her mouth. She heard his swiftly stolen breath and knew that she had pleased him, then slowly she began to move her tongue.

The light musk taste of his maleness was not at all unpleasant, and the power surging through her as she heard his agonized groan was heady in the extreme. She ran her splayed fingers up his hips and onto his belly, feeling the muscles retract in shock. She was delighted with her play and had no thought of leaving when he took hold of her wrists and drew her slowly upward. "Enough," he growled, half rising, thinking to seize her lips for another kiss.

She shook her head slowly and smiled down into his tense face. "For you and I it will never be enough," she said. She was poised above him and slowly closed herself around him. Their flesh joined, she sighed, content at last to be where she belonged.

Eben closed his eyes and allowed the wet heat to envelop him again. Never had he been so aroused, so filled with wonder by the miracle of a woman's mouth and hands and body. Whether she knew it or not, it was *she* who possessed *him* this time.

Raven would be a vital part of him from this day forward and wherever he chose to roam, he would carry her with him. For, as she had so generously gifted him with her body and her love, she had at the same time banished his loneliness forever.

This night their lovemaking held a generous measure of the tenderness born of newfound love. With each sinuous movement of her hips Raven forged anew the steel thread that bound their hearts together. By the time they gained their joint release and she collapsed on top of him, her breathing ragged, that same binding thread had been tempered well enough to last a lifetime, made to withstand a thousand trials.

Eben held her to him and stared up at the star-filled sky. The million points of light flickered, then brightened, seeming to wink conspiratorialy at his newly made plans. Tomorrow would see an end to all the uncertainty, he thought, feeling a strange kind of calm settle over him. Where he had once thought of marriage with an inner dread, he now felt only peace. Tomorrow night he would put the question to her, and afterward she would share his bed. Then every night to come. Safely pillowed in her lover's warm embrace, Raven slept, and only the stars saw his sudden smile.

A coach pulled by a team of matching grays rumbled up the last gentle grade then rolled the final mile along the south road leading to McAllister's Inn. The well-sprung vehicle had not been built to travel such deplorable roads and slid from rut to rut, swaying like a ship on choppy seas and turning the face of Senator Jameson Wharton a sickly green. The leather curtains had been rolled up and glumly he stared out at the passing countryside, wishing he were elsewhere.

"You would think a proper road would have been built by now," his wife complained from the opposite seat. Her gloved hands were braced on either side of her narrow hips to prevent her from being bounced about the plush interior.

Opposite her, Jameson sighed. There was no end to her complaining, and no way she could be mollified, save one. And this he faced with sickly dread. She needed to see that raw-edged savage again. Jameson, however, felt differently. Had he never set eyes on the man again it would have been too soon. His hatred had not lessened one iota over the years, nor had his fear. His leg throbbed, a constant and painful reminder of Eben St. Claire.

He stole a glance at his wife, who was caught up

in her brooding. She had been behaving strangely since she'd received the missive from Judge McAllister the week before, her moods swiftly running from giddiness to spitefulness in the wink of an eye. Jameson harbored no doubts to the cause of her emotional instability, for he had found and read the letter when she was out. That bastard St. Claire had come back from the West alive and triumphant, dragging with him a beautiful young woman—supposedly his ward, though privately the judge had expressed his hopes that this situation would soon change, that Eben would follow Ivory's fine example and settle down.

Jameson had scoffed bitterly at that. Ivory was a viper, and just as faithless to him as she had been to Eben St. Claire. At times when he was deep in drink and his mind reflective he considered that Ivory was his comeuppance for the part he'd played that night so long ago. Although, being saddled with a permanent and debilitating limp as well as this highborn bitch seemed too dear a price to pay for a single night in Ivory's silken bed. Two more reasons to hate Eben St. Claire. Had it not been for Eben's constant absences from Castle Ford Ivory might have remained faithful—though Jameson privately doubted she had it in her to be faithful to anyone or anything.

That rain-dappled evening more than four years ago remained a nightmare for Jameson, one that he relived daily. Each time he looked at his wife's petulant face he heard in his mind the reverberation of the bedroom door as it slammed against the wall and saw again that dark sardonic face. He felt again the unspeakable fear that had engulfed him as he'd been pushed to the window . . . and then there was nothing to catch hold of, nothing to stop his quick descent to a pain-wracked landing two stories down.

Once he'd regained his senses he'd sworn to see

that devil's spawn hanged for attempted murder. But the man had gone and Ivory was there to piece him back together.

When he could walk again they had married, and with her father's backing Jameson had run for the senate. For once things had gone his way. Ivory proved an asset. In private she was full of contempt and criticism, but in public she was the perfect political wife, full of charm and praise for the esteemed Senator Wharton, her husband. Jameson alone knew the depths of his private hell. The knowledge that it was mostly of his own making made it no easier to bear.

The horses slowed. The sprawling stone manor that served as the area's most renowned hostelry lay just ahead.

Meggie was preparing fresh venison stew to serve for dinner when Nan came into the kitchen. She looked up from her task when the girl stood before the table, waiting. "Well, what is it? We've a hundred guests coming to the ball tonight, can you find nothing to do?"

"More like a hundred and two," Nan said. "I come in to tell ya there's a coach pulled up outside."

"A coach," Meg said sharply, her head coming up. "And did you see inside?"

Nan nodded. "A woman with hair as bright as a new penny, and a gent with a cane. They're wearing getups fit for the ball and it's barely eight o'clock!"

Meggie felt a sudden cold dread. She didn't even pause to wipe her hands but pushed out of the room as if in a daze. It couldn't be, she told herself inwardly. That woman showing up now would ruin everything.

In the doorway of the common room Meggie stopped and stood gaping. The black lacquer coach was splattered to the windows with mud and showed other signs of recent abuse, as did the harassed looking man just then alighting. He was rounder than he'd been four years ago, and his hair was beginning to recede at his temples—something he'd tried to conceal by brushing it forward in curls in the current mode. As he straightened himself, he leaned heavily on his cane, then turned to aid his wife in her descent.

For an instant the woman paused in the doorway of the coach to look upward at the stone edifice of the inn. A curious look crossed her perfect features, a mixture of satisfaction and disapproval—as if finding the place unchanged after four years had justified her leaving.

She'd gone on to become a grand lady, wife to a powerful senator, while those remaining here had continued to live their dull existence, pursuing their simple country pleasures, knowing no better life existed. Her eyes sought out the proof of her musings and found it in the frail figure of Meggie, who was standing stiffly, a carving knife still clutched in her hand. Giving the woman a grim smile, Ivory took Jameson's offered hand and stepped gracefully to the ground.

"Well, I see nothing has changed in my absence," she said as she neared the porch steps. "You may inform Daddy that I have arrived, then kindly make two rooms up for Jameson and me."

"I'd be happy to carry this dire news, except that no one is here. The judge is expected soon though, and you and your husband may wait in the common room until Nan sees to your accommodations." Meggie's voice was acid. Her hatred of the judge's daughter had not lessened with the passage of time. If anything, she would have liked to spit in the younger woman's eye and send her on her way before she had the chance to settle in. There was only one thing that could have lured her to Castle Ford, and that was Eben.

"Not here?" Ivory said, incredulous. "Well, then where is he?" She was disappointed that her entrance had been spoiled. She had been planning it for miles, imagining the pleasure her visit would bring to the judge and the look of desire on Eben's face. Surely he had not forgotten her. How could he, after all that they had been to each other? No, he would take one single look at her, and he would want her.

Jameson's voice cut into her musings and she blithely ignored the strained note in it, feeling the same bitter impatience she always felt when she thought of him as her husband. "Shall we, my love? I don't wish to hasten you, but the leg is pure torture!"

He limped for effect to where she stood and offered her his arm, but finding no sympathy there, looked to Meg. "The weather, you understand."

"I understand completely, Senator," Meggie said, casting a wry look at Ivory. "The pain you put up with must be indescribable."

Inside, Ivory walked to the hearth and stood looking up at the hunting scene hanging against the smoke-blackened stone. She tugged at the fingertips of her gloves, drawing them slowly off before replacing her rings. Laying the gloves on the nearest table, she turned to Meggie. "Where is Eben? I heard that he was here."

"Now where did you get that idea?" Meggie wondered.

"From Daddy's letter, so don't try to deceive me, Meggie. I won't have it. And neither will Eben. He will want to see me, you know he will. Perhaps that's what bothers you most about my coming. It spoils all your plans." The younger woman's smile was genuine. Nothing pleased her more than to see

Meggie vexed. And nothing vexed Meggie more than the thought of Ivory and Eben being together again. "If our rooms are ready, I'd like to go up now. I'm fatigued from the journey and wish to nap and freshen myself for Eben's return."

Meggie had to bite her tongue to keep from throwing Raven and her pregnancy in Ivory's face. Nothing could hurt Ivory—or Raven—more, for bringing it out in the open would cause a violent tempest—especially since Eben remained ignorant of the situation. She held her tongue and went quickly to the stairs. "If you'll follow me," she said with feigned politeness.

Ivory and Jameson, with his awkward gait, followed her. They had nearly reached the top step when suddenly Ivory felt a strong whim to sleep in her old room. "Never mind what room you've made up, I'll occupy my own chamber tonight."

"You can't have that room," Meggie said. " 'Tis already occupied. This one here is fine. You'll be more comfortable in it—"

"Are you growing deaf?" Ivory snapped. "I said I wanted my own room, and I shall have it. I don't care at all who occupies it. Put them elsewhere."

Meggie longed to slap some color into the woman's pale cheeks. The room Ivory demanded was Raven's now, and Meg was loathe to displace her. Then it came to her. Eben's room was on the opposite side of the hall, several doors down. Next to it was an empty chamber.

Moving Raven into that room would put her much closer to Eben, which was what Meg had wanted in the first place. "All right," she said suddenly, "if you want your room, then you may have it. I'll go get Nan to help me move the current occupant's belongings. It will only take a moment."

Ivory had noticed Meggie's threatening smile and became at once suspicious. Her green eyes narrowed as she watched Meg hurry down the hall to find the serving girl. Whatever had pleased the former bondwoman was bound to displease her.

The kill had been a good one and the returning party of hunters was infected with a spirit of revelry. Most stopped off in town at the White Wolf, to linger over a mug of ale or mulled wine to wash away the dust before continuing homeward. But a small party of riders cantered on, down the south road leading to McAllister's Inn.

Raven was nodding in the saddle, dreaming of her bed and sleep, when Cadence nudged the mule she was riding and Eben's strong hands slipped beneath her arms. She felt the reins dragged from her hands and came fully awake with a startled little cry, only to find herself being settled between strong thighs. He was smiling down at her and she sighed, nestling contentedly against his strong chest.

At the inn he was the last to dismount and lifted his lady down, carrying her into the common room and heading straightaway for the stairs. Meggie caught him by the shirt sleeve so that he turned to her with a questioning look.

"Raven's room is no longer hers," Meg said softly. "I've put her things in the corner room, next to yours."

"She was comfortable where she was," Eben said. "Why did you move her?"

"Suffice it to say the winds of change have blown through here while you were gone."

In his arms Raven stirred, opening her eyes to blink at Meg. "What's wrong?" she questioned sleepily.

"Not a thing," Eben said. "I'm taking you up to bed, sweetheart."

She leaned into him again and smiled.

''The corner room,'' he said to Meg, mounting the stairs. ''It's only temporary.''

''Eben? Don't leave me,'' Raven said softly.

''Tonight is ours, little cat,'' he replied. ''Only now I can't spare the time. There are things that I must do.''

Chapter 22

Steam rose around Eben's bronze torso and swirled into the cool air of his chamber, mingling with the fragrant smoke from the cheroot he held clamped between his teeth. There was just enough time for him to finish bathing and dress before he had to join the others downstairs. He rose from the tub and caught the linen towel from where it hung on the back of a chair, wrapping it around his hips. He had only just stepped from the tub onto the carpet when Meggie knocked at the door.

"Sit," she commanded brusquely upon entering. "I've just enough time to shear your wool and don my party dress." He did as she requested and soon the floor was littered with his golden hair. When she'd finished she stood back and viewed the results with satisfaction. "I knew a gentleman lurked somewhere beneath that mane. Raven will be pleased."

"This is foolishness, trying to please a woman. She'll have to accept me the way I am. I have no wish to change."

Accept him? A slow smile crept across Meg's thin lips. Accept him the way he was . . . She picked up her scissors and went to the door, a smile still fixed on her lips. "Well, I must be on my way. I'll see you later."

He was alone again and he went to stand before

the large oval cheval glass that resided in one corner. He had never been much given to spending time staring into the glass, but now he went and looked closely at his reflection, secretly pleased with what he saw. The years of hard living had served him well so far as his physique was concerned. His middle was devoid of the excess flesh that came of high living and his muscles rippled when he moved beneath skin that was smooth and tanned. He leaned forward and studied his face for a moment, his hand straying to his unshaven jaw.

With Raven riding high before him on the return to the inn, he had been provided with an unhampered view of her bosom via the neck of her baggy shirt, and the redness put there by the chafing of his beard had not been lost on him. He frowned in indecision. "She's never seen you without it, you know. What if she doesn't care for what she sees?" The face in the mirror just looked grim in return.

Turning from the glass he found his knife, strop, and brush and began to lather his face. "Bloody fool," he accused with a wry shake of his head. "You're making a fine ass of yourself over a woman." His blade was poised for the first stroke, when he hesitated. "Her hide will toughen given time," he reasoned, all the while knowing it was not true.

The first strains of a violin floated up the stairs to remind him there was little time left him. "What matters more to you, man? Your vanity, or the wench's tender hide?" With a defeated sigh he lifted the blade and brought it expertly along his chin.

A quarter of an hour passed before Eben walked down the stairs. He checked his watch and slipped it back into his coat pocket. Raven would be making her appearance soon. He felt his stomach constrict at the thought. He had been feeling queer all day long, and wondered if it was because of something he had eaten. For the life of him he couldn't recall if he'd had a single bite all day. Even the thought of food had been far from his mind.

Below, the common room was filled with guests—most of those here Eben knew, and many pounded his back or clapped his shoulder as he passed by. He found himself detained again and again, and by the time he reached the sideboard where Zeb was holding court he was badly in need of some liquid fortification. He reached for a decanter full of whiskey and splashed a generous amount into a tumbler, instantly drawing the judge's notice.

"Here now, young man! The children's refreshment is over—" Zeb stopped in mid-sentence to gape. "Why, Eben, lad, can that be you? I barely recognized you!" Zeb stood back with his fellows, laughing at his own joke.

All eyes were drawn to his clean-shaven face, and Eben flushed beneath his tan. "Can't a man shave his face without bringing the roof down on his head?" He sipped the whiskey and took satisfaction from the way it burned a path to his empty stomach. He sipped again and felt more at ease. The glass was drained all too soon, but friend that he was, Tyler saw it replenished, filling it this time to the brim. Tyler had always had a generous hand.

The whiskey kept his belly warm and drowned those butterflies he'd noticed earlier. It added to his confidence—tonight would be perfect, he could feel it in his bones. He was gazing into space, imagining the golden days to come when he realized that the Virginian had deserted him.

"Go on now. He's waiting for you," Meggie urged.

"I never imagined I could be so nervous." Anxiety lit Raven's features and caused her dark eyes to glint. She had dreamed so long of attending a ball, of swirling around the floor amid a throng of other dancers on the arm of some handsome gentleman. The moment had at last arrived, but Raven was having second thoughts. She crept to the railing and peered down at the packed floor below. Every inch of space seemed taken, and she didn't see Eben anywhere. "Are you sure he is there?" she asked worriedly. "I don't see him."

Her bright gaze swept the room again and stopped at the very foot of the stairs where a man stood poised, one shining Hessian planted on the lowest tread as though he would mount them and fetch her if she didn't hurry. Raven's breath caught in her throat. The pale blue eyes regarding her from a face deeply tanned were the same ones she'd gazed into on the cliffs, the ones that had watched her, fascinated, as she'd made love to him. Yet the rest of him was different, and the change that had been wrought was startling.

It seemed as if each stroke of his blade had shaved away a year. And surely the man regarding her warmly from the bottom of the stairs could not be the same irascible frontiersman who had bellowed drunkenly up at her in Pittsburgh. The Eben who now awaited her looked like a gentleman, garbed as he was in tight black trousers and a matching cutaway coat. His shirt and stock were as pristine white as newly fallen snow. To look at him now, he might have been a stranger, and he was blatantly impatient to claim her.

As she stood gaping, her heart pounding wildly in her breast, he must have somehow read her thoughts, for his hand went automatically to his clean-shaven jaw, then touched the cavalier-style mustache—the only concession to his manly pride—as if to reassure himself it still graced his upper lip.

Behind him, Raven saw the Virginian, Tyler Lee, take a firm stance. Past Eben's shoulder he shot her a roguish grin, his eyes now dancing with impish delight. She had the oddest feeling that he was waiting to see if she would turn and run. But she only drew in a quick steadying breath, lifted her head, and started down the stairs.

When she reached the bottom Eben took her hand and, bowing ever so slightly over it, brought it to his lips. "My lady, you look more beautiful than any treasure I have ever beheld," he murmured in a low voice, his blue gaze smoldering. "Yet you seem startled. Is something amiss?"

She shook her head, her black curls bobbing, then glanced away as if searching the room at large. "Actually, I was rather hoping to see my guardian here tonight," she said, straining on her toes to peer around him. "Would you happen to know what has become of him?"

"I think that he has gone for good," Eben said. "Does that sadden you, mademoiselle?"

"Only a little," she replied. "I had grown rather fond of him in the time we'd spent together. I wonder what I should do now that he is gone? Am I to be on my own again, or will you perchance take his place?"

"To fill his shoes will be a herculean task. The minx he swore to protect led him on a merry chase. I confess, I feel like a beardless boy in comparison to that hoary ruffian, my lady."

Raven caught her breath. "Am I?"

"My lady?" he queried, his voice strangely warm and caressing. "I can think of none other for the position." His hard mouth curved in a smile, making the groovelike dimples deepen in his lean cheeks.

She was about to reply when Tyler Lee stepped between them, adroitly shouldering Eben out of the way. He bowed deeply before her, bringing her hand to his lips. But instead of kissing her fingers as propriety dictated, he turned her hand and touched his lips to her inner wrist. She was shocked to feel the warm roughness of his tongue against the sensitive flesh and looked with alarm into eyes that burned with blatant desire. The man's audacity was unequaled. He took liberties that should have been rewarded with a hearty slap, yet to do so with Eben looking on was nothing less than dangerous.

"M'sieur Jackson," Raven said silkily. "How very good to see you again. Now if you will excuse me?"

She would have stepped away and left him standing alone, except that her hand still rested between both of his. "Come now, Rafe," he said smoothly, "where is your hospitality? I'm a stranger here, without friends to make me feel welcome. Will you not have pity on this lonely soul and grant me just one dance?" He saw her red lips part in reply, but cut her off before she could deny him. "If it's Eben you are worried about, then let me lay your fears to rest. We two are the very best of friends. I assure you he will not mind."

"Eben does most certainly mind," Eben spoke up just behind Tyler. He had put up with the man's nonsense in the past, but he had no intention of allowing the Virginian to claim Raven for the first dance. At least not without a fight. "Sweetheart," he said, extricating her hand from Tyler's, "will you so honor me?"

Raven bowed her head and dropped into a deep curtsy. The music had just begun and the haunting strains of a waltz filled the room. She had never danced like this before, and she was sure she never would again. All around them couples swirled, turning gracefully in time to the music, yet Raven hardly noticed them. She only had eyes for this new and wondrous Eben who swept her through the movements of the dance until she felt like she was floating on air.

Her admiring gaze kept straying to his jaw. His chin was only slightly jutting and strongly molded, with a small indentation just below the sensuous curve of his lower lip. The skin of his face looked soft and smooth—so smooth that she had to resist the urge to raise her hand to touch it.

"If it bothers you so much I can always grow it back," he said, amused at her fascination.

"It does not bother me, m'sieur," Raven said. "I only wonder what brought about this sudden change."

"Change is good at times, I've found," he said. "For years I have been trying to call back the past, to somehow right the wrongs done to me and to others close to me, but now I see that I was wasting time and would have been better off had I been building for the future. We cannot go back, Raven. We can only go forward from this day forth."

"You have given it a great deal of thought." Her hand strayed around the collar of his coat to the waving strands of flaxen hair. Soft as silk it curled against her fingers. Would their son be born with hair like this? she wondered dreamily.

"I have indeed," he said, "and it is something I wish to discuss with you at length, but later, for sadly the dance is through and I see that smooth-talking jackass making his way to claim you."

"Well," Tyler Lee said, coming to stand beside them. He grinned down at Raven, ignoring Eben pointedly. "Now that you have emerged unscathed from the bearlike embrace of our unschooled friend here, you should have no qualms about treading a measure with a man more adept at the social amenities."

Eben's derisive snort only served to widen Tyler's grin. "Take care with her, my friend, if you value your continued good health," Eben warned.

He stood awhile with booted legs apart, his arms crossed before him, just watching as they circled the floor. The music went on and on, seemingly endless. He chafed that he had allowed the other man to steal Raven from him and began to suspect that Tyler had bribed the musicians to play a double measure.

The minutes ticked by and Eben's impatience mounted. The perfectly matched pair glided by, looking as if they belonged together. Even their clothing complemented each other—Tyler's blue and buff and Raven's bright vermillion. He saw Raven gazing up into the dark face of the Virginian, saying something, then saw him laugh. Selfishly, he longed to go and separate them. She was his, after all, or would be very soon.

"Why so glum, lad?" Zeb asked beside him. He spied the couple on the dance floor and knew what was bothering Eben. "Ah, lost your partner have you? Well, that's something that is easily remedied. Come and share a glass with the rest of us. It will restore your good spirits. And ready you for my surprise."

There was only one thing that would restore him to amiability, Eben thought. And that was seeing an end to this evening and all of its uncertainty, when he and Raven would close the door on all of Castle Ford, on the world, for that matter. There would be only the two of them from now on if all went well. He raised the glass Zeb had given him and drank. The whiskey slid down his throat and warmed his belly. He listened with half an ear to the judge's talk, but his gaze never once strayed from his intended bride.

"You court disaster and enjoy it," Raven was saying to Tyler just then. "What kind of man does that, I wonder?"

"A simple man, who enjoys thoroughly the feel of a beautiful woman swaying in his arms," Tyler replied smoothly. His gaze was wont to linger upon her dewy skin, her cheeks with their delicate traces of pink, the long graceful column of her throat, the uppermost curve of her bosom displayed seductively above the square neckline of her velvet gown. Eben indeed was a lucky man, he thought with an unaccustomed surge of envy. There was something about this woman that made him wish she was his own.

Her reaction to his remark was the lifting of one finely arched brow. Tyler held her body close to him and moved in ever widening circles, her vermillion skirts billowing slightly to brush his boot tops, and felt a subtle victory. The skeptical beauty was his for the moment, or as long as the musicians kept on playing.

"I doubt there is anything simple about you," Raven said at last. "What I don't understand is why you continue to pursue this reckless course, knowing it can only end in folly."

"Dare I hope that milady fears for my safety?"

"For his, is more to the point," she answered, nodding at Eben. "I have no wish to see him gain a hangman's noose, a harsh payment for defending my honor against your uninvited advances. You are bent upon causing mischief, I can see it in your eyes."

Her words delighted Tyler Lee, and he threw back his head and laughed. "The lady is not only ravishing, but clairvoyant as well. Tell me, Rafe, can you also see what's in my heart?"

"Nay, 'tis far too dark a place to see anything very clearly," Raven quipped.

"I can see why Eben wants you," Tyler said. "The only mystery that remains is what you see in him. Your brightness and vivaciousness is wasted on the likes of him."

"Another word and I will leave you—" She started to pull away, but he drew her back, unwilling to have their dance end this way.

"You can hardly blame a man for trying," he said. "Besides, he would have done the same in my place, and has a number of times. That is why he wears that scowl when he sees you in my arms. We're cut from the same bolt of cloth, Eben and I."

"That doesn't give you the right to speak this way to me," Raven told him. Tyler was an unprincipled rogue, a user of women. It rubbed her raw to think of placing Eben in the same class as him. Especially when nothing could be farther from the truth.

Knowing he had roused her ire, Tyler relented. "Come, wipe away that frown," he coaxed. "I'm sorry for the things I said. Promise me this next dance and I swear to make it up to you." He noticed how her dark eyes darted to the sideboard, and smiled. Eben had gone a moment ago, and Tyler would use his absence to his advantage. "How can he mind my keeping you entertained while he is gone?" he asked logically.

Indecision ate away at Raven's resolve. Could it hurt to dance with Eben's friend while she awaited his return? Surely there was little harm in that! She bit her lip and looked around the room. She didn't see him anywhere. If she refused and Eben didn't return right away she would be forced to sit alone and watch as the other girls and women enjoyed themselves. The music *was* wonderfully lively, the attention of this handsome rogue a little intoxicating, and he *was* Eben's friend. "All right," she said suddenly, "but only if you promise to act like a gentleman."

"Upon my honor, my dear Rafe," he said with mock gravity.

Raven raised her eyes to his and quickly hid a smile. He was an outrageous rogue, but not without a certain dark charm. She felt her earlier misgivings thaw a little. It was only one dance, and she was sure that Eben would understand.

Eben had purchased the ring in Castle Ford that very morning, after Raven had gone to sleep in the room that was next to his. Made of the finest gold filigree, it was set with a multitude of tiny diamonds that would sparkle all the brighter from his lady's dainty finger. It had cost him dearly, but was worth every dollar since it would bind the lass to him for all their days. Once she slipped it on her finger she was declaring to the world that she would share his life, his love, his bed. He could hardly wait to speak with her, and lengthened his stride as he started down the hallway toward his chamber where the ring still waited on his chest of drawers.

It took but a moment for Eben to pocket the band, then go back down the hallway, whistling as he went along.

"Ladies and gentlemen!" Zeb's voice rang out above the heads of the dancers. "It gives me the greatest pleasure to announce the arrival of two very special guests! Their coming was unexpected, but nonetheless timely. May I present my daughter, Ivory, and her esteemed husband, the Honorable Senator Jameson Wharton!"

Raven froze at the mention of the woman's name. She turned toward the dais and saw the wealth of burnished copper hair, the slanting green eyes, and the pure alabaster skin. The woman's full mouth was smiling. The judge was saying something, but Raven didn't hear—neither did Ivory apparently, for her head came up sharply, all of her attention suddenly focused on the man just then descending the stairs.

"Rafe, what is it?" Tyler asked. All of the color had drained from her cheeks. "Would you like to sit down?"

"No, no, it's nothing!" she said quickly. How was she to tell him that her worst nightmare had just come true?

Raven stood frozen, seeing Eben's pale eyes clash with those of the judge's fiery daughter. Beside her Tyler saw it too. "It seems the past repeats itself," he said dryly. "Come, Rafe, don't let either of them catch you staring. I've learned from experience that the best way to combat any injury to the heart is to laugh it off. Never let them know that blood has been drawn; it only hastens the instinct for the kill."

"You intentionally misconstrue the entire situation," she told him, starting to break away. "He looks stricken; he needs me, Tyler."

"He isn't stricken, Rafe. He's mad as hell. And you aren't going near him. I care enough for you not to let you get caught in the crossfire between two such venerable foes." He was looking down into her small countenance and felt a sudden insane urge to protect her from what he suspected would come. She was young and innocent; she didn't deserve to be hurt at Eben's hands . . . or his own for that matter. "He's a grown man. He can take care of himself well enough without you."

"You don't understand," she said. "She hurt him

before, and he has suffered enough. If I can only spare him this!"

"My God," he said low, "if one woman somewhere had shown such care for my feelings, mightn't be the jaded man I am." He heard her sniff and cursed himself for being so weak livered as to let her tears affect him. "You owe me a dance and I mean to have it. Now come."

Chapter 23

"You needn't look so murderous, Eben, everyone is staring." Ivory watched his glower blacken even further and derived a perverse satisfaction from knowing she could still affect him—even if the only emotion she could drag from him was hatred.

"And what am I to do, smile like an idiot while forced to dance with a woman I detest?" Eben growled.

"A smile from you would be suspect. Only stop scowling, or the entire town will think you are jealous of Jameson."

Eben snorted. "In truth I feel only pity for the good senator. That is the only reason I agreed to lead you out, as his leg prevents him and he asked so prettily."

"Feeling guilty?" Ivory asked, looking up at him through her lashes.

"Not precisely guilt, Madam Wharton." He gave her a look that would have made most women turn and flee. "But I feel I owe the man something. After all, the one most deserving punishment walked away unscathed. It should have been you flying out of the window that night, not Jameson. Over the years I've come to believe the man a victim of circumstance."

"I always wondered why you didn't tell," she

said, still looking up into his handsome countenance. "You set such a store by the truth in the past."

"To spare your father the pain and humiliation of knowing what a faithless jade you truly are. Better that he believes that it was you who jilted me, than to know his only offspring for a grasping and unfeeling woman."

She smiled, completely unaffected by his words. Being encompassed by his ungentle embrace was bringing back a flood tide of erotic memories. Under her hands his muscles strained with tightly leashed passion. What matter did it make that it stemmed from a mixture of rage and bitterness, when the right words, the subtle stroking she had planned could turn it swiftly into something else, something just as potent. It was true that there was but a fine dividing line between love and hate. And she could make him love her again, she was sure of it! "I think that *ambitious* is a better term, Eben," she said, smoothing the wide lapel of his black cutaway coat with one hand. "And you can hardly call me unfeeling. What I felt for you back then has never diminished."

"Your warning is well taken," he said coldly. He refused to look at her, refused to rise to her bait, even though she continued to watch him closely all the while they danced. His gaze searched for and found Raven, still locked in Tyler Lee's strong arms. It grated hard on his already sorely frayed nerves that the Virginian should have the company of his love while he was stuck with this conniving bitch.

"They make a striking couple, don't they?" Ivory asked, not really expecting a reply. So this was the foundling girl her father had mentioned. Her catlike eyes narrowed. The girl was young and beautiful—her beauty fresh and dewy with none of the lines the cruel advance of age was etching on her own fine skin. "Tell me, Eben," she said at last, "is the child your mistress?"

"Raven is hardly a child," he said, hating the woman in his arms. She knew just how to nettle him, to raise his ire until he longed to close his hands around her slim white throat and squeeze until the life drained slowly out of her. It was the only thing between them that remained the same over the years, this swelling tide of anger in him she could summon with so little effort.

"That tells me much," she said, smiling knowingly.

He scowled down at her. "You will do well, Madam Wharton, to stay out of my life!"

She was far from rebuffed, Eben could see from the way her ruby lips curved in a lazy, seductive smile. Her eyes were heavy lidded, as though she had just been bedded and the opiate of her passion still rode her hard. Any who chose to look—and many of those gathered had been watching as the tumultuous couple took the dance floor by storm—would no doubt surmise that their amorous dealings of the past were far from being ended. Thankfully, the dance slid to a close and he turned abruptly and stalked to the sideboard, leaving her standing alone.

When Raven reached him he had replenished his glass a time or two with Zeb's most potent brew and stood frowning at the shining toes of his boots. He wanted more than anything to just take Raven's hand and lead her away, to forget Tyler and Ivory and his carefully planned evening that now was in shambles, but along with Raven came the Virginian, his rival for her affections. The bastard stood hovering just behind her shoulder, boldly ogling her breasts, daring to breathe the same air she breathed.

His anger mounted dangerously within him and he shot the other man a withering glare. "So you've done with her now, have you?" He reached in his pocket and produced a clean handkerchief, which he handed to Raven. "Kindly wipe the drool off your bosom."

Raven gasped at his crudity. She felt the sting of tears and turned to leave, but his hand closed over her arm, pulling her back. "Let go of me, Eben. You have no right!"

"As your guardian I claim the right! This blackguard would only use you and then toss you aside like so much soiled goods! He is one of the most degenerate men I know and you haven't the good sense to realize why he's sniffing around your skirts!"

"Now just a damned minute!" Tyler put in, his dark face livid. "You dare to demean this genteel lady when all she did the entire time was to worry over you! By God, sir, you owe her an apology!"

Eben released her and faced Tyler. His color was high and his pale eyes gleamed with open malice. "I've had just about enough of your meddling, Jackson—" He never got to finish what he'd been about to say, for Tyler's unforgiving fist smashed into his mouth, knocking him backwards and starting a brawl that was destined to become legend in Castle Ford.

The sound of a woman's weeping guided the victor unerringly to the very edge of the creek that flowed behind the inn. It was there that he found her, crying out her heart beneath the star-bright canopy of the midnight sky.

"Sweet Rafe," Tyler said softly, "do not cry so." The ease with which she came into his arms surprised and pleased him, and as she sobbed he held her tightly to him, offering her the comfort she should have received from Eben.

"Oh, Tyler Lee," she cried, her voice tight with tears, "what am I to do? My life is ruined!"

"Come now, little love, it can't be all that bad. He regrets what he said to you, he even told me so."

She raised her eyes to his face and saw the dark swelling beneath one eye, put there by Eben's fist. "You are a liar, but without a doubt the nicest one I know. I am sorry you had to suffer because of me."

"It's nothing compared to—" He had been about to blurt out the truth, that the man who offered her insult was now slumbering peacefully on the kitchen table while Sam Ruston ministered to his wounds. "—to others I have had. Don't let it concern you. The marks will fade in a day or two."

"If only my problems could be as easily solved," Raven said. They stood a moment in the quiet night and she began to shiver. She had come outside without her cloak and the night was cold. He must have noticed for he shrugged out of his coat and carefully placed it about her shoulders. The garment still carried the warmth of his body and Raven hugged it to her gratefully. He had been so kind to her, so undeserving of Eben's biting remarks. She felt she owed him something.

"Rafe, if you had it in your power to wipe clean the slate and begin again, would you?"

"Is isn't as simple as that."

"Perhaps it is. The solution to your problems with Eben stands very close at hand," he said. "It's been ages since I've had the opportunity to rescue a lady in need."

"You are very accomplished at it, and I thank you." She tried to smile through her tears, and as she raised her eyes to his she saw something there that frightened her. The laughing devil she had so swiftly grown fond of was gone now, vanished! In his place was a sweet and caring man whom she was bound to hurt. Her fingers stole along his cheek to touch the bruise that marred his skin. "There is no easy solution, Tyler Lee."

"Rafe. Open your eyes and look at me. Do you find you like what you see?" He put his hands on her shoulders and stared down at her. "Would it be so bad, waking up to this face every morning?"

She shook her head slowly, her eyes again filling with tears. "You shouldn't say such things."

"And why not?" he persisted. "Because Eben saw you first? It seems to me that he has had his chance. I don't know that he deserves another."

"You don't understand," she said.

"But I do," he insisted low. "I don't give a damn that you're in love with him. All I ask is a chance, Raven! Just let me love you and I promise you'll never regret it!"

Before she could make any objection he pulled her to him and his mouth covered hers in a kiss of infinite tenderness, a kiss calculated to persuade. His arms were strong enough to shelter her, a wonderfully effective buffer against a callous world, and she had only to give him a simple yes to end the conflict she found herself in. He kissed her long and thoroughly and only broke the contact to breathe against her throbbing lips, "Marry me, Raven."

"You are surely mad," she whispered.

"Perhaps, I am. But I have the power to make you forget you ever knew Eben St. Claire! And deep within your heart you know it's true!"

His mouth swiftly took hers again, harder now and more insistent than before. He would be an expert lover, there was no doubt, and for the first time she began to wonder if there was some truth to what he said. Had it not been for the quickening of Eben's babe in her womb at that very instant, she might have weakened enough to accept him.

Feeling the first weak flutter come again, this time stronger than before reminded her that there was more at stake than just her injured pride. She could not accept him now, or ever. Sighing inwardly, she put one hand on his chest and slowly pulled away. The hand was but a frail barrier to prevent his claiming her again, and she knew she could not withstand another assault on her already lowered defenses.

"You don't know what you say," she said, striving mightily to put some levity in her voice. "And in the light of day you will be glad that I refused your offer." She smiled bravely up at him through the thin veil of her tears, then pulling away, turned to make her way back to the inn and Eben.

"My offer stands!" he called after her retreating figure, and strangely enough he meant every word.

It was the force of habit that brought Meg from her bed at four o'clock to make her way to the kitchen. The guests had all gone and the inn was silent except for the clock that tirelessly counted down the hour. The noisy ticking that followed only served to remind her that there were those residing under this very rooftree who seemed bent upon wasting precious time when they could have been setting everything to rights. But no more! she told herself. If the stubborn fool needed prodding, then she was the very one to wield the staff.

When she pushed open the kitchen door she saw him sitting silently by the low burning fire, both hands wrapped around an empty cup. He was brooding, was he? Well she would give him something to brood about!

"I see you're up," she said scathingly, knowing full well he had never been to bed. She went to the hearth and taking up the coffeepot, refilled his cup with the strong black brew. He would need a good bracer.

The face he turned to her was bland. "What, no hemlock, Meg? Surely you have come to see that I am punished properly." He paused before adding, "Not that I don't deserve it."

"Looking in the mirror must have been punishment enough," she said. "I'll fetch you some ice in a little."

He waved her offer away. "I won't be here to take it. I'm leaving in a little while. It's best, I think, for all concerned."

"Oh, aye," Meggie said coolly, not yet ready to ignite the fuse that would blow apart his seeming apathy. " 'Tis best that you leave. And most especially for that young rascal, Tyler. I am sure he will thank you for taking yourself off. It makes a clear way for him, you see." She paused to wet a clean cloth in cold water and wring it out, handing it to him and watching him as he pressed it to his ravaged mouth. It cost him greatly to speak at all, but with Meg in a quarrelsome mood there would be no avoiding it. He waited patiently, knowing she had more to add. "Oh, and did I tell you that he has asked Raven to marry him?"

"Somehow I'm not surprised," he replied, feeling dejected. In the pocket of his coat lay the ring he'd pinned his hopes on. It was useless now. Perhaps he should sell it. His mind balked at the idea, but he told himself logically that to remove all reminders of Raven from his sight would be the best thing—the only thing for him to do. It would not be as easy to wipe her memory from his thoughts.

"Where will you be off to this time?" Meg asked.

"Downriver. After that—I don't know. What does it matter now?"

"Well, you're having a fine time pitying yourself." He steeled himself for all of her bitterness, knowing that she had had high hopes where Raven was concerned. But then, so had he. Now all of that was gone, wiped out in one disastrous evening. "Have you given a single moment's thought to what that girl will do without you? No, of course not! You're far too occupied with your own wounded pride to see how she will suffer when she awakes to find you gone!"

She paced a little before the hearth and Eben sipped his coffee. He had thought of nothing but Raven since he'd awakened hours before. It seemed likely that once he was gone she would accept the Virginian's offer of marriage. It was probably for the best, he told himself. Tyler could give her so much that he could not. There was no way Eben could fight the other man, save with his fists.

He looked up at Meggie, suddenly aware that she had stopped before him and stood with her hands on her hips. Was it the firelight that put that calculating gleam in her eyes or just some trick of his weary brain? She was readying herself for her next salvo and from her expression he knew it must be a good one. Since he was too stiff and sore to stir himself yet, he would be forced to sit it out.

But surprisingly there was only her soft question. "Do you love her, lad?"

He stared into his coffee and was a long time answering. "Aye," he said finally, "for all the good it does either of us. Sadly, it just isn't enough."

"Oh, you great bloody fool," Meg exclaimed softly. "Love is all there is. Nothing else on this earth matters, Eben. Go to her now, before it really *is* too late and tell her that you love her. Give her what she so richly deserves.

Eben only shook his head, seeing in his mind Raven's face as she had danced with Tyler Lee. "I am not the one she needs, Meg."

"Who then, more so than you, the father of the babe she carries?"

Slowly his head came up and he stared hard at Meggie. "How do you know this?"

"I know it, never mind how."

"But she never told me."

"Did you give her reason to?" Meg asked.

Meg. Ever the voice of reason.

"Think about it, Eben," she said. "Think about your own childhood . . . then tell me you'll let your son grow up without a father!"

"Going off again, are you?" The scene that greeted Tyler was an unsurprising one and he stopped to watch with a rueful expression as Eben pulled the saddle's cinch tight and adjusted his rifle in its leather scabbard. The fact that his friend refused to look up from his work came as no surprise either.

"That should make you happy," he said, continuing what he was doing. "It paves the way for you with Raven. With me gone you'll have an unobstructed course. I wish you luck, Lee, or at least a little more than I had. You'll need it if you're going to win the little wildcat." Eben patted Cadence's neck then took up the reins and led her from the stable.

"You're a damned fool for leaving now, you know," Tyler told him. Instead of opening the way for him with Raven, Eben was in effect slamming the door in his face. His wretched sense of honor was about to rear its ugly head, making it abhorrent to compete for her love while Eben's back was turned. What really galled him was that Eben knew it.

Eben swung into the saddle. "No one knows it better than I."

"Then, hell, man, why not stay, at least long enough to speak with her. You owe her that much."

"I owe Raven some peace of mind. She's had none at all since I stumbled across her path." He leaned down and offered his hand, but Tyler would not accept it. Instead he slapped the mare's rump, hard, and sent him on his way.

It was afternoon when Raven opened her eyes to find the rose upon her pillow. She thought it the most perfect bloom she'd ever seen, a rich red spot of color against the snowy whiteness of her pillow. There was only one man who would boldly enter her chamber when she was sleeping to leave the thornless token on her pillow.

She lifted the blossom and breathed the rare perfume of the lost days of summer. It reminded her poignantly of her first weeks with Eben—at the Galloways and in Pittsburgh, before he had brought her to this place and others came between them—and how very much she longed to call those days back.

Eben's chamber was next to hers and she heard someone moving around there. He was there alone; she would thank him for the rose and then they could have this matter out between them. She had decided to tell him of his child—their child. If he made no move to right the wrong then she would have to leave.

She slipped out of bed, donned his brown robe, and went to the door, opening it just a crack. No one was in the hallway; his door was ajar. Without knocking she opened the portal and stepped inside, closing the door and leaning against it.

Nan, the redhaired serving girl, looked up from her task of sweeping out the hearth.

"Oh," Raven said in a small voice. "I thought that you were someone else."

"The one you're looking for's gone," the girl said, her ash-smudged face showing her eagerness to impart this news.

"Gone . . ."

"Threw some stuff in a bag and went off down

the south road,'' Nan offered. ''I was sorry to see him leave. He's a bold, handsome devil, you know.''

''Yes . . . I know,'' Raven replied, her voice cracking with pain.

''Ah, there you are. I was beginning to think that that damned irascible Irishwoman hadn't given you my message.'' Zeb was alone in his study, comfortable amid his bookish clutter, knowing it was the one corner of the inn that Meggie's meddling hand dared not reach. He looked up as Raven entered the room and motioned for her to close the door behind her. ''It's a private matter we need to discuss and I won't have it bandied about the inn for the amusement of others.''

Raven's spine stiffened. Just as she had thought; he was about to upbraid her about her pregnancy. She steeled herself to accept his criticism in a silence that was far from ashamed. He could say what he would, but it would change nothing. She stopped before his desk and folded her hands before her, waiting.

Zeb searched his coat pockets a moment before producing a small brass key that he fitted into the top drawer of his desk. ''One cannot be too careful in a place such as this,'' he said. He slid out the drawer and from it removed a large envelope. ''Everyone here minds everyone else's business.''

From where she stood, Raven could see her name was scrawled across it in Eben's bold hand. Her heart was beating faster now and her hands began to tremble, a fact she tried to hide by clasping them together more tightly.

''Now then,'' the judge said, taking out a pair of spectacles and placing them with care on the end of his nose. The packet was in his hands, his attention focused for the moment upon it, instead of on Raven. ''This was entrusted to me by Eben, though as I told him this morning I doubt the wisdom in going through with it. However, as you must have discovered, he can be the most mule-headed of young men, and he was set that you should be made aware of it at this point. It contains—" and here he paused, for effect perhaps, and fixed Raven with his unwavering gray stare, "—a bank draft in the sum of five thousand dollars."

"Where would he get that kind of—" She didn't finish voicing the thought. There was no need. They both were well aware how he had come by that particular sum. He must have had it all along, and was only using it to buy his freedom. It was very clear to her now—Eben would not be coming home again.

"My dear girl, you're trembling! Here, let's get you into a chair."

Raven found no will to resist as Zeb helped her into a chair. He placed the envelope in her hands and her unsteady fingers smoothed the heavy paper. "This was to be my dowry," she said softly. "I thought that it was lost, yet all this time Eben had it. Where did he find it? How?"

Zeb cleared his throat and frowned, looking at the ceiling. "Here, let's see, I believe he said that your brother entrusted it to him for safekeeping before you left Ohio. Perhaps I mistook him when he said you had no family."

"Tecumseh." Not only had he gifted them with their lives, but he had restored to her her fortune and provided her with her freedom. She was a woman of means now, and if she so wished, she could leave this place and all of its memories behind.

"Raven, I hope that you will stay and make the inn your home," Zeb said after a while. Gone was all of his courtroom manner; he slipped out of it as easily as someone shrugging off a cumbersome coat.

It rather caught Raven by surprise. He must have

known from her expression what was in her mind. "Meggie has grown very fond of you—her hopes were riding high, you know. If his absence proves of a like length as the last one, she will have need of someone."

Yes, or longer. Eben would not be here for the birth of their babe, and he would grow to manhood without ever knowing his father. But he would know of him, through her, she would see to it. And their child would never suffer the dearth of affection that Eben had known as a child.

When she gained her feet again the trembling had subsided. "I will accept your offer, Judge McAllister, with gladness. At least for the winter. And who can say what the new year might bring?" He had risen when she had, and now she went and stood on her toes beside him, straining up to kiss his weathered cheek. "Thank you. You have all been very kind to me."

The judge cleared his throat, obviously unused to any show of affection. "Well," he said gruffly, "go and console that Irish peahen. I suppose she's cried herself dry by now."

Raven opened the door to find Ivory on the other side. She could have sworn that the woman had been eavesdropping, but her expression was one of bland distaste.

"The belle of the ball, I see," the woman uttered so that only Raven could hear. "Your position as mistress to two such handsome men is enviable indeed. Pray, tell me, how does it feel to play with both of them? I can imagine it must keep you extremely busy. Especially since Eben's sexual appetite is at times—insatiable."

Raven held her temper in check with a will and managed deftly to reply in kind. "Oh? And did you find it so, Madam Wharton? How strange that he was not so with me. One might ask oneself if perhaps he found your talents lacking.''

She heard the older woman's gasp and knew that she had scored in this small battle of wits. Ivory's scathing remarks had cut to the quick as they were meant to, but as Raven made her way from the room, she kept her head held high and clung to the hope that the woman and her husband would soon be gone.

Chapter 24

"I am sorry that your wait has been a lengthy one. I was in Cincinnati visiting my sister and only just returned late last night. It wasn't till this morning that Janie told me you were here." Emery Hargraves settled back in his chair and regarded the other man with curiosity. In their brief acquaintance he had known his client to be notably short on patience, but Janie, his housekeeper, had reported that the man had appeared each and every morning for nearly a month, inquiring politely after his return. Now he stood at the window, looking out over the street as if his mind were suddenly elsewhere.

"I regret that I have so little to offer you, Mr. St. Claire," Hargraves continued. "You have come a long way for nothing. There has been no word at all from Louisiana. Of course, that doesn't rule out the chance that a reply will arrive any day. The mails being what they are, with letters sometimes passed hand to hand, any answer coming will be slow at best."

Eben's gaze absorbed the activity on the busy street, but his thoughts were far away. "It's no more than I expected," he said.

"I wish that I could do better for you," Hargraves said. "Maybe by spring . . ."

"No. I won't be making any further inquiries into

the matter," Eben said. "It's time to lay the past to rest." He took a heavy purse from his coat and tossed it to Hargraves. "This should be an ample settlement of my debt."

"It's more than generous, sir," Hargraves said, palming the coins. "If you change your mind—" he hastened to say, but regrettably the man was already gone.

Evening was but an hour old, but outside the shining panes of the common room windows the deep blue of a midwinter's eve had descended. Now and again Raven glanced up from the wreath she was fashioning for Meggie of greens and nuts and fruits to be placed upon the front portal, and observed the fat flakes of the winter's first heavy snowfall drifting slowly past the crystalline panes. This activity reminded her poignantly of her father, Henri, and of Christmastides gone by, even if these English customs weren't her own.

She heard the sound of stomping feet outside and masculine voices. The door opened to admit a blast of bitter cold that made Raven hug her lacy shawl a little closer. She smiled at the sight of the four men, Tyler among them, his dark hair sprinkled with snow, who struggled to carry the huge yule log into the room. They put it down with a chorus of groans and hurried to crowd around the wassail bowl Meggie had made earlier that evening, not even waiting for Judge McAllister to approve their work.

Only Tyler Lee abstained, opting instead to warm himself at the fireside. And if his position afforded him an advantageous view of Raven, then no one seemed concerned enough to remark upon the fact. His warm gaze was ever wont to touch her downcast eyes, her small, delicate hands so adept at turning the simple items at hand into a quaint decoration worthy of the highest praise. He had not pressed his suit since that night at the Hunter's Ball, but it remained constant in his mind. And the fact that her gowns were no longer hiding the small mound of her belly gave him a grim sort of hope. If Eben chose not to return, her babe would need a father. It mattered not at all to Tyler Lee that the child had been fathered by another; there was no question that he would love it as he already loved its mother. He was a patient man. He could wait.

A mile to the south the little mare was floundering in the deep drifts. The powdery flakes that had begun to drift lazily down from a winter white sky the previous noon had gained steadily in density and momentum, swiftly mounting until two feet and more covered the ground, clogging the roads and making travel nearly impossible.

The cold blast that had blown into the inn moments before swept ruthlessly downriver to send particles of frozen moisture flying into Eben's face and down his neck. Since he was already half frozen, it no longer carried with it the same sting as before. He was numb to pain, and only his mind stayed alert, his body having long since gone to sleep from exposure to the cold.

Christmas Eve. It had been so many years ago, but still he could not forget the spirit of revelry that infected the old stone building and its inhabitants as the holiday grew nigh. His mind was filled with the clean smell of fresh-cut pine, the aroma of baked goods from Meg's kitchen that even now, miles away in the throes of this bitter winter storm could make his mouth water. Just one mile more and he would be there, warming himself at the hearth, thawing out his frozen limbs and feeling the painful tingle as the flesh came back to life again.

All of it was a surety. It was waiting for him. But it wasn't the reason he kept pushing his mount onward when she had little heart left in her to continue wading through the deep drifts. It was the small bit of hope he had left in him that, like a flickering tongue of flame in a dying fire, refused to be extinguished, the hope that when he stumbled in the door Raven would still be waiting.

The kitchen table was groaning beneath the weight of pies and puddings, cakes and pastries Meggie had finished baking that very afternoon. Having just finished putting the final bough of pine over the last windowsill, Meg entered the kitchen to replace the shears and cord she carried. But the figure she saw hunched in her chair drawn up close before the hearth made her stop short, her hand flying to her throat as she let out a startled little cry.

The face Eben turned to her was still red from the cold, his fingers, she noted, were curled yet, as if they'd been frozen around his reins. He made no move to stand, only smiled at her a little stiffly, as though the effort cost him. "The pie smells good, Meg," he said quietly. "I swear it drew me all the many miles upriver."

"You're home!"

He put a finger to his lips. "Let's leave it between the two of us. Is she still here, Meg?"

"Aye, she's here, poor thing. Where does she have to go?"

"It seemed likely that she might opt for a warmer clime," he said.

"You misjudge her, Eben, and him. He has been a perfect gentleman, and shielded many a cruel barb from that—woman! He protected her when you did not. Raven is grateful to him, and so am I."

"She has my protection now," he said firmly. "But what is this of Ivory? Why is she still here? And what has she done to Raven? If she's harmed her in any way I swear I'll—"

"No, she hasn't. Ivory decided to remain with her father for the holiday, and Jameson, the poor fool, has been traveling back and forth from Washington. Please don't speak of vengeance. It's a holy day, a day for celebration now that you are here. The lass was fairly put out with you for not telling her you were leaving or when you would be back. But I'll wager she'll thaw quickly enough once she sets eyes on you again."

"I was fair put out with her for not telling me I'm soon to be a father," he replied. "As for thawing, could you send me up a hot bath? Damned if I don't feel like an icicle." He worked his fingers and frowned. "Is she well?"

Meggie smiled. "She's rounding nicely. Now hurry up the stairs and I'll breathe not a word. I'll bring the water directly, then you can see for yourself."

Meggie went to him and laid her hand on his shoulder. He covered it with his icy one and said, "It's good to know you're on my side, Meg." He rose to go, but instead of quitting the room directly, he made his way to the table and stood looking down at her culinary efforts.

"I had hopes you would come to your senses," she said.

"A man would be a genuine fool to miss your pie." Despite the chill of his hands he managed the knife with ease, helping himself to a generous piece that he swiftly dispatched.

"Go on with you!" Meggie said.

He gave her a grin and went up the back stairs.

An hour had passed since Eben had gone to his chamber, and now the family gathered around the long oaken board, along with a few selected guests, including Tyler and young Jedediah from the stables. Heading the table was Judge McAllister, revered for his senior years and his patriarchal status at the inn. From this position, and with a captive audience, he could manipulate the conversation as he saw fit. Senator Wharton sat at the judge's right, listening as attentively as his growling stomach would allow while his father-in-law rattled on about county matters of little interest to Jameson.

Across the board from her husband and on her father's left, Ivory picked at her food. This country fare hardly suited a palate accustomed to the finest menus Washington had to offer, though as she watched Raven through slitted eyes, she saw the girl had no such qualms or lack of appetite. Indeed, the lowborn wench seemed to be enjoying herself thoroughly as she smiled at some comment the handsome dark-haired Virginian rogue had made.

With deepening ire Ivory noticed the heightened pink of Raven's cheeks, the bright sparkle contained in the depths of her brown eyes, and how the candlelight enhanced a skin that was completely free from blemish.

The younger woman was radiant with the natural glow of youth and some deep inner happiness that she couldn't begin to fathom. She seemed not at all bothered by Eben's continued absence—but then why should she be while another danced attendance on her. He was just as handsome, and certainly his wealth far exceeded Eben's. This slip of a girl had the world on a string, while Ivory was stuck with Jameson.

If the candlelight complemented Raven's beauty, it only served to make Jameson look more like a toad in Ivory's estimation.

She frowned, her eyes sliding again to Raven, widening as she saw the dainty hand that slipped beneath the table and went almost unconsciously to the small distended round of her belly.

Ivory felt a shock go through her. The evil chit

was breeding! She chided herself for not noticing it before, but the high-waisted gowns so fashionable now hid the fact well enough from all but the most observant of eyes. It therefore followed that Meggie, with her sharp eyes, would be well aware of the fact. That would explain that smug look the former bondwoman wore. Nothing would please that Irish witch more than to have this backwoods trash whelping Eben's bastards.

Ivory's lips thinned to a line in a face gone deathly pale. There had to be some way of undermining the girl's position in the household, some sure way of having her removed from the premises before Eben returned. Covertly she continued to observe the girl, seeing how the Virginian sought to entertain her, even as her father's voice penetrated her thoughts.

Surely the honorable and revered judge would not be pleased at having his beloved hostelry turned into a breeding pen for this slut and her many suitors. The mental image of her rival being cast out into the cold brought a sudden smile to Ivory's mouth.

"How long did you think to hide it, my dear?" she asked, not bothering to lower her voice. The question stilled all conversation at the table. Jameson shifted uncomfortably in his chair, having felt the lash of his wife's tongue countless times himself. At the head of the board, the judge frowned heavily.

"I have no need to hide anything, Madam Wharton," Raven said, but her cheeks were slowly suffusing with color.

"No." Ivory laughed shortly. "You seek to flaunt your lack of morals before good folk who tried to treat you with kindness. My father took you in and treated you as he would a kinswoman! And how do you repay this kindness?"

"Ivory, shut up!" Meggie hissed from down the table. "Raven has done nothing."

"Nothing!" Ivory said scathingly. "Somehow I'm

not surprised that you would think her bearing some sireless whelp is of no importance! You are common, Meggie, and unable to understand the sensibilities of your betters."

"If being common means that I have some thread of common decency and Christian love for my own kind, then aye, Mrs. Wharton, I am very common. You would do well to use your own good sense and shut your mouth, lest you regret it."

Ivory saw the dangerous glitter in Meggie's eyes, but attributed it quite mistakenly to the older woman's rising fury. Turned as she was toward Raven and Meg and away from the staircase, she could not see the man just then descending it. Hearing Ivory's words, Eben stopped short.

"What right have you to tell me what to say?" Ivory snapped. "You're a servant! I cannot imagine why Daddy has put up with your insolent tongue all these years! Had it been up to me, I would have ordered it cropped!"

"Mrs. Wharton," Tyler said silkily, "you are tread ing dangerous ground. I would remind you that this is Christmas Eve and no time for such mean abuse of those innocent of any wrong."

"Oh, do shut up! You have no business here! I don't know your reasons for defending this Celtic hag, but your motives for defending the girl are blatantly obvious! Tell me, Mr. Jackson, who will claim the right to bounce this bastard on his knee, you or Eben St. Claire? Or could it be that there is not one among the three of you who truly knows?"

"The paternity of the child is not in dispute here." Eben's voice sliced through the heavy atmosphere, stilling every voice but Ivory's.

"Well, returns the merry wanderer," she said scathingly. "And just in time to rescue this poor homeless waif from her tormentors! Your timing always was perfect, Eben."

"Much to your regret," he said. His gaze went to Raven, who was trembling visibly, her eyes fixed on her plate. He tried to determine if she was quaking from rage or embarrassment, but could not tell as his attention was abruptly dragged back to Ivory.

"You see what you'll have with him, my dear," she said, leaning forward to look at Raven. "Leaving you alone for months at a time, then blowing in like an ill wind. Better that you take your bastard and fly before it's too late. Your pillow will ever be wet with tears, while his is empty."

"Enough!" It was Zeb who finally silenced his daughter's harping. "You abuse freely those lodging beneath my roof. Be reminded, daughter, that you are but a guest here yourself."

Raven pushed her chair away from the table and slowly made her way toward the stairs, brushing past Eben without so much as a single glance.

He grabbed for her arm, intending to beg a word with her alone, but she snatched it away from him. "Leave me be! Do you think that you can leave without so much as a word and return to have everyone bow at your sainted feet? I don't know what you want with me, but I can tell you that I want nothing from you!"

"Raven, wait!" he shouted after her, but she was running up the stairs. In a moment his low curse was punctuated by the thunderous slam of her chamber door.

"Madam," Eben snarled at Ivory. "I told you once before to stay out of my life. Now I warn you, if you prize that scrawny neck of yours you will not further abuse my loved ones." He started from the room, intending to go after Raven, but Zeb's cutting voice called him back.

"Eben, I would like to have a word with you in my study."

"It can wait, Zeb."

"It has waited long enough, I think you will agree. This has to do with Raven's future." Zeb stood, pinning Tyler with his steely gaze. "Mr. Jackson, I sense that you have a vested interest in the outcome of this matter, so you may join us."

"The hell he does!" Eben stalked angrily to the study, leaving the other two men to follow in his wake.

"I see no need for this discussion," Eben said. He refused to take the chair that was indicated, but went to stand with his back to the cold hearth.

"There is every need," the judge interjected. "Raven's future must be decided tonight, and that of her bairn. Now, I have sent Meggie to bring her here. As soon as she arrives, we can begin."

"Then at least have the decency to get him out of here. This has nothing to do with him. Your daughter's lies stem from the malice she still harbors for me. The babe is mine, and had everyone minded their own affairs I would have resolved the matter this evening. I've come back to marry her."

"Raven seems an intelligent lass," Zeb observed. "Therefore she can speak for herself and her intentions."

"That doesn't tell me what the devil he is doing here!" Eben thrust a hand in Tyler's direction, but Tyler remained seated, his expression bland. He was too calm, and Eben felt his irritation mount sharply.

"Then allow me to explain," the Virginian said smoothly. "I spoke to the judge a few days ago and expressed my intention of marrying Raven."

"I'll see you in hell first," Eben stated with deadly calm. His pale eyes were flinty as they rested on his rival, who slowly rose out of his chair.

"You are certainly welcome to try, sir."

"Sit down, both of you!" Zeb ordered. He was almost relieved when Raven's hesitant knock sounded on the closed door. He called for her to enter and offered her a reassuring smile as she came into the room.

Raven was uneasy. She closed the door behind her, unsure what to expect. Her gaze went from one face to the next. Eben was looking murderous, and a sudden thought struck her with dread. The judge, with all of his ability for judicial fairness, was trying to iron out this mess she found herself in. From the expression Eben wore, she could guess that he was being given no choice except to marry her, and he was far from pleased at the prospect. Vainly, she tried to swallow the lump that kept creeping into her throat, and glanced at Tyler Lee. His gaze softened as their eyes met, and she saw him offer her a lazy wink. She would have smiled, had she not been so nervous. He was incorrigible, and never took anything seriously.

"Come in, Raven," Zeb said as softly as he could manage. "Come and have a seat while I explain the reason you were asked down here."

"You needn't explain, Judge McAllister, and I assure you I'll be leaving just as soon as I can make the arrangements."

"You're not going anywhere!" Eben spoke up suddenly. "That's my son you carry. Do you think I will allow you to disappear again?"

"Your son?" Raven asked coldly. "As I see it this babe belongs solely to me. I neither want nor need your vigilance as guardian—nor anyone's, for that matter."

The judge harrumphed. "Both of these gentleman—and I use the term loosely—" Zeb said, peering at each man in turn, "have expressed the hope of winning your fair hand and the right to claim the child you carry as his own. I remain impartial, so the final choice is yours to make, though I would recommend that you choose one or the other, as the babe is unquestionably without guilt in this matter and should not be punished because of the foolishness of his parents—whomever they may turn out to be. What do you have to say?"

Raven opened her mouth to say that she wanted neither man, but Eben shot out of his seat and demanded to be heard. "I have a prior claim here, to both Raven and my son. Surely that entitles me to something. Zeb, for the love of Christ, grant me a moment alone with her!"

"I have nothing to say to you," Raven said. If she was left alone with him she would weaken, and she wasn't quite ready to relinquish her anger or her hurt at his having left her.

"Zeb?" he persisted.

"Five minutes, no more," Zeb allowed. "Then Raven must have her say."

"It's all I ask," Eben said, taking hold of Raven's arm and propelling her to the study door.

At the front door, Meggie waited with a vermillion cloak draped over her arm. She was smiling as she placed it carefully around Raven's shoulders. Raven felt the weight of the fur-lined velvet and looked questioningly at the woman. But Eben wouldn't allow her any time for questions as he indicated that she step into a pair of leather boots and he urged her outside into the night.

Chapter 25

The snow had slackened its pace and was now drifting down from a sky of midnight blue, fat flakes that came to rest on Raven's cloak and uncovered hair and collected on the shoulders of Eben's coat. They had only gone a little way from the inn, very near the three towering hemlocks that stood sentinel in the inn yard. It was to them Eben pulled her, and under their spreading, snow-laden boughs that he turned her to face him. His hands were cutting through the folds of her soft new cloak, hurting her arms, testifying to the intensity of his fury.

"You can't be serious about marrying Tyler," he ground out.

"Can't I?" she asked, her voice smooth as silk. His peremptory tone stirred her anger. Did he think he could just appear after a month had passed—a month during which she had resigned herself to the idea that he had abandoned her and would never return—and have her swoon at his feet? He had yet to apologize for his boorish behavior the night of the Hunter's Ball, the last night they'd seen each other, the night he had fought with Tyler. And until he did, she owed him nothing.

"What has gone on between the two of you since I left?" he asked angrily. "Is he your lover, Raven? Have you got that grinning bastard warming your bed now?"

She raised her hand to strike him, but he caught it easily. "My life is no concern of yours! If I wish to have one—or a hundred lovers—it is none of your business. Now, if you will unhand me I will go back inside."

"Not until we have this out."

"There is nothing more to say, Eben." She tried to pull free, but he held her fast in a grasp as unyielding as iron.

"You're very wrong, my lady." The feel of her sweet form wrapped in the cloak he had presented her was affecting him, draining away his anger, softening his tone. "There is much that has been left unsaid between us, and I intend to have it out. I have waited and bided my time, I have been the soul of patience while others have schemed to come between us, but no more!"

"Indeed, the very soul of patience," Raven said derisively. "Battering and bellowing your way through life as though nothing else matters save your own selfish wants and needs. I do not need to hear more from you unless it is an apology!"

"And who deserves this apology, Raven? Tyler? An unprincipled blackguard whose own blood kin do not tolerate his scandalous actions? A man who would steal you away from me simply to test my ire? I can tell you there will be no such apology forthcoming!"

"If you dragged me out here in the cold to fight—"

"No, not to fight," he said with quiet vehemence. "To set things right." He had no intention of arguing with her when he'd brought her out here, and now time as dwindling. "I cannot compete with his wealth, Raven. If it's money you want then go to him. But if you care at all for the outpourings of an admitted fool, then pray, sweetheart, listen to me."

"I listened before, that night on the cliffs, for all

the good it did me. I gave my all to you, Eben! I kept hoping—oh, it makes no difference now!"

"Hoping that I would ask you to be my wife," he finished for her. His voice was unsteady and he was grateful for the darkness, grateful she could not see how desperate he really was. "The night of the ball—I never got the chance. First there was Tyler, stealing you away, openly seducing you with his blasted charms . . . and then Ivory, with her insinuations."

"You were so hateful," she said.

"I was jealous! All my carefully made plans thwarted by a man who has so much more to offer," he said. "And I had to stand by and watch as it all dissolved before me."

"And a woman who is panting to have you back in her bed. What of Ivory, Eben? How does she fit into your life?" Raven had to know.

"She is nothing to me," he said, pulling her against him. He could feel the resistance of her body, knew that she was still angry, and yet she did not struggle to free herself. She seemed to be waiting, perhaps sensing what was to come. "Raven," he murmured, threading the fingers of one hand into the neat chignon of her blue-black tresses. With one deft motion of his hand the pins were scattered on the snow, forgotten, as his lips tenderly grazed first her brow, then her lids. "Ivory is my past, Raven. You are my future."

Raven's lids slowly came down and she felt his hard mouth take hers. What little will she might have summoned to resist him quickly vanished, leaving only Eben. It would be like this always, throughout eternity—he would lead and she would follow, to the ends of the earth if need be.

When he broke the contact and stepped back, Raven was left gazing at him in bewildered silence. As if in a dream, she saw him drop slowly to one knee in the snow. She looked down at him. This couldn't be happening, she thought. It must be some sort of waking dream. But his words came pouring out, stunning her to silence.

"I have but little that I can offer you," he was saying, "my name, my love, my loyalty. Any home that I could provide will be of necessity a simple one. This is most difficult for me, Raven. I vowed long ago never to bend to any man, and now I find I am more willing to beg you, if it furthers my case, to marry me.

"Accept my suit, sweetheart, and all I have is yours without reserve. Deny me and I will be crushed. You have it in your power to gain a fine revenge for past injustices. Deny my heart the sustenance it craves and it will wither and die, I swear! Only tell me you will be my bride and together we will build a life!"

There was a long pause during which Raven heard the front door of the inn open and close. She heard him draw a deep breath and heard his voice low, sensing within it his aching need. "Love me, lass," he asked, "please."

He waited for the yes he hoped would come, but there was only silence. Eben slowly got to his feet. Against his ribs his heart throbbed painfully. His worst fear was about to be realized. She was going to deny him, and there was little left for him to say. For a long moment he just stood before her, still holding her hands in his. Then with exquisite slowness he brought her hands to his lips, kissing first one palm, then the other.

Dazed, Raven let him lead her back to the inn. After the frigid cold of the starless night, the common room was warm and inviting. On the hearth the blaze still danced and crackled merrily. They crossed to the judge's study and Eben opened the door. Both men raised expectant faces as Raven preceded him into the room and the door was closed firmly behind them.

Zeb frowned. He had hoped that this volatile couple would resolve their differences on their own, but seeing Eben sink wearily into a chair, his expression kept carefully blank, told him that all had not gone well. Zeb cleared his throat and fixed Raven with his steady gaze. "Raven, have you come to a decision?" He had to ask the question twice before he got any response.

She slowly nodded.

Tyler glanced down at the hand that rested for the barest instant on his shoulder, but his face was grim with defeat. Somehow he couldn't summon the feeling of joy he knew should come at knowing he had won. His sympathy went to Eben as he walked from the room.

Eben knew that Meg was speaking to him, but he didn't acknowledge her anxious query. He didn't want to think just now, so keenly did he feel his loss. He only wished to drown himself in drink and hope that it would numb the pain that filled the hole where his heart once had been.

"Well, I must say that I am pleased," Zeb said. "But you had best go and find him before he throws himself from a window, or does something equally drastic." He watched Raven turn and make her way slowly from the room. Then Zeb turned his attention to consoling the loser.

"Instead of offering my condolences I will present you with something a little more substantial." His gray eyes glinted as he opened a drawer in his desk and produced a bottle of rye whiskey. "Merry Christmas, Mr. Jackson. I trust you will recover."

"You wouldn't care to join me before I attempt to drown my sorrows in the solitude of my room?" Tyler asked.

"I admire a man who can lose his heart without losing his sense of humor," Zeb said. He brought two glasses out of the same drawer and placed them within Tyler's reach. "For emergencies, mind you."

They raised their glasses. "Long life and good health, sir!" Zeb said.

"To good whiskey and warm, willing women," Tyler Lee countered with a self-deprecating grin.

The weariness that had settled in after he left the judge's study was good, Eben thought, stripping off his clothing. He always took care to fold his things and stack them neatly on his trunk at the foot of the tester bed, but this night was different. Where they happened to fall was where they remained, and in a few seconds he threw back the covers and climbed into bed, naked. The bottle of whiskey Meg had given him earlier to warm him sat on a bedside table. He pulled the cork with his teeth and spat it on the floor, then tilted up the bottle for a long draught.

He placed the bottle, devoid of its stopper, back on the table and fell back on the bed. Even the whiskey had lost its allure. For a long while he lay there just staring up at the ceiling, seeing only the muted black of the night, sensing the empty void of a bleak future stretching endlessly out before him. He must decide what he would do tomorrow. There was nothing now to keep him here, no reason to stay in Castle Ford. He would sell the land he had only just bought from Sarah Fletcher, and set out for . . . where? What matter did it make where he ventured? So long as it was far from this unlucky place and all of its ghosts.

He must have fallen asleep, for he wakened sometime later, disoriented. Someone was tapping on his door most insistently, demanding admittance. The last thing he wanted tonight was to talk, to give the impression of civility when at present he felt civil towards no one. He cursed and pounded the pillow before dragging it over his head to block out the nagging sound, but it would not relent. "Is there no peace at all for a man in this place!" he growled and climbed from the bed to stalk angrily to the door.

If his state of undress offended the sensibilities of this nocturnal pest then he considered it fair payment for the intrusion. He jerked the door open and growled at the shadowy figure before he realized it was Raven.

She was wearing his robe, he noticed. An odd thing, to wear one man's garment while intending to wed another. His eyes went over her in the brief instant they stood there—he barring the entrance with his body, she wishing he didn't look so distractingly virile, so at ease with his nudity—and he couldn't help but envy the garment that wrapped its warm folds around her sweet form, enfolding her in its softness as he so longed to do and could not.

"May I come in?" she asked finally. "Or will you keep me waiting here all night?"

"Do you think that's wise? I'm hardly fit to receive company, and your lover awaits your coming, I've little doubt. He's very jaded, you know."

"Well, I prefer to think of him as . . . experienced."

"Oh, aye, he is that!" Eben agreed. "Have you any idea of the extent of that experience? Why, I could tell you tales—" He broke off, feeling disgusted with himself for slandering the man she had chosen over him. It was jealousy that was speaking, and he was uncomfortable with that knowledge. "Raven, what do you want?"

"You are very dense, Eben," she said. "Have you been drinking?" She stepped close and put her small face to his. "You have been drinking!"

"Raven, lass, if this is some way of getting even with me for what has passed between us—"

"A woman comes to your chamber door and begs entrance and you are hesitant to let her in? Is this the Eben St. Claire of old?" She looked at him askance. "The very same who pursued me so relentlessly just months ago?"

Eben still held the latch in his hand and now his fingers tightened over it. He saw the tiny smile that curved her lips. She was taunting him, damn her, flaunting what she knew he craved but could no longer have. It was cruel of her and he felt his bitterness deepen. If she is willing to take the chance, he thought, then who are you to suggest caution?

He stepped back suddenly and held the door wide for her to enter, watching the slow sway of her hips under the robe. His body reacted to her presence with a swiftness that was almost painful. If this was some game she sought to play, pitting him against the Virginian, then she should be more wary. He had little left to lose, and the thought of having her writhing beneath him on the big soft bed a final time tempted him sorely.

"I have ever been reckless, Eben," she said softly, her fingers traveling to the belted waist of his wrapper, "treading unwisely where a more prudent woman would not think of going. Safe choices have never been my way. I realized that tonight."

He made no move to close the little distance between them, but stood very still, watching with hungry eyes as the belt loosened and the robe slipped down over her softly rounded shoulders, baring inch by lovely inch the highest curves of the silken mounds that drew and held his attention, that made his hands itch to touch them, his loins throb with the strength of his need. "Do not remind me. It is painful enough," he said.

"It is a memory I will cherish," she said softly.

"Aye, I can imagine you will hug it to you always."

The heavy sarcasm in his words made her want to throw her arms around him and end this scene between them. She did step closer to him and lay her palm against his cheek, while he looked down at her, his pale eyes wary. "And where is your intended bridegroom that you are here with me? Does he know that his most precious possession is about to be stolen by another man?"

"He is here, Eben," she murmured softly, rising on her toes to brush her mouth against his. Her tongue caressed the full sensuous curve of his lower lip before entering his mouth to playfully tussle with his.

"Do not taunt me, Raven," she heard him warn, his mouth leaving hers to blaze a scalding trail of kisses down her throat. At her collarbone he paused to nibble gently the scented flesh before continuing downward . . .

"I will never offer what I cannot give."

His head came up and he stared hard at her, as if he could by his gaze alone determine the truth of what she said. "Is this some joke, mademoiselle? For if it is, I am not amused."

"Oh, Eben, there is only you! For me there is no other man." She kissed him hungrily, pressing her naked length to his and feeling his manhood leap in primitive reply. Instinctively it pressed against the product of their joining and within her womb the child stirred. "I want to marry you . . . only you. I love you, Eben."

"And what of Tyler Lee?" he asked.

She met his gaze steadily, her long-lashed eyes a molten brown. "Judge McAllister bade me to choose. And I have made that choice. I am prepared to live with it. Are you?"

"Aye, little cat." His hands were already gliding over her, traveling up her arms and down across her shoulders to her breasts. The pearly mounds had become fuller with her pregnancy and threated to overflow his hands. He cupped them gently, his mouth tempting the sleeping coral tip to tingling life.

Raven murmured his name and kissed his gleaming hair. He was more precious to her than life itself, and she vaguely wondered how she had ever thought him less than the perfect mate. "Eben?"

"Aye?" he replied, lifting her in his arms and carrying her to the bed.

"Will you love me forever?"

"Throughout eternity," he said. He placed her on the bed and joined her there. With the quilts drawn high around them it would make a warm and cozy love nest. Eben sank back in the pillows and watched her as she moved about, seeking a comfortable spot. "No more cold and lonely winter nights," he said. "I think that this arrangement may just have its merits." He reached out and pulled her atop him. "Come hither, wench, your master is cold."

"Master?" Raven bristled. "If the only reason you are willing to marry me is to warm your bed, then I think I've changed my mind." She threw back the covers and tried to rise from the bed, but he kept a firm grasp on her arms.

In one swift movement Eben rolled and put her beneath him on the bed. "I am marrying you, madam, because I cannot live without you. And because you are the mother of my child. Is that not reason enough?"

"Eben, I will be no man's slave!"

"I was but teasing," he relented. "Come, now, be serious," he cajoled softly, his large hand settling on the mound of her belly. "Does it pain you much?" he asked when the child stirred against him.

Raven shook her head.

"And can we still—?"

Slowly she nodded, bring back the wolfish grin she once had so detested.

The world had never seen a more tender, caring lover than Eben proved to be that night. There was no need for haste; they had a lifetime of loving stretching out before them. His gentle kiss, his sweet caress prompted Raven's blissful sighs. She clung to his muscular form, wishing this night would never end. When at last the blaze of passion flaring so brightly between them had settled down to a glowing ember, Raven drifted into a peaceful sleep, safe in the knowledge that Eben would be there when she awoke.

"Do you truly like it, sweet?" Eben was pulling on his boots, but paused to look at his intended bride who sat admiring the vermillion cloak.

"It's beautiful, Eben," she replied, and went to kiss his cheek. "I shan't be cold this winter. You are most thoughtful, and I must find a way to thank you properly."

"I have a few suggestions, madam, if you would care to listen." She made a face at him and laid her cheek against the fur lining.

"Did you get the pelts during a wolf hunt?" she asked.

He shook his head. "West of the Rockies. Up on the Bighorn River."

"I have never seen a white wolf," she mused.

"It's silver, my love," he corrected her. "See these long guard hairs running down the center back, how black they are? They lend the pelt its value." He was pointing out the qualities of the pelt, but Raven was gazing at his face, thinking how happy she was to have him for her own. Their eyes met and his softened, much like winter ice melting.

"You have much to learn," he said quietly. "What do you say to living in the wilderness? If I asked you to, would you go there with me?"

"I will go anywhere," she replied readily.

"Good. Then what do you say to going downstairs with me. I'm hungry as hell."

Raven laughed. "You are always hungry. Beware, m'sieur, for if you grow fat like the senator I will leave you."

"You needn't worry," Eben assured her. "When James St. Claire was hung he was fifty-one years old, and as slim as a lad of eighteen. My mother told me before she died that I very much favored him. I only hope not to end my days in the same fashion."

Despite the warmth of the fur cape, she shuddered. "Don't speak of such things."

"It has been the way in my family to meet a violent end. However, I intend to change that tradition." He spoke evenly, almost with levity, and Raven knew she was being childish, but there was some inner fear his words had conjured up that she simply could not dispel.

That evening they gathered in the common room around a roaring fire. Outside the wind whipped around the eaves, making eerie noises that penetrated Raven's best attempt at cheeriness. She had tried hard to banish the unease brought on by Eben's words that morning, but like a dark bird of foreboding, it kept coming back to beat shadowy wings near the fringes of her thoughts.

"Have you ever skated, Raven?" Meggie was asking.

Raven raised her quizzical gaze and asked, "What did you say? I'm afraid I didn't hear you."

"For all the world, she looks frightened half out of her wits. Can it be, Eben, that she realizes too late her mistake?" Eben shot Ivory a dark look before turning away, prompting her tinkling laughter to ring out. Looking now at Raven, she feigned sympathy. "I can imagine how you must feel, dear girl. This man you've chosen to bind yourself to is at times—" she sought for the appropriate word, "—intimidating. He is bold and brash and oftimes cruel . . . even in his loving."

Raven met the woman's hostile stare with a serene expression. Ivory had no claim on Eben, Raven knew that now, and it was jealousy that was making her speak this way. "It is odd that you should find him so, madam," she said softly. "Eben has never been cruel to me. Could it by chance be that you deserved the roughness he showed you?" Raven glanced at her soon to be bridegroom and found he was watching her intently. Her cheeks warmed as his looks conjured up pictures of last night and the wondrous rapture they had shared. "I have only known tenderness at his hands."

"Meggie asked if you can skate, Rafe," Tyler put in, adroitly blocking any attempt at reply Ivory might have made. "If this weather holds the streams will soon be frozen solid. We might build a fire for warmth and have an evening of fun on the ice." He grinned up at Eben. "If this clumsy oaf can't manage the blades I know a man who'd be glad to show you how."

"Not this year," Eben said. He crossed to Raven and laid a hand on her shoulder. She was wearing again the vermillion velvet gown that she'd worn the night of the ball, and this time he knew that she wore it for him. The deep red suited her coloring perfectly, making her skin glow with health. Or was it instead the contentment he saw in her eyes when he looked at her that made her so breathtaking? "My wife will have her hands full just taking care of me," he pronounced, "and this babe will not sustain any bumps on the ice if I have anything to say about it. There will be countless other winters. . . ."

Raven covered his hands with hers and smiled up into his face. She heard, rather than saw the Ivory's disgusted hiss from across the small gathering.

Meggie heard it too, for she turned and looked at Ivory with feigned innocence. "Mrs. Wharton, could I get you a saucer of cream?"

There was a bit of laughter as the judge's daughter took herself off, her auburn head held regally high. The others turned immediately to talk of the wedding, putting Ivory from their thoughts. No one noticed her brushing past the chair where Raven's fur-lined cloak was draped, nor the sudden triumphant gleam that entered her green eyes as her fingers closed over the soft pile.

"Meg, have you seen Raven's cloak? She brought it down earlier, and now it seems to have been misplaced."

"It was on the chair right over—well, it was there before," she said. "Someone must have picked it up by mistake. I'll look into it." Meggie took the heavy tray weighted down with mugs and plates and carried it to the kitchen, Eben following behind her.

"Well, I didn't have to look far, now did I? Here it is." Meg was reaching for the velvet cloak when the smell assailed her nostrils. She spun around, alerted instantly, and checked the hearth. All was well, and only the poker had been misplaced, left thrust into the fire by a careless hand. When she turned again and saw the cloak spread wide between Eben's fingers, she muttered an imprecation.

The fabric still smoked where the hot poker had been lain to form the ugly slur. The expression on Eben's dark face was thunderous. "She's gone too far, Meg. I swear upon my mother's grave I'll make her pay for this!" He started off but Meggie grabbed his arm with both hands and hung on.

"Would you have her get away with this?" he demanded with fury.

"Not this way! Think of Raven and your child! Don't you see it yet? That harpy would like nothing more than to see you ruined! And she will go to any length to do it. The best revenge is to go on and live your own life. Be happy, Eben. It will hurt her far more than if you closed your hands around her throat."

"Eben?" Raven's voice came from the doorway. She saw him spin to face her and the look he wore struck her heart with dread.

"Go back to bed!" he ordered.

The gruffness in his tone made her blink. "I wondered what was keeping you so long. If you'd found my—you did find it! I'll just take it and go."

"Leave the bloody thing and go to bed, dammit!"

She stood a moment staring at him, and he could tell that he had hurt her. It was the last thing he'd intended, but his anger at Ivory was consuming him. He took a step toward her, but she sidestepped him and hurried to the table, where she paused. "What is that smell?" she asked, picking up the beloved garment. Her fingers found the gaping hole then and she spread the folds of soft pile to see the word harlot burned into the back of the garment. Tears pricked her eyes and clogged her throat as she buried her face in the soft deep fur.

"It's ruined," she said quietly.

Eben rested his cheek against her curls and sighed deeply. "I wanted to spare you," he said.

She sniffed. "It is my fault. I should not have baited her this evening."

"It was not your fault," Eben said. "That viper needs no provocation to strike. But I vow, she'll never touch anything of mine again."

Meggie took the cloak from Raven's hands and carefully folded it over her arm. "I'll ask Elise if she can fix it." She watched Eben as he bent and lifted Raven in his arms, then went slowly from the room. For a long while after the lovers had gone Meg just stood holding the ruined cloak. A storm was brewing, she could feel it. But it had nothing at all to do with the weather. She only prayed that they could all withstand the next few days.

The wedding was set for tomorrow evening, and the following day Eben was taking Raven to Sarah Fletcher's farm where they would spend their first winter. With Eben settled and out of reach, perhaps the judge's daughter would go back to Washington. Although at the moment, with the brooding air of the kitchen still redolent of smoke and anger, it seemed a remote hope at best.

Chapter 26

It was growing dark the following day when Eben stalked from the stable and out into the snowy dusk. Without seeing him Ivory knew that his eyes never turned her way. He had dismissed her as easily as one would brush lint from a coat sleeve, cavalierly discounting the depths her scorn could reach. But she would make him sorry, she would make him pay, and dearly.

Outside she heard the wind and the slow scrape-shuffle gait that could only belong to her spouse, and seethed with loathing for all men. The door opened and in came a chilling blast of the frigid cold that had gripped the East for days.

Wearing a knowing look on his cherubic face, Jameson stumped forward into the dim light thrown by the single lantern hanging overhead and leaning on the silver head of his cane, awaiting his wife's latest tantrum. He had only just returned from a most arduous journey upriver and had yet to announce his return when he saw Eben emerge from the stables looking as if he were contemplating someone's slow demise. There was only one person who could conjure up that evil look, and curiously he had hung back in the deepening shadows of the stable and waited until the man had gone before he made his own way inside. "Trysting amid the ordure, dear wife? he asked coldly.

She spat an epithet so foul that Jameson nearly flinched. "Your charms, it seems, have dimmed over the years," he said. "I passed St. Claire on the way here and he looked something less than pleased."

"The base-born bastard!" she spat. "When I am done with him he'll wish he'd died with his kin!"

"So," he said, amused at her hateful mood, especially since it was not directed at him, "the noble frontiersman would have none of you. Well, I can't say it surprises me. Had I a choice between you, my dear, and that sweet-fleshed beauty warming his bed at night—" Jameson never got to finish his statement as his wife gave him a sudden shove that, catching him unaware, sent him stumbling backward against the nearest stall. Unlatched, the stall door gave inward and Jameson sat down in something suspiciously warm and fragrant.

He cursed her viciously as she hovered over him, but even his meanest utterances could not block out what she was saying.

"Never speak that bitch's name to me! Do you hear, husband? I will not hear it again until it is spoken over her grave!"

"Pray tell, madam, just how you intend accomplishing that without drawing the wrath of her lover down upon your head? I could see from the look on his face that he loathes the very sight of you! He certainly would have no qualms about killing you if you managed to harm his little bride."

Ivory smiled. "She will never take his name. I will see to it, with help from you."

Jameson blanched. Surely the woman did not expect him to help her do murder! Yet even as he thought it he saw how her eyes were flaming green in the dim light of the stable. She had truly gone insane.

* * *

"What keeps her, Meg?" Eben asked. His brow was tight with anxiety and his gaze was fixed, not on the woman who stood by his side, but on the top of the stairs.

"Impatient man," Meggie said. "She'll be along in a moment or two. She only wants to look her best to please you."

He took his watch from his waistcoat pocket and checked the time. "Another moment and I will go and fetch her down!"

Beside him Meggie shook her head. Mother of God, what would he be like when the babe arrived? She could see him in her mind's eye, demanding what kept his son, threatening to deliver the child himself if he did not hurry. If the man wasn't careful, Sam Ruston would dose him well with powders so that he slept through the entire birth.

"Last minute nerves?" Tyler asked after coming to join Eben by the foot of the stairs.

Eben snorted. "Interfere and I'll see you bound and gagged and dragged off to the pantry until this ceremony is over."

"Surely you won't deny me the chance to kiss the bride," Tyler said.

"You may kiss my—" Eben began, then bit back his rejoinder as Raven appeared at the head of the stairs.

She came down slowly, a wonder in gold satin and tiny beads of irridescent crystal. The beads had been painstakingly afixed to the bodice of the gown, and more had been sewn to the gold ribbons that twined through her midnight black tresses so that when she moved she looked as if she wore a thousand multicolored jewels. Yet surely none could shine as bright as she.

"You shame the very stars, sweetheart," Eben said. He took her hand and drew her across the room, his ardent gaze never straying from her face until they halted before the judge.

Word had spread like wildfire through the countryside and many had arrived to witness the marriage of the county's most eligible bachelor and this fabled beauty. John and Bob Bently were present, though the promise of spirits in plenty was a far stronger lure than any desire to witness Eben's vows, and Sarah and Timothy Fletcher were there as well. Sam Ruston had come and was squiring one of the local girls who flushed shyly when the handsome bridegroom walked past her. Elise Goodman was there also, standing by Meggie with her kerchief ready, her other hand full of wheat, which she intended to toss on the newlyweds according to custom.

Eben, resplendent in a coat of deepest indigo over tight-fitting nankeen trousers and tall Hessian boots, looked as if he'd been made to stand at Raven's side.

"I, Eben St. Claire, take thee, Raven. . . ." He spoke the words without a heartbeat's hesitation, his voice clear and resonant, devoid of doubt. He had given her his heart and now he pledged his name, his life, eternity. Surely this was a dream, she thought, her shining eyes meeting his. Did any man give so completely once dedicated to a cause? Her mind chided her, for Eben St. Claire was not just any man! When it came her turn to speak the words she felt a surge of pride so strong she was nearly overcome. In a moment more they would be legally bound, one to the other, and no more doubts or fears would ever touch them.

But outside, at that very moment, a sobbing Jedediah was stumbling up the front steps and across the porch. He had left the stables an hour before, guilty at being an unwilling eavesdropper as Mr. St. Claire had argued with the Wharton woman. Asleep on the hayloft, it had taken Jedediah some moments once awakened to steal noiselessly across the loft and shinny down the rope that hung outside the loft door. The rope was used for butchering, and usually held the sturdy single tree that hoisted up the heavy carcasses to aid in skinning, but this night it had provided him with a convenient escape from the violent atmosphere of the barn. Now Jedediah was sorry that he had been so cowardly in leaving. Too late he considered that had he only made his presence known, the woman now lying like a broken doll in that same stable might yet breathe.

"With this ring, I thee wed." The words intoned were a warm caress, nearly as warm as the golden filigree band Eben slid over her knuckle. "And with all my worldly goods I thee endow. . . ."

Judge McAllister looked fondly down upon these two so obviously in love and thought of Jane, his first wife, dead now so many years. It was with thoughts of her in mind that he opened his mouth to say the words that would declare to the world that this couple was joined as one. But before he could speak the door burst open and all heads turned to see Jedediah make his breathless way into the room.

"Ju-Judge McAllister," he cried between sobs, "you must come n-now! Miz Wharton—in the stables! She's dead, sir!"

"What are you saying, boy?" Meggie demanded above the buzz of voices that had begun immediately at Jedediah's statement.

"She's dead, Miz Cleary. I saw her!" Jedediah cried. Tears ran unchecked over his thin cheeks and dropped from his chin. As he talked he wrung his hands in great anguish. Seeing the boy's distress and feeling pity for him, Eben went to lay his hand on the lad's thin shoulder, but the boy flinched away, a look of genuine fear on his face as he stared open-mouthed at Eben. "I think her neck's been broke," Jedediah said in a subdued voice, still looking oddly at Eben.

"This can't be!" Meggie exclaimed. "Not now, not tonight!"

"Jedediah, lad, you must sit down and tell me all you know." The crowd parted and Judge McAllister stood before Jedediah, who was being pushed into a chair. He saw the way the boy's eyes darted nervously to Eben, then rested with regret on Raven's white face. Something was very wrong here, aside from the cruel news of Ivory's death. Zeb shook his head and rubbed a knotted hand along his jaw. The loss wasn't real to him yet. The pain of grief could come later, after justice was done to his daughter's murderer. But as the boy began to speak Zeb felt a terrible wrenching pain start in his chest.

"They argued something fearful," Jedediah said, "over the new cloak he give Miz Raven, and the awful way she was treated. He said that Miz Wharton had burned the cloak on purpose and she laughed at that, and said how she only wished it had been the girl's hide she'd branded. It must have made him awful mad, 'cause I heard him curse her and she drew in a breath, like she was scared he might hit her. That was when I left the stable and shinnied down the rope." Jedediah's gaze went to Raven's stricken face, full of apology. "When I come back, Mr. St. Claire was gone . . . and Miz Wharton was layin' in the straw, her head bent off to one side."

"Were you there?" Zeb asked, pinning Eben with a steely stare that might have been directed at a stranger.

"Aye, and what the lad says is true." There was a great commotion as those gathered in the common room began all to talk at once. The noise all but drowned out the words he said in his defence. "We argued, but she was alive when I left her. I did not kill her, Zeb. I swear it."

Zeb heard the words as if from far away. He felt

suddenly and curiously detached. Was this man standing unbowed and unrepentant before him a murderer? Eben had come to this house when only a stripling, thin of body and with a spirit chiseled from ice, allowing no one save Meg, a servant, to touch him, to know him. Zeb, out of compassion, had seen the boy given shelter and food, education and guidance.

"Zeb, I swear to you, I didn't kill her."

Zeb felt very old. His daughter was dead. His only kin! "You will have a trial, and a chance to speak if you so desire."

"I did not kill her!" Eben's denial rang through the room.

"That will be determined by a jury of your fellow men," Zeb continued, refusing to look at Eben. "Until then you will be held under guard."

Zeb signaled for two men to come forward. The Bentlys were brawny, far heavier than Eben. Their escort would prevent his trying to escape. The two moved forward at Zeb's nod and took hold of the prisoner's arms, but he shook them off and turned to face the old man.

"At least give me a moment with my bride," he asked.

"Would that I had been granted a moment with my daughter . . . to say farewell." Zeb turned his gaze away. "Take him from my sight."

The two appointed guards moved forward and seized Eben by the arms, but he managed to wrench free and smash his fist into the face of the one nearest him. His newly attained freedom was short-lived. Bob Bently, enraged now and roaring like a bull, bowled into Eben's midsection and the two of them went sprawling. The crowd surged back to make room, but the fight had already been decided. Bob Bently struggled up, rubbing his knuckles and grinning through his ruined mouth at his brother. "He's quiet now."

Confusion followed as Meggie planted her bony fists on her hips and demanded that Zeb come to his senses. Across the room Raven screamed and lunged forward, her hands outstretched, the light glinting off the golden band so recently placed on her finger, only to feel Tyler's grasp holding her back. She fought him wildly, demanding he release her.

"It's bad enough," he tried to warn her. "If you go to him it can only make things worse!"

Wild eyed she stared at him, her face drained of all its color. "You don't understand! They hung his grandfather! They'll hang him too! I must help him, Tyler Lee! I'm all he has!" She struggled to get free of his hold, calling Eben's name until Tyler clamped a hand across her mouth.

"Be still and listen to me!" His voice seemed a stranger's. The words being ground out beside her ear could not belong to Tyler. His voice was always indolent, while the words she was forced to hear were anything but lazy. They came to her swiftly, and with purpose, revealing that the Tyler she had come to love was but a sham. "Yes, he has you, and Meg and me, to help him get out of here if need be. There will be no hanging, Raven. I won't allow it. You have my word."

Raven didn't hear this last. Mercifully she had fainted.

Nan's sharp eyes lit upon the stranger who quietly closed the door and surveyed the goings on in the room, seeming to debate if he should stay or venture back into the cold. She sensed, rather than saw, his brittle gaze slowly turning over every detail of the room and felt a tiny shiver chase up her spine when the man at last looked her way.

She had seen his type before, tall and dangerous,

without a penny to his name. His clothing was dark and nondescript, his boots worn and the leather cracked—nothing save the hard male body inside the clothes to catch a girl's eye. Still, what she could see of his face suggested rugged handsomeness and since Nan was without her usual bevy of male admirers this night, she decided to try him. Perhaps the stranger had a coin to spare after all for a girl who was willing to warm his bed, or some small bauble hidden somewhere in his clothes that he wouldn't mind parting with once she'd pleasured him. With this possibility foremost in mind she sauntered slowly forward, swinging her hips provocatively.

"It's druther cold to be out venturing, sir," she said and smiled a greeting, showing all her teeth. "Will you come in and warm yourself by the hearth while I see to all your needs?"

She led him to the fire and watched as he put out his hands to warm them. They were fine hands with long tapering fingers and clean well-cared-for nails, unlike the men Nan was used to whose fingernails were stubs rimed with black. They looked like the hands of a gentleman. "What can I bring you?" she asked, peering brightly into his face as if she might somehow see the brand of "gentry" stamped on that cold-reddened cheek. He returned her eager gaze with eyes that matched the chill of the winter's eve.

She stepped back involuntarily as his pale eyes raked her and fussed with her apron to cover her sudden nervousness. There was something in his eyes that was vaguely familiar, and wholly unsettling. It tugged incessantly at her memory, but she could not lay a finger to where the connection lay.

"If you've anything hot to eat, then bring it," he said. "And a bottle of your best whiskey." With that he turned to the fire, completely dismissing her from his presence.

Nan hurried to bring what he wanted. At the kitchen door she glanced back once to see him staring fixedly into the flames as if spellbound. The gold of the fire filled his eyes until not a speck of that odd clear pale blue remained. Set like golden jewels in the lean dark face, his trim black beard creeping up the hollows of his cheeks, he looked like some demon come straight from the throne of Belial. All the tales told by her granny to frighten Nan into treading the straight and narrow rose up now to haunt her. She must have stood a moment too long, just staring at that sinister countenance and not even daring to breathe, for the eyes slowly turned her way.

At that moment the door to the kitchen came abruptly open and Meggie ran directly into the gaping girl, dropping the heavy silver tray which was weighted down with a freshly brewed pot of chamomile tea.

The sudden impact startled Nan so that she uttered a cry shrill enough to tear Jase from his musings. He instantly recognized the frail woman who was busy boxing the serving girl's ears for her clumsiness and was swift to intervene.

"You clumsy wench!" the Irishwoman cried. "Is there not enough bad going on here tonight without you adding to the commotion?"

Meggie was on her knees retrieving the pieces of broken crockery to put on the tray when the shadow fell over her. With a start she raised her eyes to encounter a face that made her heart cease to beat. For a second's space she thought that she would swoon. Then she was being caught by the arms and drawn to her feet. She was grateful for the solid chair beneath her; her legs were unable to support her as she began to shake.

"Cameron St. Claire. . . ."

Her reaction shook him. He removed the hat that

shaded his face and covered the wealth of shining black hair that crowned his head and curled round his nape in back. "Megan Cleary," he said in a voice that very much resembled his brother's, "will you let your Irish imagination run wild with you, or tell me what's gone on this score of years since I've been gone."

Meggie just stared at him, speechless.

"If you knew my father's name, then surely you remember me," he said.

Her hand went to her mouth and quite suddenly she began to weep. Jase looked sharply at the serving girl who cowered yet by the door. "Bring that whiskey at once!" He watched as she scuttled to do his bidding, not caring if he frightened her.

"He's searched all these many years," Meggie said, putting her thin hand on his shoulder as if to reassure herself that he was real.

"Then it is true . . . he's alive," Jase said. "Where, Meg? Can you tell me where he is?"

Meggie wiped at her eyes with a quaking hand. How ironic it was that Jase should arrive just when Eben needed him most. "I can do better than that, Jason St. Claire. I can take you to him."

The small cell of a room was tucked up high beneath the eaves. Here there was no grate to hold a fire, and what little heat found its way up from below stairs was quickly obliterated by the sharp winter's wind whistling through the broken glass of the only window set high in the western wall. Scratch, scratch, scratch . . . the brush of the bony limbs across the remaining glass was driving Eben mad. He sat hunched where the Bently brothers had thrown him, on the scant straw of an ancient pallet. The straw smelled of mold and damp and was lightly sprinkled with snow, yet it was not his bodily discomfort that prompted Eben's thoughtful frown, but the events of the past few hours.

Around and around his mind trudged the same worn track, taking him over the events of the afternoon and evening. He relived every hateful word that had been uttered in the stable, each of his movements until Jedediah had blundered into the room with his news. He heard again and again the anguished scream that could only have come from his bride. His bride . . .

At this he laughed humorlessly. What forces worked to keep him from marrying her? It seemed that he was destined ever to have happiness elude him. And like his father and grandfather before him, he would achieve a grisly end.

His head ached terribly where Bob Bently's heavy fist had pummeled him. His movements slow, he drew up his knees and folded his arms across them, resting his head on his arms. He closed his eyes and must have slept, for he dreamed that he heard Meg's voice, calling to his guards that the judge had ordered her to fetch them down to eat. Slowly the footfalls faded away and the lonely whistle of the night wind again filled the chamber.

"Raise your head, man, and let me have a look at you." It was a long moment before the man did so and Jase finally stared into a face much like his own.

"Have I gone mad?" Eben wondered aloud. "Jase?"

"Yes, little brother, it's me," Jase said. "Come and greet me properly, we've little time allowed us."

Eben made his way to the heavy oaken door and put a hand sideways through the bars that ran vertically through the opening. "By God, it is you! You look enough like Pa that for a moment I thought it was a visitation," he said. He shook his head.

"None of this is real to me. I keep thinking I'll awaken with the lass curled at my back."

"It's real enough," Jase said. They had released hands and now he watched grimly as Eben's fists closed around the iron bars. "We have to find a way to get you out of here."

"You haven't even asked me if I killed her," Eben mused aloud. "Your trust in a brother you haven't seen in twenty years and more is phenomenal."

Jase's gaze was fixed on the dim oval of Eben's face behind the bars. "You would welcome my doubt?"

"I suppose I expect it," came the low reply. "What the boy said below was true, Jase. I was there in the stable earlier with Ivory, and I did threaten her."

"I expect you had good reason, given what Megan Cleary says of the woman."

"She must have lost her mind—the things she said about Raven and Tyler—" And every other man she could think to name. But this last Eben would keep to himself. Ivory had sought in her last hours to make him believe that Raven was a faithless jade, deserving richly the slur branded across the vermillion cloak. He would not have the aspersions cast on Raven's character brought to light to be bandied about on every gossip's tongue—especially since the one least deserving of injury would be the one most wounded. It was enough that he had heard her evil utterings. "All lies . . . "

"Megan Cleary said that the woman burned a cloak," Jase prompted.

Eben nodded. "Aye, and the foulmouthed bitch said she regretted that it was just a garment and not Raven's tender hide she'd laid the poker to." He paused, lost in recall. "She put her hands on me as she said it. How could she think that I would tolerate her touch when she sought to hurt the one person in my life I truly love?''

''What happened then, Eben?'' Jase questioned.

''It was then I warned her that if Raven came to harm she would pay with her life. She spat at me and tried to rake my face.''

''Did you strike her?''

''No,'' came Eben's firm reply. ''The only time I laid hands on her was to keep her claws at bay. I held her wrists and forced them down, then with another warning left her.''

''What happened then? Did you come inside? Did anyone see you leave the stable?''

Eben frowned. ''I went directly to my chamber to ready myself for the wedding. I bathed and shaved and went downstairs, putting the episode behind me. Thoughts of Ivory were far away . . . until Jedediah broke his news.''

''But you passed no one on your way into the inn? Saw nothing unusual?'' Eben again shook his head and looked perplexed, but Jase kept stubbornly on. ''How much time elapsed from when you left her in the stable until the body was found?''

''An hour, mayhaps,'' Eben replied. ''No more than that.''

''Was there anyone else who might profit from the woman's death? Someone who hated her enough to kill?''

Eben let go of one bar and raked a hand through his hair. ''I wouldn't know. The one to ask would be the woman's husband, and he is not here. He left last week and supposedly returns tomorrow.''

Footsteps and the sound of voices announced the guards' return. Eben knew there was little time left and there was much he wanted to say. He pressed close to the door again and grasped Jase's hands.

"Take heart, little brother," Jase said. "I'll get you out of here."

In a moment he was gone, for all the world as if he'd never been, Eben thought. He walked back to the pallet and sank down again, folding his arms over his upraised knees.

Chapter 27

The candle's glow did little to eliminate the feeling of deep melancholy that infected the very air of the bedchamber. The light of a thousand tapers would not have helped, Tyler thought, glancing once to see if the woman on the bed still slept. He had carried her here himself, to Eben's room, after she had swooned. He had fed her the chamomile tea Meggie had brought to calm her, coaxed her to seek her rest, vowed the most solemn oath he had ever sworn: to somehow get Eben out of the attic cell and away before he could be punished for a crime he may or may not have done—and now he guarded her slumber, jealous of her dreams.

Turning a blank countenance back to the frost-rimed panes of the window Tyler stared out into the moonless night, but his thoughts mounted the stairs that led to the attic cell where her lover remained locked away. With cool patience Tyler had extracted a picture of the room from Meggie. A solid door with a tiny barred opening was the only entrance, and Judge McAllister knowing very well the determined character of the prisoner had seen fit to post a heavy guard. Within the cell there was no furniture for the comfort of the accused, just an old straw pallet and a broken window set high in the outside wall.

Tyler turned the facts over in his mind. Even if Eben could somehow reach the window, it was doubtful that he could squeeze through it, and if he should succeed he would have a three story fall to the ground below, enough to break a man's bones on impact.

The window could be discounted, Tyler thought, his hand straying unconsciously to the smooth walnut grip of the pistol he'd thrust into his belt. That left only the door for escape, and the hulking minions of the vengeful judge to dispose of.

His pulse quickened as he plotted how he might liberate his friend and get the two of them away to safety. As much as he loved Raven, Tyler had been made to realize that Eben loved her even more. The two belonged together, and if there was a way that he could aid that end, then he would do all in his power to see it done.

Outside in the black and frigid night an unseen hound set up a mournful howling. Despite his calm exterior, the Virginian's nerves were taut. Even before the board creaked a warning in the hallway outside the chamber door and the latch was slowly lifted he had drawn the pistol and stood with his booted legs planted wide, waiting. Ivory's killer was still at large, and Tyler felt that his first priority was to protect Raven.

The man quietly edging open the door was no one Tyler had even seen before. There was no evidence of surprise showing on the lean countenance, and Tyler had the odd notion that whoever the stranger was, he had somehow expected to open the door and stare down the black bore of this very pistol. He stilled however, when the sound of the hammer being drawn back shattered the pregnant silence.

"Who named you the girl's protector?" the stranger asked in a voice filled with arrogance.

"She did, but as I see it it's no account to you. Now back on out the way you came. I would hate to spill your blood on Meggie's fine carpet." Tyler's varning was low pitched, but it managed to reach nto Raven's mind and shake her awake. On the bed she stirred and sat up, looking from the tall dark-haired man blocking the doorway to the look of menace on Tyler's saturnine face.

"What is going on here?" she asked. "Tyler Lee, put away that pistol."

"Not until our guest explains just who he is and what the hell he's doing stealing into your chamber while you sleep." Tyler's pistol remained fixed unwaveringly on Jase's breastbone, and as that one stepped into the room and closed the door, his finger tightened on the trigger.

"I did not mean to wake you," Jase said, strangely calm in the face of Tyler's threat. His pale gaze traveled slowly over Raven. "I needed to see what manner of bride my brother has chosen. Megan Cleary told me you were sleeping and that explains my stealth." He looked first at the gaping bore of the pistol and then up into his adversary's face, feeling some of his tension ebb as the hammer was carefully settled back into place. But the weapon was not put away and remained in the man's hand. He was cautious, Jase thought, and that was good. He might have need of him later, if things did not go the way he hoped.

"Jase . . . Eben's brother . . . my God, I cannot believe it! Everyone thought that you were dead." Raven rubbed her temples, where a dull ache had just been born.

As her father had the day of Eben's arrival at their cabin, Raven wondered if his coming wasn't somehow providential, that he had been sent, like some guardian angel, to save them from certain disaster. But looking at him, he hardly looked angelic. There was something almost forbidding about Jase St. Claire's dark persona, yet if one looked past his hard exterior as Raven did now to glimpse the man within, that same fierce demeanor he displayed to the world was strangely comforting. She could not look at him and believe that he would allow his brother to end his days on the gallows.

"I know it's hard to countenance, little sister," Jase said quietly. "I can barely believe it myself." His tones were much like Eben's and to her ears, soothing.

Her eyes were damp as she smiled up at him. "I am so very glad you've come. Please, sit down and tell me how he is. Did they hurt him much? Did he mention me?"

Jase sat on the edge of the bed and touched her cheek, offering her a rare smile of blinding brilliance. It changed his face completely, and for the space of a second she forgot it was he sitting there and not a darker version of Eben. "His every thought is of you," he said.

"I must see him," Raven said. "Will you take me to him, Jase? Please. I need to see for myself that he's unhurt."

"That isn't wise just now, but soon, I promise. You need to rest, Raven."

"How can I rest with Eben locked away!" she cried. "Whoever did this is walking free! It's not fair that Eben must pay for another's deeds, perhaps with his life!"

Jase's hands closed over her shoulders and he calmly met her frantic gaze. "Now tell me truthfully, do you think for one moment that I will let him be harmed? He is my brother, Raven. We were separated once; I will not allow anything to take him from me now. Can you not put your faith in me?"

Raven sniffed and nodded. He offered her reassurance and greedily she pounced upon it. "If you see him again, will you tell him that I love him?"

"You may tell him yourself very soon," Jase said.

"I've an idea that he'll be out of there come morning."

Tyler slid the heavy bore pistol back into his belt. "Tell us what you mean to do."

The pale blue eyes swung around to his face. "My plan is simple. I mean to find the killer."

"Sit down, son. There are evil tidings to share." The look of sorrow riding the old man's features foretold what was to come. Never in the four years of his marriage to this man's daughter had Jameson ever been addressed with anything but his given name or title. There had never been any indication that the judge held any fondness for him, and so the look of surprise that hearing it brought was to aid him in his deception as he sank into a chair. He stretched his leg before him, his cheeks red from the cold and leaned both dimpled hands on the head of his cane.

"Sir, is it Miss Cleary—" he began, then broke off as the judge shook his head.

"I wish that there was some way to soften the blow, but I know of none. It is not Meggie, but Ivory that I speak of. She is dead."

Jameson felt a wild urge to laugh, but it was quickly squashed under the heavy weight of his caution. He obviously wasn't a suspect, and so he must proceed with care. For a moment he sat as if stunned, pondering what reaction might be taken best, then he let his gaze drop to his hands. "Dead, my dear little wife . . . how can it possibly be?"

"A heinous act wrought in a fit of unbridled passion." It pained Zeb to say the words. Eben's words sprang to mind, "I did not kill her!" and were swiftly pushed away. Never before had the lad lied to him—but he had been accused, the evidence presented, and all pointed to him as guilty.

"Murder? Are you saying that someone *murdered* Ivory?"

Jameson's nerves had been stretched far beyond their limits in summoning up the courage to return here. The scenes that had run through his mind had made him quiver like some boneless thing. He had imagined being seized upon his entrance and dragged away to some dark cell where he would languish.

Doubt surged in his mind. Had anyone seen him earlier? Had he left behind some trace that could tie him to the crime? He had to know, and the best plan was the boldest one, though certainly the most difficult to play out, for it would require all of his skills at playacting. He must appear the grief-stricken husband, the loving spouse now tragically left behind. Surely he could summon up a tear or two at the thought that he was now free of that venomous bitch.

He raised his head slowly and looked at the judge, so uncomfortable in relating the facts. It was hard not to feel pity for the old man. He was now without kith or kin. Though Jameson wasn't so stirred that he felt any guilt for what he'd done.

This man's daughter had made his life a hell on earth, and had even tried to force him to do murder for her, threatening to see him ruined if he refused her. And since his dealings in Washington were sometimes less than scrupulous, he had taken the threat to heart. The very idea of being involved in plotting the murder of Eben St. Claire's bride had shaken Jameson to his toes.

Eben was half savage, and having faced his wrath once before, Jameson was less than eager to do so again, especially with the blood of the man's bride on his hands. The frontiersman would kill the man who laid a finger on her without remorse, and Jameson surmised that the method employed would be anything but pleasant. Seeing no other choice, Jameson's hands had closed easily around Ivory's neck. The look of surprise and fear on her face as she saw his intent had been worth doing murder. She had not thought him capable. The regal bitch had thought wrong.

The next question Jameson had to pose was the most difficult, but he knew it must be asked. A loving husband would demand justice be done to the man who'd taken away his spouse. It flashed through his brain that this might all be an elaborate trick to implicate him. Yet what choice was he given except to brazen it out?

He sought for and somehow summoned a look of puzzlement. "Who would do this awful thing to her? I cannot name a man who did not love her." Indeed, he thought wryly, her lovers defied counting.

"A man has been named," the judge replied wearily. He rubbed a hand across his face, and his other hand, which lay on the desk clutching his spectacles, suddenly trembled as with palsy. "The evidence is overwhelming, yet my heart recoils from believing in his guilt. Eben . . . Eben has been accused."

"St. Claire!" Jameson exclaimed, then chided himself for sounding too overjoyed. How very ironic that the two people responsible for maiming him would now be given justice with a very heavy hand. He would personally see it meted out, and quickly. "Of course, it would be him. He'd been plaguing her to renew their old affair. Being the saint she was, Ivory resisted."

Zeb's head came up and he gave the other man a sharp look. "Ivory told you this?"

Jameson nodded. "She confided in me that she was going to inform the girl of her lover's perfidy."

The judge was silent for a long moment. He knew the man was lying. He had seen the signs himself, and had even chastised Ivory in private to leave Eben be. It had not been Eben, but Ivory who sought to rekindle the flame of their romance from cold dead ash.

Zeb's eyes narrowed ever so slightly, and he watched his son-in-law more closely. He saw Jameson's tongue snake out to moisten his lips—not once, but several times, the pudgy hands fidgeted with the handle of his cane, unable to be still in his father-in-law's presence. His nerves betrayed him, and Zeb knew at once that a new suspect had just presented himself. It was hard to suppress the urge to demand the truth from him here and now, but Zeb forced himself to remain calm. The man wasn't going anywhere. "You'll be staying for the services, of course," he said.

"Of course."

"This has been hard on us all, but most of all, Meggie," Zeb said. "I'm afraid you will find supper nonexistent. The woman is put out with me for detaining Eben, and flatly refuses to cook."

"I understand perfectly," Jameson sympathized. "I find I'm not hungry anyway. I think I'll just retire."

"A wise decision," the judge said. "Tomorrow will be difficult for us all."

Jameson went out and Zeb sat for some moments mulling over the events preceding and following Ivory's death. Whatever Eben might be, he was far from stupid. If he had indeed killed Ivory, as everyone believed, then why would he remain, calmly awaiting his arrest? The Eben he knew would have simply disappeared without a trace, taking Raven with him. But instead he had remained to marry the girl who carried his child, acting for all the world like a man who had nothing to hide.

Eben's vow of innocence again echoed in Zeb's brain, this time spurring him to action. He went to the study door and beckoned Nan into the room. "Be a good lass and go fetch Jedediah's father here. Tell him it's urgent."

Five minutes passed and Joshua Jones came into the room, his hat crushed in his hands. His thick red hair was badly mussed and his face still bore traces of sleep. "You sent for me, Judge?"

"Aye. I apologize for disturbing your sleep, Joshua, but there is something that must be done and it cannot wait till morning." Knowing he could trust the man, Zeb explained. "Check all the hotels and even the brothels. Find out if the man was there and the precise day and time of his leaving, then come straightaway back. Keep in mind that Eben's life depends upon your swift return, Joshua."

After Joshua had gone Zeb sat again behind the desk. Unless the weather detained him, a day or two would bring the information he needed to clear Eben's name. Until then, and expressly to avoid arousing Jameson's suspicions, Eben would have to remain in the attic cell.

Jase closed the door of the stable and stood looking around him. The displaced straw on the stable floor indicated a struggle of some sort had taken place. He wouldn't need his skills at tracking and reading signs to uncover enough evidence to clear his brother's name, for lying nearly buried in the straw and looking as if it had been trampled was a shiny object that looked like gold.

He picked it up and held it to the light, seeing the diamond stickpin from a man's cravat catch the light. The blue-white refraction of the lamplight on the gem was the last thing Jase saw before the void closed over him.

Jameson stood looking down at the recumbent form lying on the straw. There was no mistaking the face of the elder St. Claire. Even though he hadn't seen Jase since their childhood years, he recognized the man because of his strong resemblance to Eben. Carefully he reached down and removed the stick-pin from Jase's slack fingers then paused to wipe the blood from the handle of his cane onto the fallen man's shirt.

A smile curved Jameson's plump lips into a cupid's bow. "I thank you, St. Claire," he said with a great deal of the relief he felt creeping into his voice. "This was the only thing connecting me with my wife's untimely demise. So you can imagine how glad I am to have it again in my possession."

It was no simple task for the rotund Jameson to bend and seize his victim's arms, then drag him into an empty stall where he could slumber undisturbed.

Jameson had been nearly frantic when he discovered the pin was missing and realized that Ivory must have wrenched it from his clothing during their brief struggle. But now that it was returned, he could once again relax. Without the physical evidence, Jase St. Claire could raise all the speculation he wished; without a shred of evidence he could prove nothing.

At last Tyler had gone to his own chamber and Raven was alone. It had taken some swift talking to convince him that she would be safe alone, but at last he had gone, leaving her free to do what she felt she must.

The wardrobe Eben had provided included two cloaks, a dark woolen garment for everyday wear and the vermillion velvet which was now at Elise Goodman's being remade. The woolen garment was lined with plain stuff, and thus not quite as cozy against the cruel bite of winter, but it would help to conceal her as she moved about outside.

She lifted it from the wardrobe and folded it over her arm, going on silent feet as quickly as she could manage, down the long hall to the top of the servants' stairs. As her foot touched the last tread the old case clock began to chime the twelve long strokes that counted off the midnight hour.

The kitchen fire was banked for the night and only a dull red glow showed beneath the pile of logs. It was hardly enough to light her way through the darkened room and she almost fell over Tracer, who was sleeping by the table in the deep shadows. Her heart lodged high in her throat, Raven hurried from the room and past the pantry to the rear door.

Outside she walked swiftly toward the stables, drawn by the yellow glow of lamplight flooding from the small windows to form buttery pools on the snow. Jase had left them an hour ago to examine the place and must still be there. He had promised that he would return to inform her just exactly what he had found, but oddly enough he had not come. Unable to withstand the suspense another minute, Raven was going in search of him.

Her hands found the cold, rough plank of the stable door, the frozen iron latch. She had every right to be here, she told herself as she pushed the door slowly inward. Jase could argue all he wished, but she would not be swayed. If there was some evidence lying overlooked, then she vowed that she would find it. She would do anything to save Eben from the gibbet.

The hinges needed oiling and creaked a little as the door swung inward. The lamp was indeed burning, hung from a bent nail that had been driven into an overhead beam. It gave off a wavering light in the very center aisle of the stable and made the shadows where its glow could not penetrate seem all the deeper, all the more sinister. "Jase!" Raven called softly. "I've come to help you."

The only answer was a slight furtive movement far back in the shadows, and the restless movement of Tyler's stallion, in his stall. The animal had his ears pinned back against his fine head and his eyes looked wild. He stood quivering, and as that same furtive movement came again, a dragging sound that raised the fine hairs on Raven's nape, he reared and kicked at the boards of the stall, a thunderous crack that was loud enough to wake those sleeping at the inn.

"Jason, is that you?" Raven said, screwing up her courage to move into the center aisle. She searched the shadows for the source of the noise and saw what had caused the stallion's restlessness. Protruding from the farthest stall were long booted legs that could only belong to Jase St. Claire.

Raven gave a startled scream and flew to Jase's side. He was lying facedown in the stall, a trickle of blood seeping from his black hair onto the straw. And bending over him was Senator Jameson Wharton, Ivory's husband.

Jameson came forward and seized Raven by the arm. She would have shrugged away his hold and dropped to Jase's side, but his voice instantly stilled her. "He isn't dead, but he will be if you don't come with me now."

"Come with you? You are mad. Why would I go anywhere with you?" Raven looked into the senator's round face and saw how the lamplight glistened off his sweat-dotted brow. His small animal eyes were frightened. Hope burgeoned within her. Someone must have heard her scream. Help would come very soon if only she could stall for a little time.

"Because you care a whit for your precious Eben and you wouldn't want to cause him any grief. He wouldn't thank you for allowing his brother to roast in hell's flames, even if that is where he belongs."

He stumped past her and seized the lamp from its nail, holding it aloft by a crooked finger. Raven saw it swing precariously and swallowed hard. "One murder or two, it makes no difference now," he told her.

The brothers had been so recently reunited. Raven could not bear to think of Eben's suffering if he lost Jase again, this time for good. Still on her knees beside the fallen man, she lay a questing hand on his neck and felt his pulse strong and steady. He was all right for the moment, but there was Jameson to be dealt with. She sat back on her heels and glared at him. "What do you intend?"

"I am not a rapist, if that's what concerns you," Jameson said. "I only need a way to escape, and that much you can provide, as it was for you I killed my beloved spouse."

"For me?" He spoke with so much scorn for the dead woman that Raven wondered why he had gone unsuspected until now. "You barely know me," she said, glancing back at Jase, who was beginning now to stir. "Why would you murder for my benefit?"

This time when Jameson's hand closed over her arm, she did not fight him. If Jase awoke now he would only be hit again, and she did not want him hurt.

"She wanted me to kill you so that she could get back at your husband. When she put her plan to me I knew that she had lost her senses. I refused to help her, and she threatened to ruin my career! It was all that I had left to me! I had no choice but to prevent her. Besides, I faced St. Claire's wrath once before, and the bastard threw me out a window. I had no wish to cross him again. If you know it or not, the man's a fucking savage!'' His grip on her arm tightened painfully and Raven gave an involuntary little cry. ''Now come,'' he said tersely, pulling her toward the door and freedom. ''We've far to go and little time before someone comes to investigate your scream. But with any luck I'll be gone by then.''

Chapter 28

Eben stared into the dark and listened to the snores of his vigilant guard coming from outside the small cubicle. They had left him his watch and he checked it now, and saw that it was one minute until midnight. Try as he might, he could not sleep. This was his wedding night—or should have been—but instead of resting his head on Raven's pliant breast, he was stretched on this stinking pile of straw counting off the seconds until the dawn arrived.

Somewhere beyond the dark rectangle of the window Jase searched for clues as to the identity of the murderer. Eben longed to be there with him, free of the confines of this dingy cell and any thought of what awaited him.

What would happen to Raven and his baby if he ended his life by the rope? He heaved a weary sigh and rested a forearm over his eyes, telling himself that it would not come to that.

If there was any evidence, even so much as a misplaced or broken straw, Jase would know the reason behind it. He would find out who had killed the judge's volatile daughter, and then Eben would take Raven away from this place and all its bad memories, someplace they could begin anew.

What spare comfort this vein of thought provided was instantly shattered by a woman's scream. The clear and windless night carried the sound around the inn and through the broken window of the third story room, bringing Eben instantly to his feet. With a single bound he leapt to the door and grasped the bars in his fists, cursing and giving the stalwart panel a thunderous shake.

Without, the guards stirred and heaped threats upon his head of what they'd do to him if he failed to settle down. They lay back down and ignored Eben's seeming insane ramblings about hearing a woman's scream.

"Go to sleep, St. Claire!" Bob Bently was heard to utter. "The only scream you heard is in your fewkin' head! 'Twas more than likely the judge's poor murdered daughter haunting you for doin' for her the way you did."

No amount of pleas or threats could gain his release from this damnable cell, so he would get out himself, by Christ! He turned to the window and taking off his boot, hurled it at the glass with every ounce of strength he possessed. The missile found its target and there was the sound of shattering glass as it exited, and in the hall more cursing from the Bentlys.

Eben did not wait to see if they would bestir themselves enough to investigate, but grabbed the bottom sill with both hands and oblivious of the shards of broken glass cutting his palms, hauled himself quickly upward. Lithe as any cat, he crouched on the sill, holding onto the top of the wooden frame to steady himself as he slipped sideways through the narrow opening.

And then he was climbing.

The eaves and roof's edge were his handholds, aiding in his quick, perilous ascent. There was but one way to go and that was up and over the roof to the west wing where he could drop onto the lower porch, then to the ground.

Fear for his lady drove his blood through his veins

and spurred him onward where any sane man would have been loath to go. It had been Raven's cry that had reached his ears, he knew it. She was in danger, and he could not sit and wait for someone else to act! He had to find her and see that she was safe. Afterward, if they wanted to lock him in the depths of the cellar he would not care!

Most of the snow had melted off the slate roof at the very comb. It was here, along the highest point, that Eben made his way. When he had nearly reached his goal, his foot found the loose slate. With a hiss and rattle it let go and skidded down the steep roof, Eben sliding after it. He grappled for a handhold—felt his nails tear loose—anything to stop him from going off the edge. On his belly he slid to the edge of the roof, where finally he came to a halt. Closing his eyes and for the barest instant leaning his brow against the cold slate, he let out the breath he'd been holding. Then he dug in his toes and began again to climb.

This time he arrived without incident and it was a simple matter to drop onto the roof of the porch, then lower himself from there to the ground. Inside the old stone structure he could hear yelling and questions posed and answered; boots pounded on the stairs and lights were being lit. He had no doubt the hulking guards would soon be on his tail, but he didn't linger to see if he was right. Far away he heard a woman's voice—Raven's he was sure—bouncing in a hollow echo off the snowy sleeping hills as it only could in the depths of a quiet winter's eve, and coming from the direction of the creek.

"If you don't hurry, I'll have to drag you. We haven't the time for a leisurely stroll, and the sooner we cross to the other side, the sooner you can be reunited with your recalcitrant lover. That's what you want, now isn't it!"

Jameson's hold on Raven's arm was punishing. His fingers bit into her flesh as he fairly dragged her along in the direction of the frozen creek. Behind them, and over Jameson's puffing, she could hear the sound of someone running across the frozen ground. She glanced anxiously over her shoulder in time to see the dark shape of a man sprinting across the snow. In a moment or two he would reach them, but until then Raven had to stop Jameson from taking her out onto the ice.

"Look! Someone comes!" Raven cried, hoping to frighten him into leaving her. "Let go of me and run! If you go quickly he will not catch you!"

"I cannot run! St. Claire saw to that long ago! You are my only chance at escape. With you by my side he will not dare give chase!" Jameson told her.

He pulled her forward while she struggled and kicked and tried to trip him. Grunting, he nearly went down. Her efforts to escape infuriated the desperate Jameson, and in his anger he lashed out at her, his solid blow catching her alongside her jaw.

Raven fell back with a little cry. For a second she thought she would faint as the blackness swirled around her, then just as swiftly the sensation was gone and she was dragged inexorably forward onto the ice.

Eben's enraged howl came clearly over the frozen stream, as sweet to her ears as a lover's sigh. Her brain refused to acknowledge what she knew in her heart was about to happen, and instead circled joyously around one thought—Eben was coming! Eben was coming!

Under foot the ice was slick and Jameson's awkward gait slowed their progress. They were nearing the center of the stream now where the ice was thinnest. "Please, let me go back to him! I beg of you!" she cried. Desperation mingled with foreboding, screaming at her not to take another step.

Beneath his feet the ice creaked and groaned like some wounded creature begging release from its agony. The girl dug in her heels and sobbed wildly, too much for Jameson to safely handle. With an angry curse he flung her from him, watching with crazed eyes as she fell. But no more had she slumped to the ice than a great gaping hole appeared just three feet to his left. He tried to scramble away, but not in time to save himself. The surface beneath his feet tilted, and before he could even cry out the icy flow was closing over his head.

Eben reached the crest of the bank just as Jameson disappeared. Raven was slumped at the very edge of the watery abyss. He called out for her to be still, but as he started toward her he saw her turn toward him. She looked into his face just as the fragile surface gave way. In the instant that Eben watched horrified, she sobbed his name and stretched out her hand to him, and then was gone.

"Nooooooo . . . !" The animalistic cry was torn from the depths of a tortured soul. Its keening misery flailed across the meadow, across the inn yard where the others were just now streaming out of the inn and hurrying over the frozen ground. The sound struck dread in Tyler's heart, for he knew that only one thing could have caused such anguish to come pouring from a man like Eben . . . and Eben's loss was his as well.

A hundred yards away, Eben skidded across the remaining ice and flattened himself so that he lay on his belly. She cannot die . . . she cannot! his mind screamed. "Damn you, Raven! You cannot leave me now!" The desperate words burst forth just as Tyler grabbed for Eben's heels and Eben plunged headfirst into the still black water.

In the inky depths he searched frantically with his hands in all directions, as far as he could reach. He knew that just because she had gone under here did not mean she would not surface somewhere under the ice. The cold had numbed him instantly and he could barely feel the velvet of her skirt when it brushed against his hand. His frozen fingers closed over it and he drew her toward him.

He came up gasping and scrambled to get out of the water. "Help me with her!"

Tyler was there and together they dragged her still form from Jameson's watery tomb.

Meggie removed her own cloak and tucked it around the unconscious girl. She wanted to speak, to console Eben, but there were no words. All just stood, silently watching the man who bore her to the bank and sank down to bury his face in her streaming hair.

"Oh God," Eben rasped, pressing his cold cheek to her pale one. "I beg of you, don't let her slip from me now!"

Whatever deity existed for Eben was listening, waiting for his plea, for against him Raven stirred and coughed.

She struggled to open her eyes and her lashes fluttered weakly. Something hot fell onto her cheek, scalding her skin. She slowly raised her heavy lids and gazed into beloved pale blue eyes. With a sharp pang she saw that he was crying. Her limbs were leaden, yet she managed to touch his cheek.

"I knew you would come," she said in a bare whisper.

"I could not let you go," he whispered. "Lady, you are my heart. Without you in my life there is nothing."

"As you are mine, husband," she answered, putting her arms around his neck as he rose and carried her back to the inn.

Her endearment made him smile, that same strange curling at the corners of his mouth that she had come to cherish. ''Not yet,'' he said, ''but soon, I vow. Just as soon as you are strong enough.''

He took her through the kitchen and up the back stairs, his single boot making a discordant sound on the treads as he climbed that drew Raven's attention. ''Eben, where is your other boot?''

''I threw it out the window.''

''Oh, Eben, not your new boots!''

He laughed. ''A small sacrifice for all that I have gained.''

Epilogue

St. Claire Manor
Orleans Parish, Louisiana
October 1, 1808

"Master Jase, there be a carriage comin' up de drive!" Breathless from his sprint to the main house, Tellifour hurried to impart this piece of news. The young Negro stood scuffing his bare feet on the carpet, grinning as his master stood behind the big rosewood desk and took up his coat, slipping into the garment even as he strode past Tellifour in search of Catherine.

"Have Cook prepare some refreshments, Tell," Jase ordered, then paused to bellow in the foyer. "Catherine! Where the devil are you, woman!"

Somewhere along the wide upstairs hall, a door opened and closed and the sedate click of a woman's heels progressed along the wooden floor. "Madam, they have arrived at last!" Jase called, agitated because she failed to hurry. "I want you here at my side to greet them, so hasten yourself!"

"I am coming!" replied the petite, blonde-haired woman just descending the wide staircase. "Jason, I have never seen you so unsettled. Are you sure you're feeling quite well?"

"I have never had my brother visit before, madam. I have a right to be unsettled."

Catherine's turquoise eyes lifted slowly to her husband's dark face. "It is more than just the visit, Jason."

"Yes, I freely admit I want him to stay, Catherine, and settle near us. He can build a life here in Louisiana. There is opportunity abounding for an industrious man like Eben."

Catherine smiled. His enthusiasm was catching, his energy once committed to something boundless, his determination unequalled. She had no doubt that he would convince this mysterious brother to make his home here. "You must tell Eben all of this, Jason. Now come, let's greet them together."

The coach was slowing as it rumbled up the drive. Beside it, easily keeping pace on a heavy-muscled sorrel, was a blonde-haired man who very closely resembled Catherine's husband. Her gaze went slowly over him.

Dressed in fringed leather and high black boots, he looked as tall as Jason and sat his horse as though he and the animal were one entity. "Jason, you did not tell me he was handsome."

Jase gave her a sidelong glance and grinned. "He is a St. Claire, madam."

Eben leaned toward the window and said something to the young dark-haired woman there, then kicked the roan and thundered up the drive, the horse's hooves scattering clods of mud in its wake. He reined in before them and threw himself from the animal's broad back, slapping its rump to send it toward the stables before coming to stand before his sister-in-law.

The blue eyes that regarded her were that same beloved pale color as those of his older brother, and sparkled gemlike in the dark tan of his lean face. "You must be Catherine," he said in a voice both warm and low.

''Indeed, sir,'' she said, smiling so that her dimples showed. ''Welcome to St. Claire Manor.''

He did not kiss her hand, but instead bussed her cheek, smiling down at her. ''I came ahead to warn you of the noise,'' he said, transferring his gaze to Jase who now came forward to grasp his hand. ''The little ones are hungry and setting up a hellish clamor.'

''Little ones?'' Jase said, taken aback. ''More than one?''

Eben grinned widely, his teeth showing incredibly white. ''Megan and Cameron. Twins!''

Jase laughed and pounded his brother's back. ''I can hear they have your temperament,'' he said. The outraged howls pouring from the open windows of the conveyance preceded its arrival up the drive.

The driver of the vehicle looked harassed. The little Irishwoman had scorned his driving the entire way from the city, insisting that he go slowly. It seemed that she was unused to all of this riding about at such breakneck speeds and liked to take her time to view the new countryside and all its splendor. He had thought that they would never get here, and now was glad to see the tiny harridan alight.

The blonde-haired gent who'd ridden alongside now helped her down then reached inside to take both the squalling infants, which Jason St. Claire, lord of the great manor, took in turn. Then the same man lifted down his raven-haired beauty before turning to toss the driver a purse, for which he thanked him.

Thankfully there was ample payment for the suffering he'd endured beneath the tiny woman's nagging tongue. With the trunks removed the coach was lightened considerably and the driver touched the brim of his beaver hat and whipped up the horses.

Meggie's narrowed eyes watched him fly back down the road. ''I'm glad that one's gone, and a more stubborn man I've never laid eyes on,"—her narrowed gaze switched to Eben—"save one."

Eben grinned down at her and tightened his hand on his wife's trim waist. It had taken a considerable amount of talking to get Meg here, and even a little bribery. She was a woman of means now, for just a month after Ivory's murder and several days after Tyler bade them all good-bye and headed home again, Judge McAllister had died quite suddenly, leaving the inn to Meggie, along with precisely half his assets.

The will had stipulated that the remaining half be given to Eben in recompense for what Zeb termed "an old man's foolishness." At first Eben had been reluctant to accept, but Meg had been insistent, and hence the bribery. Eben took the money, but only after he'd gained Meggie's promise to venture to Louisiana with him and Raven.

"Come, Meg," Eben said, "you must admit it is a beautiful country, and warm."

"Aye, I suppose so," Meggie said, following the others into the house. But her thoughts as she gave the land a final look were far from restful. Her home was in the North, where by now an invigorating chill would be invading the days, and scarlet and gold foliage would soon begin to appear, bathing the rounding hills in all of autumn's glory. This land was foreign to her, and she was far too old to pull up the roots she'd set so deep in the valley of the Allegheny. She looked again at the huge live oaks that lined the drive, with the shaggy gray festoons hanging from their great reaching limbs which Eben had explained was something called "Spanish moss" then shook her head and crossed the wide veranda to enter the house.

Eben and Jase were in the grand salle washing away the dust of the journey, while Raven tried to quiet the restless twins. Catherine had sons of her own and knew what needed to be done. With a word to Solomon, the houseman, she and Raven went up the stairs.

Meggie watched them go, thinking again what a curious mix the children were. The boy was as dark of hair as his sister was fair, and both had eyes of St. Claire blue. Selfishly, she had hoped to have a hand in their rearing, but it was destined not to be, since she would be going home again in a few weeks. By coming she had kept her promise to Eben, but she must begin thinking of the future. She had a business to run, after all. Meggie was so caught up in her thoughts that when Solomon spoke to her she started.

"Would madam care to rest before dinner?" the liveried black man asked.

"Why, yes," Meg said quickly. "It's Mistress Megan Cleary. And I find I am a bit fatigued. It's a far piece from Pennsylvania. I own an inn there. Do you know of it?"

"No, mistress. My home is in the parish."

"Oh, well. You don't know what you're missing. It's beautiful there, and wild. Very different from this place." Her voice slowly faded as she followed the servant up the stairs.

The chamber where Raven fed the twins was high ceilinged and cool even in the heat of late afternoon. She sat on the brocaded lounge and surveyed her surroundings as Cameron suckled at her breast, pinching her soft flesh between his tiny fingers as he watched his *maman* with his father's eyes.

Strangely enough, Raven felt at home here. The place had a certain graceful order to it that was somehow lacking in Castle Ford. Catherine had intimated before she'd left that Jase was hoping they would make their home here. The final decision belonged to Eben, but Raven privately considered that this would please her very much. Castle Ford and all of its memories belonged to the past, and Eben was determined that they begin again. With her husband invading her thoughts, Raven was unsurprised when he entered the room. It often was so with them, that one knew what the other was thinking.

He went directly to the bed and sat down to remove his boots. The quilt she had spread there earlier made him smile. It was the quilt that Elizabeth Galloway had given her for their marriage bed. At the time he had never considered that it would be warming them both at night. But that was ages ago, and much had changed since then.

Raven's gaze rested softly on her husband's countenance as she waited for him to speak. In a moment, her patience was rewarded. He rose and walked to the French doors, closed now against the hot Louisiana sun, and stood there looking out at the lush green stretching away to the wide river in the distance. "Jase wants us to stay," he mused. "He says there is some prime land coming up for sale. Good enough to raise horses on, and sons."

A companionable silence stretched out between them as Raven put away her breast and placed a now sleeping Cameron in the nursery with Megan. When she returned Eben had not moved, and his broad-shouldered form was silhouetted in the ruby light of the setting sun. She pressed her cheek to his back and wrapped her arms around him. "Would that please you, M'sieur St. Claire?"

"The winters here are mild," he said, "the summers hot and long. I've had my fill of snow and ice."

"And what of the farm in Castle Ford?" she asked. He owned it still, Sarah Fletcher's farm. They had lived there until the twins arrived, yet it had never seemed like home.

"We can always sell it," he said, turning to face

her. He looked down at her, and she could see the eager light that had entered his eyes. "Would you be unhappy here?"

"I can be happy anywhere," she answered, "as long as I'm with you."

He took her then, there on Elizabeth Galloway's marriage quilt. The future could wait until tomorrow. Tonight was destined for love.

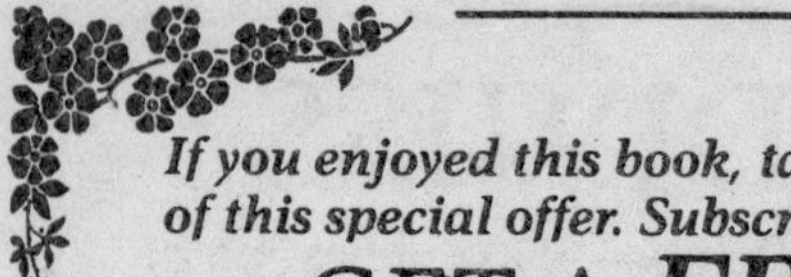